"That ... book. I can't go anywhere without it being the topic of conversation."

Dorsey glanced at Adam, her expression bemused. "It has a title, you know," she pointed out.

"I can't say it without gagging. Every woman in America is adopting that book as her bible. *How to Trap a Tycoon* is wreaking indigestion on most men."

"Well, not every woman's adopted it," Dorsey said. "But it's hardly surprising you wouldn't care for it. Seeing as how you're the perfect prey for any potential tycoon-trapper out there."

And as Dorsey glanced up at him, there was a flicker of humor sparking in her eyes. Not for the first time, Adam marveled at how green they were, how they were a color he'd never seen anywhere before. A color that reminded him of the waters lapping at a certain Caribbean island ... and he was very tempted to invite her to accompany him there for a very intimate visit ...

Other Avon Contemporary Romances by
Elizabeth Bevarly

HER MAN FRIDAY
MY MAN PENDLETON

ELIZABETH BEVARLY

How To Trap a Tycoon

AVON BOOKS
An Imprint of HarperCollins*Publishers*

This is a work of fiction. Names, characters, places, and incidents are products of the author's imagination or are used fictitiously and are not to be construed as real. Any resemblance to actual events, locales, organizations, or persons, living or dead, is entirely coincidental.

AVON BOOKS
An Imprint of HarperCollins*Publishers*
10 East 53rd Street
New York, New York 10022-5299

Copyright © 2000 by Elizabeth Bevarly
Inside cover author photo by Chuck King
ISBN: 0-380-81048-4
www.avonromance.com

First Avon Books paperback printing: June 2000

Avon Trademark Reg. U.S. Pat. Off. and in Other Countries, Marca Registrada, Hecho en U.S.A.
HarperCollins® is a trademark of HarperCollins Publishers Inc.

Printed in the U.S.A.

WCD   10   9   8   7   6   5   4   3   2   1

My family tree has been remarkably fruitful when it comes to producing strong, outspoken women, women who flew in the face of a society that would much rather have kept them docile and quiet. They are women who influenced me profoundly throughout my life—in childhood and adolescence, especially, but in adulthood, too. It has only been in the last several years that I've really begun to understand just how fortunate I've been to have such women in my family, and how much they molded me and meant to me as I was growing up.

During the writing of this book, I lost two of them, both great-aunts. So this book is dedicated to them, and to their memories, which I will always carry with me, very close to my heart.

With much love, admiration, and gratitude,
for Ina Bevarly Brady
and Girlie Mae Hensley Goben.
The world won't be the same without you.

Acknowledgments

As always, there are many people I need to thank for guiding me (i.e., keeping me sane) through the writing of this book. First, a *huge* thank-you to my editor, Lucia Macro, a woman of infinite patience and limitless understanding, for being infinitely patient and limitlessly understanding.

Thanks, too, to my two muses, Teresa Hill and Christie Ridgway—Teresa for always answering her phone, even when she had to know it would be me asking, "What do I do now?" and Christie for her tremendous literary insight. And thank you to Teresa Medeiros, who kept sending me cheery, supportive E-mail to get me through some difficult weeks, even when I didn't have it in me to reply.

I'd like to acknowledge musical inspiration for the book, the way I am wont to do, but all my CDs got waylaid in a move to a new house where nothing went right, and then the tape deck broke in the car and . . . Well, it's a long story, but it was all in keeping with the way the rest of the year went. Anyway, thanks to WFPK in Louisville for always playing *some*thing cool on the radio, whether it be on "Roots and Boots" or "Thistle and Shamrock." And thanks to all the local pop stations, whose rotations are normally pretty mediocre, for playing "She's So High" by Tal Bachman about a million times a day. That, more than anything else, I suppose, inspired me musically this time around.

Mostly, though, as always, thank you to my husband David, who, while guiding me (i.e., keeping me sane) through the writing of the book (as if that weren't enough), also guided me (i.e., kept me sane) through more life upheavals and icky stuff than any family should have to experience in a single year. Or in ten years, for that matter. And thanks to my incredible son, Eli, for being the most understanding five-year-old in the whole, wide world (the most understanding six-year-old in the whole, wide world by the time this book comes out). You guys are both amazing. Thank you.

Chapter 1

The fourth time it happened, it really got Dorsey's attention.

The first time, she put it down to coincidence, because, after all, it was bound to happen sooner or later. The second time, naturally, she shrugged it off as a fluke. The third time came as no surprise at all, because, as the saying goes, things come in threes. However, by that fourth time, Dorsey MacGuinness realized that she was clean out of explanations. There was just no good way to account for that fourth time, so it really got her attention.

The coincidental first occurrence, um . . . occurred . . . shortly after she began her lecture in her eight o'clock Intro to Sociology class. Dorsey wasn't happy to be teaching as many intro classes as she was, but that was what teaching assistants like her were for, weren't they? To babysit the students taking sociology as an elective and keep them off the streets, where they might otherwise get into trouble. Only *real* professors got to teach sociology to *real* sociology students. So Dorsey would just have to settle for being a pretend professor until after she defended her doctoral dissertation in six months.

Soc. 101 classes were always, in a word, uncooperative. Except, of course, for eight o'clock Soc. 101 classes, which were always, in a word, unconscious. Today was no exception. Dorsey faced the twenty odd—"odd," being a term of more than one definition here—students in her class, and was in no way surprised to find a good half of them dozing.

What she *was* surprised to find was that one of them was quite wide awake.

In the very back of the room, a female student—which was redundant, really, because *all* the students at Severn College were female, was not just very much awake, but also very much focused on her studies. Unfortunately, those studies did not include sociology. Not the kind of sociology Dorsey was trying to teach in this particular class, at any rate.

"Ms. Jennings," she called out in her best teaching assistant voice. It held a tone that gave even the best— *real*—professor voice a run for its money.

But Ms. Tiffany Jennings was not impressed by Dorsey's best teaching assistant-almost doctor voice. Because Ms. Tiffany Jennings offered no indication whatsoever that she had even heard Dorsey summon her by name. She was far too wrapped up in the book that she held open before her face. Not her fat Soc. 101 textbook, but a slim paperback. A slim paperback titled *How to Trap a Tycoon*, authored by the undoubtedly pseudonymous—and utterly ridiculous—Lauren Grable-Monroe.

"Ms. Jennings," Dorsey tried again.

This time, the voice worked a trifle better, because two or three of the dozing students pried open their eyes. Ms.

Tiffany Jennings, however, only continued to read.

With a resigned sigh, Dorsey tossed her stubby piece of chalk into the tray and strode forward, adjusting her oval, wire-rimmed glasses as she went and raking both hands through the rioting, dark-auburn curls that tumbled past her shoulders. As she covered the dozen or so steps between the blackboard and her uninterested student, she tugged her baggy, oatmeal-colored sweater down over faded Levi's.

Severn College was a tiny, tony women's liberal arts college situated in the tiny, tony Chicago suburb of Oak Brook, but staff and student body alike had long ago succumbed to a casual atmosphere. It was only one of the things Dorsey liked so much about both studying and teaching here. The school itself had been founded more than a century before, and the building where Dorsey did the bulk of her teaching and learning attested to that fact.

The scarred wood floors softened the sound of her rubber-soled hiking boots, so that Ms. Tiffany Jennings neither heard nor saw Dorsey's arrival beside her desk.

Not until Dorsey snatched the book right out of her hands.

"Hey!" the student then exclaimed, "I was just getting to chapter seven, the one everybody says has all the good stuff."

Dorsey closed the book and read the title aloud. "*How to Trap a Tycoon*, Ms. Jennings?" she asked. "Are you really interested in trying?"

The girl nodded her head with much enthusiasm. "You bet. Who wouldn't be?"

Dorsey could think of a few people off the top of her head—she herself, of course, would be in the number one spot—but declined comment. Instead, she opened the book to the table of contents and perused the offerings held within.

" 'Chapter Seven. Keeping the Tycoon in the Bedroom.' Yes, I can see where the concentration of good stuff, as you call it, Ms. Jennings, would most certainly be in that chapter. One can only shiver with delicious anticipation at the prospect of bedding a man whose entire focus in life is adding more dollar signs to his name." She peered at Ms. Jennings from over the tops of her glasses. "While you're doing all the work, he'll be mentally undressing his board of directors in the hope of figuring out what makes them tick. And, naturally, looking at all those boxer shorts and black socks would make any tycoon feel randy, wouldn't it?"

Since the question really required no answer, Dorsey returned her attention to the top of the table of contents. " 'Chapter One,' " she read. " 'The Best Tycoon Bait.' "

"That one's about how to give yourself a makeover that would make you more attractive to tycoons."

"Oh, my," Dorsey remarked. "How have I made it through twenty-seven years of life without having this information at my fingertips?" She flipped to the chapter in question and quickly scanned a few pages. "According to this, if I want to trap myself a tycoon, I should rush right out and spend a small fortune—which, of course, I don't have, seeing as how I have yet to trap myself a tycoon, a development that rather negates the entire premise of the book, doesn't it?—on a wardrobe full of . . . what does it say here?"

She lifted her glasses to the top of her head and squinted at the paragraph in question. " 'Sporty separates, cute little Chanel suits, seductive peignoirs, and diaphanous gowns." She glanced back up at Ms. Jennings. "Do they even make diaphanous gowns anymore?" she asked the girl. When Ms. Jennings only shrugged, Dorsey turned to the rest of the class. "Anyone?"

"I saw some diaphanous gowns in Better Dresses at the Marshall Fields on Michigan Avenue," one of the students offered.

Dorsey and Ms. Jennings both eyed the girl intently, the former with much disappointment, the latter with much hope.

"Thirty percent off," the other girl added. "But only through Sunday."

At the announcement, everyone in the classroom opened her notebook—for the first time that morning, Dorsey couldn't help but realize—and hastily jotted down the information. As Dorsey studied the student offering up shopping tips, her attention inescapably fell to the open backpack leaning against the student's desk. Sure enough, stuck haphazardly in the side pocket was a copy of *How to Trap a Tycoon*. Dorsey bit back an exasperated sigh and glanced once again at the copy she held in her hands, contemplating the chapter headings in the table of contents.

" 'Identifying the Tycoon's Lair,' " she read aloud. " 'Stalking the Wild Tycoon. Keeping the Tycoon in Captivity.' Goodness," she added, "one would expect a chapter on 'Stuffing and Mounting the Tycoon,' so clear is the author's intent to have every rich man in America taken to the taxidermist and turned into a trophy for whichever desperate female most perseveres in the hunt."

She closed the book, then pretended to study its cover with great interest. "You know," she said, "the fact that the author clearly took a pseudonym should tell you everything you need to know. For example . . . Oh, I don't know . . . Maybe the fact that she's ashamed to admit she's responsible for writing such tripe."

"Nuh-uh," Ms. Tiffany Jennings countered. "She's a career mistress, and she's spilling trade secrets. And she's afraid she'll be sued if she writes under her own name. She's been with *a lot* of tycoons. It's all there in the introduction. That's why she took the fake name. She just doesn't want anyone coming after her."

"She took the pseudonym," Dorsey corrected the girl, "because she knows that what she's penned here is sensationalistic claptrap that panders to the masses."

"Yeah, and she's gonna make a fortune off it, too," Ms. Jennings said, "because every woman on campus is reading that book. You can't log on the Internet anymore without seeing it mentioned a dozen times. Every chat room I've been in lately, sooner or later, the conversation turns to *How to Trap a Tycoon*. Even my mom wants to read it after I'm done."

Dorsey digested the information with a response that was rather mixed. And with results that were rather mixed, too, seeing as how her stomach pitched and rolled upon hearing it.

She closed the book, handed it back to Ms. Jennings, and replied, "Yes, well, do please try to keep your tycoon hunting for after class. That shouldn't be a problem, seeing as how Severn is just swarming with them, after all."

That last was added dryly, of course, because in addition to there being no men among the student body at Severn, there were few tycoons to be had there. Or any tycoons, for that matter. Virtually all the students were here on academic scholarship, and few of them would have been able to afford a similar education elsewhere.

Dorsey was like any other Severn student. It was her brain that had landed her in her current position. She had no background or money—or even family, unless she counted her mother, which she only did on days when her mother wasn't driving her crazy, which meant that today, as usual, Dorsey had no family to speak of.

Even after returning the book to Ms. Jennings, she was left feeling a bit troubled by the episode. Shrugging off her anxiety as best she could, Dorsey continued with her class—and her day—in the usual fashion. She taught dozing, uninterested students things they would remember only long enough to record them in a blue book come midterm—if they remembered them at all. And, eventually, she really did stop dwelling upon the episode with the tycoon book.

Until the second time.

Which came when Dorsey was standing in line at the Severn College bookstore, waiting to pay for her lunch— a mondo-sized Snickers bar and a Diet Pepsi. *How to Trap a Tycoon* was displayed in an enormous cardboard contraption at the front of the campus bookstore, and the enormous sign on top of the enormous cardboard contraption fairly shrieked its presence in enormous red letters. And three Severn students were gathered about the enormous thing, perusing the book in question with much—dare she say enormous?—interest.

Honestly, Dorsey thought, there was no accounting for tastes. She shook her head with disbelief as, after a few moments of animated conversation and giggling, all three of those students took their copies of the book to the cash register and plunked down good money for them.

The third, charmed, event likewise took place that day, while Dorsey was riding the El to her second job. She glanced up from a new biography of Ghandi, which she had been anticipating for months, only to find herself staring at yet another copy of *How to Trap a Tycoon*. The reader was, yet again, a young woman of college age, and she was reading the book hungrily, as if it offered answers to the darkest mysteries of the universe.

Dorsey sighed in bemusement, swallowed what tasted very much like fear, and went back to reading about non-violent passive resistance. However, she was beginning to feel anything but nonviolent or passive or even resistant, for that matter. No, what she was beginning to feel was homicidal. Or perhaps suicidal. She hadn't quite decided yet who she wanted to kill—Lauren Grable-Monroe or herself.

It was a quandary that continued to bother her right up until the fourth, and attention-getting, episode.

After alighting from the El inside the Loop, Dorsey hustled into an impressive glass-and-steel high-rise, rode the elevator to the sixteenth floor, then hurried down a hall to the employees' entrance for Drake's. As quickly as she could, she tugged off her glasses and hiking boots and shrugged off her sweater and jeans, then tossed them, along with her backpack, into her locker. At the same time, she withdrew a white man-style shirt and black man-style trousers.

Within minutes, she had donned those, along with the black man-style shoes and the brightly patterned necktie that completed her bartender's uniform. And then she was standing at the sink, gazing into a badly lit mirror, trying to weave her unruly, shoulder-length tresses into a fat French braid. Not having quite mastered the procedure yet—she only bound her hair when she worked at Drake's, and only then because it was a requirement of the job—a few of the dark-auburn tresses . . . or maybe several . . . or perhaps dozens . . . oh, all right, *hundreds* liberated themselves from the rest, scattering like a pack of rioting teamsters.

Dorsey watched with dismay as they unfurled in loose corkscrew curls around her face. Her boss, Lindy, would no doubt write her up for looking so unkempt, but she didn't have time to mess with her hair right now, because, as had become her habit of late, Dorsey was late. So, waving a hand in surrender at her reflection, she returned to her locker for the final accessory that would complete her bartender's uniform.

Her wedding ring.

When she'd purchased the simple gold band at a pawnshop six years ago, it had only set her back twenty dollars, but it was one of the best investments she had ever made. Shortly after she'd started tending bar, she'd discovered that when it came to female bartenders, men were constantly searching for more than the perfect martini. And her wedding ring—even if she'd never had a husband to go with it—was the best defense she'd found to ward off untoward advances.

And if her tips had always been a bit lighter because her customers thought she was married, well, that was just the price she had to pay. She made less than the blond bartenders, too, but that hadn't made her want to color her hair. And anyway, she wasn't working at Drake's because she needed the money, was she?

Although it wasn't yet four-thirty in the afternoon, the club was bustling. Well, as much as a bunch of buttoned-down and uptight, overfed and underjoyed old guys could bustle, at any rate.

Dorsey marveled, as she always did, that anybody could be as dry and stuffy as the pin-striped clientele of Drake's without being mummified. Then again, there were one or two who might have given Tutankhamen a run for his money—in both the gold *and* the shrivel departments. Honestly. A good, stiff wind would have blown some of them away like the parchment upon which they'd written the Declaration of Independence.

Independence for *men*, anyway, she thought, seeing as how women had been completely excluded from the document that had made this country what it was today, by God. And if these guys had had their way—and now that Dorsey thought about it, many of them did still have their way—women would continue to be neglected possessions left at home, overseeing the polishing of the silver of generations and squeezing out heirs to inherit it.

A healthy handful of men was scattered about the luxuriously appointed club room as Dorsey passed quickly through it. Some were seated in leather wing chairs reading newspapers and annual reports, while others relaxed on strategically arranged burgundy leather sofas. Many were murmuring into cell phones, no doubt looking to buy some stock or place a bet on the seventh race at Saratoga or line up a date with someone other than their wife.

As questionable as she found the appeal of Drake's clientele, though, Dorsey certainly couldn't criticize the decor. Lindy Aubrey, the woman who owned and operated the place, had utterly impeccable taste and knew exactly how to make a man feel comfortable and pampered. Fine English antiques and oil paintings of hunt scenes complemented the elegant furnishings, and Persian rugs and crown molding further enhanced the mood. The effect, on the whole, was one of old money, old bloodlines, old boys.

Other than Lindy, who was pretty much an old boy herself, the only women allowed here were the ones who served—quietly, unobtrusively, and without complaint. Frankly, that was the toughest part of the job as far as Dorsey was concerned, being obsequious and pleasant. But doing so suited her needs—for now, at any rate. She wasn't above—or below, for that matter—sucking up for the few more months it would be necessary. Once she had achieved her goal here, she'd happily kiss good-bye—and kiss off—the illustrious Drake's. Until then, however, like women everywhere, she was content to do what she had to do.

The posh European decor carried from the club room into the bar, which was also filled with men, even so early in the evening. Then again, it was Friday, she recalled, and most of these guys could afford to leave work early and get a head start on the weekend. Because, by and large, these guys owned the weekend. Not to mention every other day of the week. They were the men in charge, unlike the majority of working stiffs who had to punch a time clock. And, by God, they rarely let anyone forget it.

They sat lining the bar like thumbtacks, each affixed to his stool and nursing a drink. Dorsey noted all of the usual suspects as she passed by them, identifying each by what he drank.

Seven-and-Seven sat next to Salty Dog, who was followed by the gin twins, Gimlet and Gibson. After them came Anchor-Steam-Draft, Heineken-in-a-Bottle, and Kir Royal.

Kir Royal, Dorsey mused, not for the first time, as she considered the huge, hulking, dark man who cradled a delicate wine glass in his hand. Honestly. He was the CEO of a *trucking* company, for heaven's sake. If the guys driving the big rigs ever found out what he drank, they'd mutiny.

Next in line came the Scotch brigade—Rob Roy, Rusty Nail, Scotch-and-Water, and Dewar's-Straight-Up. And then, at the point where the bar began to curve around, seated in his usual spot . . . Dorsey bit back an involuntary—and very wistful—sigh.

Then came Oban-over-Ice.

Oban-over-Ice was, hands down, Dorsey's favorite of

her regulars, which wasn't saying much, because she didn't like any of her regulars *except* for Oban-over-Ice. Still, she did like him—probably more than she should.

Outside Drake's, his name was Adam Darien, and she'd learned quite a bit about him over the course of her month-long employment at the club. He was, after all, in the bar more evenings than not, and he often ate his dinner seated right where he was now. They'd shared more than a few interesting and often animated conversations.

She knew that he was the editor-in-chief of *Man's Life* magazine, which, in her opinion was really far too elitist and sexist a publication for *any* self-respecting woman—rich or poor—to condone, but it did usually contain a very nice fiction piece, and once, she'd found a great recipe for a Manhattan in there, and the arts section was far superior to anything she found in any other publication. But other than that, the magazine was pretty much an affront to womanhood everywhere. Even if Janet Reno *and* Gloria Steinem had both given profiles in the magazine recently. Really good ones, too.

Dorsey also knew that Adam Darien had just recently purchased a new, jet-black, Porsche 911 cabriolet. She knew that, because the two of them had discussed at length the pros and cons of that car and the new Jaguar roadster. Mr. Darien had been leaning toward the Jag until Dorsey had assured him the Porsche was one fine piece of automotive machinery, and when you compared German and British engineering, well . . . say no more. Unless he was willing to import a mechanic named Nigel, he was much better off with the 911.

Had Mr. Darien been any other kind of man—one who wasn't incredibly handsome, successful, intelligent and self-aware—she might have thought his frequency at the club was a result of loneliness. But there was no way—

no way—she would ever believe a man like him was lonely. Doubtless he simply enjoyed the camaraderie and excessive testosterone levels at Drake's. After all, he always left well before bedtime. Even if he didn't wear a wedding ring—something she just happened to notice one day when she *hadn't* been looking, honest—she was sure there was some woman, or perhaps women—he did rather seem that type—waiting for him at home.

But that was all beside the point.

Because Mr. Darien was, when all was said and done, a member of Drake's. He was a suit-and-tie-wearing, establishment-supporting, stock-and-bond-owning, woman-objectifying . . . man.

And anyway, regardless of how much she knew about him, she scarcely had time to think about him, had she? He only braved entry into her brain once or twice—or ten or twenty—times a day, and only during those few—or several—off moments when she had nothing else to think about. She especially didn't have time to think about him while she was here at Drake's, even if, every time she turned around, she saw him sitting there staring at her.

Like right now, for instance.

With those incredible brown eyes.

And that impudent little grin.

And that dark hair that would never quite stay tamed, as if he ran his fingers through it in exasperation constantly, hair that Dorsey always found herself wanting to reach out and ruffle herself. Over and over and *over* again. Preferably while both of them were somewhere other than Drake's. Somewhere alone. In the dark. Horizontal. And naked.

And then there was the way his jacket was always hanging on a nearby peg, and the way his vest was always unbuttoned, and the way his necktie was always askew, as if he only conformed to the suits because he had to, and if he had his choice, he'd much rather be wearing something else entirely—like maybe a sexy denim shirt and some tight Levi's or something. Or some sexy silk pajama bottoms with no tops or something. Or nothing at all or something.

Um, where was she?

Oh, yeah. She was thinking about how she *never* had time to think about Adam Darien—she was far too busy with . . . stuff. Besides, doing things like thinking about him, and, oh . . . imagining what he looked like naked would only make him that much harder to forget when the time came for Dorsey to leave her position here at Drake's. And the time would definitely come. In just a few months, too. So Mr. Darien would always remain on the fringes of her thoughts. And he would never, ever be naked when he was hanging around those fringes.

Well, okay, *almost* never.

Twisting the wedding band on her left hand, Dorsey covered the short distance between herself and the bar, trying to pretend that she didn't feel his gaze consuming her, noting that, in addition to her regular customers who had shown up early this cloudy, fallish Friday afternoon—one of whom, she couldn't quite help but note again was Mr. Darien—one of Edie's regulars was still hanging around.

Edie Mulholland was the daily lunchtime bartender at Drake's, and Straight-Shot-of-Stoli was the most regular of her regulars.

According to Edie, he came in every afternoon at two-thirty, and Dorsey had seen for herself how he stayed until a few minutes after she left for the day at four.

Had Dorsey been a more charitable woman, she would have assured herself that Straight-Shot-of-Stoli cared for

Edie the way a man his age might care for one of his daughters. But even if he'd never made a pass at the other bartender, Dorsey was reasonably certain that Straight-Shot's intentions toward Edie were anything but honorable.

He looked to be in his mid-forties, something that would make him more than two decades older than Edie. But Dorsey had to grudgingly admit that he was a very handsome man. His black hair held only a few negligent threads of gray, and his blue eyes suggested a wealth of intelligence and good humor. Beneath the pin-striped power suits he favored, his body was slim and firm and fit.

There was, unfortunately, one problem. Like Dorsey, he sported a wedding band on the third finger of his left hand. And she was fairly certain that his reason for doing so didn't quite mirror her own. It was something that rather compromised any feelings—whether honorable or not—he might have had for young Edie.

That didn't stop him, however, from visiting with the other bartender pretty much every day. Or from saying things like—

"Edie, you need someone to take care of you."

—as he was saying when Dorsey pushed up the hinged section of the bar and strode quickly behind it.

"I know, Mr. Davenport, I really do need a keeper," Edie said in response, just as she always did. And, as always, her voice was the picture of politeness when she said it.

Which was no surprise at all, because Edie Mulholland was, without question, the nicest, most courteous person on the planet. And had Edie's remark about needing a keeper come from any other woman, Dorsey probably would have lost every bit of respect she had for her. Then she probably would have smacked her open hand against the other woman's forehead and cried, "Snap out of it!" They had, after all, come a long way, baby. The last thing Dorsey's gender needed was for some sweet, young thing like Edie Mulholland to hurl them all back into high heels and pearls. Or, worse, chastity belts and those funny little pointed hats with the scarves attached.

But Edie *did* need someone to take care of her. Because in addition to being the nicest, most courteous person on the planet, she was also the sweetest, the most generous—and the most trusting.

She was exactly the kind of person that predators— predators like, oh, say, Straight-Shot-of-Stoli—came after. And she wouldn't know what hit her until it was too late.

"And believe me, I'm working on it," she added in an aside to Straight-Shot as she lifted a hand in greeting to Dorsey. "If all goes well, I'm going to find exactly the person I'm looking for. Soon."

"Edie, I'm sorry I'm late," Dorsey said as she slung her white apron over her head and reached behind herself to tie it. "I was at the library, and time just got away from me."

"That's okay," the other woman said as she repeated Dorsey's action in reverse—unfastening and tugging her apron over her head. "I can still make it before they close," she added as she fingered her delicate blond bangs to straighten them.

"I'll come in a half-hour early on Monday, okay?"

Edie smiled, her blue eyes full of a genuine happiness at the simple pleasure of being alive.

Some people, Dorsey supposed, were just decent folks. And Edie Mulholland was their queen.

"Don't worry about it," she said, reaching beneath the bar to collect her things—history and humanities textbooks for when the bar was empty, fashion magazines for when the regulars began to trickle in. Because smart women generally received lousy tips. "It's no big deal," she added. "Honest."

"I'm still coming in early to relieve you on Monday."

"Fine," Edie said. "But have a nice weekend between now and then, okay?"

Yeah, right, Dorsey thought. With a barely begun dissertation that was due in six months waiting for her at home? With volumes of research to perform and analyze? With papers to grade and a midterm to create? Not likely.

Nevertheless, she assured Edie that she would do her best, and only then did the other bartender wad up her apron and throw it in the linen bin beneath the bar. Then Edie quickly began to pack up her own backpack. She was zipping it up when Dorsey realized she'd left a book behind, a lone paperback sitting on a shelf beneath the bar.

"You forgot one," she said, reaching out to grab it. She was handing it to Edie when she noted the title of the book and frowned. "Oh, Edie," she added, unable to mask the disappointment in her voice when she saw what it was. "Not you, too. I can't believe you're reading this stuff."

Edie blushed as she made a grab for the book in question. "Hey, it's headed straight for the best-seller list," she said in her defense. "Everybody says so. Lots of women are reading it."

"What is it?" Straight-Shot asked.

Unwilling to give the man any insight into Edie—especially insight like *this*—Dorsey pretended she hadn't heard the question and handed the book back to her co-worker. But Edie evidently had no qualms about letting Straight-Shot know what she was looking for in life, because she turned the book face out toward him.

"*How to Trap a Tycoon*," she said.

Man, Dorsey thought, she didn't even have the decency to sound embarrassed about it.

"By Lauren Grable-Monroe," Edie added.

She didn't stuff *How to Trap a Tycoon* into her backpack with the other books, however, only turned to hand it back to Dorsey, who, not surprisingly, was reluctant to claim it. "I'm leaving it for Renee," Edie told her. "She wants to read it. And then Alison wants it after Renee." She smiled knowingly at Dorsey. "You want me to put you on the waiting list?"

Dorsey shook her head. "No, thank you," she said blandly.

Edie chuckled. "Yeah, that's our Dorsey. The last woman in the world who would want to trap herself a tycoon."

"And why is that?" a second male voice piped up.

Dorsey spun around at the remark, only to find Adam Darien gazing at her with much interest—way more than usual, and that was saying something—from the other side of the bar. He smiled before adding, "Oh, yeah. I forgot. You're already married, aren't you, Mack?"

As much as Dorsey MacGuinness hated to be called Mack, she never challenged Adam Darien on the nickname. She told herself it was because of Lindy's rule— give the customer what he wants . . . or else. But really, it was because the way Adam Darien spoke the name, the way he murmured it low in that rough, husky voice of his, that voice that reminded her of very good cognac pooling in fine crystal and warming in the palm of a gentleman's hand, the way he wrapped his tongue around her name and fairly purred it, so that it sauntered indolently into her ear, leaving a ripple of heat in its wake that traveled down her throat to her breasts and points beyond. . . .

Ahem.

Well, suffice it to say that when Mr. Darien called her Mack, it just didn't quite bother her as much as it did when others called her Mack, that was all. Because, hey, considering the way her social life had been lately—or, more correctly, the way her social life had *not* been lately—the heady thrill she received from hearing the way he spoke her name was about as close as she was likely to come to sexual fulfillment for some time. Not to mention that, quite frankly, the way he said her name gave her considerably more sexual fulfillment than most women probably received in a lifetime. Certainly more than Dorsey had received in her own.

And my, but wasn't it warm in Drake's this afternoon? she thought further, reaching up to loosen the knot in her necktie. What did Lindy have the thermostat set on, anyway?

"I have to run," Edie said, giving Dorsey the perfect opportunity to avoid responding to Mr. Darien's comment—or the call of his libido. Whatever. Edie ducked underneath the bar, then, realizing she was still holding *How to Trap a Tycoon*, she tossed the book easily back to Dorsey, who caught it capably in one hand.

"You better not let Lindy catch you doing that," Dorsey said. "Or else."

But Edie only grinned as she lifted a hand in farewell and hoisted her backpack over her shoulder. "See you Monday. Have a great weekend!"

Straight-Shot turned completely around on his bar stool to watch her go, never uttering a word as he did. Dorsey shook her head in disbelief. How obvious could the guy be?

Only when Edie had passed through the door and was out of sight did he spin back around to stare at what was left of the vodka he swirled in the bottom of his glass. "That girl needs someone to take care of her," he said before swallowing the last bit.

"And I suppose you consider yourself a likely candidate for the position," Dorsey replied sarcastically, quietly, the response intended for his ears alone.

It was the kind of comment—spoken in the kind of voice—that could have gotten her fired if Straight-Shot complained, but Dorsey couldn't quite stop the words from coming. If he did decide to say something to her boss, Lindy would be matter-of-fact and in no way hesitant about inviting Dorsey to clean out her locker. Pronto. Lindy Aubrey stated flat out at the interview that her workers, in addition to being attractive young women, should be thoroughly willing to be dominated by the exclusively male clientele. Or else.

To her credit, however, Lindy paid her employees very well, certainly well enough to make submitting to such a rule easier than it might have been in another establishment. Nevertheless, the membership of Drake's was generally of the variety that very definitely enjoyed dominating. A lot. Straight-Shot, she was certain, was no different. But somehow, Dorsey couldn't quite help putting her friendship with Edie first.

To her surprise, however, Straight-Shot didn't seem to be put off by her remark. Instead, he placed his empty glass back on the cocktail napkin before him and offered her a mild smile.

"Maybe I do think I'm a likely candidate," he said. "Edie's a sweet girl. Why wouldn't I want to take care of her?"

Dorsey's gaze fell pointedly to the thick gold band encircling the ring finger of his left hand. But she said nothing more. No sense pushing her luck.

"Ah," he said, dropping his own gaze to the accessory in question. "Yes, that does rather complicate things, doesn't it?"

"So then maybe Edie should be looking for someone else," Dorsey said.

"Judging by her choice of reading material, it would appear that she is."

Dorsey nodded and pretended that the two of them were on the same wavelength. "Well, if she trapped herself a tycoon, that would certainly take care of her troubles, wouldn't it?"

She gazed back down at the book in her hand as she uttered the question that invited no response. The cover of the paperback was bent in a couple of places, the spine cracked, suggesting frequent handling and heavy reading. The swirling, dark-crimson words *How to Trap a Tycoon* took up most of the pink-tinted background of a satin, tasseled pillow. And a single row of words at the bottom, in the same color, stated the author's obviously phony name: Lauren Grable-Monroe.

All in all, it was a harmless-enough looking package, she supposed. Still, she was beginning to get a very bad feeling about things.

"I do believe I hate this book," she muttered.

Then she put it out of her mind by tossing it back onto the shelf where Edie had originally left it. Dorsey did, after all, have more important things to do with her time than speculate about what Lauren Grable-Monroe had intended to accomplish with her book. Especially since she already knew *exactly* what Lauren Grable-Monroe had intended to accomplish. Dollar signs. Lots of them.

Dorsey knew this because she was, after all, the author of the book in question. *She* was Lauren Grable-Monroe.

Chapter 2

Adam Darien watched as Mack pitched *How to Trap a Tycoon* back beneath the bar, listened to her murmured words of disapproval, and could scarcely believe his ears. A woman who actually hated that damned book? A woman who wasn't greedily consuming every last word of it as gospel and arming herself for the hunt? He was ready to leap over the top of the bar and kiss her.

Of course, that wasn't necessarily because of her reaction to the book. He'd been wanting to do that since the day he'd walked into the club and seen her standing behind the bar, splashing Courvoisier into a snifter for Lindy Aubrey. The first thing Adam had noticed about Mack was that she had excellent taste in neckties. The Hermès silk she'd been wearing that day was one he'd nearly bought for himself a few months before. The second thing he'd noticed about Mack was that he was noticing a beautiful woman's midsection for the first time

22

and wasn't noticing what he usually noticed when noticing a woman's midsection for the first time.

It rather took his notice.

In the month that had passed since Mack had started working at Drake's, there hadn't been a single day go by that Adam hadn't considered asking her out. But the slim gold band encircling the fourth finger of her left hand had been a pretty effective deterrent in that regard.

So far.

Not that Adam was the kind of man to go after a married woman. There were far too many moral, ethical, and philosophical considerations with regard to such an endeavor—not to mention a real problem with timing. But in some ways, flirting with a married woman was more fun than flirting with a single woman, because there was little chance of anything materializing. And Mack did return his flirting, outrageously at times. It was fun. That was all. And Adam had so little fun in his life. What was the harm in enjoying it with Mack?

Even if she was a married woman.

"You hate that damned book?" he echoed incredulously, nudging aside his other, less comfortable thoughts. "How can you hate that damned book? Every woman in America is reading and loving that damned book."

Mack's expression would have been the same if he had just slapped her with a big, wet fish. "Excuse me?" she said, genuinely puzzled and surprised.

"That damned book," he said again, gesturing impatiently toward where she had thrown it. "I can't believe you just said you hated it. I can't go anywhere these days without that damned book being the topic of rabid conversation among whatever women happen to be present."

She glanced over her shoulder at where she'd thrown

the paperback, then back at Adam, her expression bemused. "It has a title, you know," she pointed out.

"I know," he conceded grudgingly. "But I can't say it out loud without gagging."

"You should see a doctor," she told him.

"I'm sure it's just a natural reflex to an unnatural phenomenon. Every woman in America seems to be adopting that damned book as her bible. It's not surprising that it would wreak indigestion on most men."

Mack's gaze fell some. "Well, not quite *every* woman has adopted it as her bible," she said dryly.

Adam bit back a chuckle of delight. She really was too good to be true. He'd suspected as much since the day she'd started working at Drake's, and now he was positive of the fact. Mack was more like one of the guys than she was . . . one of *them*. Recollections of her midsection aside—which, of course, he had noticed eventually, several times, in fact—Adam could talk to Mack. Really talk to her. They were on the same wavelength. She was as straightforward as they come. She didn't have any secrets at all.

"But you have read it, yes?" he asked her. "I mean, you would have had to, if you hate it."

"Um, yeah," she told him, sounding a little uneasy for some reason. "I've read it. Have you?"

He shook his head vehemently. "To put it succinctly, hell, no, I haven't read that damned book. It's a crime against nature and society and the way things are."

She narrowed her eyes at him thoughtfully. "Actually, that wasn't very succinct," she observed. "You could have just replied, 'No.' That would have been succinct. What you said was actually kind of—"

"No."

"Well, that was certainly succinct."

"So you read it and didn't like it?" Adam asked again.

She sighed heavily, and again he got the impression that she was uncomfortable about something. "Let's just say I don't like the way it's been received by the general public," she told him.

He eyed her thoughtfully in return for a moment, then pushed his empty glass forward in a silent request for another drink. "That's an interesting way to put it. What don't you like about its reception?"

She went about the motions of her job automatically as she replied, "It seems to be conducive to mass hysteria, that's what. And mass hysteria leads to everything from nihilism to jingoism."

Immediately, he began to feel wary. "Uh-oh," he said.

She glanced up curiously from her task, the bottle of Oban suspended above his glass. "Uh-oh?" she echoed.

"Nihilism," he repeated. "Jingoism. That's the sociology student in you talking, isn't it? You're about to go off on another one of your sociological tangents, aren't you? You're going to start using words like 'esoteric' and 'exegesis' and 'dogma.' I hate it when you do that."

Mack chuckled as she went back to pouring his drink. "Oh, come on. You know your cocktail party chitchat quotient has gone sky high since you met me. Admit it."

"That's beside the point."

When she glanced up to look at him again, there was a flicker of humor sparking in her eyes. Not for the first time, he marveled at how green the irises were, how they were a color he'd never quite seen anywhere before. It was a color that reminded him of the waters lapping at a certain Caribbean island of his acquaintance and he was tempted to invite her to accompany him there for a *very* intimate visit sometime.

And it bothered Adam a lot to realize he had the capacity to entertain ideas like that about a married woman. Hell, about any woman. The last thing he needed in his life was a very intimate visit with someone, married or otherwise. Intimate visits had a habit of turning into permanent conditions. Or, rather, in his case, semi-permanent conditions. The presence of his ex-wife in the world attested to that. And he wasn't likely to make such a mistake again.

"No, that's the human being in me talking," Mack replied, scattering his thoughts.

He loved her voice. It was perfect for a bartender, low and throaty and husky, redolent of smoky bars and bluesy guitar riffs and good Scotch over ice.

"Being a sociology student—or instructor, for that matter—has nothing to do with it," she continued in her smoldering, whiskey riff. Then she smiled. "However, if you'd like to discuss it in terms of the millennial *Zeitgeist*, I'm open."

He narrowed his eyes at her, stifling a growl. "No thanks," he said. Then, brightening, he added, "I hate that damned book, too. *And* its reception by the general public." Then, in case that wasn't enough to emphasize his point, he continued, "And I hate its cover. And its size. And the promotional campaign used. And the fact that it's written in English. And the font it's printed in. And the ink they used. And—"

She laughed as she finished free-pouring a generous amount of Oban over ice. "Yeah, well, it's hardly surprising that you wouldn't care for it. Seeing as how you're the perfect prey for any potential tycoon-trappers out there."

"It's not just that," he denied.

She set his fresh drink before him and smiled knowingly. "Oh, isn't it?" she asked, likewise knowingly.

He shook his head adamantly. "It's nothing personal," he assured her. "I consider that damned book to be an affront to men everywhere, regardless of their economic situation."

She crossed her arms and leaned forward, all signs of her previous uneasiness and discomfort having vanished. This was the Mack he knew and loved, the witty, confident, take-no-guff pal.

"Oh, is that all?" she asked mildly.

"I'm serious, Mack," he insisted. "Thanks to that damned book, the men in this country are being completely outmaneuvered in the mating game. We've become quarry, for God's sake. And that's just not how nature works. It's . . . it's . . . Well, it's unnatural, that's all. We—the men—are supposed to be the hunters. Not the women. But how can we hunt when we can't even figure out what rules the women are playing by on any given day?"

"You can figure that out," Mack told him. "Just read whatever book is on the best-seller list that day. Like, oh, say, *How to Trap a Tycoon*."

"Very funny."

"It's true," she said. "Sexual politics have always been a part of the whole man-woman thing. They just change with each new best-seller, that's all."

"Hmm. You may have a point," he conceded. "And, to be fair, I suppose Ms. Grable-Monroe's book is no more irritating than any of the other best-sellers of recent years that have made a man's life difficult. At least this book isn't telling women to avoid us or, worse, to psychoanalyze us. Or worse still, to turn us into apron-wearing, hummus-eating Yanni listeners. But," he interjected when Mack opened her mouth to comment, "this book does flat out objectify men. It turns us into status symbols, possessions to be acquired."

"Which," she said, "when you get right down to it, is exactly what men have been doing to women throughout history."

"It's not the same," he said.

"It's exactly the same," she assured him.

He shook his head before reiterating, "It's not the same, Mack."

She grinned, an impish little grin that both chilled and heated him. What a strange—and not unpleasant—sensation. "It's not the same," she said smoothly, "because *you're* the one being objectified and turned into a status symbol this time."

"It's not natural," he said again, ignoring her comment because—well, just because, that was why. "Women aren't the pursuers. Men are."

"Not anymore," she said softly. "Don't know much about biology," she misquoted, "but I am familiar with a little theory that some biologists find interesting. It's called Evolution." She enunciated the word carefully, as if she were speaking to a three-year-old—or perhaps to a sexist, elitist, chauvinist pig. "Maybe you've heard of it, Evolution. Things, animals—even men—do change." She paused a telling beat before adding, "Eventually."

Adam said nothing, mainly because she was gazing at him in a way she had that made his entire body go on red alert. It was a feeling no self-respecting single man should experience when faced with a married woman. Because it was the kind of feeling that made him want to forget all about her husband. The kind of feeling that made him want to make *her* forget all about her husband.

He pushed the feeling aside as far as he could—which, granted, wasn't all that far. "Don't you find offensive, though," he said, "the suggestion that a woman should go out and find herself a rich man to take care of her? I mean, hasn't your gender been fighting for decades to obliterate this kind of thing?"

Mack shook her head. "No, my gender has been fighting for decades to provide women with choices and opportunities. We never had those before. What each woman *chooses* to do with the choices and opportunities she has available to her is entirely up to the individual. But it's that choice we've been fighting for. Besides," she added, "Ms. Grable-Monroe's book isn't necessarily telling women to go out and find rich husbands to take care of them."

This was news to Adam. "And just how the hell do you figure that?"

She shrugged. "I see her book as more of a social satire."

"A social satire?" he repeated incredulously. "In what way? This is a book that tells women that money—someone else's money—would solve just about every problem they have."

She met his gaze levelly again. And once again, Adam found himself forgetting all about that husband of hers, who must be waiting for her at home. Then again, maybe he worked nights, and he'd never notice if Mack got in a little late for once. . . .

"Money *would* solve just about every problem women have," she said. "And the reason it has to be someone else's money is because personal wealth is something women have constantly been denied throughout history by men. Even today, at our highest earning power, we're still not allowed to make as much as men do who are performing the same work."

He narrowed his eyes at her. "Does everything have to become a sociology lecture with you?"

"Don't try to change the subject."

He sighed his exasperation. "Do you really believe that?" he asked. "That women don't make as much as men do for performing the same work? Here I've been under the impression that that was one of those urban legends."

She straightened, then rolled her eyes heavenward and tapped her chin with her index finger, clearly feigning thought. "Gee, do I really believe that? Let me think about it a minute. Yep, I really do believe that," she immediately answered herself, returning her gaze to his.

He shook his head at her in disappointment. "And here I've been thinking you're such an intelligent woman, Mack."

"I am an intelligent woman," she said matter-of-factly. Then, evidently discerning again his attempt to change the subject—she was, after all, an intelligent woman—she reverted to what they were initially discussing. "Men can't afford to let women earn the same amount of money that they do. Because with money comes independence. And men, who, alas, do still rule the world—for now, at least—can't afford to have us independent."

"Why not?"

She waited until he turned his attention fully to her face, then pinned her gaze on his yet again. "Because we would enslave you, that's why."

For a moment, he was so stunned by her response that he simply could not form a reply. But he regained his composure again eventually and smiled. At least, he hoped he was smiling. His face—not to mention other body parts—still felt a little stiff at hearing the whole enslaving thing suggested. My, but the prospects were just too intriguing to bear.

"Gee, there's nothing I'd love more than to continue

this conversation," he said, "but something tells me it's not one I should be having with a married woman."

She colored a bit at that, as if she, too, had forgotten all about that husband of hers. Well, well, well. Wasn't this just the most interesting conversation that he and Mack had never had?

Thankfully, their nonexistent discussion was interrupted then by the arrival of Adam's most recently acquired and very existent—sometimes too existent, in Adam's opinion—staff writer. As he watched Mack answer the summons of another club member halfway up the bar, Adam told himself she was *not* fleeing, and turned to greet his associate.

Lucas Conaway, age twenty-four, was fifteen years and a lifetime younger than Adam. In his Dockers, white button-down shirt and Animaniacs necktie, he was the sartorial antithesis of Adam, who had opted today for a three-piece, pin-striped Hugo Boss number—which, admittedly, was currently in something of a state of disarray. Likewise, the kid's blond, blue-eyed, gee-whiz good looks were at odds with what Adam cheerfully claimed as his own dark and brooding demeanor.

Normally, he would readily concede that their differences ended there. Despite the physical and temporal disparities, employer and employee were virtually two of a kind. Both were equally ambitious and driven when it came to the magazine they worked for—and, in Adam's case, owned—and both were equally irreverent and cynical when it came to life in general. Neither accepted any guff from any swine. And neither backed down an inch from what he wanted.

Adam could already sense that it was that last shared quality that was about to cause some trouble. He could tell by the look of intent on Lucas's face. Oh, well, he thought, it wouldn't be the first time they'd gone head to head on something. Nor, he was confident, would it be the last. And that, he told himself, was what made for good journalism. Even if that journalism found its way into a publication that was targeted less at hard news and more at—he might as well admit it—frivolous masculine pursuits.

Nevertheless, *Man's Life* magazine was Adam's pride and joy, his friends and family, his offspring, his better half, his reason for being. He had launched the glossy monthly a mere six years ago, and already its circulation was higher than any other magazine of its kind. Devoted to covering the finer things in a man's life—fast cars and fine wines, great books and good cigars, beautiful, intelligent women . . . and other such masculine acquisitions—*Man's Life* had become everything he had envisioned. And in his role of publisher as well as editor-in-chief, Adam was exactly where he wanted to be.

"I have a great idea for a story," Lucas said as he folded himself onto a neighboring bar stool. Without giving Adam a chance to reply, he hastily continued, "Three times yesterday, I encountered the same thing. Three times. To me, that means it's newsworthy." He lifted his hand toward Mack, who nodded an acknowledgment that she would be right there.

"Three times, huh?" Adam asked, his curiosity reluctantly piqued. "I suppose that counts for something."

"It's a sign," Lucas assured him. "On three separate occasions yesterday, in three separate places, I saw women reading that new book *How to Trap a Tycoon.*"

"Oh, no," Adam said, rolling his eyes. "Not again. Not that."

"So what could I do but go out and buy myself a copy, too?" Lucas asked.

Adam eyed him with much disgust. "How could you? You've betrayed your entire gender."

Lucas shrugged off the charge. "Hey, the book is topical. It's a current event. I'm a journalist. Sue me."

"Don't tell me you actually read the thing."

"Of course I read it. And it really fired me up, too."

"To do what? Go out and trap yourself a tycoon?"

Lucas grinned in a very wicked way that Adam found more than a little intriguing. "Nope," he said simply. "It made me want to go out and trap Lauren Grable-Monroe."

Well, that sounded promising. "And do what with her?" Adam spurred.

Lucas's grin turned positively malicious. Adam was liking this more and more. "My intention is to go out and trap myself Lauren Grable-Monroe and then completely expose her for the fraud I'm certain she is."

His announcement was punctuated by the sound of shattering glass, something that gave it a rather ominous implication. When Adam glanced up, it was to find Mack gazing at Lucas with wide eyes, her mouth slightly open, her face drained of all color—except for her cheeks, which were faintly stained with the hint of a blush. Strangely, she was holding her hand out before her, but her fingers, though curved, held nothing. Pushing himself up from his stool, Adam glanced over the top of the bar to find that, yep, just as he'd suspected, Mack was the one who had broken the glass. It lay in about a million pieces on the tile floor behind the bar.

As he sat back down, he tried to imagine what would have caused such a reaction in her. Not only did Mack never lose her composure over anything, but she never broke anything, either. She was amazing when it came to tending bar. Ultimately, all he could figure—and it was a lame deduction at best—was that maybe she had been overcome by Lucas's boyish good looks. In which case Adam would have no choice but to transfer the kid to the Spongemop, South Dakota, beat, thereby reducing the competition. Bad enough Adam had to sit around waiting for Mack's husband to go to his final reward. *Man.*

Then Adam remembered that he couldn't transfer Lucas to Spongemop, South Dakota. Because Lucas had single-handedly upped *Man's Life* subscriptions by six percent with that Wall Street exposé he'd written for the June issue. So if the kid wanted to turn his journalistic attentions—and intentions—to Lauren Grable-Monroe now, Adam sure as hell wasn't going to stop him. Then again, a story on Ms. Grable-Monroe meant *Man's Life* would be giving that damned book of hers free publicity. Did he really want to do that?

And why was Mack still staring at Lucas that way, her green eyes lambent—he could safely say he now knew what that word meant—her mouth full and ripe and luscious-looking, her face glowing with a mixture of caution and something he was hard-pressed to identify, and . . . and . . . and . . .

And, man, it was getting hot in here. What did Lindy have the thermostat set on? *Jeez.*

He reached up to loosen his already loosened necktie, then told Lucas, "I'm not sure I want Lauren Grable-Monroe in my magazine."

Lucas smiled but turned to Mack. "Gimme a Tanqueray and tonic."

Mack, of course, was way ahead of Lucas on that score. It was remarkable how she kept a catalogue of the drinking preferences of Drake's entire membership and began pouring the preferred beverage the moment she noted the member's presence at the bar. She set Lucas's prepared drink before him, then dropped the Tanqueray bottle back into the well. But she didn't scurry off afterward, as Adam had assumed she would. Instead, she continued to study Lucas. With much interest.

Dammit.

"This is a story," Lucas finally continued, oblivious to Mack's interest, "that the readers of *Man's Life* would find very interesting."

"And that would be because . . ." Adam spurred him.

Lucas's smile turned predatory. "Because I intend to locate Ms. Lauren Grable-Monroe and find out just what her credentials—so to speak—are that would make her the self-appointed social guru of today's women."

Adam sighed heavily but said nothing. He was torn between the dread of giving space to Lauren Grable-Monroe in any form and the ecstasy of filling that space with what might be a really satisfying diatribe against her. If anyone could write a flaming exposé of Lauren Grable-Monroe, it would be Lucas Conaway. The kid was a truly gifted writer.

There were times when Adam frankly wondered what had made the kid accept a position at *Man's Life* when he could have gone pretty much anywhere he wanted. Certainly his salary was competitive with any number of similar publications. But Lucas was a writer who should be covering human rights violations and sneaky, underhanded governments. Not which Cuban cigars best complemented California cognacs.

"Why would you want to expose Lauren Grable-Monroe?"

The question came not from Adam but from Mack, who seemed to be genuinely curious about the answer.

Lucas sipped his drink and sighed with much contentment, then turned his attention to Mack. "Because she's fast becoming the latest icon of popular American culture," he pointed out. "She's a good sound bite. Like I said, she's topical. She's controversial." He hesitated for only a moment before adding, "And something tells me she is really *hot*, too. Have you read the book?"

Mack nodded, but once again her cheeks were stained faintly with pink. Adam thought it made her look rather adorable. Then he immediately berated himself for allowing the word "adorable" into his masculine verbal repertoire. What Mack looked, he corrected himself, was rather . . . Oh, dammit. Adorable. That was what she looked.

"So that means you read chapter seven, right?" Lucas asked. "The one called Keeping the Tycoon in the Bedroom. Man, that chapter alone's worth the price of the book." He turned to Adam. "You would not believe some of the stuff she writes in that chapter. And so matter-of-fact she is about it, too. There's this thing with crème de menthe . . ." He threw another look toward Mack, then halted himself. "Well, let's just say that that Lauren has got some mouth on her. And I'd like to have it on me, too. Very arousing reading material." He smiled wickedly.

"Arousing," Adam echoed blandly. He decided not to look and see how Mack had taken Lucas's mouth references. He was afraid she might have gone way beyond adorable by now. And that way lay madness. "I think 'annoying' would probably be a better word for Ms. Grable-Monroe," he concluded.

"Yeah, well, I guess I can't expect a man your age to respond to a sexy woman the way a man my age does. But, hey, you'll always have Viagra."

The last thing Adam wanted was to be part of a discussion about Viagra in front of Mack. "Please spare me.

It probably hasn't been that long since you took your Pamela Anderson Lee poster down off your bedroom wall."

Lucas's smile grew broader. "Who says I took it down?"

"I think Mr. Darien is right," Mack piped up. "You owe it to your readership to avoid this kind of sensationalism. It's just popular, mass-market-driven propaganda. And in case you haven't noticed," she added parenthetically—if a little sarcastically—"the typical *Man's Life* reader is an elitist, sexist snob."

"Oh, I've noticed that," Lucas assured her.

Adam nodded. "Me, too."

Mack narrowed her eyes at both of them, but only continued, "Your typical reader has worked hard and sacrificed a lot to preserve his elitist, sexist, snobby way of life. You might want to be careful to not offend him. Elitist, sexist snobs have a way of not minding how much money they spend to read about elitist, sexist snobbery. Lauren Grable-Monroe doesn't pander to that."

This time Adam was the one to narrow his eyes. "You know, Mack, I think I speak for both Lucas and myself when I say, '*Huh?*' "

She frowned at him but said nothing, which was just as well, because Lucas started up again.

"I want to do this story, because I think Ms. Grable-Monroe has acted irresponsibly."

"In what way?" Adam asked.

Lucas thought for a moment before responding. "Well, she could cause a lot of unhappiness in the world," he finally said. "Women will be crushed when they don't land the man of their financial dreams even after following the instructions in the book."

In response to his assertion, Adam covered his mouth and yawned.

"She could cause a lot of disappointment," Lucas added.

Adam, in turn, glanced down at his watch.

"A lot of heartache."

Adam tugged gently at a hangnail.

"You know, the least you could do is listen to what I have to say."

Adam crossed his legs and rubbed at a spot on his shoe. "I will, once you start saying something that doesn't make me want to throw up. Hey, I had sushi for lunch. It could get ugly."

Lucas gazed down at his drink, then ran his thumb slowly, thoughtfully, along the rim of the glass. "I want to do a story on her, Adam."

"Why?"

"I have my own reasons."

"Care to tell me what they are?"

Lucas glanced up and met his gaze levelly. "No."

Adam studied the other man with much interest but didn't pursue the matter. Not because he wasn't curious about whatever was going on in the wily head of the hotshot writer, but because, suddenly, he began to get a pretty good idea of his own for a story. Before he could stop it, the idea had taken root, and even more quickly, it began to blossom.

It was a good idea for a story, he thought. A really good idea. One that would definitely appeal to his readership. Because it was, without question, elitist. And sexist. And snobby. And it was also, he had to admit, not a little sensationalistic.

Okay, so sensationalism had its uses, he conceded.

Elitist, sexist snobs were only human. In their own unique sort of way.

"Fine," he told Lucas, even before the idea was fully formed. "Let's do it. Let's do a story on Lauren Grable-Monroe. But," he quickly interjected when he saw Lucas snap to attention again, "it's going to be on my terms. With my spin."

The other man's disappointment was almost palpable. "Oh, come on, Adam. That's not fair."

"My magazine. My rules."

Lucas gazed at him sullenly.

"Don't worry," Adam told him. "You're going to like this. Because you, my fine, young, ruthless writer, get to go hunting."

The younger man shook his head, still looking ticked off. "I don't like the sound of that. You know how I feel about the cruel and senseless slaughter of innocent animals."

"You couldn't care less about the slaughter of animals," Adam said. "But not to worry. For this assignment, you won't be hunting an animal." He smiled with grim satisfaction. "You'll be hunting a woman."

Lucas brightened some. "Oh, well, in that case, I'm your man."

"Good boy."

"Now, then. About this assignment," he continued, dipping his head forward with much interest. "Will I, by any chance, be hunting a woman in lingerie?"

Adam chuckled. "Hey, if you want to wear lingerie when you go hunting, it's none of my concern."

"You know what I mean."

Adam eyed him thoughtfully. "I guess it depends on how successful you are in your hunt."

"I'm always successful, Adam. You know that."

"Yes, I do. Which is why you're going to be the perfect candidate for writing this story the way I want it told."

"And the story the way you want it told would be . . ."

This time Adam was the one to smile the predatory smile. "Lucas, since you're such a fan of the book, I want you to use it to go out and trap yourself a tycoon."

Lucas's rapt interest suddenly shifted to vague suspicion. "Come again?"

"The way I see it," Adam began, "even though Ms. Grable-Monroe wrote her book for women who want to land themselves a rich husband, there's no reason why a *man* can't use the book to land himself a rich *wife*."

"Whoa, whoa, whoa," Lucas objected immediately, raising his hands before himself palm out in a gesture of what was clearly self-preservation. "You want me to go out and trap a rich wife? Are you crazy? I don't care how much money she has. No way do I want to be married and miserable for the rest of my life."

"Not a real wife," Adam told him. "You don't have to marry the tycoon you trap. Just use the instructions in the book to snag yourself . . . you know . . . a sugar mommy."

Lucas shuddered visibly. "I think that's the single most revolting thing anyone's ever said to me. I do *not* want to go there."

Adam ignored the comment. "Look, just write me a story for the magazine that offers a man's view of this whole thing. I want to see what happens when a young, ambitious guy like yourself reads the book and takes the advice to heart in the quest for a rich woman. It should make for a nice piece."

"A nice piece," Lucas repeated flatly. "I'm not even going to touch that comment."

"Hey, you don't have to touch anything you don't want to. No reason to get tawdry. Just get me a good story out of this," Adam reiterated. "One that will appeal to our readership."

"Oh, I can definitely do that. It should be really interesting," Lucas said blandly. "And, gosh, really fun, too. And, whoa, very educational. And it should put to rest once and for all my father's theory that it's as easy to fall in love with a rich woman as it is with a poor one. Would that he had followed his own advice," he added in a voice that prohibited further probing.

"You say that because you don't believe in love, period," Adam said.

Lucas tilted his head to the side. "Excuse me, but I'm only a twenty-four-year-old bachelor, unlike the thirty-nine-year-old bachelor who is also sitting at this bar. Is it just me, or does this seem like an odd statement for the old guy to be making to the young guy in such a situation?"

Adam ignored the comment, thinking he was getting pretty good at ignoring Lucas. Now, if he could just be as effective in getting the kid to shut up in the first place, he'd be okay. Of course, the fact that Lucas refused to be shut up was probably what made him such a good journalist to begin with.

Damn, Adam hated these catch-22s. But he did love the way Lucas worked.

"I'd still like to expose Lauren Grable-Monroe," his hotshot writer said. "How about I write an exposé on her as a companion piece to this story?"

Adam opened his mouth to tell Lucas no, to state quite adamantly that such an exposé had no place in *Man's Life* magazine. And when he did, the oddest thing came out instead.

"No way, Lucas," he told him.

"Why not?"

Unbidden, a feral little smile curled Adam's lips. "Because," he said, "Lauren Grable-Monroe is *mine*."

Chapter 3

"**W**hat do you think, Dorsey? The blue or the green?"

Dorsey heard her mother's question and told herself it would be polite to answer. Unfortunately, she was far too busy doing other things—things like, oh, panicking, reeling from shock, quaking with fear, choking on terror—to form an adequate reply. She couldn't even bring herself to glance up from where she had buried her face in her hands after collapsing onto the edge of Carlotta MacGuinness's pink-satin-covered, king-sized bed. Because one terrible, terrible sentence kept echoing and spinning through her brain.

Lauren Grable-Monroe is mine.

Adam Darien's proclamation still made Dorsey shudder when she replayed it, even though a full weekend had passed since she'd heard him utter it aloud. She'd spent the entirety of that weekend trying to convince herself that she was worrying over nothing. That there was no way the two men could possibly uncover Lauren's true identity. That her editor and publisher were more than capable of maintaining her anonymity—they had, after all, promised. That her life, as she knew it, was going to be just fine.

.And now, on this bright, sunny, cheerful Monday afternoon, she realized she had wasted her entire weekend. Because she knew she was lying through her teeth.

She'd spent the bulk of Friday evening listening to Adam Darien and his trained python, Lucas Conaway, as they'd gleefully outlined the downfall of Lauren Grable-Monroe. And because both men had been completely clueless that they were unfolding their plans in the company of their very quarry, they had been quite vivid—and inventive—in completing their plotting.

And oh, what plotting it had been.

Between the two of them, by evening's end, they'd had Lauren stripped naked and covered in honey, staked out spread-eagle beneath a blazing desert sun, with a big ol' "Come 'n' get it!" sign posted for a nearby platoon of hungry army ants. And although she'd had to admit that the naked and covered with honey part had held a certain, odd, oh . . . allure . . . in its initial state when Adam Darien had proposed it—she hadn't even minded the staked out spread-eagle part, really—Lucas's introduction of carnivorous insects had pretty much spoiled the fantasy.

They were going to expose her. They were going to investigate Lauren Grable-Monroe and find out that she was really Dorsey MacGuinness, almost Ph.D., sociology professor wannabe at utterly respectable Severn College. That, she decided, was a given. It was only a matter now of how long she could hold them off and what damage it would do to her credibility in the academic community—and in every other aspect of her life—once it happened.

Dorsey had read *Man's Life* magazine, in spite of its elitist, sexist snobbery, and she knew that Adam Darien and Lucas Conaway, when left to their individual devices, could be formidable. Combined, however . . . She didn't even want to think about what they could achieve.

All in all, it had made for a rather gloomy weekend.

And the mood had carried over to today, because Dorsey had walked home from Severn to catch a late lunch before going to work at Drake's only to find that she had absolutely no appetite whatsoever. The unmitigated terror that filled her belly at being exposed by Adam Darien left little room for something as mundane as ham and cheese on whole wheat.

Her mother, of course, didn't suffer from so grave a condition as fearing for one's way of life. After all, nobody was threatening to expose *her*. Nobody was going to stake *her* out naked under a burning desert sun, oh no. Because *she* wasn't the author of *How to Trap a Tycoon*, was she?

No, Carlotta MacGuinness was only the driving force behind it. The impetus. The genesis. The reason for its very existence. That was all *she* was.

Therefore, the only condition plaguing Carlotta this crisp autumn afternoon was whether to wear the blue or the green. Forcing her hands away from her face, Dorsey made herself look up at her mother's reflection in the bedroom mirror, if not at her mother herself. As always, she found Carlotta looking cool, composed, and cosmopolitan. Her platinum blond hair was blunt cut to chin length, and not a strand of it dared stray out of place. She was dressed in her stay-at-home leisure uniform of velvet leggings and tunic, having opted for lavender today. The color highlighted the pale blue of her eyes, and the cut of the outfit showcased her trim, petite figure spectacularly well.

No one would ever guess that there were twenty-five years separating them, Dorsey thought. Carlotta Mac-Guinness was doubtless as fit and beautiful at fifty-two as she had been at twenty-two. In many ways, she was probably more stunning now than she had been three decades ago. Because now she had a knowledge and experience of life that women of twenty-two could never possess. And over the years, she had used that knowledge and experience in a way that most women—of any age— would never understand.

Dorsey fell into that "most women" category. Although she loved her mother dearly—in spite of those occasions, frequent as they were, when Carlotta's behavior threatened to drive her stark, raving mad—she would never, ever understand any of the choices Carlotta had made over her lifetime.

"The blue, I think," Carlotta decided without further consultation with her daughter.

Well, except maybe for that choice, Dorsey amended. Blue really was a better color on her than green. Other than that, though, most of Carlotta's life decisions made no sense at all. And making decisions on her own was pretty much par for the course for Carlotta. She was very much her own woman, in spite of having spent her adult life being kept by so many men.

"The blue is nice," Dorsey agreed. If a tad shorter than most fifty-something women would wear. Carlotta, she was certain, would pull off magnificently the brief, sleeveless silk sheath.

"Where are you going tonight?" Dorsey asked her.

"Hollis Barnett is celebrating her fiftieth birthday this

evening with what promises to be great excess," her mother replied.

"Wow," Dorsey said. "That's some milestone."

Carlotta held the green dress before her again, just for good measure. "I suppose," she replied blandly. "But it's a bit anticlimactic, seeing as how Hollis actually passed said milestone seven years ago." She spun around and, clearly still undecided about which dress to wear, she tossed both carelessly onto the bed beside Dorsey and contemplated them from that angle instead.

"You could come with me," she said, smiling sweetly. "You could wear the green. It would look wonderful on you."

Dorsey eyed the even briefer strapless cocktail dress that was—almost—made of shimmering emerald satin. Then she drove her gaze down over her standard teaching assistant-post-grad student uniform of blue jeans, hiking boots, and nondescript flannel shirt. "Gee, I don't know, Carlotta. Somehow, it just doesn't scream *me*."

Her mother sniffed indignantly. "It could, you know, if you'd just forsake those awful jeans and sweaters and"—she shuddered for effect—"flannel shirts. Honestly, Dorsey, you dress like a lumberjack. You should change your name to Lars."

"Lars?"

Belatedly, Dorsey realized she had spoken the comment aloud, and immediately, she wished she could take it back. She'd learned long ago not to encourage her mother to elaborate on such remarks. Too often, Carlotta's elaborations went on for days.

"Yes, Lars," Carlotta said before Dorsey could come up with anything that might sidetrack her. "I once knew a lumberjack named Lars. Randy as a bear he was, too. Really, his name should have been Bjorn. Bjorn is Swedish for 'bear.' Did you know that, Dorsey? I don't know what Lars is Swedish for. Probably 'flannel shirt.' I couldn't get him to wear anything else. Of course, sometimes, that was rather nice—the not wearing anything else part, I mean—but other times, well . . . Come to think of it, maybe he should have been named Randy instead of—"

"Carlotta," Dorsey interjected as discreetly as she could.

Her mother glanced up, her face etched with surprise at the interruption. "What?" she asked.

"Um, we were talking about something else, I think?"

Thankfully, Carlotta nodded and moved on. "So we were. We were talking about you putting on that green dress and coming with me tonight."

Dorsey shook her head. "No, we were talking about how that dress"—she pointed toward the garment in question—"was not going to work on this body." This time she pointed at herself.

Her mother smiled. "Dorsey, you put that dress on, there wouldn't be any *work* involved, I assure you."

Dorsey ignored the comment. "It's not my style," she said simply.

"Oh, pooh. You've got an incredible figure," Carlotta told her daughter, "and cheekbones that cost other women thousands of dollars. Not to mention those amazing green eyes and that auburn hair you inherited from your father."

And it went without saying, her eyes and hair were the only things she would be inheriting from her father. But Dorsey didn't say that—it did, after all, go without saying—and neither did Carlotta. Reginald Dorsey was *persona non grata* around the MacGuinness household. That was because he was also *in absentia*. And, at least as far as Dorsey was concerned, he was *non compos mentis*, too. Et cetera.

"It's only your . . . deportment . . . that needs work," Carlotta added.

Dorsey laughed. My, but her mother was being uncharacteristically charitable today. "In other words, if I change everything about myself, I have a chance of—what? Trapping myself a tycoon? Thanks, but I'll stick to working on my dissertation."

Her mother's normally full mouth flattened into a thin line. "Dissertations don't put food in a hungry belly, Dorsey."

"Maybe not," Dorsey agreed, "but they feed other things that need just as much nourishment."

Carlotta arched an elegant blond eyebrow in speculation. "You come to Hollis's party with me tonight in that green dress," she said, nodding toward the tiny garment on the bed, "and I guarantee you that you'll catch every male eye in the place. By evening's end, you'll be set for life."

Oh, now, *that*, Dorsey decided, was open to debate. Not just because her idea of set for life and her mother's idea of set for life were crashingly at odds, but also because, as much as Carlotta resisted specifics, no man had ever set her for more than a few years. And even Dorsey's father, Reginald, had kept Carlotta—and Dorsey—for less than a decade before moving on to his next female acquisition.

"Thanks, Carlotta," she said magnanimously, "but I have to work at Drake's tonight. Besides," she added before her mother had a chance to go off yet again about how Drake's was the biggest pond for fishing and how could Dorsey refuse to even sink a lure. "I don't think

Hollis Barnett would be too happy about an uninvited guest showing up at her party."

"Oh, Hollis wouldn't mind a gate-crasher," Carlotta said. "That's how she met Mr. Barnett, by crashing his first wife's birthday party." She hesitated, then added thoughtfully, "Come to think of it, that's how I met Mr. Barnett, too." She shrugged the memory off quite literally and contemplated her choice of dresses once again. "But he ended up married to Hollis, didn't he?"

"Obviously," Dorsey replied obediently.

"It's just as well," her mother said with a quick wave of her bejeweled fingers. "He had terrible breath. I don't know how Hollis has managed all these years. She must have invested quite heavily in Binaca stock."

Dorsey chuckled. She was about to offer further commentary when the telephone on the nightstand purred with a delicate whir. Everything about Carlotta's room was delicate, from the rose-trellis wallpaper to the pink, poofy canopy bed, to the fringed ivory chaise longue, to the crystal lamps, to the floral, pastel rug. No one would ever accuse Carlotta MacGuinness of having anything even remotely resembling a Y chromosome, that was for sure. She was the very definition of femininity. Dorsey often wondered how they could possibly share the same strands of DNA.

Her mind still focused on the conundrum, she leaned over to answer the phone, muttering a perfunctory greeting as she pressed the receiver to her ear.

"Dorsey! Hi! It's Anita!"

Instinctively, Dorsey reacted as she always did when she heard Lauren Grable-Monroe's editor's voice coming through the phone line. First she shivered as cold fingers of terror began clawing at the back of her throat. Then she swallowed that terror until it ran amok as a cyclone of panic and discontent in the pit of her stomach. Then she battled a cloud of black foreboding and clung desperately with brittle fingers to what little composure she had left.

Then she told herself to stop being so melodramatic— unless she planned to have her option book be a Gothic romance—and switched on the speaker phone. Conversations with Anita Dixon, after all, always included Carlotta, too.

"It's Anita," she told her mother as she completed the action.

"Hallooo, Anita," Carlotta sang out as she reached again for the two dresses on the bed. She turned toward the mirror and held the green up before herself once more, her expression contemplative. "The last time you called," she said over her shoulder, "it was to tell us that *How to Trap a Tycoon* was going into its third printing. What delicious news do you have for us today?"

Dorsey could envision Anita Dixon sitting at her desk, a dark-haired, energetic waif furiously smoking a cigarette, having completed her lunch of Twinkies and espresso. She'd never met her editor in person and had no idea why she pictured Anita in such a way. The other woman simply sounded young, hyper, and brunette.

"Two words," Anita announced. "Book tour."

Book tour? Dorsey thought. *Book tour? Oh, no. No, no, no, no, no.* "I don't like those words," she told the editor. "Choose two more. Like 'good' and 'bye.'"

"How about 'network' and 'television'?" came Anita's response.

"No, I like those even less," Dorsey assured her.

"Get used to them, Dorsey," Anita told her. "Because Lauren Grable-Monroe is about to go national."

Oh, no, Dorsey thought. *No, no, no, no, no.*

Evidently taking her silence as a positive sign, Anita continued blithely, "The book is selling like crazy, and readers and booksellers are clamoring to meet Lauren. You wouldn't believe the mail we've received and the feedback our sales force is getting."

"But, Anita—" Dorsey cut in feebly.

So feebly, obviously, that Anita didn't even hear her. Because the editor continued quickly, "The American public wants Lauren. Badly. And Rockcastle Books wants to give her to them."

Give her to them? Dorsey echoed to herself. More like toss her to them. "Them" being not the American public, which actually connoted a rather warm, comfortable gathering of moms, baseball players, and grandmas holding apple pies, a fate that wouldn't be without its merits, actually. No, the "them" she visualized at Anita's assertion was a group more consistent with a pack of howling, rabid wolverines that were frothing at the mouth.

"But, Anita," she began to object, "how—"

"A book tour is the logical way to do that," her editor interrupted her. Again. "We want Lauren to speak and sign books in some of the larger cities, starting, naturally, with Chicago. And we're setting a place for her at Book Expo in the spring."

"But, Anita, how are you—"

"It's incredible, the response to this book, Dorsey. *Good Morning America* has already called twice. *Twice.* We can't put them off any longer. We don't *want* to put them off any longer. Do you know how hard it is to get time on national television? Yet they're calling *us*! It's phenomenal."

A wave of nausea rolled through Dorsey's midsection as she waited for Anita to come to a stopping point. The instant she heard her editor taking a breath, she jumped in, "And how are you going to manage this, Anita? Need I remind you that Lauren Grable-Monroe *doesn't exist*?"

Immediately, she regretted voicing the question. Not because she feared offending Anita, but because she feared the reply she just knew her editor was going to give her.

There was a thoughtful pause from the other end of the line. Then, softly, "No, Lauren doesn't exist," Anita agreed. "But, Dorsey . . . you do."

Aaaaagggggghhhh!

The silent scream unrolled in Dorsey's head, and it was with no small effort that she kept it silent. Yep. That was pretty much the reply she had feared, all right.

"Yes, I do exist," she agreed. "But I'm not a sexy former mistress full of tips on how to bag a tycoon. I'm an academic striving to carve out a career in research and teaching," she reminded her editor. "If the head of the sociology department at Severn finds out I'm the one who authored *How to Trap a Tycoon*, she'll never let me teach again. It might even compromise the reception my dissertation will receive this spring."

"Dorsey, your dissertation is a scholarly, sociological treatise on stuffy old-boy men's clubs and how they exist as a microcosm of a male-dominated society," Anita reminded her. "Two words, darling: *big yawn*. Nobody's even going to be able to finish it, so why are you so worried about defending it?"

Dorsey reined in the comment she wanted to make. Hey, maybe it wasn't destined to be a best-seller, but she was proud of her work. Her dissertation, she was certain, would be a hit with the faculty of Severn's sociology department when it came time for her to defend it.

Unless, of course, Anita Dixon and Rockcastle Books had their way. Should it ever get out that Lauren Grable-

Monroe was actually Dorsey MacGuinness, then Dorsey might very well be barred from teaching at the college she loved.

And in addition to blowing her credibility, the revelation that she was Lauren Grable-Monroe might also compromise the financial aid Dorsey had been receiving for years. Even if she wasn't benefiting from the profits of the book—every last cent of the advance and royalties were being paid to Carlotta—Severn would view Lauren Grable-Monroe as a wealthy woman. They might very well demand that Dorsey repay the thousands of dollars' worth of tuition that she had received over the years, based on her economic situation. And that was a lot of money to have to repay. Especially seeing as how Dorsey would never have it.

Somehow, she quelled the ripple of hysteria that had begun to bubble just beneath her surface and tried to focus again on the conversation at hand. "I can't be Lauren," she told her editor. "I can't. I'm a sociology Ph.D. candidate, not a social butterfly. Furthermore, my mother has just accused me of dressing like a lumberjack. And you know what, Anita? She's right. I *do* dress like a lumberjack. I'm not some former mistress-slash-party girl like Lauren in any way, shape, or form. I'm not Lauren, period."

There was another one of those pregnant pauses, followed by Anita's carefully stated, "You could be."

Aaaaagggggghhhh!

"Oh, no, I couldn't," Dorsey stated immediately, adamantly, swallowing another silent scream. "Lauren and I have absolutely nothing in common. If it hadn't been for Carlotta, I never would have written this book. The content is hers, not mine. Hell, the *earnings* are hers, not mine."

"But the *writing* is yours, Dorsey," Carlotta interjected. "All I did was list a lot of pointers and suggestions. The wit, the wry humor, the irreverence . . . that's all you."

"She's right," Anita agreed. "And those are the things that define Lauren."

"Anita," her mother said. "Maybe if you let me talk to Dorsey—"

"There will be no talking," Dorsey stated clearly, first to her mother and then to the telephone. To Anita, she added, "You agreed going into this thing that I'd be able to preserve my anonymity."

There was a rather dubious silence from the other end of the line, followed by a rather ominous sigh. "We need to rethink this anonymity thing, Dorsey," Anita said carefully.

"No, we don't," Dorsey told her. "You assured me, before I even signed the contract, that taking a pseudonym wasn't going to be a problem."

"That's not the problem," Anita told her. "That, actually, especially in hindsight, was a very good idea."

"You also assured me," Dorsey continued, "that my personal life wouldn't be jeopardized at any time. That there was no reason to disclose the fact that Lauren Grable-Monroe is, in fact, a Ph.D. candidate in the sociology department of Severn College."

"That's not the problem, either," Anita replied. "Quite frankly, the last thing I want is for Lauren to come forward as a stuffy academic from some snooty women's college."

Dorsey tried not to feel offended—even if she did have to concede that she was rather stuffy and Severn was rather snooty—and went on, "You also promised me that keeping Lauren Grable-Monroe under wraps would be a piece of cake."

"See, now *that's* the problem."

"Anita . . ."

"Look, Dorsey," her editor interrupted her—again. "Just think about this for a minute. Book sales have been phenomenal with Lauren lying low behind the scenes. If—*when*—we bring her out, the numbers are going to go through the roof. Through—the—roof," she reiterated slowly. "We're talkin' *New York Times* list, baby. We're talkin' 'More than a million books in print.' We're talkin' foreign sales out the wazoo."

"All the more reason to maintain my anonymity," Dorsey said, her tone pleading.

"No, Dorsey, you're not listening," Anita replied. "We're talkin' incredible royalties. Way beyond your initial advance. We're talkin', potentially, many hundreds of thousands of dollars. Financial security for the future," she added pointedly, and, as far as Dorsey was concerned, that was the lowest of blows. "I thought that was what you wanted. I thought earning a nice little nest egg for your mother's retirement was the whole point of writing *How to Trap a Tycoon*. How can you turn that down?"

She couldn't turn it down. Dorsey knew that. The promise of cold, hard cash was what had generated this whole fiasco. Carlotta, as charming as she was, had absolutely no head for financial planning, and she'd always made her way on someone else's ticket. Nowadays, those tickets were coming fewer and farther between. The proceeds from *How to Trap a Tycoon* were supposed to fund Carlotta's future, so that she could spend the rest of her life in relative comfort without relying on a benefactor. Dorsey just wished she didn't have to sell off so much of herself to guarantee her mother's health, happiness, and well-being.

In spite of the feeling of defeat that gripped her, Dorsey said halfheartedly, "Anita, I can't identify myself as the author of this book."

Anita's exasperated sigh was followed by an impatient "Why not?"

Even as the reasons unfolded in her head, Dorsey knew her editor would never understand them. She scarcely understood herself why she was so reluctant to do what Anita was asking her to do. All she'd ever wanted from life was security. Not just financial security, but personal security, too. Psychological security. Emotional security. In her own small way, she had won, or was about to win, all of those things. She was about to earn her Ph.D., was close to nailing down a position at Severn College that would someday lead to tenure. She had a stable income and regular rituals she observed in her life, along with a daily routine that was wonderfully routine. There were no ups and downs for her these days, no unforeseen curves, no hidden trapdoors.

It was exactly what she wanted after growing up in an atmosphere where she and Carlotta had often, quite literally overnight, gone from living in posh apartments to the streets. One day her mother would be bringing home carryout from five-star restaurants for Dorsey's dinner, and the next day they'd have trouble scraping up enough for McDonald's. The quality of their lives had always depended on whether or not Carlotta had a benefactor lined up, and as often as not, those benefactors would disappear without warning. These days, more than anything else, Dorsey craved stability. Security. Routine.

The financial reward that Anita was promising, should Dorsey pose as Lauren Grable-Monroe, would give her mother all of those things, and Dorsey, too, by extension. Contrary to popular belief, she knew money *could* buy happiness. Because money could buy security. And security was everything—*everything*—she had ever wanted. For herself *and* Charlotta.

In spite of that, very softly, very slowly, Dorsey said, "I don't want to identify myself as the author, Anita, because, for the first time in my life, I'm enjoying a quiet, orderly existence. Something like this would wreak havoc in my life, with absolutely no guarantee of anything more. And I don't like havoc. I like even less the absence of guarantee. I'm going to be defending my dissertation in six months. If everybody knows I'm Lauren Grable-Monroe, it's going to totally blow my credibility in the academic community. There's a very good chance they wouldn't let me teach at Severn anymore."

"Dorsey, your mother will have piles of money," Anita reminded her. "You won't need to teach at Severn anymore."

"But what if you're wrong?" she asked. "What if those piles of money never materialize?"

"I'm not wrong."

"But what if you are?"

Anita seemed to sense Dorsey's distress, and, like any good New Yorker, she pounced on it. Ruthlessly. "Dorsey," she said, "if you come forward as Lauren to promote this book, it'll spur sales even higher. It'll garner your mother a *fortune*. Charlotta could potentially make a *ton* of money. I thought that was the whole point. How can you even think of balking at an opportunity like this? Lauren Grable-Monroe needs to come out of the closet. Now. We have to put her in the public eye. Now. She has to be made real. Now."

"She's right, Dorsey," Carlotta said, her voice somber, all traces of playfulness gone. "We did this for the money. I know I'll be the one benefitting from the profits—at your insistence—and I hope you don't think me frightfully selfish, but I do wish you'd reconsider."

This time Dorsey was the one to sigh. As cheerful and happy as Carlotta was now, she knew her mother feared growing old like nothing she had ever feared before. Although Carlotta had been the recipient of enormous financial backing over the years, her backers hadn't been heavy on cash. They'd been more amenable to investing jewelry, dinners, and lingerie, with a car or vacation thrown in as a year-end bonus.

They hadn't embraced any long-range goals where their investments were concerned either. They'd stayed for as long as they were interested, and then they'd pulled out—if one could pardon the incredibly tacky pun.

And as Carlotta had aged, her investors had become less frequent and less generous. Certainly she was still an attractive, vivacious woman, one who was capable of doing just about anything she wanted, should she set her mind to it. But what Carlotta wanted was to be cared for by a wealthy man. Nowadays, there just weren't that many wealthy men who wanted to take care of her.

Dorsey couldn't ever understand her mother's ambition. Or, rather, her lack of ambition, as she was more inclined to view it. Her mother was intelligent, resourceful, spirited, and in the prime of her life. Carlotta was capable of achieving so much, with or without a man involved. Convincing Carlotta of that, however, was next to impossible.

As much as Dorsey had tried to dissuade her, her mother was certain she could do nothing but what she had been doing since she was eighteen. Her entire adult life had been defined and made possible by the fact that she was young and beautiful and witty and because of that, rich men enjoyed being with her. She had never worked—well, not at anything that required punching a time clock—had never graduated from college, had never been trained to do anything that might lead to a career.

And because her benefactors these days were more infrequent and less inclined to hang around for long, Carlotta was convinced that she would die a desperate, destitute old woman, having nothing of interest to offer anyone of the male—and economically enhanced—persuasion.

Her position over the years—or, perhaps, positions, if one wanted to be gauche, which of course, Dorsey didn't, but that was how her mind worked sometimes, unfortunately—hadn't provided Carlotta with a nice retirement package. So she'd decided to create her own little financial nest egg. How to go about that, however, had eluded her.

Until the day cable television had brought them the Classic Movies Channel.

Carlotta had been watching one of the network morning shows one day when she'd seen coverage of a wildly best-selling how-to book that instructed women on the dos and don'ts of husband-hunting. Immediately after the show, she had changed the channel—to the Classic Movies Channel—and found herself watching *How to Marry a Millionaire*.

And then, at the very back of Carlotta's brain, a little light had flickered on.

Carlotta MacGuinness had never wanted a husband. But she had always wanted a millionaire. She'd grown up poor and neglected and wanted to be rich and well cared for. So she had devoted her life to creating just such an existence for herself. And she had been very good at what she set out to do. She'd had lots of millionaires over the years. So it made sense that she would author a book about, if not marrying a millionaire, then certainly about having one. Or two. Or more.

The only problem was that Carlotta couldn't write a sentence to save her life. Her daughter, however, the academic who was used to years of term papers and theses and dissertations, could write up a storm. Or a book. Or, evidently, a national best-seller.

Mother and daughter had made a nice team. Provided, Dorsey thought, one didn't mind one's entire way of life being blown into bits. Carlotta, it seemed, didn't mind at all. Then again, it wasn't Carlotta's way of life on the line, was it?

"If what Anita says is true, and I come forward as Lauren Grable-Monroe," Dorsey told her mother, "my life will become a media circus."

Carlotta smiled. "It sounds rather fun to me. I always liked the circus. In spite of the proliferation of clowns. What on earth were they thinking to put makeup on men, for heaven's sake? And so much of it! How could they think children would like that? Not only is it frightfully macabre, but it skirts the surreal, and no child—or adult for that matter—is comfortable with the surreal. Why, look at Dali and that odd clock painting, for heaven's sake. Who would possibly find that anything but—"

"Carlotta," Dorsey interjected as discreetly as she could.

"What?"

"Um . . . we were talking about something else?"

"So we were. We were talking about how you should come forward as Lauren."

Dorsey shook her head. "No, we were talking about how I *shouldn't* come forward as Lauren."

"Oh, come on, darling. It would be fun."

Dorsey brightened. "Then *you* come forward as Lauren."

Ruefully, her mother shook her head. "As much as I'd like to, there are two reasons why I can't. Anita," she added, spinning around to face the telephone. "Dorsey and I need to talk about this. We'll call you back in an hour."

"Fine, Carlotta," the disembodied voice of their editor answered. "You two talk. But we need to get this settled today."

"I promise you," Carlotta said, "it will be settled within the hour."

Dorsey opened her mouth to disagree, but Carlotta lifted a hand, palm out, to halt the flow of words. So, with a sigh, Dorsey disconnected the phone, then scooted over to make room for her mother on the massive bed.

For one brief moment, she flashed back to her childhood, when she would climb into her mother's bed at night after a particularly bad dream, of which there had seemed to be many when Dorsey was growing up. Dreams of abandonment and solitude and loneliness. Whenever such dreams had plagued her, her mother had always gathered her close and tugged the sheets higher around them both.

And then she had always said, in a quite matter-of-fact way, "Dorsey, there will be abandonment, solitude, and loneliness in your life. You can't escape that. People will come and go, and they'll find what they need in you and overlook the rest. But your mother will love you—all of you—no matter what happens. And I will never, ever abandon you."

As Dorsey grew into adolescence, the speech became more specific, as her mother had traded the word "people" for the word "men." And over the years, her mother's was a prediction that Dorsey had seen fulfilled. Carlotta had always been there for her, had always loved her unconditionally. And people, including men, had come and gone in Dorsey's life—though not with the frequency or the intimacy that they had with her mother. Dorsey made certain of that. And people, especially men, did seem to find what they wanted in her and overlook the rest.

For some reason, that made her think of Adam Darien. To him, she was simply Mack. One of the boys. A pal, a bud, someone with whom he could speak frankly and nothing more. She couldn't imagine him seeing her as a woman. Unless, perhaps, she was someone like Lauren Grable-Monroe. Party girl, sexpot, tycoon-trapper.

Hmmm . . .

Having Lauren come forward into the public eye might possibly deter any exposing that Adam Darien and Lucas Conaway might undertake. If they saw Lauren in the flesh—or at least in the print and television media—then they might not be so inclined to dig deeply into her background. If Lauren saturated the market, then they might just leave her alone. They might never find out that she was, in fact, Dorsey MacGuinness, sociology instructor and stuffy academic.

That thought brought her back to the matter at hand. She looked at her mother beseechingly, but she knew going in that the battle was already over. Because she'd already fought the hardest conflict with herself—and lost it.

In spite of that, she asked her mother halfheartedly, "Why can't you be Lauren?"

Carlotta smiled a bit sadly. "Actually, there's nothing I'd enjoy more than being the center of attention with a book tour and network television," she began. "Especially if it was that nice Matt Lauer doing the interview. But as I said, there are two reasons why I can't."

"And they would be?"

She expelled a quick sigh. "Reason number one is that there are too many men out there who, were I identified as the source of the material, would recognize themselves in the book. And worse, whose *wives* would recognize them in the book. The lives of those men would be thrown into an uproar, should I come forward as the author. Those men have been good to me, Dorsey. I owe them discretion."

"You owe them nothing," Dorsey countered.

"I owe them more than you realize," Carlotta countered. "More than you will ever know." She paused only a moment before adding, "And even if I didn't, they all have battalions of attorneys at their disposal, attorneys who could ultimately claim every nickel from those piles of money Anita has promised."

"So you'd rather have your daughter's life thrown into an uproar?" Dorsey asked.

"No," her mother told her. "But I think that you would bounce back from uproar much more quickly than any of those men would. Men are such frail creatures, after all. We do so have to shelter them, Dorsey. And who knows?" she added with a smile. "You might just like uproar, if you'd only give it a chance. I don't know why your quiet, peaceful, academic existence is so all-fired important to you."

No, of course she wouldn't know that, Dorsey thought. Carlotta would never understand her need for quiet and permanence. But all she said was, "And the other reason?"

This time her mother's smile held resignation. "The other reason is that nobody wants Lauren Grable-Monroe to be a fifty-something woman who only has a few good years left in her."

"Oh, Carlotta, you don't honestly think—"

"What I know to be true, Dorsey," she said, "is that the American public would much rather see you as Lauren than they would me."

"A peace-and-quiet-loving academic who dresses like a lumberjack?" Dorsey asked. "I doubt it."

"Dorsey MacGuinness is the peace-and-quiet-loving academic who dresses like a lumberjack," her mother corrected her. "Lauren Grable-Monroe is no such thing. Lauren is a blond bombshell party girl who knows men. Or, at least, she will be when I get through with her. Through with you. Whatever."

Dorsey narrowed her eyes at her mother curiously. "What are you thinking?" she asked.

In response, Carlotta stood and extended both hands toward her daughter, silently bidding her to rise as well. Reluctantly, Dorsey did, then allowed herself to be guided over to the full-length mirror affixed to the closet door. Her mother positioned her to face it, then turned back to the bed and swept up the discarded dresses.

"We'll have to go shopping for a good wig and a few wardrobe pieces that don't scream Great White North," she said as she held up both dresses to inspect first one and then the other. "And it goes without saying, we'll also need to get you a Wonderbra."

"Carlotta . . ."

But her mother ignored what Dorsey had hoped was an unmistakable warning in her voice. "We will also," she continued, "without a doubt, have to make a rather substantial investment at the Lancôme counter. But we will pull this off, Dorsey. I promise you that. When you go out into the world as Lauren Grable-Monroe, no one will ever suspect Dorsey MacGuinness is hiding there."

"It'll never work," Dorsey told her. "There's no way we'll make it work."

Instead of commenting on Dorsey's conviction, however, Carlotta moved to stand behind her and placed first one dress and then the other in front of her. Then she grinned impishly. "So . . . what do you think, Lauren? The blue or the green?"

Chapter 4

Adam Darien had adopted a new role in life, but it wasn't one he could see himself adding to his resume any time soon. Because—call him unrealistic—Skulker just wasn't the kind of position that led to prodigious promotion. Not in any of the professional capacities in which he wanted to find himself, at any rate.

Yet here he was skulking. Skulking through a major retail establishment, at that, the Borders Books and Music on Michigan Avenue, where Lauren Grable-Monroe was about to launch a national book tour by signing her runaway best-seller, *How to Trap a Friggin' Tycoon*.

The only thing that made Adam's new role tolerable was that he had drafted Lucas Conaway to man the position of Skulker's Assistant. Lucas, curiously, had no qualms whatsoever about skulking. In fact, he'd approached it with relish. Adam, too, found himself putting skulking in a whole new light, because in an effort to locate the best vantage point for Lauren Grable-Monroe's arrival, he had been forced to position himself in the psychology and self-help section of the store. Right in front of the books on—he tried not to look—impotence.

Oh, how the mighty had fallen. So to speak.

"Ooo, this one looks good," Lucas piped up from beside him, plucking a slender tome from a high shelf—where just about anybody could see him, for chrissakes. *Me and My Penile Implant: One Man's Journey to Enlightenment and Self-Discovery.* I just don't think I can wait for this bad boy to show up in paperback. I think I'll have to take this home and start reading it tonight. Gosh, I hope it has a happy ending."

Adam rolled his eyes and clenched his jaw, then smoothed a nonexistent wrinkle out of his charcoal suit jacket. He'd come to Borders straight from the *Man's Life* offices, because he hadn't wanted to miss a minute of Lauren Grable-Monroe's seven o'clock debut. Now, however, in his three pieces of dark wool—even if he had unbuttoned two of them—and his discreetly patterned necktie—even if he had loosened it—he was feeling significantly overdressed among the shoppers. Lucas, naturally, in his rumpled navy sweater and khaki trousers, didn't seem at all out of place.

"Oh, just shut up and drink your Starbucks, will you?" Adam instructed the other man.

The Skulker's Assistant dutifully reshelved the book, but instead of sipping from the steaming cup in his hand, he scanned the titles for another. "*Know Your Scrotum,*" he read from one spine. "Gosh, now, there's a philosophical quandary for you. Can any man truly know his scrotum?"

"Lucas . . ."

"Oh, now, here's one that might actually have some

potential," he said, reaching for yet another book. "*Love Me, Love My*—"

"*Lucas.*"

He shoved the book back into place and sighed heavily. "Boy, you are in some state tonight," he muttered irritably to Adam.

Yeah, and it wasn't the state of Rhode Island, either, Adam thought. He couldn't remember the last time he'd felt so agitated. And all on account of a woman he had yet to even see up close and personal. Though, certainly, over the past several weeks, he had seen more than his fill of her in just about every other context.

In the past month, Lauren Grable-Monroe had appeared on all of the morning news shows, in virtually each of the weekly news and lifestyle magazines, and on too many call-in radio shows to count.

She was saturating the market more pervasively than her book was. And that was saying something. Because in the few short weeks since the author had gone public, her book had blasted into the top ten of every nonfiction best-seller list in the country. At the rate it was selling, Adam thought, it would soon shoot right to number one.

Certainly the book had staying power. Because there were millions of potential buyers for it—all those women who fell into that "more likely to be abducted by a pack of kilt-wearing, spumoni-eating, Elvis-impersonating aliens than to be married after age thirty" statistic. And doubtless each new generation of females was going to want to know the whys and wherefores of trapping their very own tycoons.

It wasn't a particularly cheerful prospect, as far as Adam was concerned.

Lucas continued to scan the shelves as they waited, but evidently nothing more came close to capturing his interest, because he finally gazed around the store. "She's late."

"She's a woman," Adam reminded the other man unnecessarily.

"A late woman," Lucas concluded.

"Which is redundant," Adam remarked.

"Not that I don't share your opinion of the fairer sex," Lucas said, "but I know why I feel the way I do. What's your excuse?"

The question brought Adam up short. Not so much the question itself, or even the speculative tone of voice in which Lucas had uttered it. No, it was the fact that the other man had put voice to it at all that gave Adam pause. Lucas's was a personal question, and Adam wasn't used to getting personal with people. It was something that his acquaintances understood, and was probably why he had so few true friends and so many acquaintances. He rarely moved beyond the introduction phase of any relationship.

Lucas, it would appear, had no such qualms. Then again, Adam reminded himself, Lucas was from a brave new generation, one that had come of age in a more cooperative social environment, overrun by MTV, Nike for Women, and Mars and Venus in Every Room in the House.

Still, that didn't mean that Adam had to cross the generational line. So all he said in explanation was, "I used to be married."

"Ah," Lucas replied.

And that, evidently, was all that needed to be said. Because, surprisingly, Lucas went back to sipping his Starbucks. And Adam, in turn, went back to trying to pretend that he had no idea the impotence books were shelved right in front of him, well, would you look at that, who knew?

"I see an entourage," Lucas announced suddenly. "I do believe Lauren Grable-Monroe has entered the building."

As, indeed, she had. Somehow, Adam sensed her presence before he even saw her. A quick frisson of heat swept through him, as if someone had applied a small electrical charge to the base of his spine. But what startled him more than anything was the realization that he suddenly felt very much as if he'd just been transported back to adolescence.

To be specific, back to the first day of ninth grade, when Mitzi Moran had been assigned the desk right next to his in Biology. And in honor of the opening of football season, Mitzi had worn her jayvee cheerleader uniform to school. The one with the microscopic red skirt. And the skintight yellow sweater. And those little cotton socks that to this day he found so inexplicably erotic.

Man, that had been a great day. And an incredible feeling Adam had never thought to feel again. But suddenly, right in the middle of Borders Books and Music on Michigan Avenue, he was reliving that same hormonal, almost narcotic, surge.

He told himself it was only because he'd been anticipating this event for more than a month, ever since *Man's Life* had received a press release from Rockcastle Books that announced the great coming-out party of the illustrious Lauren Grable-Monroe. It wasn't the press release, however, that had most captured Adam's attention, teeming though it was with interesting—in a rabid, overblown, sensationalistic kind of way—tidbits about the author of *How to Trap a Freakin' Tycoon*.

Lauren Grable-Monroe, it seemed, was a resident of this very city, a factoid that had settled in the pit of his stomach like a piece of badly cooked veal. Rockcastle Books made no bones about the fact that the moniker

Lauren Grable-Monroe was a pseudonym flagrantly lifted from the three actresses who had starred in the film *How to Marry a Millionaire*. However, they *had* made bones—really big ones, too—about divulging who, exactly, had adopted the pseudonym. They had insisted that to divulge Ms. Grable-Monroe's true identity would endanger her position in the social community she loved, not to mention open them up to defamation suits.

According to her bio, whoever Lauren Grable-Monroe was, she had grown up on Chicago's Gold Coast, the only child of a wealthy commodities broker and his socialite wife. Her parents had, however, lost their fortune some years ago after a hushed-up scandal, the details of which, at least in the press release, were sketchy, at best. Thus their daughter, a former debutante, had made her way in the world by "making herself available" to numerous and sundry tycoons whose fancy she had captured along the way. And now that her parents were no longer alive—and, presumably, couldn't be embarrassed by her antics—she was hoping to recoup her family's financial losses by offering professional tips in a runaway best-seller.

Adam, of course, knew her entire biography was a lot of hooey. He'd grown up on the Gold Coast, too, and although he'd never troubled himself with idle gossip—or even active gossip—he would have heard about any scandal that had left anyone broke. More than that, though, he would have known about a socialite daughter making herself available the way Ms. Grable-Monroe claimed to have made herself available. Because Adam had *always* enjoyed available debutantes. Had her story been true, Lauren Grable-Monroe, whoever she was, would have been his—at least for a while.

But even the outright phony details of her life hadn't

been what had captured Adam's eye when he'd received Rockcastle's press release. No, what had caught his eye— among other body parts—was the publicity photo that had been included with it. Because it had been the kind of photo that could make a man lose sleep. And lots of it. In her glossy picture, Lauren Grable-Monroe evoked an image of a fabulous forties film star, all posh glamour and sex appeal. A fall of shoulder-length, platinum blond hair swept down over one eye in a pretty effective Veronica Lake "do." Her brown eyes were at half-mast, heavily shadowed and lushly lashed. And her mouth . . .

God, her mouth.

Her full, ripe lips were painted red, red, red. Her chin was resting on her hand, and she clutched a slender cigarette holder between two fingers tipped in crimson lacquer. But what Adam had noted most of all was that, judging by the expression on her face, she appeared to be *this* close to a shattering orgasm.

And it didn't stop there. Her voice, he knew, thanks to repeated television appearances and an NPR interview that he hadn't quite been able to bring himself to switch off, mirrored the image she projected—a deep and husky timbre, one that reflected her complete and unapologetic confidence in both her femininity and her effect on the opposite sex.

And speaking of sex, her voice reeked of it—of sex and sex appeal, of sexual knowledge and sexual power. And of something else, too, something Adam hadn't quite been able to identify. Something that had grabbed him by his libido and yanked hard.

Lauren Grable-Monroe, he had decided some time ago, was one hot tomata, no two ways about it. And hell, he hadn't even seen her in more than two dimensions yet.

Now, finally, he would be able to discover for himself

if the reality lived up to the media promise. Craning his head and pushing himself up taller, he gazed over the bookshelves and in the direction that Lucas was watching himself. And he realized right away that . . . *whoa, baby* . . . the reality looked to be pretty damned promising.

Blondness was the first thing Adam noted from this distance and this angle. Pale blond, the color of good champagne, flowing in a straight, silky cascade past her shoulders. Curviness was the second thing he noted. A tight, chocolate-brown skirt hugged her hips to midthigh, and the legs extending from beneath—all eight miles of them—were slim and elegant. A short jacket of the same dark fabric fell to her waist and hung open over a pale-gold top that scooped low over high, full breasts. Although a solid twenty or thirty feet separated him from the table where Ms. Grable-Monroe took her seat, he had a clear line of vision from which to take her in.

And, boy, did Adam want to take her in. Every last luscious inch of her.

"Wow."

The observation came not from Adam but from Lucas. Nevertheless, Adam couldn't think of a single thing to add. Unless it was to put the word into capital letters. And italics. With an exclamation point or two following behind. Because *WOW!!* pretty much summed up Lauren Grable-Monroe.

He watched as the entourage broke apart and scattered, then watched some more as she folded herself into a chair behind a table laden with what appeared to be . . . oh . . . about a billion copies of her book. Seated in chairs before the table and standing around at a respectable distance were what appeared to be, oh . . . about a billion women clutching copies of that book in their hands.

Most were young, Adam noticed, college age or even

younger, but many—too many—appeared to be his age, too. Several more were older than he, some by as many as three or four decades. The desire to marry money— or, at least, to trap it—evidently transcended generational lines.

"Ladies—and you few gentlemen," a young woman who was evidently an employee of the bookstore called out to the surrounding crowd. Adam couldn't help noticing that she clutched her own copy of *How to Trap a Tycoon* in her hand. "Borders is pleased tonight to be hosting best-selling author Lauren Grable-Monroe on the first stop of a multicity book tour. She'll speak briefly about her book, answer questions for twenty minutes, and then sign as many copies as she's able to sign. Please be patient, as the line promises to be long. And please join me in welcoming Lauren Grable-Monroe."

The fans, as they say, went wild. Because the applause that clamored up around the author was nothing short of feral. The author herself smiled brightly and wiggled expertly manicured, red-tipped fingers in greeting. "Hello," she said in that throaty, musky voice of hers. "And thank you all for coming tonight. Wow, I didn't expect such a crowd. This is amazing."

Oh, the hell it was, Adam thought. Rockcastle Books had spared no expense in promoting its latest best-seller. Still, he watched and listened and observed for the rest of the hour as Lauren Grable-Monroe charmed and captivated and entranced her already adoring—hey, her already worshipping—public. And he himself had to admit that there was definitely something rather . . . tempting . . . about her. Much to his surprise, he even found himself smiling and laughing at a few of her responses to some of the audience's rather pointed questions. Stranger still, Adam found himself wanting to raise his hand and ask a few of his own.

So, Ms. Grable-Monroe, just what is it about your book that everyone finds so damned wonderful?

Well, Mr. Darien, chapter seven seems to be of particular interest to most of my readers. It's about keeping tycoons like yourself in the bedroom.

And just what is it in chapter seven that everyone keeps raving about? Aside from that crème de menthe thing I've heard mentioned so frequently?

Why don't you read the book and find out for yourself?

What? And ensure that you receive an added royalty from my purchase? That's not my style.

Ooo, and just what is *your style, big boy?*

Why don't you read me and find out for yourself?

It occurred to Adam suddenly that although the self-help section in which he stood might be of some use after all—just where did they shelve the voices-in-my-head books, anyway?—anything on impotence was pretty much unnecessary at the moment. No, what he needed was something he really didn't want. Well, he *wanted* it, he just didn't *want* to want it. Unfortunately, judging by the looks of Lauren Grable-Monroe's reception, he was going to be surrounded by it—by her—for some time to come.

He stood in the bookstore watching her, until she had finished signing books for her devoted followers. And all the while, one thought kept circling in his head. He really, really, really wanted to take Lauren Grable-Monroe *down*. He just wasn't quite sure yet what he would do with her once he got her there.

"How's your story coming, Lucas?" he asked his staff writer as he watched his quarry blow kisses of farewell to her applauding fans.

"Not so good," Lucas replied. "I'm having trouble finding female tycoons."

Adam turned to face him. "You're joking, right? There are plenty of female tycoons in this town."

Lucas shrugged. "Not the right kind."

Adam narrowed his eyes. "What's the right kind?"

Lucas expelled an exasperated sound. "The kind that will give me the time of day, okay?"

Adam laughed. "Having trouble with the fairer sex, are we?"

"I'll get the story," Lucas assured him. "Just give me another week or two. I'm following a new lead." Before Adam had a chance to pry further, Lucas turned the tables. "How's *your* story coming?"

Only then did Adam recall that he had sort of announced his intention to investigate the elusive author himself way back when he'd assigned Lucas his story. Somehow, though, he'd never quite gotten around to undertaking that investigation.

Why not? he wondered now. It had seemed like a good idea at the time. And it had been more than a little enjoyable sitting at the bar that night plotting Lauren Grable-Monroe's downfall with Lucas—particularly that part about staking her out naked and covered with honey, spread-eagle, beneath a hot desert sun. It was an image that still crept into Adam's thoughts from time to time, and at the oddest moments, too, especially since he'd seen her publicity photo, because then he'd been able to put a face—a gorgeous, seductive, alluring face—on that body—that lush, rounded, bronzed, naked, sweaty, honey-covered body—and . . . and . . . and . . .

And where was he? Oh, yeah.

Other things had come up, so to speak, and his plans for Lauren had been put on hold. Recalling the honey-covered image again, however, Adam couldn't begin to imagine why he had let other things prevent his investigation. And now that he'd seen the author in the flesh—and quite nice flesh it was, too—albeit from a distance, he discovered, not much to his surprise, that he suddenly wanted to undertake his investigation again.

"I'm on the case," he assured Lucas.

"Yeah, you're on something, all right," the other man said.

"Yeah, and it's not Viagra, either."

"Are you going after her, or what?"

Adam turned back to where Lauren Grable-Monroe had been sitting mere moments ago and smiled. "Oh, yeah. I'm going after her. I'm going to find out who she is, where she comes from, and what the hell she was thinking to write a book like *How to Trap a Flaming Tycoon*."

"And then?" Lucas asked enthusiastically.

Adam hesitated. "I'm not quite sure yet. But I have a couple of ideas." One included honey and stakes and a hot desert sun, he realized. And the other . . .

Well, the other was nowhere near as polite.

"Lucas," he said, still preoccupied by his thoughts, "help me find out where they keep the books on the Gobi Desert and carnivorous insects."

Dorsey nibbled her lip anxiously as she flicked her gaze to Fran Schott, the publicist Rockcastle Books had assigned her for her book tour. "Are they gone yet?" she asked the tall young blonde who had entered the small stockroom.

Fran shook her head as she closed the door on a murmur of voices that slunk in from the other side. "There are still about a dozen people out there who want a few more words—or something—with Lauren. Most of them are male. And few of them look respectable."

Dorsey sighed fitfully. "Tell them Lauren has left the building."

"Believe me, I have," Fran assured her adamantly. "But a couple of Lauren's fans saw her—you—pass through this door, and they're not leaving until they see her—you—come back out again. You're—she's—just going to have to wait them out."

Dorsey didn't want to wait. She *couldn't* wait. If she had to be dressed in her Lauren costume much longer, she was going to scream. Her wig itched, her clothes pinched, her cosmetics weighed more than Mount Rushmore, and her Wonderbra made her feel like she was going to fall forward face first and suffocate on her own foam rubber inserts. Still, all things considered, her first public appearance had gone surprisingly well, especially in light of the fact that she'd been utterly terrified during the entire episode. Now, however, she just wanted to go home, take a bath, and return to Dorseyhood.

"You might as well make yourself comfortable," Fran said.

"I'd rather go home to be alone. I feel kind of ... strange."

"I'm not surprised. These things can be nerve-racking in the best of situations." The publicist smiled sympathetically. "And I don't imagine this is the best of situations."

Fran Schott had been apprised of the actual situation when Rockcastle Books had assigned her to escort Lauren on her book tour. She'd also been apprised of the fact that should she reveal the truth to anyone, she'd never work in publishing again.

Now the publicist shrugged apologetically. "I had no

idea it would be like this," she told Dorsey. "Had I suspected, I would have had a car waiting for you outside.
I just assumed that once the signing concluded, everyone
would scatter." She tilted her head toward the door.
"They might still, if you go out there and exchange a few
more words with them."

Dorsey shook her head. Vehemently. Through much
practice and rehearsal over the last month, she had managed to pretty much master the art of deception in creating Lauren Grable-Monroe. After she and Carlotta had
collected a suitable vamp's wardrobe from the department stores and couturiers along Michigan Avenue and
had amassed cosmetics the like of which Dorsey hadn't
even realized existed, they had spent the better part of an
afternoon creating the physical manifestation of Lauren.
With the addition of blond wig and brown contact lenses,
with the application of two or three—or ten—layers of
eye shadow, blush, lipstick, and whatever else filled those
little tubes and tubs that Carlotta had insisted were es-
sential, with the body-altering Wonderbra and stiletto
heels, Dorsey had seemed to become someone else entirely. Dorsey *had* become someone else entirely. She
had become Lauren Grable-Monroe.

Until she opened her mouth.

That part had taken a bit longer to master. She'd had
to mask her voice, and she had been obligated to master
the art of—she shuddered now to think about it—repartee. Most difficult of all, she had been forced to get in
touch with her sexuality, something she'd never really
bothered to do before.

It wasn't that Dorsey didn't like sex. On the contrary,
on those few occasions when she had experienced it—
long ago, in a galaxy far away—she was reasonably certain she had enjoyed herself. She was simply opposed to

using sex as a marketing tool, that was all. Especially since she was the one carrying the toolbox. So to speak. Lauren needed to be presented as a sexual being. Dorsey was not a sexual being. Therefore, she could only sustain the illusion for a brief time.

And besides, her wig really did itch a lot.

She remembered then that she had changed her clothes and donned her makeup at Severn earlier that evening before meeting Fran on campus, and that the publicist had then driven her to the bookstore. Now Dorsey's blue jeans, hiking boots, and lumberjack sweater were packed safely away in her backpack. The backpack which—hey, what do you know?—just so happened to be leaning haphazardly on a shelf right behind Fran. Dorsey also recalled that there was a tiny employee washroom behind the door to Fran's left.

"I'm leaving," she announced suddenly, crisply.

Fran arched her blond eyebrows in surprise. "Going to send Lauren right through the gauntlet out there, are you?" the publicist asked. "You're a braver man than I."

Dorsey smiled and tugged at the fake fingernail glued on her left index finger, snapping it clean off. "Lauren's staying right here," she said. "*I'm* the one who's leaving."

Fran eyed her warily but said nothing as Dorsey snatched the backpack from the shelf behind her. Fifteen minutes later, she was once again green-eyed, bespectacled, and auburn-haired. She tugged her baggy, olivedrab sweater over her cotton undershirt and faded blue jeans, then pushed her glasses to the top of her freshly scrubbed nose. And then, rather gleefully, she crammed every last remnant of Lauren Grable-Monroe—suit, cosmetics, and sky-high heels—into the faded blue backpack.

Something oddly satisfying wound through her as she zipped the pack up tight. Something even more pleasant wandered through her as she smiled and tossed it at the publicist, who, even though clearly surprised by the action, caught it in capable hands.

"Fran," Dorsey said as she strode to the stockroom door, "I'm going downstairs to the coffee shop for an iced cappuccino."

The publicist blinked once in confusion, then asked, "But how will you get home?"

"I'll catch a cab," Dorsey told her. She nodded once toward the backpack and grinned wickedly. "You'll keep an eye on Lauren for me, won't you?"

And with that, she turned and strode casually—happily—out the door.

Chapter 5

Had he been watching where he was going, Adam wouldn't have bumped into the young woman who appeared suddenly from behind a stack of best-sellers at the front of the store. Nor would he have knocked her cup of coffee right out of her hand. Nor would he have reached out to steady her when it looked as if she was going to go down along with said cup of coffee. Nor would he have felt the surge of utter . . . utter . . . What was the opposite of impotence? he wondered idly. Utter . . . *virility*—yeah, that was it—that thundered through him when he found himself gazing down into familiar, if startled, pale-green eyes.

So he was pretty damned glad he hadn't been watching where he was going.

"Mack," he said softly, a warm ripple of genuine delight purling through him when he recognized the gift that fortune had quite literally—and quite liberally— dropped into his hands.

Right on the heels of that recognition, however, came the even more delightful realization that after months of thinking about it, dreaming about it, fantasizing about it, he was touching Mack—actually touching her—for the very first time. And just like that, the ripple of warmth became a crashing tsunami of heat.

It was a rather . . . stimulating . . . sensation.

Before he had a chance to contemplate that particular revelation further—not that extensive contemplation of anything was of primary importance to him at the moment—she righted herself, straightened herself, steadied herself . . . and took a *biiiiig* step backward.

And that was when Adam realized that Mack looked a little different from how she usually did. Her hair, instead of being caught back in the elaborate braid she normally wore at Drake's, tumbled free in a riot of wild, dark-auburn curls about her face and shoulders. Her face, too, was different, due to the presence of oval-shaped, wire-rimmed spectacles that perched pertly on the bridge of her nose. Strangely, instead of detracting from her looks, her glasses only enhanced them. Her eyes seemed larger, somehow, clearer, more expressive.

And the expression he noticed most was . . . fear? But that was ridiculous. Why on earth would Mack be afraid of him? After all, looking the way she did right now, all soft and pretty and touchable, she was a hell of a lot scarier than he was.

"What are you doing here?" he asked her, nudging aside the impression of fear—both hers and his. Then, immediately, he answered his own question. "Oh, wait. Don't tell me. Let me guess. You came to see the newest official spokes-icon of the women's movement."

She narrowed her eyes at him curiously. "And who would that be?"

He smiled indulgently. "Nice try," he said. "But you'll never convince me that you didn't come here as a devoted disciple of Her Most Royal Commodity, Lauren Grable-Monroe."

"Oh, her."

"Oh, please. Don't act surprised."

Oddly, though, she didn't seem to be acting. She really did seem to be surprised. Just not by the presence of Lauren Grable-Monroe, that was all. Clearly, her surprise—and something more, he just couldn't quite say what—had been generated by his own presence in the store.

Then again, he reminded himself, it was only natural that she and he, for that matter, might feel a bit awkward, seeing as how the two of them had never met in surroundings other than Drake's. And at the club, their roles were always clearly defined. Plus, they were always separated by the bar—among other things. Adam really had never laid a hand on Mack until a moment ago. Now, suddenly, with all the barriers, both physical and psychological, gone, he realized he wanted to lay more than just his hand on her. He, too, felt a bit surprised. By, of all things, his own uncertainty. He'd never felt uncertain about anything in his life.

Oh, except for Mack, of course.

"Well, it was interesting seeing you, Mr. Darien," she said, stooping to pick up the cup of coffee that had spilled on the floor between them. It had been covered by a snug plastic lid, so the mess was reasonably well contained. Still, there was a small beige puddle spreading rapidly by the time she scooped the cup up. "I'd better find somebody to take care of this," she added. "See you at Drake's."

In other words, Adam translated, Beat it.

"I'll help you," he said.

But instead of stooping alongside her, he lifted a hand to hail one of the bookstore employees. Evidently one of them had seen the collision, because the young man was approaching with a roll of paper towels.

"And I'll buy you another . . ." Adam gazed down and noted the proliferation of ice cubes and foam mingling with the beige and bit back a gag. How anyone could do something like that to a perfectly good cup of coffee was beyond him. "Another . . . whatever it was you were drinking," he finally concluded.

Mack stood when the bookstore employee assured her he would take care of the mess, then apologized profusely for the spill, even though Adam had been the one responsible.

"I'm the one who should apologize," he said.

She met his gaze levelly, her green eyes flashing with . . . something. "Yes, I know, but you didn't apologize, did you?" she asked pointedly.

He narrowed his gaze at her, then turned his attention to the young man on the floor. "Sorry," he said. Without awaiting a reply, he turned to Mack. "I'll buy you another one."

She expelled a soft sound of disbelief and shook her head. "Do you *ever* defer to *anyone*?"

This time he was the one to utter a sound of disbelief. "Of course not," he told her. But he offered no further explanation. After all, he figured, none was necessary, was it?

She nodded. "No, of course not," she echoed. "I stand corrected."

Yeah, she stood something, all right, Adam thought, unable to keep his gaze from roving hungrily over every inch of her. He was trying to figure out if this was the first time he'd seen her from the waist down. Surely not. Then again, he was pretty sure he'd remember a below-the-waist like hers.

Her baggy bartender uniform, although very appealing, hadn't prepared him for the trim, surprisingly long legs revealed by her snug blue jeans. Her sweater, unfortunately, was not so snug, but during the collision, the scooped neck had fallen off one shoulder, revealing a strap of white cotton undergarment—not to mention creamy shoulder—beneath. And that more than made up for any lack of shape the sweater suffered. Not that Mack was particularly well endowed, Adam noticed, and not for the first time. But what she did have was quite . . . fetching.

"I'll buy you another cup of coffee," he said for the third time, irritated that she hadn't yet taken him up on his offer. Or his edict. Whatever.

"That's okay," she said, her voice sounding rushed and anxious. "It's not necessary. I really need to get something to eat anyway."

"All the better," he told her. "I skipped dinner myself. There's a great restaurant a couple of blocks away. We can eat there. My treat."

Again she threw him that incredulous look at the way he tossed around orders, as if he were czar of all he surveyed. Okay, fine. So maybe he was a little . . . commanding. Adam preferred to think of it as being a good delegator. All right, a good dictator. Details, details. *Jeez*.

"Um, that's okay," she told him yet again. "You don't have to buy me dinner. Thanks, anyway."

It took a moment for Adam to realize that she was determined to turn him down. And it took him a moment more to realize how much that bothered him.

"Oh, come on," he cajoled. "It's just dinner. What's the big deal?"

The moment he voiced the question, Adam remembered what the big deal was. Her husband. As big deals went, that one was sort of . . . big. At least, he'd always visualized Mack's husband as being big. About six foot six, to be precise. Weighing in at three hundred pounds at least. With no neck. And a nasty overbite. And a hairy back. And knuckles grazing the tarmac. A really big beer belly. And a really tiny—

Before his thoughts became too distastefully graphic, Adam dropped his gaze down to the third finger of her left hand, to the slim gold band that always served to remind him of his folly. Much to his surprise, however—not to mention his profound interest—he discovered that Mack wasn't wearing her wedding ring.

Oddly, that made him remember that she hadn't worked a number of her shifts at Drake's over the past few weeks. She'd always had one of the other bartenders filling in for her, but she had missed quite a few nights. He wondered now if the reason for her absences at work might have something to do with the absence of a ring on her left hand. Like maybe her marriage wasn't all it was cracked up to be these days. And then he recalled once again their surroundings and couldn't help but think that Mack had come to the bookstore tonight to hear a best-selling author tell her how to trap herself a tycoon.

"Dinner's not a good idea," she told him. But, Adam noticed, she didn't say exactly why.

"It's an excellent idea," he countered. Then, before she could object—and because he just couldn't quite help himself—he reached out and wrapped his fingers lightly around her upper arm, urging her gently forward. And, talking as fast as he could, he added, "Besides, there's something I've been wanting to talk to you about for a long time now, and Drake's just isn't conducive to frank conversation."

Dorsey had no idea how Adam Darien talked her into joining him for dinner, but fifteen minutes later, she found herself seated across from him at a cozy—really, it was too cozy—table for two, in a quiet—really, it was too quiet—restaurant near the bookstore. Actually, that wasn't entirely true. She was, in fact, fairly certain she knew how he had talked her into joining him for dinner. She had let him. That was how. She just wasn't sure she knew *why* she had let him.

Oh, all right, that wasn't exactly true, either. She was pretty sure she knew why she had let him. Because number one, he had caught her completely unawares when he had invited her. And number two, he had simply looked too scrumptious to resist.

And that was precisely the problem, Dorsey remembered now too late; she had found him irresistible since day one. He was an enigma, and she'd never been able to let go of puzzles she couldn't solve. He was everything she should deplore in a man—autocratic, self-centered, elitist, rich—but there was just something about him. . . . She couldn't quite put her finger on what.

But some undefinable thing in him called to something equally undefinable in her. She could think of no other way to describe it. A rare, unifying element of some sort that they had in common. Whenever he strode into the bar at Drake's, every sense she possessed went on alert. She could have her back to the door, could be focused completely on a complex and unfamiliar drink recipe, but the second Adam Darien entered, she knew—she *knew*—he was there.

And her reaction to him, so unlike any she had experienced to anyone else, was something she couldn't help but want to explore.

Too, somehow she sensed that his exterior—as hard and impenetrable as it seemed to be—was little more than a facade, one that hid behind it a completely different creature from the face he presented to the world. Her conversations with him, full though they were of his dogma and opinions, were always animated—the two of them were evenly matched. He wasn't quite so full of himself that he didn't listen, and listen well, to what she had to say. And even when he disagreed with what she said, which was pretty much all the time, he still showed respect for her evaluations.

He was an intriguing mix of contradictions, first gruff, then gentle, at once antagonistic and agreeable, both chauvinist and conversationalist. As a result, he was that most irresistible kind of man for a woman to find—one who challenged her, both on a human and a feminine level.

Plus, she had to admit as she glanced over the top of her menu to inadvertently watch him inspect his, he really was very cute.

More than cute, she admitted grudgingly. It wasn't only what went on inside his head that appealed to her. As much pride as Dorsey had in her intellectual achievements, she was by no means above succumbing to a primitive physical attraction. And the attraction she felt toward him was certainly primitive. Potent. Relentless. Rawly sexual. Which, now that she thought about it, was probably a very good reason for her to avoid him. It was a long time since she had been sexually attracted to a man, never so powerfully as she was to Adam Darien. She'd just as soon it not be happening now, when her own sexuality was being manipulated by someone else—namely, Lauren Grable-Monroe.

"So what looks good to you?" he asked suddenly, glancing up from his menu before she had a chance to avert her gaze. He smiled—rather smugly, too—when he caught her ogling him.

What looked good to her, Dorsey thought, he would be better off not knowing. Because it would only lead to trouble. "Oh, gosh. I can't really decide," she hedged.

"Interesting," he countered smoothly, fixing his gaze on hers. "Because I know exactly what I want."

A surge of heat hummed through her at his softly uttered assurance, and she had no idea how to respond. All she could do was damn Lauren anyway for using up all the good repartee hours ago.

Thankfully, their server arrived with the drinks they had ordered—or, rather, that Adam Darien had ordered. God forbid he should consult her first, after all, she thought, as the waiter placed a glass of very expensive Merlot in front of her. "It was cold walking here, and you need warming" had been his reason for ordering red wine instead of the iced cappuccino he had promised her earlier. The way he'd voiced the "you need warming" part, however, had gone a *loooong* way toward remedying that particular problem. Still, there was no reason *he* had to know that.

Dorsey mumbled her thanks to the server and, resigned to her fate, lifted the glass to her lips for an idle sip. The wine was dark, smooth, and mellow, and she had to admit that it felt good going down. But it was nowhere near as intoxicating as the dark, smooth, mellow look in his eyes. And she couldn't help wondering if he'd feel just as good going—

Uh-oh.

Their waiter hastily scribbled down their dinner orders as they gave them—an amazing feat, as far as Dorsey was concerned, seeing as how she herself couldn't understand a word of what she said in that regard—then conveniently disappeared. She opened her mouth to say something, anything, that might do something, anything, to alleviate the frantic heat arcing between them—or, at the very least, the frantic heat smacking her upside the head—when Adam took matters out of her hands by speaking first.

And, oh, what a speech it was.

"So, Mack, tell me about this husband of yours."

It was the last thing Dorsey had expected to hear from him. Although he had commented once or twice at Drake's on her phony marital status, it had always been some silly little flirtatious thing that meant nothing. "Mack, if you weren't a married woman, I'd take you away from all of this" or some such thing. He had never actually asked her about her husband. And why the subject should come up now she couldn't imagine.

She remembered then that her wedding ring—the one her nonexistent husband had allegedly slipped over her finger on their imaginary wedding day—was currently lying on the top shelf of her locker at Drake's. Hoping Adam didn't notice, she slowly withdrew her left hand from the table and tucked it between her leg and the chair.

And just when had she taken the next, Herculean step, toward thinking of him as Adam instead of Mr. Darien? she wondered. Unfortunately, she couldn't find an adequate answer to her own question. Nor could she find one for his. So she answered him with one of her own.

"Why do you ask?" she replied.

He lifted his shoulders and let them fall in a shrug that

was in no way casual. "You mentioned once in conversation that you thought money could solve all of a woman's problems." He leaned forward, resting both elbows on the table, folding his arms one over the other. It was a harmless action that seemed very intimidating somehow. "If that's true," he continued, "then why didn't *you* marry for money? Why didn't *you* go out and trap yourself a tycoon? Seems like that would have made your life a whole lot easier."

"Who says I didn't marry for money?" she replied evasively.

Adam chuckled low, a wonderfully masculine sound that seemed to meander indolently through her entire body. And oh, *boy*, did it feel good.

"Well, there's the fact that you attend Severn," he said, "a college whose student body is comprised of those less financially endowed than others. And there's also the small matter of your job at Drake's," he added. "Call me presumptuous, but I'd think that had you gone to all the trouble to find a rich man, you probably wouldn't have been admitted to Severn, and you probably wouldn't be tending bar to supplement your college expenses. A nice girl like you in a place like that, I mean."

She hesitated before responding, not so much because she wasn't sure what to say this time, but because of the way he had uttered the words "A nice girl like you." Simply put, he had voiced the phrase as if he'd meant it exactly as he'd said it—that he did indeed consider her to be a nice girl. That was completely at odds with what the rest of her patrons at Drake's seemed to think. A woman bartender was to them, evidently, the equivalent of a prostitute. Except that they could get a bartender for a lot cheaper, and she'd fix a helluva nightcap after they had sex.

"Maybe I work at Drake's," Dorsey replied dryly, "because I like the social interaction and fascinating conversation."

He eyed her skeptically as he fingered the base of his wine glass in a way that set her heart to racing again. He had nice hands, she noted. Big and square and blunt-fingered, exactly what a man's hands should look like.

"And maybe," he said, "an asteroid the size of Lithuania will crash into the Earth while we're sleeping peacefully in our beds tonight."

She shrugged. "Hey, it could happen."

He laughed low in that very masculine way again before cajoling, "Come on, Mack. Tell me about the forthright, upright, do-right guy you're married to."

She sighed, hedging again. "Um, gee, what's there to tell?" she finally asked. Aside from the fact that he didn't exist, of course. Which, now that she thought about it, made him infinitely more appealing than most men of her acquaintance.

Present company excluded, naturally.

"What's his name?" Adam asked.

"Why do you want to know?" she stalled yet again. "I mean, I don't ask you about your girlfriends, do I?" she asked pointedly.

"Girlfriends?" he repeated, clearly surprised—and a bit scandalized?—by her charge. "As in plural? Isn't that pushing it?"

She scrunched up her shoulders again. "I don't know. Is it? You seem like the kind of guy who—"

"What?" he asked with a wicked grin when she cut herself off.

"Nothing," she replied quickly, wondering what had possessed her to suggest such a thing to begin with. "It's not important."

He opened his mouth, clearly to object again, but closed it and eyed her with much consideration. "But then, we were talking about you," he finally said, deftly turning the topic right back to where he had initially assigned it. Dammit.

"I don't want to talk about me," she told him.

Hastily, she scrambled for some other topic to discuss, something that would lead to their normal philosophical differences. Because at Drake's, invariably, the more contentious their conversations became, the more Adam smiled—and, oddly, the better he tipped her. And the more he smiled, the more contentious Dorsey's remarks became. Not just because she liked the big tips, but because she liked his smile, too.

She liked his smile a lot. Even more than the big tips. And tonight was promising to make her a very wealthy woman indeed.

"I bet he's blue collar," Adam said suddenly, grinning again.

"Who?"

"Your husband," he reminded her. "I bet he operates heavy machinery for a living, am I right?"

She couldn't quite help the bubble of laughter that erupted at that. "Heavy machinery," she repeated blandly.

He nodded. "A forklift, I'm guessing. No, wait," he corrected himself. "A bulldozer. Yeah, that's it. I'm right, aren't I?"

Dorsey opened her mouth to comment, but quite frankly had no idea what to say.

Evidently taking her silence as affirmation, Adam went on, "I knew it. I know women. I know what kind of man attracts them. You would definitely go for the heavy machinery type."

She nodded slowly. "I see. And what else can you tell

me about this bulldozer operator that I'm supposedly married to?"

He seemed to give that some thought. "Well, let's see now," he began. "He probably has some really straightforward, hardworking name, too. Like . . . like . . ."

"Knute?" she suggested, biting back a giggle. "Rocky? Axel? Bull?"

He narrowed his eyes at her. "Actually, I was thinking more along the lines of . . . Dave."

"Dave the bulldozer operator," she repeated.

"Tell me I'm wrong."

"What you are," she told him, "is remarkable. Truly. Remarkable."

His grin turned smug. "Well, I hate to say I told you so, but . . ."

Someone at a neighboring table laughed loudly at something then, but the sound seemed to come from very far away. For a moment, Dorsey simply could not look away from Adam Darien's beautiful Bambi-brown eyes. It was as if he were drawing her into himself, slowly and thoroughly, until she just couldn't quite get away.

And then the sweet, peaceful moment vanished, shattered as it was by the comment he made next.

"Well, at least it's nice to know *you* haven't been sucked in by this tycoon-trapping nonsense," he said, gazing down into his wine before lifting it to his lips for an idle sip. "If I ever get my hands on Lauren Grable-Monroe," he continued as he lowered his glass to the table again, "she'll find out that a tycoon trapped is one mean fuh . . . uh, friggin' animal, that's what. Oh, *man*, would I like to get my hands on that woman."

Dorsey told herself to say nothing, to just ignore the remark and move on to another subject, something harmless and bland that wouldn't become a forum for debate—religion, politics, women's rights, fashion dos and don'ts, that kind of thing. But being the kind of woman she was—namely, impulsive and incautious—and seeing as how she rather took his attack personally she just couldn't quite let it go by.

So very quietly, she asked, "Who says I'm not a complete convert to Ms. Grable-Monroe's book?"

He arched his eyebrows in surprise, parting his lips slightly. Just enough so that, had she wanted to, she could have leaned across the tiny table and tasted him, right now, this very minute, in front of God and everybody. But of course, she didn't want to do that. Heavens, no. Not right here in the middle of the restaurant. Just what kind of girl did he think she was?

Much better to do that in private.

"You've been converted to Ms. Grable-Monroe's book?" he asked. "Does this mean you're planning on leaving your husband to find a man with money?"

And did he actually sound hopeful when he asked that? she wondered. Surely not. She tilted her head to one side and said, "That depends."

He eyed her with much interest. "On what?"

She strove for a cocky grin. "On whether or not he's done the laundry when I get home tonight."

Adam looked absolutely scandalized by the mere suggestion. "You make the poor sap do the laundry?"

Dorsey looked positively incredulous in response. "Hey, half of the dirty underwear would be his, you know. Why shouldn't he do the laundry?"

"Somehow, I can't imagine Dave the bulldozer operator sorting socks."

"Hey, you might be surprised what Dave the bulldozer operator could do."

In no way did Dorsey mean for the comment to be

suggestive, but somehow, it came out sounding exactly that way. She supposed it was because, no matter how much or how little time she spent talking to Adam Darien, somehow, at some point, their conversation always became suggestive. And that, she supposed, was because she found him so attractive. And, she knew, he found her attractive, too. In spite of that, he'd never overstepped the bounds of propriety, probably because of her alleged marital status. Still, that didn't keep them from being attracted to each other. Nor did it keep their conversations from straying into dangerous waters.

"So what else is Dave . . . good at?"

Really dangerous waters.

The way he voiced the question made a quiver of heat dance around Dorsey's entire body, and she didn't trust herself to say anything more. Adam, however, seemed not to share her problem. Because he continued to eye her expectantly as he lifted his glass again and filled his mouth with wine, his gaze never, ever, not even for a second leaving hers. She couldn't help but be fascinated by the way his strong throat worked over the swallow, nor could she prevent the heat she felt creeping into her face as she watched.

Worse than all that, though, was the fact that he smiled—very knowingly—as he placed his glass back on the table. And then, more softly than she had ever heard him speak, he asked, "More important than that, though, what else are *you* good at, Mack?"

Chapter 6

Adam never found out what Mack was good at. Not from her, at any rate. Not during dinner. Now, as he drove her home—after practically picking her up and carrying her to his car when she'd kept insisting she would walk to the El instead, alone; yeah, right—he still wasn't sure what he'd expected to find out when he'd asked her about her . . . goodness. But he hadn't been able to help himself in voicing the question. The way she danced around the subject of her husband—or, at least, her alleged husband—had driven him nuts. He still wasn't sure what the hell was going on.

Was she married? Was she separated? Had she ever actually had a husband to begin with? Adam honestly wasn't sure now. The absence of her wedding ring and the fact that she had never specifically answered him one way or the other about Dave the bulldozer operator really had him wondering.

Was she married? And why was he so obsessed with finding out the answer to that question?

As the Porsche rumbled confidently down a quiet street in Oak Brook, it murmured its contentment with the cool night air outside. Which was good, because nobody else was saying a damned thing. Even their conversation over dinner had been surprisingly sparse. Which was odd considering the animation of their discussions at Drake's, where there were definite parameters and boundaries to inhibit them.

But he and Mack hadn't been at Drake's tonight. Therefore, those parameters and boundaries were immaterial. There should have been neither restraint nor hindrance to the topics the two of them could broach. Yet that very freedom of speech had hampered them both. They'd forsaken the meaty subjects they normally tackled in favor of—Adam swallowed his revulsion—chitchat. As a result, they hadn't discussed much of anything at all.

Especially Mack's husband. Or lack thereof.

Was she married?

The question echoed again in his mind, and no amount of ignoring it would squelch Adam's curiosity. Over the past hours in Mack's company, he was inclined to think that no, she wasn't. Not just because of the absence of her wedding ring. And not just because she had sidestepped each of his questions regarding her spouse. No, it was because of the way she had been looking at him all night. As if she was going to forsake all the luscious tidbits on the dessert cart in favor of something else entirely. Yep, crème brûlée and tiramisu had nothin' on Adam Darien, if the look in Mack's eyes was any indication. No married woman would look at an unmarried man that way. No happily married woman, at any rate.

Was she married?

If she was, regardless of whether or not it was a happy union, Adam wasn't the kind of man to violate the marital bond—his own or anyone else's. He knew too well what it felt like to have such a trust betrayed, to be on the receiving end of spousal infidelity. If Mack was married, no matter the state of her matrimony, he wouldn't press his luck. Or her.

If she *wasn't* married, however . . .

Well, even then, he wasn't sure it was a good idea to get mixed up with her in anything other than a mixed drink capacity. Ultimately, they could wind up in a much more difficult position than simply being shaken or stirred. He and Mack had a nice friendship. Did he really want to mess with that?

"It's on the right," she said suddenly, scattering his ruminations. Her soft voice sounded unnaturally loud in the close confines of the previously silent car. "Number seventy-three, second to last from the corner."

Adam slowed the Porsche as he approached the quaint—he could think of no other word to use, even though "quaint" was one he normally, manfully, avoided—townhouse, coming to a halt beside a sleek Jaguar sedan. It was a quiet street, devoid of traffic at this hour on a Monday night. In the bluish-tinted light of a corner street lamp, he developed a quick visual impression of wrought-iron railings on tidy front stoops, window boxes full of bright chrysanthemums, beveled glass in bay windows, and lace curtains.

Townhouses around here didn't rent cheaply, he couldn't help but observe. And mortgages here were even more costly. Mack's address amounted to awfully nice digs for a bartender-student and her bulldozer-operator husband. If, in fact, these were her digs. And if, in fact, she shared the digs with a bulldozer-operator husband who may or may not be real.

Was she married?

Only one way to find out.

"I'll walk you up," Adam said, telling himself that the simple offer did *not* sound like a royal command.

He double-parked, flicked on his emergency flashers, and switched off the engine. Then he turned to find that Mack was already opening her door and scrambling out of the car—or, more accurately, fleeing from the car. The minute she was out, she hurried between two luxury sedans parked at the curb beside her toward the front porch of the building she'd identified as her home.

"Hey!" Adam called after her as he raced to catch up.

He did so just as she cleared the top step and alighted on the front stoop. Unable to quite help himself, he curled his fingers around her elbow in an effort to slow her escape. The small action must have caught her off guard, though, because Mack stumbled a bit as he tugged her gently back. Instinctively, as he had earlier in the bookstore, he extended his other hand to once again prevent her from falling. This time, however, he was ready for her when she righted, straightened, and steadied herself. And this time, he stopped her when she tried to take that *biiiiig* step in retreat.

"What's your hurry?" he asked softly, breathlessly. Though he couldn't begin to imagine why he should feel breathless after such a short, quick sprint. Then he looked down at Mack's face and knew exactly why. And what little breath was left him evaporated completely.

She had slipped off her glasses at some point during the evening—an action whose significance Adam decided not to ponder just now—and her eyes seemed brighter, even greener, thanks to the spill of light from the street lamp behind them. Her lips, plump and dewy and oh-so-sexy, were parted softly, though whether in surprise or for some other reason he chose not to contemplate. And her hair, those fiery tresses that had danced about her shoulders all night, just begging for a man's touch, danced about her shoulders now, just begging for a man's touch.

How could he resist?

Lifting a hand gingerly to her shoulder, he captured one errant coppery curl and twined it around his forefinger, twisting slowly, leisurely, deliberately. As he completed the gesture, his hand drew nearer her face, and his other fingers skimmed lightly over the elegant line of her jaw. Mack gasped softly at the contact, opening her eyes wider, parting her lips more. And then, without thinking, without questioning, Adam dipped his head toward hers and claimed her mouth with his.

Fire flashed in his belly when he tasted her for the first time and he savored the mingling essences of wine and woman. Wanting more, he stepped forward and closed what little distance still lay between them. The hand he'd caught in her hair framed her face just as easily, and he tipped her head back some, so that he could plunder her mouth at will. At the same time, he slipped his other hand around her waist, splaying it open at the small of her back to push her gently forward into his embrace.

For just the briefest of moments, she stiffened, doubling her fists loosely against his chest. But she made no effort to push him away. And then, without warning, she melted into him, curving one hand over his shoulder, threading the fingers of her other slowly through his hair. Tightening his arm around her waist, Adam pulled her upward, closer to himself. He buried his face in the delicate curve where her neck joined her shoulder, nuzzling the soft, fragrant skin he encountered there. She sighed, murmuring a feather-light sound of contentment, then tilted her head back even more. When she did, he felt the ends of her hair brush over the hand he held at her back, a sensation that was surprisingly arousing.

She smelled incredible, a heavy, heady, intoxicating scent that seemed both perfectly suitable and entirely inappropriate for her. It tempted him, lulled him, drew him closer still. Nosing aside the wide neck of her sweater, he pressed his lips to her throat, dragging light, open-mouthed kisses up and down the slender column before running the tip of his tongue along her collarbone.

She murmured another low, provocative sound and crowded her body closer to his, and his heart hammered wildly at the gentle thrust and fluid motion of her soft breasts against his chest. The hand he had pressed to her back fell to the curve of her bottom, and he pushed her forward, upward, rubbing her belly languidly against the swollen, heavy hardness that swelled urgently against his trousers.

A torrent of desire flooded him as their bodies met, and a ballast of need rocked him. And for one very brief, very scary moment, Adam thought he might never recover.

Too far, too soon, he thought. Way, way, too far. Way, way, too soon.

Somehow, he rallied his resources to retreat, but not by much. He nuzzled her neck again, more slowly, less urgently this time, then looped his arms loosely around her waist and tucked her head beneath his chin. Mack clung to him and buried her face in his shoulder, breathing erratically, her entire body trembling. Somehow, he sensed she was reluctant to look at him. And he wasn't sure whether that was a good thing or not.

For one long moment, Adam only held her in silence, wondering what the hell had just happened. Gradually, he managed to will his own heart rate to settle, and slowly, he goaded his libido into submission. Eventually, Mack lifted her head from his shoulder, but she didn't pull herself away. Nor did she look up to meet his gaze. Instead, she focused her attention on his chest, and idly—nervously—fingered the lapels of his jacket.

But she didn't say a word.

So Adam spoke instead. Sort of. "You're, um . . ." Finding that particular effort a bit difficult to manage, he cleared his throat and tried again. "This is just a shot in the dark, but . . . You're not . . . married, are you?"

Mack expelled a single humorless chuckle, then glanced up at him for the merest of moments before looking away again. Nevertheless, it was time enough for him to see that she was a little dazed and a lot confused. Maybe even as confused as he was himself.

"Gosh, figured that out all by yourself, did you?" she replied quietly. She shook her head slowly. "No, I'm not married," she added. "I wear a wedding ring at Drake's to keep the members from hitting on me, that's all."

He nodded, even though he wasn't sure he understood or approved of the deception. "Ever been married?" he asked further.

She gazed out at the dark street and shook her head again. "No."

"There's no Dave the bulldozer operator?"

"No."

"No one at all?"

This time she hesitated before replying. And she continued to avoid his gaze.

So Adam clarified his question. "No one special who fills your head during the day and your bed at night?"

She squeezed her eyes shut tight for a moment, then opened them again. Very, very slowly, she looked up to meet his gaze. "There's no one in my bed at night, no."

Suggesting that there *was* someone who filled her head during the day, Adam concluded. Somehow, though, he couldn't quite bring himself to ask her who that might be.

"You doing anything tomorrow night?" he asked her impulsively.

She hesitated before answering, but she didn't look away. "I have to work."

He nodded. "Right. I forgot." Hoping he didn't sound too desperate, but worried that he did—desperate was, after all, exactly what he was feeling—he asked, "Can you get someone else to take your shift?"

With clear reluctance, she told him, "No. I can't. I've already asked Lindy for too many nights off lately. I don't think she's going to tolerate too many more."

Adam wanted to ask her about all those missed shifts, was curious as to just why there had been so many of them lately. But the question that came out of his mouth instead was, "When's your next night off? I want to see you again."

For a long moment, she only gazed up at him in silence, her dark brows arrowed downward in very clear concern. Adam couldn't imagine what she had to feel worried about. In spite of all the uncertainty tying him up in knots, he hadn't felt this good himself for a long, long time.

"I'll be off Thursday," she told him. "But I, um . . . I'm busy. I can't see you. I'm sorry."

"How about this weekend, then?"

She shook her head again, harder this time. "I can't. I have to . . . I have something I have to do."

A knot of anxiety closed tighter inside him at her response. After the way they'd just responded to each other, he'd begun to think that maybe the two of them . . . Well. He wasn't sure what to think the two of them might do. But he had been thinking in terms of *the two of them*. And that was more than a little unsettling.

"Is it because of your job at Drake's?" he asked. "Because Lindy would fire you if she found out you and I were going out? Because if that's the reason, Mack, she'll never have to know. Or if that makes you uncomfortable, then I can talk to her, and maybe—"

"It's not that," she interrupted him.

"Then what?"

A slash of disappointment darkened her features. "I just have things to do, okay?"

Things to do, he echoed to himself. He couldn't recall ever being brushed off quite so vaguely. *Things to do*. Yeah, that was pretty clear.

"Fine," he muttered blandly. "No problem." Nodding once, he dropped his hands from around her waist and took a step away, then turned toward the stairs.

"Adam—"

It was the first time he'd heard her say his name aloud, and there was a pleading, plaintive tone to her voice when she said it. As if she was torn between what she wanted to do, and what she felt she should do. Even though it was probably pointless to make the effort, but unwilling to leave things as they were, Adam spun back around and reached for her again, pulling her roughly toward himself until her body was flush against his. He buried his hand beneath her hair, cupping it around the nape of her neck. And then he bent and covered her mouth with his again. This time when he kissed her, it was fiercely, insistently, possessively.

She had just sighed her surrender, was just beginning to melt into him again, when the porch lamp above them flashed on, bathing them both in a slice of garish yellow light. In one swift motion, they separated, Adam leaping backward, Mack jumping toward the front door. Before she even had the knob in her hand, however, it opened inward, to reveal a pert, petite blonde standing on the other side.

The newcomer blinked wide blue eyes, then arched delicate blond brows in not particularly convincing surprise. "Why, Dorsey," she said, turning her attention first to Mack and then to Adam. "I had no idea you were out here. I was just going to run next door to check on Mrs. Hoofdorp's cats."

She looked at Adam again and smiled. "Mrs. Hoofdorp is traveling," she added parenthetically. "We have no idea where she is—I suspect she's in Betty Ford again, because that's where she was the last time she was *traveling*, if you follow my trail, but I'm much too polite to ask her—and since we have a key to her place, we're feeding Moochie and Jester while she's gone . . ."

"I feel it's my civic duty to warn you," Mack interjected quietly, nodding her head toward the blonde, "that if you don't stop her right now, then she'll just keep on talking."

Adam eyed her quizzically but said nothing. Why would he, when he had absolutely no idea what she meant?

"Not that Moochie and Jester necessarily need feeding," the woman at the front door continued, just as Mack had said she would. "Why Jester is so fat, he could pass for that . . . that . . ." She fluttered a hand restlessly in front of her face. "Oh, who's that fat, pompadour-wearing, checkered-pants boy who holds the hamburger up over his head?"

"Uh . . . Big Boy?" Adam supplied helpfully.

"That's the one," she said with a smile. "And as for Moochie, well. He rather reminds me of that actor who played one of the criminals in the old Batman TV show. It wasn't one of the ones who wore spandex, though— or is it latex?" she asked. "I always get those confused. Anyway, it wasn't one of those, though I always rather liked that Frank Gorshin outfit. But this other actor I'm thinking about wore something Egyptian, I believe. Yes, in fact I know it was Egyptian because I took a class in Egyptology during that half-semester I spent at Brown. Actually, I spent half-semesters at quite a lot of universities, so it may not have been Brown. Not that I was really paying attention, anyway. I only went to college because I was hoping to meet some cute boys. And it worked! Because not only did I meet some cute boys, I—"

"Carlotta," Mack interjected again. And with surprising delicacy, too, Adam thought.

"What?" the rambling woman asked.

"Um, we were talking about something else?"

"So we were." She smiled at Adam again, but her words were clearly offered to Mack. "You were about to introduce your little friend to me."

Actually, Adam recalled, they'd been talking about cats, but he sure as hell wasn't going to put them back on that track.

Mack sighed in a martyred, taxed-patience sort of way, and Adam got the feeling that this was a scene the two women had played out before. Too often, if Mack's pained expression was any indication.

"Carlotta, this is Adam Darien," she introduced him

halfheartedly, as if she were unwilling to give Carlotta that information. "Adam, this is . . . this is my mother. Carlotta MacGuinness."

So Mack lived with her mother, did she? Adam thought. A mother who had a tendency to switch on the porch light just when things were starting to get good. Well, well, well. That had no doubt hampered Mack's past dating habits a bit. For some reason, the realization reassured him—until he realized it would also hamper her future dating habits a bit, as well.

"How do you do?" Mack's mother greeted him pertly.

"Mrs. MacGuinness," he returned. "It's nice to meet you."

"Oh, it's *Miss* MacGuinness, dear," she corrected him mildly. "I've never been married."

Well, well, well, Adam thought again. There was just no end to the surprise package that Mack presented. "*Miss* MacGuinness," he amended. "It's nice to meet you."

"Dorsey, of course, is *Ms*. MacGuinness," her mother continued. "And I don't guess I need to tell you how embarrassing *that* is for a mother to acknowledge."

"Carlotta . . ." Mack groaned.

Her mother waved another airy hand, this time evidently in surrender. "Are you coming in, dear?" she asked her daughter.

Mack nodded obediently, but she made no real effort to move forward.

"Anytime soon?" her mother asked further.

Mack sighed in that martyred way yet again, then turned to Adam. She still looked a little dazed and confused by the evening's events and not a little wary. "Thank you for dinner," she told him.

"Thank *you*," he countered.

She offered him a puzzled smile. "For what?"

He leaned forward, lowering his voice as he spoke, shamelessly excluding her mother from the conversation. "For everything else," he murmured softly close to her ear. And then, because he couldn't quite help himself, he brushed a quick, chaste kiss along her neck.

Okay, so it wasn't so chaste, he thought. Not when he took into account the way his groin ached as he performed the gesture. It was quick. Just not so quick that Carlotta MacGuinness didn't see it. He was also reasonably certain that she'd seen him out here on the front stoop trying to consume her daughter in one big bite a few minutes ago and that—not the impending starvation of poor Moochie and Jester next door—was why the porch light had snapped on when it did.

Instead of calling Adam on the fact that she'd just caught him mauling her daughter, however, Carlotta MacGuinness only inspected him for a moment in thoughtful silence. "Darien," she finally said. "You're Nate and Amanda's boy, aren't you?"

Adam couldn't mask his surprise. "You know my parents?" he asked.

"Well, perhaps I know your father a little better than I know your mother . . ." she said, her voice trailing off cryptically as she completed the remark.

"*Carlotta.*"

This time there was no taxed patience or martyrdom in Mack's voice. This time she was spitting fire.

"Oh, Dorsey," her mother replied indulgently. "Not like *that*."

"Like what?" Adam asked.

"Nothing," Mack assured him, the word coming out clipped and cool. "I have to go," she continued hastily, before he had a chance to challenge her. "Thanks again for dinner, Adam. I'll see you at Drake's."

And then she slipped through the door past her mother without a single glance back in his direction. Adam was left standing alone on the porch with Miss Carlotta MacGuinness, having no idea what to say or do next.

Fortunately, she seemed to have no such problem. "It was lovely meeting you, dear," she said sweetly. "Thank you for bringing Dorsey home safely." And then, without further comment, she closed the front door and switched off the porch light, effectively—though very politely—communicating her desire that he scram.

Bringing Dorsey home safely, he echoed to himself as he turned toward the steps and began to make his way back to his car. That, he decided, was open to debate. Certainly he had brought Mack home tonight. As to her safety, however . . .

Well. He supposed he was just going to have to wait and see what happened there.

Chapter 7

Lucas Conaway was in a worse than usual mood by the time he arrived at Drake's—and that was saying something, because even his good moods were generally pretty lousy. His most recent irritation had been stirred up at the bookstore, generated by Lauren Grable-Monroe's incessant—and pretty damned effective—sexual innuendo. It had only grown—his irritation, that is . . . although that wasn't the only thing that had grown, now that he thought about it—when he'd realized there was no outlet in sight for his current state of . . . irritation.

As a result, he was kind of irritable.

Add to that the fact that he still hadn't found a female tycoon to trap for his *Man's Life* story, and the combination made for one sulky guy.

Man. What was it with wealthy women? he wondered. All modesty—what little he had—aside, Lucas knew he was a reasonably good-looking guy of higher than average intelligence. He wasn't socially embarrassing or medically contagious. He could be charming when the occasion called for such nonsense, and he waded through the minefields of society bullshit and cocktail party chit-chat better than most men. So why the hell hadn't he been able to trap himself a tycoon?

He'd been following the rules of Lauren Grable-Monroe's book to the letter—well, except that stuff about diaphanous gowns and Chanel suits; there was, after all, only so much a man could be expected to do to get his story, regardless of how dedicated he was to his journalistic pursuits. Yet not one woman he had targeted for trapping had fallen into his snare. Every time he fired up his sales pitch and flexed his come-hither muscles, the women in question only gazed at him with faint amusement, fairly patted him on the head, and sent him home to have a cup of warm Bosco.

At this rate, he'd be lucky to trap himself a date to the senior prom.

Still feeling frustrated—and, of course, irritable—he wasn't paying attention to who was manning the bar. Or, rather, womanning the bar, as was the case at Drake's. So he didn't much care who was the recipient of his lousy mood when he dumped himself onto the leather stool he generally occupied and snarled, "Gimme a Tanqueray and tonic. And make it snappy."

When his drink didn't magically and immediately materialize before him on the bar—an extremely odd development at Drake's—Lucas glanced up to find that the woman to whom he had just barked out his order was none other than Drake's illustrious and infamous owner, Lindy Aubrey. And he understood right away what he'd just done: namely, put his life—and more important than that, his manhood—in very grave peril.

Lucas had nothing but respect for Lindy Aubrey. Like

every other member of Drake's, he was too terrified of her not to have respect for her. Although he didn't know her well—or at all, for that matter—she was something of a celebrity in Chicago. Since opening Drake's, she had received extensive and not just local press; Adam himself had often commented to Lucas that he'd considered doing a story about Lindy for *Man's Life*. She'd grown up in one of the city's most notorious neighborhoods, was a survivor of the streets, and had been on her own since she was fourteen years old.

In spite of her mean and meager beginnings, however, she had, through mysterious ways she'd never revealed, raised the money to open Drake's a few years ago. Since then, she had turned the club into one of the country's premier establishments. She was completely unapologetic about its masculine exclusivity and employed some of the best attorneys in the nation to fight and win numerous court battles to maintain the club's purely male membership.

She was a man's man in many ways, yet her femininity was inescapable. In her mid-forties, she was a striking-looking woman. Lush, dark hair tumbled past her shoulders, and clear gray eyes reflected both intelligence and wry wit. Tonight, she wore a screaming-red suit, the short skirt showcasing what Lucas, even terrified, had noted long ago were spectacular legs. Bright gemstones sparkled on nearly every finger, around both wrists, around her neck, in her earlobes. It was rumored that she carried a revolver in her purse everywhere she went, and that it had been fired on more than one occasion.

Lucas believed the rumor quite readily.

She had been sifting through some papers when he had growled his command, but she had halted, mid-sift, to smile at him in a deceptively benign way. Now that she had his attention, she pursed her lips in a manner that another man—one who wasn't terrified of her, say—might find sexy. Lucas, on the other hand, just about wet himself.

"Well, aren't you cute," she cooed softly. "And whose little boy are you?"

"Oh, uh . . . hi, Lindy . . . um, Ms. Aubrey . . . uh, ma'am," Lucas stammered. "I didn't realize it was you standing there."

She continued to gaze at him in that unnervingly bland I'll-huff-and-I'll-puff-and-I'll-have-your-shorts-for-dinner manner. "Obviously," she murmured in response.

Lucas shifted a bit nervously—okay, a bit terrifiedly—on his stool. "I'll just, um . . . I'll just go, uh . . ." *Go wet myself,* he finished lamely. "Uh . . . I'll just wait for one of the bartenders to get my drink for me."

Lindy's smile turned knowing. "Yes. You will."

Unable to help himself, Lucas noted again the proliferation of jewelry adorning Lindy's not at all unattractive person, and unbidden, an idea popped into his head. Though, he had to admit right away, it wasn't a very good one. Because the idea that braved entry into his brain just then was that maybe he could target Lindy Aubrey as his tycoon to trap. She was rich, obviously, and a good-looking woman. Intelligent, wry sense of humor, sexy in her own man-eater kind of way. Hmmm . . .

Of course, there was that small matter of him wanting to wet himself whenever she came within a hundred feet of him, he reminded himself. That could potentially put a damper on things, so to speak. Probably it would be best if he found someone else.

Lindy continued to gaze at him in that bored, I'm-done-with-you-now way of hers, then, "Edie," she tossed over her shoulder at the bartender who stood nearby.

Then she went back to sifting through her papers, and—just like that—dismissed Lucas with all the concern of a jackal that had finished bloating itself on a piece of ripe carrion.

The good news, as far as Lucas was concerned, was that he no longer had Lindy Aubrey's attention. The bad news, however, was that he did have Edie Mulholland's.

Oh, great, he thought. Little Edie Sunshine. Just what he needed to make a lousy night lousier. Little Edie Two Shoes. Mulholland of Sunnybrook Farm. A woman who was so nice and so kind and so sweet and so polite and so . . . so . . . God, so *blond*, she could make the Olsen Twins vomit.

"Hi, Mr. Conaway," she greeted him pertly with a cheerful little smile.

Pertly. Cheerful. *Ew*. Lucas tried not to lose his dinner all over the bar. And the "Mr. Conaway" thing was just too nauseating for words. He knew that referring to him as "Mr." was required by her job, and really, coming from another woman, he might find the address kind of . . . well, kind of arousing, actually, now that he thought more about it. But the fact that it was Little Edie Sunshine saying it revolted him for some reason. She was probably the same age he was, give or take a year, but she seemed so much younger somehow.

Her pale blond hair was swept atop her head, held in place by some invisible means of support. A few errant tendrils had escaped to frame her face, giving her an ethereal, almost angelic appearance. He couldn't help comparing her to a Pre-Raphaelite madonna with her delicate build, her huge, blue eyes, and her high, elegant cheekbones. Her mouth, too, seemed more beatific than the average woman's was, as if she had been touched at birth by some holy hand and was divinely blessed as a result.

She was just so naive, so ingenuous, so damned happy, Lucas thought uncomfortably. She couldn't possibly have even a nodding acquaintance with reality. Wherever Edie Mulholland lived, he knew it was, without doubt, an enchanted kingdom populated by fairies and sprites and unicorns and rainbows. Trolls and dragons like him would be completely unwelcome in such a fantastic place.

"Edie," he said by way of a greeting, trying not to gag on the word. Jeez, even her name was nice and sweet and pert and blond. "What are you doing here? I thought you only worked days."

She smiled easily. "I'm filling in for Dorsey. She had something she needed to do tonight."

"Oh." Then, without further ado, Lucas said, "Gimme a Tanqueray and tonic."

"Coming right up," she replied—happily, of course.

Lucas tried not to hurl.

And he tried not to be fascinated by the deft, capable way she prepared his drink and set it without flourish on the bar before him. As sweet and nice and polite and blond and nauseating as she was, Edie Mulholland, he had to admit, was one helluva bartender.

"Thanks," he said as he reached for the glass.

"Don't mention it," she replied—sunnily, he couldn't help but note.

He enjoyed a healthy taste of his drink, realized she was still standing in front of him, almost expectantly somehow, then remembered that Little Edie Sunshine was one of those bartenders who like to—he bit back another gag—make small talk. Uncertain why he felt compelled to indulge such a filthy, disgusting habit, Lucas found himself asking, "So. Edie. How was your day?"

Not surprisingly, she grinned brightly, and somehow, he refrained from curling his lip in disdain. "It's been great!" she announced with much animation. "Well, except for this afternoon."

Resigned to his fate, Lucas asked halfheartedly, "Um . . . what happened this afternoon?"

Edie frowned unhappily. He rejoiced at the sight. Very softly, very somberly, she told him, "I committed adultery."

Whoa! Now this was a newsworthy bulletin! Lucas was about to leap up and dance the dance of righteous victory when he remembered that Mulholland of Sunnybrook Farm was a single woman. "Edie," he said. "How could you commit adultery? You're not married."

She gazed at him blankly for a minute, clearly confused. Then, suddenly, her expression cleared, and she blushed like a summer rose. "Oh, not *that* kind of adultery," she said, lowering her voice even more. Then, in a clearer voice, she added, "I'd *never* do something like that. *Hair* adultery. I committed hair adultery."

"Hair adultery?" he echoed before he could stop himself.

She nodded. "I needed a bang trim really bad, but my usual stylist was out. So . . ." She glanced first right, then left, as if to make sure no one was listening. Then, lowering her voice again, she said, "So I made an appointment with a *different* stylist."

Evidently, this was a grave sin among women, Lucas surmised, because Edie looked as if she might shave her head in penance for committing such an egregious act of betrayal. "Uh . . . I see," he lied.

"What's worse," she continued, even though he had silently willed her not to, "the new stylist? She did a better job than my usual one. Now I want to go back to her next time. I feel *so* guilty."

He eyed her blandly. "Gee, I can see where that might cause some real turbulence in your otherwise happy existence."

She nodded. "Other than that, though," she concluded genially, "it was a really nice day."

Before he realized he was even thinking the question, Lucas heard himself ask, "Edie, do you ever wake up in a bad mood?"

She smiled—happily. "Never."

"Why not?"

She shrugged—pleasantly. "It's a waste of time."

"A waste of time," Lucas echoed incredulously.

She nodded—merrily.

He enjoyed another sip of his drink, then stated, "You're a Stepford Wife, aren't you, Edie?"

She laughed—spiritedly.

"Come on," he cajoled. "Admit it."

"I'm not a Stepford Wife," she denied—good-naturedly.

"Then you must be one of those pod people from outer space," he decided. "The real Edie Mulholland has to be snoozing in a space pod somewhere, where the body-snatchers left her. I bet *she* wakes up in bad mood. If she ever wakes up again."

Edie's eyes twinkled—gleefully. "I'm not a pod person from outer space, either. I just don't see the point in carrying around a lot of negative energy, that's all."

Lucas gaped at her in disbelief. "Hey, negative energy is what made this country great," he told her. "Negative energy has been responsible for some truly significant historical achievements all over the world."

"Like what?" she asked—dubiously but nonetheless cheerily.

He thought for a moment. "Well, like the Roman Empire, for example," he said. "Talk about your negative energy. Those guys had downright bloodlust going for them. Gladiators fighting to the death, peasant-eating lions, crucifixion. And look at all the amazing things they accomplished. That was one phenomenal civilization."

Edie eyed him—pleasantly. "The Romans actually learned everything they knew from the Etruscans," she pointed out. "And the Etruscans were pretty easygoing people. Well, except for that pesky human sacrifice business," she qualified. Hastily, she added, "But they were a primitive people. At any rate, they knew the value of living a good life."

Lucas narrowed his eyes at her. "Okay, I'll give you that one," he conceded. "But once the Romans got things up and running, nobody messed with them. Nobody."

"Actually, the Celts did," Edie objected—mildly. "They kicked Roman butt."

Lucas frowned. "Oh. Yeah. I forgot about that."

"And the Celts," Edie continued, blithely, "wild men though they were, still appreciated the beauty and tranquility of the natural world that surrounded them."

Lucas thought for a moment more. "Okay. Then how about the race for space? We landed men on the moon because we were pissed off at the Soviet Union. Negative energy, I'm tellin' ya."

But Edie only smiled again—joyfully—and waved a hand—jovially—in front of herself. "We didn't put men on the moon because we were mad at the Soviets," she told him sweetly. "We did it because we were *optimistic* that we could. *Positive* energy. Positive energy did that. Not negative."

Clearly, there was no point in arguing with her, Lucas thought. No matter which way he looked at things, Edie was bound to see them from the opposite side. To her, the glass would always be half full. To him, it would always be . . . well, quite frankly, it would always be empty.

Thankfully, another one of Drake's members summoned her from the other end of the bar then, and Lucas glanced up to see . . . Davenport, he thought the guy's name was . . . beckoning to her. Funny, but he'd never seen the guy in here at night before, only in the afternoons . . . when Edie was working.

So he was one of those, was he? A man who lusted after his bartender. Nothing so unusual about that, though, Lucas conceded. Hell, he himself lusted after most of the women who worked at Drake's. Except for Little Edie Sunshine, of course.

Who could possibly lust after someone who was so sweet and nice and kind and happy and blond and nauseating? Not Lucas. No way. She wasn't his type at all. He liked his women dark and brooding and convenient and temporary. Edie, he was certain, was the kind of woman who pined for wedding cakes and rugrats and white picket fences.

He shrugged off his ruminations before they could wander into the realm of forbidden fantasizing, then went back to moping in silence. Unfortunately, his moping was shortly interrupted by Edie's lyrical and, inescapably, happy laughter.

Involuntarily, he turned his attention to the end of the bar, where she was laughing at something Davenport had said to her. Davenport was laughing, too, then he uttered something that Lucas had heard him say a million times before: "Edie, you need someone to take care of you."

And then it was with no small amount of surprise that Lucas watched the man reach over the bar and run the pad of his thumb lightly and with great affection—or something—over Edie's cheek.

And it was with no small amount of astonishment that Lucas watched Edie jerk her entire body back in response out of Davenport's reach, lifting her own hand to her face as if she'd just suffered a bad burn.

She recovered quickly, seeming to realize how much she'd overreacted—at least, Davenport seemed to think she'd overreacted, judging by the stark surprise etched on his face. Lucas, on the other hand, was thinking she should have heaved a coffeepot at the guy. But she forced a quick smile and mumbled something Lucas couldn't hear, something that made Davenport smile in return. Nevertheless, Edie, Lucas could tell, was still pretty shaken by the man's action.

Something inside him tightened coldly at witnessing the episode. Not just because Davenport had broken one of Lindy Aubrey's clear but unspoken rules of Drake's membership—nobody, but nobody, touched her employees—but because of the way the man continued to look at Edie. As if he knew something she didn't know. As if he planned to act on whatever that something was. As if he intended to make Edie his own, in whatever way he could.

It gave Lucas the creeps.

And it took a hell of a lot to give Lucas Conaway the creeps. Davenport, with one simple action, had set off every alarm bell Lucas possessed. And hell, it wasn't even Lucas the man was bothering.

"Hey, Edie, come here," Lucas called out, unsure when exactly or even why he had decided to divert her attention that way.

Clearly puzzled, but seeming nonetheless grateful, she excused herself to Davenport and carefully made her way back down to where Lucas was holding his—he just now realized—barely touched drink. Well, hell, now what was he supposed to say when she got there? What other reason would he possibly have for catching her attention, if not because he wanted another drink? Without thinking, he lifted the glass to his mouth and tipped it back, consuming the entire contents in three hasty gulps.

If Edie's expression had been puzzled before, now it was absolutely flummoxed. Flummoxed also described how he felt when two ounces of good gin splashed hotly into his belly. *Wow.* That was actually kind of cool. He should do that more often.

"Yes, Mr. Conaway?" Edie asked as she approached him.

For the first time since he'd met her, she wasn't quite so annoyingly chipper. But she was still smiling, he noted. And really, he supposed, when he got right down to it, it wasn't such a bad smile after all. Not nearly as irritating as he'd initially thought it. Of course, the fact that he currently had two ounces of good gin buzzing into his system might have something to do with taking the edges off Edie. It was certainly taking the edges off him.

"I'm ready for another drink," he told her.

She eyed him a bit cautiously, and he really couldn't blame her for that. "Are you sure?" she asked. "I mean, that first one—"

"Is gone," he finished for her. "Which is a very good reason for me to have another one."

She arched her eyebrows in idle speculation, then capitulated. "Okay," she said as she reached for his empty glass.

And as she fixed him another drink, as he watched her small, delicate hands move so gracefully over glass and bottle, Lucas turned his attention to the man seated at the other end of the bar. Now Davenport was eyeing *him* cautiously, clearly as unconvinced of Lucas's motivation in summoning her as Edie was.

Too bad, old man, Lucas taunted him silently, having no idea why he should suddenly be feeling so combative, so strangely protective. Nevertheless, part of him wanted to stick out his tongue at the other man and sing, "I've got her no-ow, you ca-an't have her, nyah, nyah, nyah, nyah, nyah."

He glanced back at Edie, feeling oddly triumphant for some reason. Then he heard himself say, "And tell me something, Edie. Just how do you know so much about the Romans, anyway?"

Edie Mulholland was just finishing up her lecture on the Pax Romana when Lucas Conaway fell off of his barstool. She shook her head in bemusement and leaned over the bar to evaluate the outcome of his tumble, hoping he hadn't hit anything important. Fortunately, he appeared to have landed on his ego, and with all that padding, she was more than certain he was okay.

What on earth had come over him tonight? she wondered. He never drank to excess, rarely even ordered a second drink. Yet every time she'd turned around tonight, he'd been calling her over to fix him another one, then asking her some question like, "So those aqueducts—what's up with that?" or "Remember Appian Way Pizza? Man, I loved that stuff."

Actually, it wasn't every time she'd turned around that he'd claimed her attention, she thought as she watched him brush off his ego and climb back aboard his stool.

It was only when he'd seen her talking to Mr. Davenport. Then again, Mr. Davenport had left Drake's a half-hour ago, and Lucas hadn't stopped talking. On the contrary, over the last thirty minutes, their conversation had taken a few, not particularly welcome, turns toward the personal.

Of course, she had easily sidestepped those personal questions by returning to the topic of the Romans. Because there was nothing like dry, dusty history to put a damper on a man's—even an intoxicated man's—ardor, however dubious. Men hated rehashing stuff, after all. History was something they very seldom remembered. It was something that Edie, however, could never forget. And not just because it was her major, either.

"Are you okay, Mr. Conaway?" she asked as politely as she could, watching with some concern as he righted himself and folded his arms and hands very carefully over the top of the bar. Clearly, he was not okay. Clearly, he was three sheets to the wind. But Edie was much too courteous to call him on the fact. Besides, Lindy would fire her like *that* if she told a member to his face that he'd had a snootful.

"I'm fine, Edie," he insisted. "And please, call me Lucas."

Oh, yeah, right, she thought. It was one thing to think of him as Lucas in her head, quite another to address him by his first name here in Drake's. Hey, if she was going to do that, then while she was at it, she might as well just tell him he was three sheets to the wind, too. And then she should empty all the cash registers and stuff her pockets with the evening's receipts. Then, as a final farewell, she could jump up on the bar and dance *La Vida Loca* while she quoted Goethe. If she was going to get fired, she ought to at least go out memorably.

She knew she should alert Lindy that Lucas Conaway was snookered, because Lindy insisted on being informed of such things. She absolutely did not tolerate overly inebriated members in Drake's. But something prevented Edie from doing so. Unlike some of the other members of Drake's—drunk *or* sober—Lucas Conaway was harmless. And it wasn't like this had happened before. Everybody had days when they felt the need to tie one on. Well, everybody except Edie, of course. But that was only because she couldn't afford to tie one on.

So instead of telling Lindy, she told Lucas, "I'm going to call you a cab."

He smiled, not a little seductively. "I'd rather have you call me sweetheart," he murmured, slurring the last word a bit before breaking up in hysterical laughter and slapping his open hand against the bar.

Edie shook her head but couldn't help smiling back. At least he wasn't a mean drunk. She'd seen more of those in her day than she cared to think about.

"Maybe some other time," she told him. "Right now, you need a cab."

"I need you more," he told her. This time, however, there was no laughter, no slapping the bar. This time his eyes darkened dangerously, and he seemed completely focused, completely sober.

Edie expelled a quick, unexpected breath and wondered why her heart was suddenly racing so. Lucas Conaway had never once flirted with her. On the contrary, he seemed to go out of his way to make sure she knew he didn't much like her. Not that he'd ever been mean or snide to her, but she knew he called her Little Edie Sunshine and Mulholland of Sunnybrook Farm behind her back.

Not that such labels bothered Edie. She'd worked long and hard to become a sappy sentimentalist, dammit. She wore her bleeding heart proudly on her sleeve as a badge of honor, by God. She hadn't always been Mulholland of Sunnybrook Farm. Oh, no. She'd clawed her way up from the very dregs of despair to be as abominably happy and as nauseatingly cheerful as she possibly could be. Nobody—but *nobody*—was going to take her good will and contentment, her sappy sentimentality, away from her. Nobody. Certainly not some sarcastic little pessimist like Lucas Conaway.

She didn't care how cute he was.

Which still didn't explain why she was suddenly so overcome at the sight of him intoxicated and tempting and . . . and . . . Reluctantly, her smile returned. And *happy*, she realized. Even if it had been brought about by the contents of a bottle, Lucas Conaway was honestly, genuinely happy. She'd never seen him in such a state. And she could only wonder why he became this way when his guard was down.

Best not to think about it, Edie, she told herself. *It's none of your business. He's none of your business.*

"What you need is a cup of hot coffee and a cold shower," she told him, assuring herself that was *not* affection she saw glittering in his eyes.

He smiled again, the fuzzy, dreamy little smile of a man who was much too inebriated for his—or her—own good. "Why, Edie," he murmured in that fuzzy, dreamy voice again, "you little vixen, you little minx, you little spitfire, you little tigress, you little . . . little . . ." His pale-blond brows arrowed downward in confusion for a moment. "Where was I? Oh, yeah. You little firebrand, you. If you want to take a shower with me, just come right out and say so."

Okay, time to call Lindy, Edie thought.

But he seemed to realize he'd gone too far. "I'm

sorry," he told her. He leaned back a bit, lifting his hands lightly in surrender, seeming genuinely chastened. "You're right. I've had far too much to drink, and there's no way I can drive myself home. Here," he added further, reaching into his trouser pocket. "Here are my keys. You take them."

Before she could decline and before she realized what he intended to do, he reached across the bar and took her hand gently in his. Instinctively—because she simply could not tolerate the feel of a man's hands on her—Edie jerked her own hand back out of his grasp. He looked as startled by her reaction as Mr. Davenport had earlier that evening, and she felt as angry now at Lucas as she had then at the other man. Now, however, for some reason, she was less inclined to cover her feelings, and she glared at him openly if silently.

Dammit, why did men feel like they could just reach out and take whatever they wanted, without so much as asking first? she wondered, not for the first time in her life. And why did they have to take more than a person was willing to give?

"I'm sorry," Lucas said, clearly dumfounded by her sudden and vehement withdrawal. "I didn't mean . . . I mean, I know Lindy forbids . . . That is, I know I'm not supposed to touch you, but . . . ."

"Then why did you?" Edie demanded.

He blinked once, his blue eyes reflecting his puzzlement at her reaction. "I was just . . . I was going to give you my keys, that's all."

Her heart still racing, Edie nodded once. "Fine," she told him. "Just set them on the bar then."

Without comment, Lucas did as she'd requested, and it was with no small effort that Edie hid her surprise. He didn't seem like the kind of man who would obey a woman's command without grumbling something snide in response. Hey, he didn't seem like the kind of man who would obey a woman's command, *period*. Even when he was slightly intoxicated, she was no match for him, and they both knew it. If he wanted to give her a hard time, he could do it very easily.

Yet he'd backed down. Quite willingly, too. Edie wasn't used to wielding such power over a man. Or any power over a man, for that matter. And she had no idea how to interpret his response. So for now, she decided not to think about it.

Gingerly, she reached for his keys, and she tried to forget that he had touched her the way he had. She tried to forget that his fingers had been warm and gentle and playful against her flesh, not cold and rough and demeaning. And she tried to forget that there had been something different in his eyes when he'd touched her, something that hadn't been there before. Something that had almost made her feel warm and gentle and playful inside. Confused by her reaction, she folded her fingers over his key ring and focused on the cold, ungiving metal instead.

"You sure you want me to have these?" she asked him. Not that she would give them back, she thought. He really was in no condition to drive.

"I trust you," he said.

Well, that made one of them, she thought.

"Where do you live?" she asked. "I'll call you a cab to take you home and give your keys to the driver so you can get inside once you're there."

He gazed at her for a long time without answering, long enough to make Edie wonder if maybe he was too far gone to understand anything so elaborate as a three-part direction. Honestly. He really hadn't had that much to drink. And he was a big man, six foot two, she guessed, and probably around a hundred and eighty pounds. Certainly she could see how the amount of liquor he'd consumed this evening would make him feel happy, but it wasn't such a huge serving that his brain would turn into hasty pudding.

"Mr. Conaway?" she prodded him. "Where do you live?"

His smile, the one that had been so seductive a moment ago, suddenly turned playful again. "I don't think I want to tell you where I live," he said.

Well, that would certainly complicate things, she thought. Aloud, however, she only remarked, "Why not?"

He tilted his head to one side, gazing at her in a way that was far too appealing. "Because then you'll have to take me home with you instead," he told her. "To your place."

Oh, I don't think so, she thought. She arched her brows imperiously. "I beg your pardon."

"Actually," he said more quietly, leaning in toward her, "I'd rather have you begging for my—"

"*Mr.* Conaway," she interrupted, irritated by such a blatant come-on. Until now, she'd kind of . . . sort of . . . almost . . . been having fun with their flirtatious exchange. But now Lucas had gone too far.

Why did men always do that? she wondered. Why couldn't they leave well enough alone? Then again, she supposed she should be relieved that Lucas's pushing had only been verbal. So far, anyway. You never could tell with men.

"I think you've overstepped the line now," she told him frankly. "Tell me where you live, and I'll call you a cab. Otherwise, I'll have to tell Lindy about this, and she could very well bar you from the club."

He seemed unconcerned. Leaning back again, he muttered, "It doesn't matter. I'm going to lose my membership soon, anyway."

"Why?" she asked, telling herself she really didn't care. Honest. She didn't. She was just curious, that was all.

He expelled an impatient sigh, one that bordered on a growl. "Because I'm having a damned problem writing a damned story for my damned magazine about a damned book that's been no damned help at all," he told her. Then, to punctuate his frustration, he concluded, "Dammit."

Still assuring herself that her interest was only casual—honest, it was—Edie asked further, "What are you talking about?"

"I'm having trouble finding someone," he told her cryptically.

"Oh, well, aren't we all?" she replied before she could stop herself.

He eyed her with some confusion. "I don't know. Are we all?"

She said nothing more, hoping he'd move on to something else. But of course, being Lucas Conaway, he leaped on that little tidbit like a rabid Great Dane on a bone.

"Who are *you* looking for?" he demanded.

She shook her head quickly. "Nobody," she told him.

"Well, you must be looking for somebody," he countered, "otherwise you wouldn't have answered the way you did."

"I was just making conversation," she hedged. "I'm not looking for anybody."

He obviously didn't believe her, but, surprisingly, he

said nothing more about it. In an effort to change the subject and get on with her life, Edie held his keys aloft and gave them a single meaningful jingle.

"Oh, all right," he finally relented. "Call me a cab, if you must. God knows I've been called worse things in my life."

So Edie did. She did call Lucas a cab. Twice, as a matter of fact. But by the time Lindy closed the bar, no taxi had shown up to take him home. In the meantime, she fed him a steady diet of black coffee, and he seemed to be coming around a bit. He still wasn't fit to drive anywhere, but he had at least eased up on his dubious flirtation. And he'd finally stopped asking her who she was looking for.

"Edie, you're a flower, you are."

Okay, so he hadn't stopped his flirtation completely, she amended. At least he was calling her a flower now instead of minx or vixen or spitfire. Honestly. She hadn't been any of those since she was seventeen.

Still, she had rather liked the way he'd said "minx" and "vixen" and "spitfire." She couldn't recall any man ever using those specific words to describe her. Others, certainly, none of them worth repeating, but never in such an affectionate tone of voice. And never with a smile that had curled her toes and warmed her all over in a way that she'd never felt warm before.

She noticed that Lindy was watching them and was clearly going to ask Lucas to leave—or rather, demand that he leave . . . or else; Lindy Aubrey never *asked* anyone to do anything. So before her employer had the chance to put Lucas out on the street—literally—Edie leaned forward, ostensibly to take his coffee cup from the bar, and said very softly so that Lindy couldn't hear,

"Meet me downstairs in the lobby in fifteen minutes, and I'll drive you home myself."

He snapped his head up at that, his lips parted in obvious surprise.

"To your place?" he asked hopefully.

"To *your* place," she corrected him.

He smiled lasciviously.

"But only as far as the front door," she hastened to add. "Don't be getting any bright ideas, Romeo."

"Oh, trust me, Edie," he said, "the ideas I'm having right now are anything but bright."

Lucas's apartment, when they arrived there a half-hour later, wasn't at all what Edie had expected it to be. Lucas, on the other hand, behaved pretty much as she would have expected him to. As she pushed the front door open, he shoved past her without warning—it was only at the last minute that she leapt aside and avoided touching him—and without an acknowledgment or thanks. And he didn't stop moving until he'd crossed the room to his couch and promptly collapsed onto it.

She frowned as she watched him go, then wrestled the key from the lock so that she could pitch it to him and be on her way. Momentarily intrigued, however, she couldn't quite bring herself to leave. Lucas seemed like the kind of man who would go for minimal, functional, no-frills living, and not warm and cozy. Yet the place looked like something out of *Martha Stewart Living*. Certainly it was a masculine domain, but the colors were softer than she would have expected, the furnishings less boxy, the accessories less obnoxious.

The walls were the pale-yellow color of butter, countered by an overstuffed sofa of Wedgwood blue. Two fat club chairs were printed with a wide plaid that mingled the two colors, and a plush area rug of the same hues and geometric design spanned much of the hardwood floor. On the walls were Art Deco prints of what appeared to be famous Caribbean hotels, mixed with brightly painted posters of Spanish bullfights. The mantelpiece boasted a few odds and ends from his travels abroad, and two largish bookcases were crammed with books.

Not surprisingly, however, there were few personal touches. Actually, she realized, there were no personal touches. No framed photographs, no comfy throws crocheted by Grandma Conaway, no athletic trophies or educational citations, no tumbling plants—nothing that needed nurturing or tending or noticing. And nothing that offered any insight into the man. Really, the place was almost too tidy. Lucas Conaway obviously took great care to maintain his home.

"*Bienvenue à chez Lucas,*" he mumbled from where he had sprawled himself comfortably on the couch.

He threw one arm upward against the sofa's back and rested it in an arrogant arc above his head. The action caused his dark-blue sweater to ride up above his khaki trousers, and Edie couldn't stop herself from fixing her gaze on the brief ripple of naked, rock-hard abs beneath. Evidently his apartment wasn't the only thing that Lucas took great care to maintain, she thought, her mouth going dry at the sight of his lean torso. Hastily, she glanced away.

"*Mi casa es su casa,*" he added further. "Bet you didn't know I was trilingual, did you?"

When she forced her gaze back to his face, she found him grinning in a way that seemed self-mocking somehow. She arched her brows and crossed her arms over her midsection, pretending she was completely immune to him.

"Do tell," she said as blandly as she could.

He nodded. "Actually, I'm quadrilingual. In addition to French and Spanish—and English, natch—I also speak German fluently." To illustrate his accomplishment, he inhaled a deep breath and announced, "*Ich bin ein Berliner.*" He waited for her reaction, and when she offered none, he sighed. "Not that I want you to think I'm bragging or anything."

"Traveled overseas a lot, have you?" she asked.

He shook his head. "Never."

"How come?" she asked, honestly curious. "You're unattached, you have a good job, you can afford it. Fear of flying?"

He shook his head again. "Fear of life."

She opened her mouth to ask him what he meant, but before she could voice the question, he pushed himself up from the couch and strode toward the kitchen. "Coffee?" he asked her as he went. "Clearly, I'm not quite sober yet. I think I could use another pot or two. I'm much too chatty tonight." He voiced that last as if he were confessing to the most vile of crimes.

This time Edie was the one to shake her head. "No, thanks," she told him. "I have to get home."

He spun around quickly, the expression on his face alarmed for some reason. "Don't," he said, his voice clipped, cautious. He must have detected her surprise—or perhaps her own alarm—because he immediately softened the command by adding, "Please." He took a few steps toward her, and for one brief, insane moment, she thought he might actually reach out to her. But he only stopped where he was, dropped his hands to his hips, and said, "Just stay for a little while, Edie. Talk to me. I'm way too het up to sleep."

All the more reason for her to go, she thought. No way did she trust the wee hours of the morning, and right now, they were about as wee as they came. Just because she never managed to sleep through them herself didn't mean she had to spend them with someone else. On the contrary, those were the hours of the night when she absolutely had to be alone.

She jutted a thumb halfheartedly over her shoulder, hoping the gesture looked casual. "I, um . . . I really do have to go," she told him, taking a step back. "I have an eight o'clock class in the morning."

He nodded, though somehow she could see that it was less in understanding than it was in resignation. As if he'd expected this reaction from her and was for the most part content to let it go.

Strange, she thought. She suddenly felt guilty for cutting out on him. It wasn't like the two of them were friends, she reassured herself. And it certainly wasn't like she owed him something. Until tonight, they'd barely spoken a civil word to each other. Just because he'd had a few too many drinks and had revealed a side of himself she'd never seen before . . . Just because it was a side of him she found oddly endearing somehow . . . Just because it was a side of him that, under other circumstances—like maybe if she'd lived an entirely different life from the one she had—she might honestly want to explore . . .

Well, just because of all that, it didn't mean she had to do as he asked. It would be lunacy—idiocy—for her to stay here and share a cup of coffee with Lucas Conaway. Not just because there could be no future in it, but because her past *was* in it. And her past being what it was, the evening would only end badly. Of that, she had no doubt.

"I, um . . . I'll see you at Drake's," she told him, taking another step back until she found herself framed in the open doorway.

Only then did she recall that she still held his keys and, with a quick shake to warn him, she tossed them the length of the room. He caught them capably in one hand, no easy feat seeing as how his eyes never left hers as she performed the action. So handsome, she thought. He was so handsome. Intelligent. Funny. Interesting. Really, it was just too bad that—

She cut off the thought with a deep sigh and lifted a hand in halfhearted farewell.

"Edie," he called out as she turned away.

Reluctantly, she spun back around.

"Thanks," he said softly. "For everything."

"No problem," she replied.

He emitted a single humorless chuckle. "No problem," he echoed unhappily. "Yeah, right. That's what you think, sweetheart. That's what you think."

Chapter 8

A week after telling Adam she couldn't see him, Dorsey sat in the locker room at Drake's and marveled at how very accurate her prediction had been. Because during that week, she had seen neither hide nor hair—nor suit nor tie—of him anywhere. When she'd told him that night on her front porch that she wouldn't be able to see him, she'd meant socially. Romantically. Personally. She hadn't meant she wouldn't see him at all.

But it was actually kind of a relief, because she had no idea how she was supposed to act around him now, anyway. She felt so odd about things. Before last week, their roles had been clearly defined, and they'd both been reasonably comfortable playing those roles. Now, however, the line between them was blurred. Whereas before, she'd had no trouble toeing that line, now Dorsey had stumbled off of it completely. And she couldn't rightly say on which side of it she had fallen. But what was most troubling of all was that no matter where she landed, Lauren

Grable-Monroe would be right there with her.

There was no way Dorsey could start something with Adam—or anyone else, for that matter—without Lauren getting involved in it, too. And even though Lauren's baser nature would probably relish the idea of a three-some, Dorsey just wasn't that kind of girl.

Of course, the night that she had kissed Adam, for those few moments that she lost herself in his arms, she sure had felt like that kind of girl. Not a day—not an hour—had passed since their embrace that she hadn't re-lived in her head those two searing, combustible kisses. He had felt so good, so exciting, to hold onto. It had been like corralling wild energy, unrestrained force. Like clasping a cyclone to her breast and pulling some of its limitless power and vast fury into herself.

In addition to arousing her sexually, powerfully, kissing Adam had made Dorsey feel strong, potent, infinite. That such a man would lose control over her, lose control *with* her, was a heady sensation indeed. She'd never felt anything like it before. Something told her she would never feel anything like it again. And the realization of that had just made her miss Adam all the more.

But she'd also missed their friendship. She'd missed their easy banter and mildly dangerous flirtations. She'd missed his low laughter and reluctant smiles. She'd missed his totally erroneous masculine assumptions and his laughably misguided chauvinist deductions. She'd even missed the pangs of wistful melancholy that invariably shot through her every time she had to stop herself from reaching out a hand to run her fingers through his hair.

She'd just missed *him*. Very much. And she couldn't stop thinking about those two kisses they had shared on her front porch. She couldn't erase the memory of how his hands had felt curling over her bottom, how his mouth had felt rubbing insistently against her throat. She recalled every sigh, every scent, every seductive sensation. And more than anything in the world, she wanted to experience it again. All of it. And more.

But she also wanted to recapture their familiar camaraderie. And she couldn't come up with a solution that would combine both a romantic and a friendly relationship with him. Certainly not while she was leading a triple life as Dorsey MacGuinness, sociology prof wannabe, Mack, the bartender, and Lauren Grable-Monroe, cultural icon. It was just too weird to think about it all right now. All things considered, she supposed it was just as well that she hadn't seen him for a week.

But she sure did miss him.

Then again, the week had passed in such a blur, she hadn't seen much of anything at all. Lauren Grable-Monroe, it seemed, was hitting the peak of her popularity. In one week she had signed books at a shopping mall in Schaumburg, had spoken to a group of sex therapists in Champaign, and had still fitted in an early-morning radio talk show in Chicago.

That last event, having occurred only yesterday morning, was still fresh in Dorsey's mind, and she was still feeling a bit uneven because of it. Whereas she had gone to the radio station thinking she'd be fielding the usual sorts of questions for Lauren—fun, frivolous queries about the book or the author's fictional personal life—some of the callers had been a bit less than enthusiastic in their responses. True, there had been the usual assortment of giggling schoolgirls cutting class, but there had also been disenchanted housewives shouting over squalling babies and frustrated men berating Lauren for ruining women everywhere. Dorsey had left feeling slightly smudged. As if the smooth, clean lines of Lauren Grable-Monroe's self-assurance had been soiled and stretched and damaged.

And now here Dorsey sat with barely ten minutes to go before the start of her shift at Drake's, trying to conjure enough energy to change from her teaching assistant clothes to her bartender clothes. In her backpack, she also carried Lauren Grable-Monroe's clothes, because she'd had an early-morning appointment with a writer for a local weekly, which had gone, if memory served, fairly well. But she hadn't had time to go home between Lauren's meeting and Dorsey's first class at Severn. She hadn't had time between Severn and Drake's, either. In fact, Dorsey could barely remember when she had last spent any amount of time at home. It seemed like a very long time ago . . .

She closed her eyes for just a moment—only long enough to rest them, honest—then was immediately jarred to awareness by a not so gentle shove to her shoulder. Snapping her eyes open again, she glanced up to find Lindy Aubrey standing over her, hands fisted on her hips, one eyebrow arched in silent query, clearly none too pleased to find her bartender here in the locker room. Which was odd, Dorsey thought, because for the first time in weeks, she was actually a few minutes early for her shift. You'd think Lindy would be happy about that, but—

"Do you know what time it is?" her employer asked.

"Ten till four," Dorsey replied.

Lindy shook her head. "Try five after."

Dorsey glanced down at her watch. Sure enough, she was five minutes late for her shift and not even dressed in her uniform yet. "But that's impossible," she said. "I got here fifteen minutes early."

"Then what have you been doing for the last twenty minutes?" her employer asked.

"I've been . . ." *Sleeping*, she realized. Good heavens, she'd actually fallen asleep sitting on the bench and had stayed that way for fifteen minutes. "I—I . . . I guess I . . . I just didn't realize . . . I mean I . . ."

Lindy crossed her arms over her midsection, looking all too menacing in her sleek black suit. "Dorsey, this has gone on long enough," she said. "For the past month, you've missed more shifts than you've worked. And my patience has just about come to an end."

"But I've always had someone covering my shifts for me," Dorsey pointed out. "I've never left you short-handed."

"That's beside the point," Lindy said. "I hired you to work thirty hours a week, and you agreed to work thirty hours a week. Now, I don't mind accommodating you when you need a night off here and there, but this is getting out of hand. If you can't handle the work load, I'll hire someone else who will. Do I make myself clear?"

Dorsey nodded.

"Fine. I don't want to hear that you need another night off for a while. Or else."

"But—"

"Not one night. If you need more than your regularly scheduled nights off, then don't bother coming in at all."

Dorsey hesitated only a moment before deferring to her. "Yes, Lindy."

"That said, I need you to work an extra shift this week. Saturday night. Drake's is catering a cocktail party for one of its members, and I'm down a bartender. You can start setting up at six o'clock. Here's the address." And then, without even awaiting a reply—there could, naturally, be only one reply . . . or else—she thrust a scrap of paper into Dorsey's hand.

"Six o'clock," she repeated. Then, very clearly, she cautioned, "Do *not* be late."

"I won't," Dorsey assured her.

Lindy was about to turn and leave when her gaze lit on something on the top shelf of Dorsey's locker. Not the wedding ring, which she knew—and approved—of Dorsey wearing to fend off unwanted advances, but the stack of spiral notebooks that had doubled in number over the last month. Her notes for her dissertation, Dorsey realized. Four volumes, so far. In hindsight, she supposed it wasn't such a good idea to leave them here at Drake's where anyone could find them. But she never worried about the sanctity of her locker being violated, and she often liked to review past notes when recording new ones. Still, if Lindy ever took it upon herself to investigate . . .

Nah. That would never happen. Dorsey was confident of that. Lindy was a total privacy freak where her own life was concerned, and she always respected others' rights in that respect, too. She guarded Drake's membership roster like a mother polar bear protecting its young, and she afforded her employees no less a privilege. She asked few personal questions of anyone, and expected the same courtesy in return. She wasn't the kind of woman who would pry into someone else's affairs. Or someone else's locker, either.

With one last warning glance at Dorsey, she spun on her heel without comment, clearly certain that Dorsey would not only show up on time Saturday evening, but would also now scurry right out to the bar.

Which, of course, she would.

Just as soon as she found the energy to move.

With a final sigh, Dorsey went to work on the buttons of her flannel shirt and tried not to think about the weekend ahead. She had really, really, *really* been looking forward to having Saturday night off. Not just because she'd been run ragged all week trying to be Dorsey at Severn, Mack at Drake's, and Lauren in too many places to name, but also because she had so much catching up to do in each of those lives. She had papers to grade, research to perform, writing to complete. And, dammit, she needed to rest. She and Lauren and Mack were all starting to look a mite bit peaked.

But she knew she'd be showing up to work the cocktail party. Not just because Lindy would fire her if she refused, but also because, she had to admit, it might be kind of fun, if she could stay awake for all of it. Although she'd observed a lot of the elusive domestic tycoon's predation and mobbing behavior at Drake's, where he was surrounded by like members of his pack, working this party would give her the added opportunity to analyze some of his social behaviors. With any luck at all, she might even witness his mating habits. Or, at the very least, his courtship rituals. Viewing the tycoon's mating habits, after all, could put her off her lunch for days.

Only then did Dorsey remember that Lauren had an engagement of her own that weekend, speaking and signing books at Northwestern University. But that was on Sunday afternoon, Dorsey reminded herself. Lauren— and Dorsey—were both free on Saturday night.

When she saw that it was Adam Darien who opened the front door to the posh penthouse suite to which Lindy had directed her Saturday night, the first thought that went through Dorsey's head was that she really should have seen this coming. The second thought was that he looked too yummy for words.

His white dress shirt and charcoal suit were utterly faultless and very sexy—though not quite as sexy as they were when he was all rumpled and disheveled at Drake's at day's end. And his brightly printed Valentino necktie was totally bitchin'. Dorsey felt a momentary pang of covetousness, and she had half a mind to slip the accessory from under his collar and pocket it for herself. And, hey, while she was at it, she thought further, she might as well unbutton his shirt and slip it, with his jacket, right off his shoulders. Probably, he'd want to remove his own shoes and socks, but she could certainly help him out of his trousers, and then she'd be free to run her hands all over his naked—

"Hi, Mack. Long time, no see."

Pffft. Another perfectly good fantasy interrupted just when she was getting to the good part. That had been happening to her a lot lately.

"Uh, hi," she responded lamely, not sure what else to add.

Actually, that wasn't quite true. There was, in fact, one question that was circling through her mind at a pretty steady clip at the moment, but she was fairly certain this wasn't a good time to ask him if he had any plans to put his tongue in her mouth again any time soon, and if so, when, because she had absolutely no plans after the party was over.

"I'll be working your party tonight," she told him instead. "Lindy needed an extra ton—Uh . . . hand."

"Ah." Then, stepping aside to extend an arm toward the interior, he bade her, "Come on in."

Dorsey tried not to be too hurt by the fact that he seemed to not even remember what had happened the last time they were together. Hey, the least he could do was look a little melancholy, feel a little hungry, the way she did herself. But he appeared to have moved on to other things. *Other women?* she wondered before she could stop herself. And he seemed to have forgotten completely that scarcely a week ago he had been trying— and succeeding really well, she recalled a bit breathlessly—to cop a feel on her . . . front porch. Among other places.

Fine, she thought. She could be just as indifferent as he could. She'd just stroll right into his apartment and not notice him at all, not notice just how . . .

Wow. Okay, so she wouldn't be able to completely ignore her surroundings, she realized immediately. Because in addition to Adam looking just too, too yummy, dammit, his penthouse was the most sumptuous place she'd ever seen.

The far wall was all windows, offering a spectacular view of the Chicago skyline, spattered with lights and washed in the pinks and oranges of a setting sun. The furnishings were utterly masculine—dark woods and neutral leather, and the floors were covered by massive Oriental rugs with abstract designs. The mantelpiece of the dark mahogany fireplace was fairly obscured by antique models of ships, and it bisected floor to ceiling bookcases that boasted hundreds of leather-bound volumes. On the wall between them, above the fireplace, was a painting of what looked to be a turn-of-the-century harbor full of more boats.

The dining area lay near the windows, and Dorsey could just make out the entrance to the kitchen on one side. The cacophony of clanking dishes and clinking glass told her someone was in there preparing hors d'oeuvres. She knew she should be getting to work, herself, setting up the bar in preparation for his guests' arrival.

"Mack. You coming?"

She heard Adam call to her from the other side of the room and only then realized that she had been standing there by the front door, gaping at her surroundings while he had moved blindly on to other matters. Now she turned her glance in his direction and found him standing framed by an elegant archway on the other side of the room, still acting as if nothing had happened between them.

Judging by his response, she might very well have dreamed the entire episode. There was nothing in his expression, nothing in his voice, nothing in his posture, to suggest that the two of them had shared the intimacy they had. Maybe she really *had* dreamed the whole thing, she thought. Maybe the entire exchange had simply been a fantasy conjured by her overwrought brain. Maybe he really hadn't pulled her into his arms and kissed her senseless. Maybe he really didn't feel anything for her at all beyond a fond friendship. Maybe all of her dreams and hopes and memories were little more than smoke and sparkle.

"I thought we could set up the bar here in my library," he told her, tipping his head at the room on the other side. "It's fairly centrally located and large enough to accommodate a good number of people."

Dorsey barely heeded what he was saying, because she was too busy trying to make sense of her feelings. This was what she wanted, wasn't it? For him—and her, too—to forget about what had happened a week ago and return to the way things had been before. Adam seemed perfectly willing and capable of doing exactly that. So why couldn't Dorsey do likewise? It would be disastrous to

wish for more with him, impossible for anything significant to come of it. Any relationship beyond friendship
that might arise between them was doomed from the
start. Even their friendship would probably suffer a fatal
blow if Adam ever found out that Lauren Grable-Monroe
was actually Dorsey "Mack" MacGuinness. Rank deception did tend to wreak havoc on a personal relationship,
after all. Go figure.

She should be grateful for his indifference, she
thought. And she should mimic it herself. So why did
she want so badly to walk across the room right now and
cover his mouth with hers and lose herself in another one
of those potent, relentless embraces?

Probably, she thought, because he looked so very kiss-
able right now, that was all. If she'd thought him handsome in the elegant atmosphere of Drake's—and
certainly, she had thought him handsome at Drake's—
then he was doubly so here in his own home. As skill-
fully arranged as everything was, there was a casualness
about the place that mirrored what she had sensed was a
part of his own personality. He seemed more at ease here,
more comfortable. More confident. She wouldn't have
thought such a thing was possible, but here in his home,
Adam Darien was even more self-assured than she'd ever
seen him, and somehow that made him sexier than he'd
ever been before.

Her heart hummed in an irregular, hip-hop rhythm, but
she managed to force her feet in his direction. He didn't
move at all as he watched her approach, only stood
framed in the arched doorway. As she drew nearer, and
he didn't alter his position, she slowed her pace some
and waited for him to step aside. Belatedly, however, she
realized he wasn't going to step aside. And also belat-

edly, she realized it wasn't a particularly wide archway that framed him.

She hesitated.

He didn't alter his position.

She came to a halt.

He didn't alter his position.

She gestured toward the room on the other side and raised her eyebrows in silent query.

He smiled. But didn't alter his position.

"Um, do you mind?" she asked pointedly.

"Not at all. In fact, I'm rather looking forward to it," he said.

Her heart hammered harder. "Adam, move out of the way."

He feigned confusion. "I'm sorry?"

"You're standing in my way," she told him pointedly. "Please move."

He pretended he was just now noticing. "Oh, that. I'm sorry. I didn't realize I was blocking you." But he didn't move.

Clearly he wasn't going to move, no matter what she did, so Dorsey inhaled a deep breath and pushed sideways through the archway as best she could. Her best, however, was none too good. Because just as she thought she'd make it through, Adam turned his body so that the two of them were face to face. Toe to toe. Chest to breast. And he smiled down at her in a way that was quite—

Whoa, baby.

Okay, so maybe it hadn't been a dream.

And oh, but it felt so good to be this close to him again. Better than anything—anything legal, at any rate— had the right to feel. She told herself to ignore the flash of heat rocking her and continue on her merry way. She told herself to forget how good Adam Darien felt to hold.

But she couldn't ignore the heat, and she didn't want to forget how he felt in her arms. Especially since she had promised herself most definitely that it would never, ever happen again.

Somehow she made her body move forward, only to halt it again when Adam dropped an arm across her path and planted it firmly against the wall on the library side of the archway. Oh. Okay. So then, *probably*, it would never, ever happen again, she amended. *Possibly*, it would never, ever happen again. Maybe. Perhaps. Um . . . what was the question again?

Because of Adam's change of position and Dorsey's brief forward motion, her upper torso now pressed lightly against his forearm, and a hot shaft of desire speared through her at the contact. Immediately, she tried to back up, but he hastily lifted his other arm to flatten his hand on the opposite wall.

And then Dorsey found herself effectively penned against one side of the archway, an opening that was barely a foot wide. There was no way she could avoid touching Adam, no way she could avoid acknowledging him. No way she could prevent the ragged trip-hammering of her pulse or the quickening of her breath or the heat that flushed her face. Instinctively, she re-treated a step, an action that pressed her back against the hard wood of the arch. And before she realized what was happening, Adam claimed a step forward to compensate for her withdrawal, bringing his entire body within a hairsbreadth of her own.

"Adam . . ." she began to object halfheartedly. But whatever lame protest she had thought to utter died be-fore she could give voice to it. Probably, Dorsey thought, that was because she didn't want to protest what she could see coming.

"I've missed you this week," he murmured softly. Then, without a single hesitation, he dipped his head forward and covered her mouth with his.

It was an extraordinary kiss. Adam picked up right where he had left off the week before, brushing his lips lightly over hers once, twice, three times, before deftly slipping his tongue inside. Dorsey opened to him willingly, eagerly, curving her hands up over his shoulders, around his nape, into his hair. At her silent encouragement, he deepened the kiss even more, pressing his body into hers from thigh to chest.

His heat surrounded her, his scent enveloped her, and she wanted nothing more than to join herself with him, lose herself in him forever. Oh, she had missed him, too, this week. Even more than she had realized. Certainly more than she should.

The last thing she needed was for someone from Drake's to stumble upon them this way. But before she could utter her concern aloud, Adam withdrew, nuzzling the sensitive hollow at the base of her throat before pulling his head back to gaze down at her. She murmured a soft sound of disappointment but let him go. Before retreating completely, however, he dragged his lips, briefly and with aching tenderness, one more time over her own.

The entire episode passed so quickly and was so wondrous she could almost believe she imagined it. Almost. Then she saw the way his face had grown flushed from the embrace, noted the way his pupils had expanded with his desire, marked the way his chest rose and fell in a rhythm even more ragged than her own respiration. More than that, she saw her own passion mirrored in his expression. And she realized that what had just happened was very, very real.

And very, very arousing.

"We need to talk," he said softly.

"Adam . . ." she said again, pleading for she knew not what, but pleading just the same.

"I can't stop thinking about you," he said softly, ignoring her protest. "About what happened the last time I saw you. I thought maybe if I stayed away from the club this week, it would be better for both of us. But I still think about you all the time. And something tells me you've been thinking about me, too."

"Adam, please, I . . ."

In response to her unspoken request, he pressed two fingers lightly over her mouth. "We'll talk later," he told her. "Make up some excuse to stay late tonight after everyone else has gone."

Dorsey tried to tell herself it was a bad idea and ticked off all the reasons why. He wasn't her type. He was the kind of man she'd sworn to avoid. They had nothing in common. He wasn't into long-term relationships. *She* wasn't into long-term relationships. Her mother had hinted at a rather questionable liaison with his father. And—the big one—Adam and Lauren Grable-Monroe would never get along.

Then again, Dorsey thought, *she* and Lauren Grable-Monroe didn't get along particularly well, either, so that was something she and Adam had in common, and that totally erased reason number three. And probably her mother hadn't really been with his father—Carlotta did so love to tease—which eradicated reason number six. And really, when she thought about it, there might be one or two things to be said for long-term relationships, so she ought to exclude reasons number four and five until she had more to go on. Which left her with only, gosh, two reasons not to go through with it.

And, hey, two wasn't so many.

"Okay," she told him softly. "We'll talk later."

He didn't drop his arm right away, however, and as she turned to squeeze past him, Dorsey bumped into him instead, breast to biceps. Touching him that way was, she decided, a very nice feeling, one she wished other parts of her body could experience, too. Adam seemed to agree, because instead of pulling away from her, he uttered a low sound of wanting, and his entire body began to draw nearer.

"Later," she repeated reluctantly. "We'll talk later."

"Talk," he reiterated blandly. "Yeah, we'll do that, too." Then, with obvious unwillingness, he dropped his arm and let her go.

Unfortunately, Adam thought, as he watched Mack cross to the bar on the other side of his library, between now and later he had a cocktail party to get through. Damn. He hated hosting parties to begin with, but it was a good way to conduct business in a laid-back atmosphere, to learn things about both his colleagues and competition that he might not learn in professional surroundings. And because the guest lists of his parties generally consisted of a pretty eclectic assortment of people, it wasn't uncommon for Adam to get a nice story for *Man's Life* here and there in the process.

He'd always hired Drake's to cater the things because it was convenient and by now Lindy knew how he liked things done. But it had never occurred to him that Mack would work as one of the bartenders, because Mack didn't normally work weekends. Now, suddenly, here she was, in his home, a place he'd fantasized having her on more than one occasion. "Having," of course, being a relative term in this case, because he'd also fantasized *having* her in a variety of other places as well—including, but certainly not limited to, the top of his desk at the *Man's Life* offices, the deck of his sailboat, the back seat of his car, a Ferris wheel, a canoe, and one of the fitting rooms at Carson Pierie Scott. And now . . . and now . . .

Damn. He'd lost his train of thought. Something about having Mack . . .

Oh, yeah. Here he finally had her in the privacy of his own home—relatively speaking—and she was working for him, for God's sake.

This wasn't how he'd planned for their first encounter in his home to unfold. He'd rather hoped to have her as a guest. And he certainly hadn't pictured her here dressed in her bartender uniform. He'd had her wearing something considerably more revealing and infinitely more feminine.

Stop it, he ordered himself. If he kept this up, he was going to be so focused on Mack tonight that he would forget all about the people—who was it he had invited again?—who were coming to his party. Including—

Oh, no. Oh, man. Oh, jeez.

Desiree.

Adam had been so wrapped up in his thoughts, or rather fantasies, or maybe plans—hey, a guy could dream, couldn't he?—for Mack that he'd completely forgotten that he would have a date for his party tonight.

This, he thought, might pose a problem. Especially if Desiree got it into her head that she would be spending the night after the party. Which wasn't entirely unthinkable, because the last time he'd had her at his place— wow, had it been almost two months ago?—he had, well . . . *had* her at his place.

What the hell had he been thinking to invite her tonight? he wondered now. Then he recalled the last night that she'd spent here and what she'd—almost—been wearing under her dress. Oh, yeah. He remembered now. He'd been thinking about her—

Well, that really wasn't important at the moment, was it? he told himself. Because what he hadn't been thinking when he'd invited Desiree tonight was that he would, at some point, discover that not only was Mack a single woman, but that she felt damned nice to hold in his arms. And once those little revelations about Mack had started playing out in his mind—over and over and over again, too, dammit—the last thing Adam had thought about was Desiree. About Desiree coming over tonight. About Desiree's probable expectation that she would be staying until dawn.

And now Adam was going to have his work cut out for him trying to figure a way to juggle two women without hurting either of them—or himself, for that matter, seeing as how one of those women had such sharp fingernails and the other had such a sharp tongue.

As if to punctuate his dilemma, the doorbell rang rather ominously. With one final, longing look at Mack, he forced himself to go and answer it.

Oh, man, he thought again. It was going to be a *loooong* night.

As a clock somewhere behind Dorsey chimed softly nine times, she concluded that this was going to be the longest night of her entire life. Although only two hours had passed since Adam's guests had begun to arrive, the evening had seemed interminable. Of course, that was probably because one of the first of those arrivals had been Adam's date. His date, for crying out loud. This after he had asked Dorsey—no, commanded her—to remain after the party. *To do what?* she wondered now. Make cocktails for Emperor Odious the First and Princess Dainty during their romp in the royal love shack?

It didn't help at all that Adam's—she tried not to choke on the word—*date* was a pink, poofy powder puff of a woman, nor was it at all heartening to overhear an introduction of her and find out she was named Desiree. Truly. Desiree. What was worse, she was tiny and trim and bubbly, with elfishly cut, pink-tinted—*I mean, really*—blond hair. Still worse, she was dressed in a cute little Chanel suit the color of blush wine.

A Chanel suit, Dorsey reflected again. A cute little Chanel suit, too, exactly the kind Lauren Grable-Monroe described in *How to Trap a Tycoon*. Somehow, Dorsey couldn't help but speculate further that Desiree had sporty separates, seductive peignoirs, and at least one diaphanous gown in her closet, as well, and that she was looking to trap herself a tycoon, a tycoon like, oh, Dorsey didn't know, maybe Adam Darien, for example, and it was all Lauren Grable-Monroe's fault, and damn, damn, damn, what the *hell* had she been thinking to write that stupid book to begin with?

Dorsey had always considered herself to be an average-sized woman, but she felt like a great, hulking ogre next to Desiree. Everything about the woman was just so dainty and so cute and so perky and so . . . pink. She'd even come to the bar and, when she couldn't remember the name of the drink she usually had—it *was* something pink, though, she did remember that part— had asked Dorsey to fix her something that would match her suit. And Dorsey, damn her evil little mind, had recommended a cosmopolitan which, in addition to being a lovely shade of rose, was pretty much straight liquor and might just cause someone who was tiny and perky, someone like, oh, say, Desiree to pass out in the bathroom—

or, as would be the case for her, the *powder* room—at some point during the evening.

So far, Desiree had consumed four of them. Any minute now, it ought to start getting interesting.

Likewise interesting was the look on Adam's face now as he hastily approached the bar, because he looked uncomfortable and annoyed, and Dorsey was just superficial and ticked off enough to be happy about it. Hey, why should she be the only one who was having a lousy time?

"What the hell have you been serving Desiree all night?" he demanded without preamble.

Dorsey shrugged as innocently as she could. "Cosmopolitans," she told him benignly.

He narrowed his eyes thoughtfully. "That doesn't sound too bad. What's in a cosmopolitan?"

"Vodka."

"What else?"

"Triple Sec."

"What else?"

"A little splash of cranberry juice for color."

"What else?"

"A lime squeeze."

"What else?"

"More vodka."

He gaped at her in alarm. "Are you trying to tell me she's been drinking straight liquor all night? Do you realize what that will do to a woman her size?"

"Make her really, really fat?" Dorsey asked hopefully.

Adam frowned but said nothing.

"Well, it can," she insisted. "Of course a little thing like her could use a few extra pounds."

Clearly detecting her malice, Adam countered just as coolly, "Oh, I don't know. I kind of like the way Desiree is arranged."

"Yeah, you would," Dorsey muttered. Then, unable to help herself, she added, "She'd better be careful her Wonderbra doesn't suffocate her. Those things can be fiercely hard to manage."

Adam eyed her blandly. "Gee, you talk as if you speak from experience. No offense, Mack, but you don't seem the Wonderbra type." He dropped his gaze to the part of her that was most likely to don such a contraption and added, "Obviously."

If she hadn't set herself up for that comment, Dorsey would have slapped him silly for making it. "I, uh . . . I wore one to a Halloween party once," she told him, feeling stung by both his blatant ogling and the fact that she'd come up lacking—in both his eyes and her own bra.

"Mm," he replied noncommittally. Then he added, "Actually, if you must know, Desiree doesn't wear a Wonderbra."

A little stab of jealousy pricked Dorsey's ego—oh, all right, a huge, razor-edged broadsword of jealousy rammed itself right through her heart—and before she could stop herself, she replied, "No, I didn't must know, actually, but since you told me anyway, it sounds like *you're* speaking from experience."

He grinned at her with a little malice of his own. "Maybe I am."

Once again, Dorsey realized she'd just set herself up for being torn down. "Oh," she said in a very small voice. "Well. I see."

Adam sighed heavily, then rubbed a hand over his forehead as if warding off a wicked migraine. "Look, Mack, I'm sorry. I invited Desiree before you and I . . ." He expelled another restless breath. "Whatever I had with her—it was a long time ago, okay?" he told her.

Dorsey eyed him suspiciously. She told herself to drop the subject, that he'd said all he needed to say on the matter, that it was none of her business, that she was only setting herself up for more disappointment if she pushed the issue. In spite of all her admonitions, however, she heard herself ask him, "How long ago?"

He hesitated before responding, then, "Months," he said. "It was months ago."

"How many months?"

"Lots of months."

"How many?" she repeated.

He expelled an impatient sound, then said through gritted teeth, "So many, I can't remember."

After another thoughtful moment, Dorsey said, "I'm guessing it was two months."

He rolled his eyes but said nothing more. Nor would he meet her gaze. *Bingo*, Dorsey thought. Men were so transparent. "I'm right, aren't I?" she cajoled. "It's only been two months since the two of you—"

"All right," he conceded. "It's been two months."

"Two months isn't very long," she observed.

"Not in woman years, maybe," he conceded. "But in man years, Desiree might as well be dead."

The difference in opinion heartened Dorsey not at all. "I suppose you've changed your mind about wanting me to stay late tonight after everyone else goes home."

He met her gaze levelly. "No, I haven't."

"But with Desiree here—"

"Desiree won't be here."

A little flutter of something warm and hopeful skittered around Dorsey's heart. "She won't?"

"No," Adam told her very decisively.

"Oh."

Evidently, this was something he had yet to discuss

with Desiree, because, as if she'd been conjured from thin air by their speculation, she appeared magically at his side. Then she pressed herself into him as if she were trying to absorb him through osmosis. It soon became clear, however, that it was an entirely different scientific experiment that she wanted to perform on him this evening. Not osmosis so much as metamorphosis.

"Adam," she said petulantly, twirling her empty glass by its stem. "When are we going to get married?"

Adam went absolutely rigid beside her, mimicking Dorsey's own icy posture. *Married*? she thought, horrified by the prospect.

"*Married*?" Adam echoed, clearly horrified by the prospect.

The petite blonde nodded and, although Dorsey would have sworn such a thing was totally impossible, she crowded her tiny body even more closely into his. "Yes, *married*," she said insistently. "For the last four months, I've been setting my tycoon trap for you, and you still haven't stepped into it."

Wow. If Dorsey had thought Adam was angry before, she was severely mistaken. Because at Desiree's casually offered comment, he suddenly went utterly still, utterly silent, utterly . . .

Uh-oh.

"You, uh . . . you've been setting a tycoon trap since you met me?" he asked very softly.

She nodded. "I've done everything that Lauren Grable-Monroe told me to do. I found you exactly where she told me I'd find you, and I did all the things she said to do in her book, but I still don't have you trapped. I mean, you didn't even notice the new diaphanous gown I wore the last time I was here." She turned her face up to look at him and—*unbelievable*, Dorsey thought—didn't even seem to notice that he was absolutely livid.

"Do go on, Desi," he said, once again speaking in that soft, scary voice.

"So, Desiree, looks like you could use a refill," Dorsey cut in quickly, hoping to defuse the tension. She reached across the bar to snatch the woman's empty glass out of her elegantly manicured—and, inescapably, pink—fingertips.

Desiree smiled her gratitude. "Thank you. You've been so considerate and so helpful tonight. Adam's so lucky to have you." For a moment, Dorsey felt guilty for all of the mean-spirited thoughts she'd been having all night about poor Desiree. Then, "Good help is *so* hard to find," poor Desiree said.

Dorsey's fingers tightened on the glass. "So. Desi. You were saying something about luring Adam into your tycoon trap. And here I've been thinking that he's the kind of man who would chew his own foot off before he'd let something like that happen. I do wish you'd go on."

The other woman brightened. "Oh, have you read *How to Trap a Tycoon*?" she asked.

Dorsey nodded indulgently. "Chapter seven had me glued to my chair," she said.

Desiree's expression clouded. "That's funny. Chapter seven had me squirming in mine. That whole crème de menthe thing was just so . . ." She squinched up her pink little face in something akin to deep thought, then added, "Although maybe if I'd done the crème de menthe thing, Adam would have proposed by now. And then I wouldn't have to do it anymore, because wives aren't expected to be so inventive. All they have to do is lie there and—"

"Desi," Adam interrupted. He intercepted the drink that Dorsey had eagerly extended toward her and set it back down on the bar. "I think you've had enough. God knows I have. I'm going to find Lucas Conaway and ask him to drive you home."

It was at that point that Edie Mulholland, who had been working alongside Dorsey much of the night, returned to the bar to refill a serving tray with flutes of champagne. "What are you, nuts?" she interjected when she heard Adam's statement, drowning out Desiree's halfhearted protests. "You get Lucas Conaway to take her home, she'll never get there."

Adam threw her a funny look. "What are you talking about?"

"Just . . . you know . . . Lucas Conaway," she repeated, as if that were explanation enough. At Adam's still befuddled expression, she added, "How can you trust him to behave himself with a woman in her condition?"

"What, are *you* nuts?" Adam asked this time. "Lucas is the only man here I *can* trust to behave himself with a woman in this condition."

This was obviously news to Edie, Dorsey noted, and she couldn't help but wonder why the other bartender was taking such an interest in the matter, anyway.

"Why? Is he gay?" Edie asked pointedly.

Adam shook his head and laughed. Hard. "Lucas Conaway gay? Ah, no. But taking advantage of intoxicated women isn't his style at all."

This, too, was clearly news to Edie. And to Dorsey, too, for that matter. After all, Lucas Conaway had been the one who wanted to put carnivorous ants all over Lauren Grable-Monroe's naked, staked-down, honey-covered backside. If that wasn't taking advantage, Dorsey didn't know what was.

The clock behind her chimed again, once this time, announcing the quarter hour, and Desiree evidently took it as her cue to lose consciousness. Because it was right about then that her delicate eyelids began to flutter, and her tiny body went slack. It was only at the last possible moment that Adam caught her, before she would have fallen face first into her untouched cosmopolitan—bonking her head on the bar in the process, no doubt—something Dorsey realized belatedly that she would rather have liked to see.

Adam sighed heavily and glanced down at his watch. "Damn," he muttered under his breath. "Will this night never end?"

Chapter 9

It was after one A.M. when Mack finally finished breaking down the bar, and Adam didn't think he'd ever seen her looking more exhausted. She seemed to be stretching herself pretty thin these days, what with working on her Ph.D. studies, working on a dissertation, working at Drake's, working at Severn . . . Hell, all Mack seemed to do in life was work on something, he thought now. Funny, he'd never noticed before that the two of them had that in common.

But where Adam thrived on his work, Mack's was obviously beginning to wear her down. And for what? he wondered. He himself had a lot to show for all the time he put in for the magazine. He'd gone out of his way to take advantage of the financial rewards inherent in a position like his. And he felt not a twinge of guilt for buying himself all the expensive toys he had purchased over the years. He'd worked his ass off to earn every last one of them, even if his work wasn't the primary source of his wealth; that had been in his family for generations.

Mack, on the other hand . . .

God knew she worked hard enough to earn more for herself than what she had to show for it. She lived with her mother and didn't own a car. She didn't seem to go out or travel—as if she had the time. He knew her tuition was paid at Severn by the work she performed there as a teaching assistant, and he also knew she made a decent wage at Drake's. So just what the hell did she do with the money that she did make? he wondered. And why did she work so hard? Especially since she had a mother who lived in a posh neighborhood and who dressed like a spread out of *Vogue*. Why did Mack work herself to exhaustion?

"Have a drink with me, Mack," he heard himself say suddenly. "You look like you could use one."

She had just folded down the flaps on the last of the liquor boxes, and when she straightened, she tossed her head a bit to dislodge a couple of unruly curls from her forehead. The rest of her hair was still bound in the elaborate braid she always wore, and Adam had been itching all night to loose it. *Soon*, he told himself. *Very soon*.

She had loosened her necktie, at least, some time ago, and now it hung from her collar. Somewhere along the line, she had also freed the top two buttons on her white shirt and rolled back the cuffs, and the casualness of her uniform, usually so starched and pressed at Drake's, made him smile.

So she could relax when the occasion for such a thing arose, he thought. That was good. Because right now, he felt like relaxing himself.

"All right," she conceded with a tired smile. She retrieved a cocktail glass from beneath the bar and filled it with ice, poured in a conservative amount of Johnnie Walker Black, then splashed a little water on top.

Adam sighed with much disappointment, tipping his head at her choice of beverage. "You drink like a girl," he told her.

She lifted the glass to her lips, sipped it daintily, then softly retorted, "Do not."

He chuckled. "You're right. At least you drink Scotch, like a man. A man who's a total wuss, granted, drinking blended—and with water, no less—but still . . . At least you don't drink anything that's"—he shuddered for effect—"pink. Call me a traditionalist, but I don't think liquor was ever meant to come in pastel colors."

She eyed him indulgently. "Gee, next you'll be complaining about the feminization of pro basketball."

"Actually," he told her, "I've already complained about that. A lot."

"What? You don't think women have as much right to wear silly-looking shorts, get all sweaty, and chase a ball pointlessly through a gymnasium, as guys do?" She smiled mildly. "Gosh, this'll just ruin the enlightened, sensitive, beta-male image of you that I carry tucked secretly in my heart."

Adam smiled and enjoyed a very alpha-male swallow of his own unblended and unwatered Scotch. "You women are taking everything away from us men," he complained.

She expelled an incredulous sound. "Oh, hang on a minute. Let me go get a bucket to catch the flow from my bleeding heart."

He chuckled. "Well, you are. Don't you read my monthly rants in *Man's Life*?"

"I don't read *Man's Life*," she replied readily, unflinchingly.

"Liar," he said with a smile. "You've offered enough commentary on my views over the last few months to assure me that you read my magazine with some regularity."

Her expression remained impassive as she said, "I suppose you feel violated by that, don't you? A woman invading your man's world."

"Not really," he told her honestly. "Contrary to popular belief, I'm not a chauvinist, a sexist, or a lout."

Her eyes widened in mock astonishment. "I'll alert the media."

He laughed. "I'm not," he insisted. "Never once have I intimated that one gender is superior to the other."

She eyed him intently now, running the pad of her middle finger slowly, methodically, around the rim of her glass. For some reason, as he watched that finger make its slow revolution, Adam's mouth went dry. Hastily, he lifted his own glass for another sip, but the mellow liquor that cooled his throat did nothing to quell his thirst. Instead, as it splashed in his belly, it only warmed him in ways that he really didn't need to feel warm right now.

"You think men and women are the same, then?" she asked him.

"No," he told her. "I think they're totally different from each other."

"And you don't think that's a sexist opinion?"

"Of course not. I don't think either gender is better or smarter or more capable than the other. They're just different, that's all. Each has its own inherent weaknesses and strengths. Actually," he added, "when you get right down to it, the two genders complement each other ideally."

Now she gazed at him with much interest. "What do you mean?"

He shrugged. "Men might have greater physical strength, but women have greater emotional strength. Where men analyze a situation in terms of black and white, women can distinguish the necessary shades of gray. Where men see the quickest, most direct path between point A and point B, women see side trips that can make the journey more interesting and more profitable."

She eyed him with frank astonishment. "Amazing," she said. "We actually agree on something for a change."

"You think men and women are inherently different?" he asked, unable to mask his surprise. "I'd think you were one of those people who considered them to be exactly alike. You seem like such a rabid feminist to me."

"I am a rabid feminist," she said readily. "But just because I think both genders are equally important to the global village, that doesn't mean I think they're the same. I agree with you that men and women are built differently," she told him. "They see things differently, they say things differently, and they operate differently. And only in acknowledging their differences can they put them to good use."

"And that's the whole point to *Man's Life*," he said with a nod of approval. "It's a publication that celebrates what makes a man a man. It's vital information for my gender to use in furthering the cause."

She digested that for a moment, then smiled. "Just like *How to Trap a Tycoon* is vital information for *my* gender to use in furthering the cause," she said.

He arched his eyebrows in surprise. First that she would bring that damned book up again, when she knew how he felt about it, and second that she would actually equate it with *Man's Life*. "Oh, I don't think so," he said.

"Sure it is," she retorted. "*Man's Life* is a magazine

that celebrates all the nice things that men have. *How to Trap a Tycoon* is a book that tells women how to go about getting those nice things, things they don't already have because they've been denied them by men."

Adam rolled his eyes and pushed himself away from the bar. "Oh, great. Here we go again. Men have everything and women have nothing."

He made his way to a leather sofa near the fireplace, where a few orange and yellow flames still danced and flickered. Then he set his drink on a side table and sat down, folding his hands over his midsection. Mack wasn't the only one who had forsaken sartorial splendor for comfort. Adam had shed his jacket and shoes some time ago and had freed his own tie from its mooring, along with the top couple of buttons on his shirt.

"Believe it or not, Mack," he continued, "I got that the first time you said it months ago. And the second time you said it. And the third. And the fourth. And the—"

"Until the problem is rectified," she interrupted him, "it bears repeating. For thousands of years, men have deliberately denied us our rightful economic rewards. And there's no end to that tradition in sight."

She, too, moved from behind the bar and strode across the room, taking her seat at the opposite end of the sofa without awaiting invitation. Then she kicked off her shoes and tucked her feet beneath her, leaning back into the corner of the couch as if she owned the place. Adam smiled at the picture she presented and considered her lack of inhibition to be a very good thing.

"Hey, men don't deny women anything," he told her. Although his tone was vehement, his pose remained quite casual, and he could only deduce that it was because this was the most comfortable he'd felt for quite some time. A week at least. Man, he'd missed his little chats with

Mack. Hell, he might as well admit it—he'd missed Mack.

He'd missed her a lot.

"Women like being dependent on men," he added. "That's their reward for their hard work. They get protection. They get affection. They get us."

She laughed. "You have got to be kidding. Like that's some prize."

He shook his head. "Of course I'm not kidding. Men *are* a prize. That's why *How to Trap a Tycoon* is such a phenomenal best-seller. That's why Lauren Grable-Monroe has become such a guru to the modern woman. As annoying as I find her, at least she has the balls to come right out and say what women actually want."

Mack smiled indulgently. "And what, pray tell, is it that women actually want?"

"They want to be taken care of. By men. They want to be protected. By men."

She lifted a hand to her forehead and shook her head slowly, as if she was having trouble processing the words he was saying. "Oh, please," she finally replied. "You have no idea what women want. You have no idea what it's like being a woman in a man's world, nor do you have any idea what it's like to *not* have money. Not only have you been wealthy from the day you were born, but, well . . ." She shrugged. "You're a guy."

Adam eyed her thoughtfully for a moment, thinking that the two of them were finally getting around to something they should have gotten around to a *loooong* time ago. "Gee, Mack, I thought you'd never notice."

"Adam . . ." she murmured, the warning in her voice unmistakable.

He held up his hands, palm out, in surrender and returned to the matter at hand. "And you do, I assume," he said. "Know what it's like to do without money, I mean," he quickly clarified. "The being a woman in a man's world part, well . . ." He couldn't help making a slow perusal of her person, taking in the loosened necktie, the open collar of her man-style shirt, and all the soft, round places of her body that her masculine attire did nothing to hide and everything to enhance. "Well, that goes without saying, doesn't it?" he concluded.

She pretended to ignore his perusal, then, just when he thought she was going to ignore that comment, too, she told him, "Yeah. I know what it's like to do without money. I'm a woman, after all."

"So I've noticed."

"Adam . . ."

"Is that why you majored in sociology?" he asked, this time ignoring her—or, at least, her warning. "Because of your economic disadvantages?"

He was honestly curious about her answer. He really had always wondered why Mack had chosen the major she had. She was a smart woman, certainly capable of excelling at whatever topic she decided to study. Why sociology? Why not something that would enable her to, oh . . . *make a living*, perhaps? Just a thought.

She shook her head. "No. I chose sociology because of my own gender disadvantages."

He threw his hands up in mock surrender. "Oh, boy. Here we go again."

"Hey, you asked."

"So I did," he conceded, dropping his arms to fold them back over his midsection. "And I suppose the least I can do is allow you to respond."

Dorsey eyed Adam with a mixture of longing to be close to him and a desire to escape him. How on earth had they wandered down this road? The last thing she wanted to talk about was why she'd chosen her field of academic study.

She sighed fitfully and shoved a handful of curls off her forehead as she propped an elbow on the back of the couch. It really was much too late to get into this tonight. She should just go home and forget about how nice it felt to be with Adam again. Forget about how much she had missed being with him this way, just talking. Forget about how much she wanted to be with him in another way, too. Forget about how wonderful it would be to sit here all night with him, just talking. Or . . . something.

Instead of forgetting all that, though, she heard herself saying, "You know my mother, of course."

Adam nodded. "She's a charming woman."

"Yes, Carlotta is that," Dorsey agreed.

He considered her with much interest. "Why do you call her Carlotta?" he asked.

"Oh, gee, I don't know," she replied mildly. "Maybe because that's her name?"

He chuckled. "No, I mean, why don't you call her Mom?"

She grinned. "Does Carlotta honestly seem like a Mom to you?"

He thought about that for a moment. "Well, no, now that you mention it, I suppose not. But it's still kind of unusual."

"Maybe. But I've never called her anything else. I guess she just always referred to herself as Carlotta when I was a very young child, so I learned to call her that, too. But we digress," she said pointedly.

"Yes, we were talking about how charming your mother is."

Dorsey nodded. "That's because being charming is Carlotta's life's work."

"And why is that?" he asked.

She sighed heavily, set her drink on the end table beside her, and dropped her hand into her lap. "Because being charming—among other things—is pretty much how my mother makes her living."

A flare of bewilderment crossed Adam's face. "What do you mean?"

Dorsey inhaled deeply again before continuing very carefully, "My mother has . . . made her way in the world by . . . being kept. By whatever man will have her, whatever man can afford to keep her for any length of time."

"Kept," Adam repeated, his expression clouding a bit more. "I'm not sure I follow you."

Dorsey smiled benignly. "Oh, I bet you do. You're a smart guy. Think about it."

He opened his mouth to speak, said nothing for a moment, then ventured, "Are you saying that your mother has spent her life as a man's mistress?"

Dorsey smiled again, though it wasn't as happily as before. "Actually, I think Carlotta prefers to think of herself as a courtesan, and she's actually been more than one man's mistress, but . . . Yes. For the most part, my mother"—she adopted her best Blanche Dubois, crushed-magnolia voice—"has always depended on the kindness of strangers."

Adam said nothing for a moment, just seemed to mull that over for a bit before continuing. Dorsey let him mull, because she knew it wasn't every day that a man found himself chatting with the product of an illicit love affair. If, of course, one could call Carlotta's relationships love affairs. Which, of course, Dorsey didn't. Had there been love involved in any of them, neither she nor her mother would be alone these days. Carlotta's relationships had been founded for economic reasons, at least on her part.

As to why her benefactors had entered into the union, well . . .

Dorsey still wasn't quite sure what they'd gotten from the arrangement, other than the obvious—sex. They certainly hadn't entered into the relationships out of love.

"Your mother mentioned that night at your house that she had never been married," Adam said, stirring her thoughts.

"No, she hasn't been," Dorsey agreed.

He hesitated a moment before continuing, "Even so, I assumed that she and your father . . ." But he left the statement unfinished.

Not that it needed finishing, she thought. She had known this was coming, had set herself up for it. It made sense that Adam would be curious about such a thing, and neither Dorsey nor her mother had ever tried to hide the circumstances surrounding her birth, though they never named Reginald Dorsey specifically as her father.

And it wasn't like this was the first time Dorsey had had to explain to someone the absence of a father in her life. Ever since she was six years old—the last time she'd spoken a word to her father—she had been spinning one tale or another to explain why he wasn't around. First for her friends, then for herself. Somewhere along the line, though, she'd forgotten which of those tales was true and which were wishful thinking.

What it all boiled down to was that Reginald Dorsey had been one of her mother's patrons for almost ten years. It was evidently as close to a love affair as Carlotta had ever come. During that time, she had become pregnant with Dorsey. Reginald had been attentive enough to his daughter those first six years—when he'd been around—but once he'd tired of Carlotta, he had, of necessity, shed his daughter, too. Since then, Dorsey hadn't exchanged a single word with him.

Oh, she knew quite a bit about him, and not just through Carlotta's recounting of the past. He was a prominent local businessman who had been happily—to the outside world, at least—married until his wife's death more than a year ago. He claimed three grown legitimate children, all older than Dorsey, and lived alone now save the servants in a big, beautiful Tudor mansion in Hinsdale.

In fact, since he and Carlotta traveled in the same social circle, her mother still ran into him from time to time. On those occasions, according to Carlotta, the two of them would exchange polite conversation for as little time as they could manage. Rarely, though, did he ask about his—other—daughter.

Dorsey's social circle was considerably less affluent than Reginald's and Carlotta's was, so she never ran into the man. Nor did she ever ask after him, either. Carlotta had forgiven him for his abandonment of her two decades ago, ascribing it to hazards of the job. Dorsey, however, had never been employed by Reginald. Therefore, she had always reasoned, she didn't have to forgive him.

"My father," she told Adam, "was one of my mother's benefactors. Many, many years ago," she added unnecessarily.

"You say that in the past tense," he noted.

She nodded. "That's because all of it is in the past."

"He's not a part of your mother's life anymore?"

"No."

"Not a part of your life?"

"No."

"Do you know who he is?"

Dorsey felt herself coloring and fought the heat back

down. She had no reason to feel embarrassed, she told herself. She wasn't responsible for her illegitimacy. And these days, there was little stigma attached to such a birth. Had it only been that way when she was a child, too, things might have been a little easier.

"Yes," she told Adam. "I know who he is."

"And he knows about you?"

"Yes."

"Yet he's not a part of your life."

"No."

"Nor your mother's."

"No."

His interrogation having evidently concluded with that, Adam studied her in silence for a long moment, his focus never wavering, his posture never changing, his eyes fixed intently on her face. Dorsey, too, said nothing, waited to hear what his reaction would be before acting one way or another. Finally, just when she thought he would never speak again, he did respond, in a very, very soft voice.

But all he said was, "Ah-hah."

She narrowed her eyes at him. "Ah-hah?" she echoed, just as quietly. "What does that mean?"

"It means, my dear Mack, that you're finally beginning to make sense to me."

Gee, that makes one of us, Dorsey thought. She decided not to ponder how his casually offered endearment punched the puree setting on her pulse rate. Best not to think about that right now, she told herself. So instead of pursuing his odd statement, she decided to answer the question he had asked her what seemed now like a lifetime ago.

"And that's why I chose to major in sociology," she told him. "Because, having grown up watching my mother's . . . social habits, I've always been fascinated by the dynamic between men and women. As much as I've spouted off about men ruling the world—and I do believe they rule it—it often seems to me that there's a pretty blurry line between who really controls whom."

Adam's features knitted in puzzlement once again. "Don't you mean who really controls what?" he asked.

Dorsey shook her head. "No. Men control the world. There's no question there. But so many men in positions of power have risked it all or lost it all or thrown it all away because of some indiscretion or obsession with a woman. It makes for a fascinating paradox," she said, warming to her subject. "If men control the world— which they do—and women control men—which they do—then doesn't that put women in the position of supreme power? And if it does, then why haven't women made the most of it? Why are we still second-class citizens?"

Adam gazed at her blandly now. "That's an easy one, Mack."

She gazed blandly back at him. "Then tell me the answer."

"Because women don't control men," he said simply. "Your whole hypothesis is skewed."

"Is it?"

"Of course it is. You yourself just said that your own mother has only survived in this world by depending on men. She didn't control them. They controlled her."

"I'm not necessarily arguing with you," Dorsey said. "But think about it. Who really controls whom in a relationship like that? It's generally men who are in the highest positions of power who indulge in this kind of relationship. Yes, the man provides the woman with compensation for her companionship. But he wouldn't be involved in that relationship with her—often an extramarital one, I might add—if the woman didn't have some kind of power over him, some kind of control. Something that he needs and can only get from her."

Adam sat up straighter, his interest clearly more than piqued. "You're a Ph.D. candidate, and you can't figure that one out?" he asked her, smiling in a way that made her insides go slack with heat.

"No, I can't," she told him frankly. "Not really. Not sufficiently. Even after writing my master's thesis on the topic, I'm not satisfied with the conclusions that I drew."

He shook his head in clear disappointment. "All that research, and you still don't see the most obvious thing in the world," he said. His smile grew broader, and somehow she got the feeling that he was laughing at her. "I think you need a study partner."

"No, I don't," she countered, battling a sudden rush of heat and wanting that came out of nowhere and threatened to run rampant through her body. "I have all the sources and resources that I need right at my fingertips."

"Mm," he replied. "Wish *I* had all your sources and resources—among other things—at *my* fingertips. And other places, too," he added before she could stop him.

"Adam . . ." she began, striving for another warning that never quite materialized.

Without further comment, but with much purpose, he pushed himself out of the corner of the sofa where he had been so adorably slumped. Then, little by little, he made his way down to the other end, where Dorsey was sitting. She had thought it would be a long trip, considering the size of the furniture in question. Somehow, though, it took him no time at all to cover the distance.

And when it finally occurred to her what he had on his mind, when she finally realized his desire—nay, his intent—she shifted her position, prepared to excuse herself from what she could clearly see coming, what she was in no way prepared to pursue. But just as she stood, he snaked out his hand and deftly wrapped his fingers around her wrist. Then, very gently, he tugged once to pull her back down. Dorsey had no choice but to fall back to the sofa beside him, landing in his arms, just, she was sure, as he had planned.

"You want to know who controls whom in a relationship like that?" he asked, fairly purring the words into her ear. "Well, now, Mack, why don't we just find out for ourselves?"

Dorsey told herself that the reason she didn't immediately withdraw from Adam was because she was too exhausted to make the effort. But when he brushed his fingertips lightly along her throat, when he stroked his thumb leisurely over her collarbone, when he dipped his head to nuzzle the sensitive skin beneath her ear, she realized that exhaustion had nothing to do with her capitulation. Because suddenly, Dorsey wasn't tired anymore. Suddenly, she experienced a renewed surge of energy that would allow her to do just about anything she wanted.

And she wanted. Oh, how she wanted.

She wanted Adam. Every hard, muscular, arrogant inch of him. She wanted him stretched out beside her, nestled on top of her, moving behind her. She wanted his hands roving hungrily over every part of her body, wanted to explore every part of his in return. And the moment Adam cupped a hand over her nape and bent his head to hers, the second he covered her mouth with his and plied her lips tenderly with his own, he shattered any objection Dorsey might have uttered.

Especially when the fingers that had strummed along her collarbone moved lower to free a few more of the buttons on her shirt. Instead of protesting—why on earth would she?—Dorsey lifted one hand to thread her fingers through Adam's silky hair, looping the other around his neck to hold him close. She returned his kisses with equal fire, equal passion, equal need. And with each brush of her mouth over his, with every sample of him she enjoyed, her desire for him multiplied, her hunger for him amplified, her need for him intensified.

He just tasted so good. And he felt so good. Everything in her life that had come before tonight seemed to fade to nothingness somehow. In that moment, Adam was everything to her. He overshadowed her past, filled her present, became her future. He dominated every thought, every feeling, every response she had. The totality of the experience should have overwhelmed her. Somehow, though, it all seemed to fit so perfectly. And Dorsey decided then to make the most of the evening. Of Adam. Of their time together. She simply would not think about how long that time might be.

When he pulled his mouth from hers, she reluctantly let him go. But he didn't want to go far. His face hovered just over hers, his brown eyes seeming darker than usual somehow, his lips curved into a tempting little smile. He smelled of smoky whiskey and sweet cigars, the twin vices only enhancing his already potent allure. In that moment, Dorsey knew she was done for. But she could think of no better way to go down.

"Is it just me?" he murmured softly as he lifted a hand to wrap an errant curl around his forefinger. "Or is this something we should have done a long time ago?"

She chuckled low. "It does seem rather silly that we've avoided it, doesn't it?"

" 'Silly' doesn't quite seem the right word to me," he told her. " 'Amazing' is more like it."

She spread her hand open over his rough jaw, raked her thumb lightly over his masculine mouth. "I just hope we're not making a terrible mistake."

He loosed the curl he had twined around his finger and placed that finger gently over her lips. "Don't," he said. "Don't ever once think that this is a mistake. It's not. No matter what happens, Mack, this, tonight, is *not* a mistake."

She opened her mouth to speak again, but he silenced her with a kiss. And then another. And another. And another. As he took her mouth again and again, he reached around to free the band that held what little of her braid remained in place. He pulled back as the dark auburn tresses tumbled free around her shoulders, then buried his fist in a particularly lush collection of curls. Gently, he tugged her forward, and Dorsey went without hesitation. Then he bent toward her to nuzzle her throat again, dragging his open mouth lightly up and down the side of her neck.

Too late, she realized his ministrations were meant to distract her while he freed a few more buttons on her shirt and tucked his hand casually inside it. Before she could object—not that she necessarily wanted to—he found the champagne-colored lace of her brassiere beneath and deftly began to explore. At first, he only grazed his thumb along the upper and lower lines of the garment, over the sensitive flesh of her upper torso and each elegant rib he encountered.

Little bonfires erupted everywhere his fingertips met flesh, and before she even realized she intended to speak, very, very, softly Dorsey murmured the word, "Please." Please what, she couldn't possibly have said. She only knew that what he was doing wasn't quite enough. She wanted more. She needed more. Of Adam and all that he promised.

Her soft, single-word petition was all the encouragement he needed. He dragged his lips back up along her throat, over her ear, her jaw, her chin, then finally covered her mouth with his. Dorsey answered his demand in kind, opening to receive him, to make herself fully accessible for his erotic plunder. And plunder her he did. He thrust his tongue full into her mouth, tasting her deeply, his slick passion nearly overwhelming her.

His big body pressed into hers, urging her backward, until Dorsey lay half on her back, her head cushioned in the palm of his hand. He positioned his own body sideways alongside and over hers, so that she lay between him and the back of the sofa. Strangely, Adam seemed larger lying down than he did standing up, and a small tremor of anticipation shook her as he crowded himself more insistently against her. The fingers that had been dancing along the lacy perimeter of her bra dipped lower, and he filled his hand with her, palming the tender peak of her breast with much affection. She heard the soft whisper of tearing fabric, felt her shirt gape open wider, then the kiss of warm air over her naked breast.

As enjoyable as that warmth was, though, it was nothing compared to the even more pleasurable sensation of Adam's hand rubbing over her swollen breast. That sensation, too, was soon surpassed, however, when he trailed a series of brief butterfly kisses down her neck, along her shoulder and collarbone, between her breasts and finally, finally over the tender mound of flesh. He opened his mouth wide over her nipple and sucked as much of her inside as he could, laving her with the flat of his tongue before doing his best to devour her whole.

Oh . . . that felt so . . . delicious, Dorsey thought. So delectable. So decadent. Her fingers tightened convulsively in his hair, and she urged him closer still, silently begging for more. So Adam gave her more. He licked the undersides of her breasts with long, lingering strokes, taunted the stiff peaks with the tip of his tongue. And with every salacious taste, he pushed a hand lower, loosing the fastenings of her trousers, dipping inside, skimming along the waistband of her panties.

Dorsey was so focused on enjoying the scintillating pleasure she was feeling that she didn't pay much attention to where Adam's seemingly aimless wandering was taking him. Not until he scooped his hand lower, beneath the silky fabric of her panties. Not until he buried three fingers in the damp, delicate folds of flesh that he found between her legs. At that shocking contact, she went absolutely rigid, clenched her fingers more tightly into his hair, expelled a rough sound that wasn't quite objection, wasn't quite acquiescence.

Adam halted his invasion then, as if awaiting a signal from her. Dorsey's gaze found his, and she saw that he was smiling, a predatory little smile that indicated he was enjoying himself immensely. But when she offered no indication that she wanted him to either withdraw or continue, his smile fell some. Not because he was unhappy, she soon realized. But because he had his mind on other things.

The fingers pressed against her moved again, slowly, gently, almost imperceptibly, two of them enclosing that most sensitive part of her, one of them reaching lower, to softly penetrate her. Dorsey's eyes fluttered closed at the keenness of the sensation, and her mouth fell open in an effort to draw in more air. Adam's fingers moved again, backward, forward, gliding effortlessly, insistently, through her slick heat.

"Oh, Adam . . ." she whispered. "Oh, that feels so . . . Oh . . ."

She heard his rough chuckle but couldn't quite bring herself to open her eyes. Because what she was feeling was quite unlike anything she had ever felt before, and she was reasonably certain that she didn't want it to end just yet. Which was good, because he showed no sign of ceasing his actions anytime soon. And with each eager, capable motion of his fingers, Dorsey fell back a bit more until her head lay cushioned on the sofa arm and her body lay open to Adam's onslaught.

Vaguely, she registered the removal of her trousers and her panties, her socks and her shoes. Vaguely, she sensed Adam removing some of his own clothing, as well. Vaguely, she felt him shove a throw pillow beneath her hips. And vaguely, she sensed him drawing near again. But there was nothing vague about her response when, instead of returning his fingers to the damp, raging heart of her, his mouth went there instead. Dorsey's eyes snapped open wide, and she cried out in both surprise and scandal at the sensations that swamped her when he flicked his tongue against her. No one had ever . . . It was completely unexpected . . . There was no way she should allow . . . Surely he wasn't planning to . . .

She never completed any of those thoughts, so far gone by now was she that she could scarcely remember her own name. She had ceased to be Dorsey, had ceased to be Mack, had ceased to be even Lauren Grable-Monroe. At that moment, she was simply a woman—nothing more, nothing less. And for making her feel that way, more than anything else, she would always be grateful to Adam.

And then even that fey, indistinct thought evaporated, melted away into a capricious whirl of others even less defined. All Dorsey could do then was *feel*. Feel and marvel at the kaleidoscope of sensation and emotion that wheeled through her, until even those shattered into a billion shards of joy.

She cried out her completion and instinctively groped for Adam. Clutching his shoulders, she pulled him back up to her breast, captured him, clung to him. But before she could say a word, he pushed himself between her legs and coaxed them wider still. She moved her hand between their bodies to find his ripened, rigid shaft and was surprised to discover that it was already sheathed in a condom. But her disappointment that she wouldn't have the opportunity to explore him more completely quickly turned to anticipation when she felt the solid length of him pressing against her hand. He was so . . . oh . . . Instinctively, she opened her legs wider, thrust her hips forward, and guided him to where she wanted him to be.

With one swift, arrogant thrust, Adam buried himself as deeply as he could, filling Dorsey in a way she had never been filled before. With that one, single maneuver, he seemed to be everywhere inside her, overflowing places she had never known were empty, warming parts of her she had never realized were cold. For a moment after entering her, he stilled, remained motionless, as if he couldn't quite believe what he had done. Then he withdrew and pushed himself forward again, even more deeply than before. And Dorsey knew in that moment that regardless of where he might be in the future—or, perhaps more realistically, where he would not be— Adam would never, ever leave those places inside her that he had filled. Not completely. He would be with her always. No matter what.

Then she gave up thinking at all, because his movements became more rapid, more rhythmic, more insistent than ever before. Again and again he drove himself inside her, deeper and deeper, faster and faster, harder and harder and harder still. Dorsey bucked her hips upward to meet every swift thrust, wrapped her legs and arms tightly around him, until their damp, heated bodies seemed to fuse into one. And just when she thought they had accomplished that very thing, just when she was certain the two of them had united to become one, Adam's thrusting ceased, and his entire body went rigid atop hers.

Had it not been for the man-made barrier he'd donned to protect her, he would have emptied himself inside her then, would have mingled his physical essence with her own. Something in Dorsey grieved for that loss, even with her certainty that he had done the right thing. The joining of their spiritual and emotional essences had been more than complete, she told herself. And that was what was truly important.

After one final thrust, Adam withdrew from her, then deftly maneuvered their bodies so that he was flat on his back with Dorsey lying atop him. "Next time, Mack," he gasped against her hair, "we do this in a bed. Agreed?"

Somehow, she found the strength to nod. "Agreed."

After the passage of approximately two seconds, he added, "Okay, I'm ready for next time. How about you?"

Chapter 10

Edie still had a full block to cover before reaching her car when she finally accepted the fact that she was being followed. She had felt someone's gaze trailing her almost since she'd stepped out of the elevator and into the lobby of Adam Darien's building five minutes ago, but she'd brushed the sensation off, had tried to convince herself that she was imagining things. She was tired, it had been a long night, and no woman in her right mind savored a solitary walk in the darkness.

Edie had told herself she was just creating monsters where there were none. And heaven knew she could spot a monster from this distance. And she was certainly no stranger to dark urban streets.

In spite of the quick pep talk, however, she'd been fighting off a major wiggins ever since leaving Adam's place. She'd even ducked into a coffee shop and ordered a café au lait to go, hoping that whoever belonged to the gaze following her would continue on his merry way and find someone else to creep out. Within seconds of leaving the coffee shop, however, that eerie sensation of being watched had washed over her again, and she'd heard the sound of not so distant footsteps echoing her own.

She hadn't planned on leaving Adam Darien's place by herself, had figured she'd help Dorsey finish cleaning up, and then the two of them could walk out together. But Dorsey had insisted she could close things down by herself and had encouraged Edie quite adamantly to go on home. Had Edie explained the situation and said she didn't want to walk so great a distance by herself, Dorsey—and probably Adam Darien, too, for that matter—would have no doubt come to her aid.

But with one look at Dorsey and another at Adam, Edie had been reluctant to say another word. The tension in that room had been thick enough to hack with a meat cleaver. No way did she want to get caught in the downswing of whatever was coming next.

She never would have guessed anything was going on with those two. Not only because they didn't seem to have anything in common, but because Edie had always figured Dorsey was way too smart to get caught up in something like that.

Man, you never could tell with some people.

Still, it was none of Edie's business. Dorsey and Adam were adults, and they both knew what was what in this world. Besides, Edie had infinitely more pressing matters to attend to right now. Not the least of which was the source of the footsteps that were gradually beginning to catch up on her.

This part of Chicago, during the day, would be bustling with people, but at nearly one A.M., it was pretty much deserted. Well lit, certainly, something for which Edie was grateful, but deserted. Still, there were a number of restaurants serving a few final customers, and she'd seen a lone police cruiser pass by shortly after leaving Adam's building. If she screamed horribly at the top of her lungs, she was sure someone would come running. Probably, anyway. Nevertheless, she wished she hadn't had to park so far away.

Why couldn't life be like TV? she wondered, not for the first time. On TV, people always got a parking spot right by the door. Of course, on TV, people found true love and profound happiness, too. Most of them had dream jobs and chic apartments and fabulous clothes and adoring families. TV was a fantasy, she reminded herself. Nobody in reality ever got what they wanted. Certainly not true love or adoring families. And not parking spots by the door, either.

Experimentally, she stopped walking, ostensibly to study a menu in the window of one of the restaurants she was passing. The footsteps shadowing hers stopped, too, not surprisingly. This was ridiculous, Edie thought. There was no way she was going to lead this person right to her car and invite him to commit whatever heinous acts he was intent on committing. And besides, she *was* feeling a little hungry.

The café she entered was charming, a little slice of the Mediterranean brought to the Midwest. Crisp, white linen tablecloths covered the crowded tables, and frescoes of olive groves and Greek villages splashed the walls. She smiled when she heard the voice of Pavarotti serenading her with a mellow, operatic rendition of *La Vie en Rose*.

The last thing she needed was to stay up late tonight, she thought. She'd already gone nearly twenty-four hours without sleep, and what sleep she'd had then had been anything but restful. Then again, her sleep was rarely good, even at the best of times. But she was still feeling anxious about being followed, and something about the little café called to her, cocooned her, made her feel safe.

"Are you still serving dinner?" she asked a bartender who was wiping down the bar. He was big and round and smiling, with arms the size of rain barrels, and Edie sensed in him immediately a brave and noble spirit.

"Only appetizers," he told her. "And only for another half-hour at that. We close at two."

"That'd be okay."

He waved a hand expansively at the otherwise empty room. "Have a seat anywhere. I'll get Margie to take your order."

"Thanks."

Edie chose a small table midway between the bar and the door—well, perhaps it was a *bit* closer to the bar than it was to the door—one that was well lit and set for two. Then she plucked the menu from between the salt and pepper shakers and gave it a quick perusal. A woman as big and round and smiling as the bartender came out to take her order, and since Edie already had her café au lait from the coffee shop, she ordered a baked Brie to go with it.

Hey, she had no romance in her life, she thought, and there would certainly be none forthcoming. Who cared if she ate an entire Brie and swelled up to the size of France? At least she'd be happy.

Content with her decision, she unzipped the backpack that she carried with her everywhere and withdrew a battered textbook. If she was going to stay up too late and eat foods rich enough to keep her awake for hours, then she might as well get a little studying done.

She had just turned to the assigned reading on the Peloponnesian War when she felt someone watching her again. She glanced up just as the café's front door opened, and her mouth fell open in surprise when she saw who strode through.

Lucas Conaway was still dressed in the blue jeans, white oxford shirt, and black blazer he had been wearing at Adam Darien's party, but his necktie was loosened now, and he'd unfastened the top two or three buttons of his shirt. His icy blue gaze was fixed intently on hers, and Edie felt certain then that he was the one who had been following her.

How dare he? she wondered, outraged by the realization. How dare he scare the life out of her the way he had? What was the matter with him?

Without greeting her or awaiting an invitation, he walked purposefully to her table, pulled out the opposite chair with an ominous scrape, then dropped into it, landing in a careless sprawl. But he remained silent, only stared at her as if it were she and not he who had just committed some grievous sin.

"Well, gosh, just sit yourself down," she told him wryly. "Don't do something so crass as wait for me to invite you."

"Do you mind?" he said blandly.

"What if I do?"

His only response was a shrug, but there was nothing at all casual about the gesture.

"Fine," she conceded shortly. "Join me." Then, as rudely as he, she dropped her gaze back down to her textbook and pretended to read, pretended to dismiss him without another thought.

"Thanks," he said. "I think I will."

Before Edie could point out that her comment had been sarcastic—something she was certain he would be able to appreciate, seeing as how he was the reigning king of that particular realm—her server came back to take his order, too. Before she could stop him, Lucas asked for a cup of coffee but nothing more. And evidently realizing that the table was fully laden with tension and ill will, their server didn't suggest anything else and beat a hasty retreat.

Edie spared a glance back up at Lucas then, but she said nothing, silently indicating that it was up to him to go first and explain what he was doing here. For a moment, he only continued to stare at her in that plainly disgruntled way, then, very slowly, very intently, he bent his body forward, folded his arms one over the other on the table, and frowned.

"Just what the hell were you thinking to leave Adam's place all by yourself this time of night?" he demanded.

She arched her eyebrows in disbelief. "Excuse me?" she demanded right back. "What were *you* thinking to follow me and scare me half to death?"

"You *should* be scared to death," he countered. "A woman walking alone in a deserted city in the middle of the night. Anything could have happened to you out there."

"Hey, I can take care of myself," she told him.

His cool smile indicated just how seriously he took that assurance. "Yeah, right," he muttered.

"I can."

He looked nowhere near convinced. "Uh-huh. Sure. Okay. Whatever you say."

"And even if you don't believe that, it didn't give you any right to follow me," she told him.

He hesitated only a moment—a moment he used to glare at her even more—then said, "*I* wasn't the one who was following you. I was following the guy who was following you."

Okay, now she was really confused. "What are you talking about?"

He sighed heavily, then threw her another one of those looks that suggested she was responsible for ruining his whole evening. Hey, his whole life. "I was sitting in my car across the street from Adam's place, about to pull away, and—"

"You got a parking space that close?" she interrupted, unable to help herself. Figures a guy like him would get a break like that. Lucas Conaway was the kind of person who got every break life had to offer. Good looks, massive intelligence, expensive education, fabulous job right out of the gate. Of course, there was that small matter of him completely lacking a soul, she thought further. But then, nobody was perfect, right?

He eyed her in a way that made her feel like she was about two years old. "Ye-ess," he said, drawing the word out curiously. "I got a parking space that close. Is that a problem?"

She shook her head. She wanted to ask him if he'd found true love and profound happiness, too. She'd already seen for herself that he had a dream job and a chic apartment and fabulous clothes. He no doubt also had an adoring family and maybe even true love, as well. Then again, she didn't really want to know about it if he did have all those things. It would only reinforce her conviction that the universe was in no way balanced. Why should Lucas Conaway get all the breaks? she wondered. Especially since he obviously didn't appreciate them.

"No," she told him. "It's not a problem. Just interesting, that's all."

"In what way?"

In response, Edie only shook her head and told him to go on.

"Anyway, I was getting ready to pull away from the curb," he continued, "when I saw you leave the building. I watched you go, and—"

"Why?" she interjected, her curiosity getting the better of her.

He said nothing for a moment, then leaned forward again and fixed his gaze even more studiously on her face. And then, very softly, he told her, "Because I like the way you move."

When she noted the way he was looking at her—all hungry and agitated and intense—a strange heat circled up from her belly to coil around her heart. All she could manage in response to his revelation was "Oh," in a very small voice.

Thankfully, their server returned with his coffee then, giving Edie some small reprieve to collect her thoughts. Unfortunately, she discovered that she'd lost most of them. And she doubted she would be finding them anytime soon.

Lucas said nothing as their server set his coffee before him, only continued to study Edie's face as if it was something he honestly found worth studying. Hah. What a laugh. She knew she was in no way study-worthy, with her makeup long gone and the stain of embarrassment darkening her cheeks. She had to fight back the urge to lift a hand to her hair and brush back the straggling bits of blond that had escaped her topknot, faint tresses she could feel dancing around her face and neck. She'd tugged on a massively stretched-out, faded green Severn College sweatshirt before leaving Adam's, and she was certain the shapeless garment only enhanced her utter lack of appeal now.

Nevertheless, in spite of her certainty to the contrary, Lucas must have found her intriguing, because his gaze roved hungrily from her eyes to her hair to her cheeks to her mouth, where it lingered for some moments more. The heat that had flooded Edie's face moved lower then, to her heart, her belly, her womb, then exploded somewhere lower still, somewhere deeper, somewhere she hadn't felt heat ever before. And on the heels of that heat came a wanting, a needing, a desiring that was completely alien to her.

Never in her life had Edie desired a man. Never had she wanted one. She had certainly never needed one. And she was stunned to discover that, after all this time, after all her certainty to the contrary, her body would feel something like this and betray her so thoroughly. Especially now. Especially here. Especially with someone like Lucas Conaway.

"Anyway," he finally continued, scattering her thoughts again—for now. "I watched you go, and then, as I was getting ready to pull out, I saw some guy leave the building behind you and take off in the same direction."

"What made you think he was following me?" she asked.

Lucas smiled again, but, as usual, there was no happiness in the gesture. Such a bundle of contradictions he was, she thought, not for the first time.

"What can I say?" he muttered. "I always expect the worst from people."

"Yeah, well, I can't say that's exactly a surprise," she muttered back.

"I didn't like the thought of you being out there alone if this guy tried something," he went on, as if she hadn't spoken, "so I left my car where it was and took off after him. I just wanted to make sure you were okay, all right?" he added apologetically. But the apology seemed to come less because he had scared her and more because he was ashamed of himself for caring.

"I don't know who it was," he said further when she opened her mouth to ask him exactly that. "And when you ducked in here, he just kept on going. Probably because by then he knew he was being followed, too, by me. But *he* was following you, Edie. Not me. Him. I wouldn't do something like that to you. I wouldn't try to scare you."

You might not try, she thought, *but you do a damned fine job of it anyway.*

"I can't imagine why anybody would be following me," she said.

He chuckled low, without an ounce of humor. "You can't imagine," he repeated.

She shook her head slowly but said nothing.

"A beautiful woman alone on a deserted street in the middle of the night?" he cajoled. "And you can't imagine what it is about that scenario that would inspire a man to commit mayhem? Or worse?"

Well, of course she could imagine when he put it like that. In fact, she could do much more than imagine. She had, after all, lived the reality. She just didn't want to think about it if she didn't have to. And damn Lucas for making her recall it now.

But when she responded to his comment, all that came out was a very surprised, "You think I'm beautiful?"

The moment she said it, Edie wanted to crawl under the table and hide. Instead, she squeezed her eyes shut tight and just hoped like crazy that Lucas hadn't heard what she said.

"For chrissakes, Edie," he countered, squelching her hope. "How have you made it through life this long without someone taking complete advantage of you?"

Her eyes snapped open again at the vehemence that had crept into his voice. He sounded like he wanted to hit something. Hard. "Who says no one's ever taken advantage of me?" she said softly.

The retort was out of her mouth before she could stop it, so rattled had she been by the anger in his delivery, so fast was her heart racing when she remembered how he'd called her beautiful. Immediately, she regretted giving voice to the comment and wished she could call it back. But it was too late. Lucas was looking at her in a completely different manner now, one full of startled surprise and newfound interest.

"I mean, uh . . ." She tried to backpedal. "That, um . . . that didn't come out right."

"Didn't it?"

"No."

But her voice shook a little when she spoke, and she could tell that he didn't believe her.

"Who's taken advantage of you, Edie?" he asked softly.

"Nobody," she replied.

He eyed her with much speculation. "The other night, when you took me home," he said, rousing more memories in her brain that she would just as soon not have roused, "I told you I was looking for someone. And then you told me you were looking for someone, too."

"No, I told you I *wasn't* looking for anybody," she countered quickly. A little too quickly. Even she could tell she was lying now.

"I didn't believe you then," Lucas told her. "And I don't believe you now." Before she had a chance to contradict him again, he hurried on, "So are you, by any chance, looking for the person who took advantage of you? Could Little Edie Sunshine be looking for something as nasty and cold-hearted as revenge?" He smiled grimly. "I didn't think you had it in you, sweetheart. Way to go."

She told herself to change the subject—now—to a safer, more mundane topic. What Edie was looking for was none of Lucas's business. For some reason, though, she found herself revealing, "I'm not looking for revenge." Not the way he thought, anyway, she added silently to herself. "I'm looking for my mother. My biological mother."

At her revelation, his grin fell, but his expression remained totally impassive. "I didn't realize you were adopted," he said.

She nodded. "When I was an infant. My adoptive parents are both dead now." Somehow, she refrained from adding, *May their putrid, disgusting, miserable souls rot in the coldest pit that hell has to offer*, and continued, "I've just always been curious about my natural mother and the circumstances surrounding my birth and why she gave me up and where I come from and what kind of heritage I might have and if there are any medical conditions I should be aware of and—" She cut herself off when she realized she was beginning to sound hysterical. She cleared her throat indelicately and tried again. "Anyway, I've just always wondered where I came from."

Lucas nodded. "I take it you're not from Chicago."

"I was born in Kentucky. I moved from Hopkinsville to Naperville with my adoptive parents when I was ten."

"So then you probably come from Kentucky," he remarked blandly. "There. I've solved the mystery for you. Now you can stop wondering."

She emitted a soft sound of surprise at his easy conclusion. "Yeah, well, as much as I appreciate your, uh . . . your help, there's a little more to where a person comes from than the geographic location of their birth."

"Is there?"

She eyed him curiously. "Well, yeah. I mean, where are you from originally?"

He hesitated a moment before replying simply, "I was born in Wisconsin."

"That's it?" she asked. "Just 'I was born in Wisconsin'? No town, no house, no family, no history?"

In a very low, very flat voice, he told her, "No."

"None?"

"None worth mentioning."

Gee, why all the melodrama? Edie wondered. From what she'd seen of Lucas Conaway, he seemed to have enjoyed every advantage life had to offer. Still, she knew it took more than financial stability and the presence of a family to make a person content. Boy, did she know that.

"Unhappy childhood?" she asked mildly.

"Slightly," he told her, the word coming out cold and clipped.

She nodded her understanding. "I know the feeling."

"Oh, I sincerely doubt that."

Edie wasn't about to sit here and play What's My Whine? with Lucas Conaway. Not just because it was much too late for that kind of thing, and not just because the two of them would look pathetic, and not just because she had no desire to rehash her past history with him—or to learn more about his, for that matter. No, the reason Edie didn't want to compete with Lucas in the I've-had-it-rougher-than-you-have department was simply because she knew she would win, hands down.

Such a conclusion had come about because it was a simple statement of fact and was in no way inspired by an immersion in self-pity. On the contrary, she had long ago turned loose the resentment she'd once had about how the capricious fates had dealt her such a god-awful hand in the game of life. Because if she didn't turn it loose, she knew she would become one of those stark, ugly creatures who ate out of trash cans and slept in society's refuse. And she'd seen enough of those people during her months living on the streets that she didn't want to become one herself.

So she said nothing to start such a disagreement. Instead, she turned the tables on Lucas. "So who are *you* looking for?" she asked.

He expelled a few more of those dry, humorless chuckles and deflected his gaze from hers, staring at some point over her left shoulder. "A tycoon," he finally mumbled. "I'm looking to trap myself a tycoon."

Lucas had no idea what provoked him to reveal his professional quest to Edie Mulholland. What was the point of talking to such a raging goody-two-shoes about anything other than the most mundane superficialities? Even if what they'd discussed over the last several minutes had been anything but mundane or superficial, never mind goody-two-shod.

What the hell had he been thinking to follow whoever had been tailing her? he wondered. Okay, some misguided sense of chivalry, maybe. He could live with that. He could accept that somewhere deep down inside himself, there still flickered some small gasp of decency, however remote. But once the guy following Edie had sensed Lucas's presence and kept walking past the café, why had Lucas gone inside? Why had he sat down—uninvited, no less—with Edie? And what had possessed him to tell her he was looking for a tycoon?

He supposed he'd just wanted to say something—any-thing—that would banish that haunted, hungry look from her eyes. Man, for a minute there, perky, cheerful, genial, blond Edie Mulholland had actually looked unhappy. Morose. Bitter. And it was because of something he'd said. As many times as Lucas had been nauseated by her blind sweetness, he hadn't necessarily wanted to see her lose it. Not really. Yeah, putting up with her being chipper and happy and blond all the time was certainly depressing, but now he realized it was worse to see her sad.

You are such a sap, Conaway, he chastised himself. And hell, he hadn't even been drinking this time.

He remembered again how much he had revealed that night he'd gotten drunk at Drake's when she'd had to take him home. He remembered telling her that he wanted her, remembered asking her—no, begging her, he reminded himself ruthlessly—not to leave him alone in his apartment. Worse, he remembered how much he had wanted her to stay. He remembered how much he had needed her. And he remembered how much it had hurt to hear his front door click shut softly behind her when she left.

And Lucas didn't like it that he had felt hurt. He liked it less that he had felt need. He didn't need anybody, he told himself now. And he sure as hell wasn't going to let anybody hurt him ever again.

"A tycoon," Edie repeated, bringing him back to the present. "Um, aren't you surrounded by them every day at Drake's?"

"Not the kind I need."

Their server returned then with a massive wheel of baked Brie surrounded by slices of apple and pear and a small bunch of grapes and accompanied by a big basket of baguettes and brioches. And Lucas decided right then and there that there was no way he could allow Edie to consume all that by herself.

"This is an appetizer?" she asked their server, her thoughts clearly mirroring his.

She nodded as she told them, "*Bon appetit.*"

"Let me help you with this," Lucas offered magnanimously as he plucked a grape from its stem. "It's the least I can do."

"Yeah, the very least," Edie murmured—dryly, if he wasn't mistaken.

"Hey, you can't eat baked Brie alone," he told her. "It's a fact of life."

She eyed him dubiously. "You learned this fact of life on your fictional trip to Paris, I assume."

"*Touché,*" he said.

She smiled. "I forgot you speak the language fluently."

"*Mais, oui,*" he told her.

"Can you say anything that's not a cliché?" she challenged him.

"There, see?" he countered. "You speak French, too. You said *cliché* like a native."

"But then, we were talking about some tycoon you're looking to trap," Edie said, spoiling what had promised to be some pretty righteous chitchat.

Lucas sighed his resignation. "Yeah," he said, reaching for a slice of apple to dip in the soft, fragrant cheese. "Adam wants me to find a rich woman to take care of me."

Edie had just swallowed a bite of Brie-laden brioche when Lucas tossed off his careless announcement, and it must have gotten lodged somewhere on the way down. Because suddenly, she went still. Then she made a very unladylike sound, and then she began to hack. A lot. Lucas stood quickly and moved around the table, ready to administer the Heimlich on her if he had to. At least, he would have administered the Heimlich on her . . . if he'd ever bothered to learn how to perform it. Since he hadn't, he opened his hand over the center of her back instead and began to pat her with some vigor.

Or, at least, he tried to pat her. But the second his hand made contact with her back, Edie jerked up out of her chair at the speed of light and spun around fast enough to send that chair clattering to the ground.

Lucas told himself that the reason she looked so terrified was because she was in the process of choking to death. But she inhaled a deep breath, and he realized that whatever had been blocking her windpipe was now free. Nevertheless, she sputtered uncomfortably a few more times. And nevertheless, she still looked terrified.

He remembered then how she had reacted at Drake's that night when he had tried to place his keys in the palm of her hand. He remembered how she had reacted when Davenport had reached across the bar to skim his thumb lightly over her cheek. Innocent gestures, both, but Edie had reacted as if rabid hyenas were launching themselves at her jugular. Both times she had lurched her entire body backward, as if she feared for her very life. She seemed to feel exactly the same way right now.

"Edie?" he asked quietly, taking an experimental step toward her.

She in turn took a very deliberate step backward.

"Are you all right?" he asked further. He righted the chair that had toppled over when she'd rocketed out of it and silently bade her to sit down. Amazingly, she did so without comment.

"I'm fine," she said a bit hoarsely once she was seated.

Lucas inhaled a slow, deep breath and returned to his own seat. "I probably shouldn't ask what that was all about, but then, I've never much been one to do what I know is right, so . . . Just what was that all about?"

She looked at him with wide, innocent eyes, eyes that appeared even larger and bluer than usual, thanks to the dampness that lingered there after her coughing fit. At least, Lucas assumed the tears were a result of her coughing. What the hell else could have caused them?

"What was what all about?" she asked him innocently. "I just swallowed the wrong way, that's all."

He frowned at her. "Don't start, Edie. Don't try to lie to a liar like me. It won't wash. You know exactly what I'm talking about."

"I just swallowed the Brie wrong," she insisted.

"You just about jumped out of your skin when I put my hand on your back," he corrected. "The same way you just about jumped out of your skin at Drake's that night when I tried to give you my keys."

Her blank expression turned vague. "And your point would be . . . ?"

He muttered a ripe curse under his breath. "You got a problem with being touched, Edie?"

She met his gaze levelly. "Yes." But she offered no further explanation.

Never known for his tact—or his courtesy, for that matter—Lucas asked, "Why?"

Something in her eyes went absolutely glacial at his question. But her voice was the very essence of politeness when she said, "That, Mr. Conaway, is none of your business. Now then. Back to what we were talking about a moment ago. You're looking for a rich woman to take care of you, is that it?" Her tone was decidedly less polite as she added, "You? Want to be taken care of? By a woman? With money? This is something that frankly surprises me."

Lucas smiled when he realized how badly he'd misspoken—and how badly she'd misunderstood. No wonder she'd nearly choked on her Brie. "I meant that Adam wants me to use the book *How to Trap a Tycoon* to find a rich woman to take care of me for a story. It's for the magazine, Edie," he clarified, his smile growing broader. "For *Man's Life*. What, you thought I was really looking for a sugar mommy?" His smile turned into chuckles. Real chuckles, too. Not the phony-baloney sarcastic ones to which he'd become so accustomed.

Wow. That felt really good. He couldn't honestly remember the last time he had laughed at something because it was funny. Because he enjoyed it. Because it made him feel happy. He should try to do that more often. Interesting it being Edie who had generated the spark within him.

She had the decency to look chagrined for assuming what she had. And when she did, Lucas laughed some more. He hated to say it, but she really was cute when she was embarrassed. Even if she was Mulholland of Sunnybrook Farm, she wasn't quite as annoying as he'd suspected she would be at close range. Funny how he'd never noticed that before tonight.

"A story for the magazine?" she asked a little sheepishly.

"A story for the magazine," he told her.

"Gee. I, uh . . . I guess I should have figured that one out for myself, huh?"

Lucas shrugged, and with that single, careless gesture, he felt a few of the chips he'd carried around since childhood tumble right off his shoulders. *Wow.* That felt really good, too. Amazing. Two questionable evenings with Edie Mulholland, and suddenly, he felt almost like a human being. This could get interesting.

"Yeah, well, Edie, it's not like I've ever given you any reason to look for the best in me, have I?" he asked. "And that's probably the reason I'm having so much trouble finding myself a tycoon to trap," he further speculated.

She said nothing in response to his assertion, probably because no response was necessary. Then, carefully, as if she wasn't quite sure of her reception, she said, "I could help you out."

Lucas Conaway had never asked for or accepted help from anyone in his entire life. Whatever he had to show for who he was, he'd damn well earned it all by himself. Now, however, he met Edie's gaze with much interest. "What do you mean?" he asked.

She tore off another piece of baguette and used it to scoop up a generous serving of Brie. Before popping it into her mouth, however, she told him, "I'm good at finding people, Lucas. I'm close to finding my mother right now. And God knows I've had a lot of experience with tycoons."

He assumed she was talking about her work at Drake's, and decided he didn't want to know any particulars of the situation if she wasn't. At any rate, all he said in reply was, "Oh, yeah?"

She nodded. "Yeah. You want to trap yourself a tycoon? I'm just the woman who can help you."

Chapter 11

Dorsey awoke Sunday morning to the most pleasurable sensations she had ever experienced. The cool crush of satin pillowed her cheek and naked breasts, cascaded over her bare back and bottom. Faint strains of a Bach piano concerto serenaded her from somewhere nearby, the light, joyful noise mimicking the happy pulsing of her heart. She inhaled deeply her contentment and was further greeted by the rich aroma of strong coffee, a fragrance that roused her from the last remnants of sleep. When she finally opened her eyes, it was to see Adam entering his bedroom wearing naught but a pair of sapphire-colored silk pajama bottoms and carrying a tray. A tray, she noted further, gratefully, that carried, among other things, the promise of nourishment.

She could use some nourishment after the night she had just spent, she thought, feeling muzzy-headed and pleasantly achy. Drowsily, she eyed the basket of sweet breads, the carafe of black coffee, the two simple white mugs, and the single apricot-colored rose in a silver vase. Goodness. What a romantic Adam Darien was turning out to be.

In the pale light filtering through the half-open window blinds, she got her first good look at him in dishabille. Her insides turned to warm butter at viewing such a sight first thing in the morning. His broad, naked chest was dusted from shoulder to shoulder with dark-brown hair, hair that arrowed downward to disappear into the waistband of his pajama bottoms. His belly was as flat and firm as a steam iron, and his arms were corded with muscle and sinew. His hair was adorably rumpled, and his eyes were lit with warm affection. He had the fat Sunday edition of the *Tribune* tucked under one arm, and she couldn't help thinking that he meant to spend the entire morning sharing his bounty with her right here in his bed. The mahogany sleigh bed that was surrounded by all manner of luxurious furniture and accessories, from the matching wardrobe and armoire to the richly patterned Oriental rugs scattered about beneath. The walls were painted a deep forest-green, adorned here and there by oil-on-canvas renditions of the English countryside.

The effect, on the whole, was one of enormous wealth and lush hedonism. And as Dorsey watched Adam draw nearer, carrying his sumptuous feast, surrounded by his luxurious belongings, one thought—and one thought alone—circled through her head: *Oh, I could get used to this. I could get used to this very easily.*

Suddenly, the idea of trapping herself a tycoon wasn't nearly as unappealing as she'd once considered it to be. In fact, suddenly, Dorsey was questioning every conviction she'd ever had. Because she was also beginning to think that it might not be so bad relying on someone else for a change. It might not be so bad being taken care of once in a while. And it might not be so bad to be shackled to another human being for all eternity. Because if this was how it felt . . . If she could experience these wonderful sensations every morning when she awoke . . . If it meant having Adam Darien all sleepy-eyed and rumpled in her bed . . .

Well. Maybe Lauren Grable-Monroe was onto something after all.

Dorsey smiled sleepily and stifled a yawn and tried not to dwell on the fact that nothing had ever felt so utterly right in her entire life than this particular moment did. "Good morning," she murmured as she pushed herself up from the mattress. As unobtrusively as she could, she wrapped herself in gold satin as she went.

Funny that she would feel modest after some of the things the two of them had done to and with each other over the last several hours. She certainly hadn't been shy during the night, she recalled now, the heat of her memories warming her entire body. Of course, neither had Adam. Then again, she thought further, when she noted the way his pajama bottoms were tied so haphazardly— and so low—on his hips, he didn't seem to be feeling particularly modest himself at the moment. On the contrary, if that sly little smile playing about his lips was any indication, he had every intention of—

Oh, my. She might never leave this bed again.

"Good morning yourself," he replied, his voice a rich rumble of contentment as he set the breakfast tray on the upholstered bench at the foot of the bed. "I thought you were going to sleep the whole day away."

A momentary panic shook Dorsey as she searched frantically for a clock and found none.

"It's not even nine-thirty," Adam told her, chuckling.

"What's wrong? You got a hot date somewhere I should know about?"

Although he seemed to be striving for levity, something in his voice held an undertone of uncertainty, as if he feared she might very well have another romantic obligation this morning. Goodness, could he possibly be feeling jealous? Feeling possessive? she wondered as a curl of something warm and fuzzy slowly unwound inside her. And why did the prospect of such a possibility make her feel so wonderfully delicious? The absolutely last thing on earth she wanted was to be possessed by a man. Wasn't it? Of course it was. Then again, she was feeling a bit possessive about Adam this morning, too.

Oh, dear. This was certain to wreak havoc on her dissertation.

"I have to be someplace this afternoon," she told him, nudging the thoughts aside for now and forcing herself to relax. "But not until three." Impulsively, she added, "I'm yours until then."

The smile he bestowed upon her in return was one of the greatest prizes Dorsey had ever won. Without further comment, he poured her a cup of coffee and brought it around to her side of the bed, setting it on the nightstand within easy reach. She mumbled her thanks but didn't pick it up right away. She was having too much fun feeling sleepy and disoriented and wanton, and she didn't want her wits about her just yet.

Adam, too, neglected the cup he had poured for himself, leaving it on the tray near where he had tossed the newspaper. "I should warn you," he told her without preamble, "that although I'm not a churchgoing man, I do have a rigid Sunday morning ritual that I religiously observe."

"Oh?" she asked innocently.

"I stay in bed until noon, reading every last word of the *Tribune*."

She smiled. "Even *Broom Hilda*?"

"Yep."

"Wow. That's impressive. And you don't mind if I'm here to intrude?" she asked. "I won't be a distraction to you?"

"Oh, I'm counting on it," he assured her.

Ignoring the newspaper, he climbed into bed and prowled like a predator toward her, then seated himself, cross-legged upon the mattress, before her. For a moment, he said nothing, only studied her with much interest, as if he were trying to decide exactly what to say. Then, suddenly, he grinned. A slow, sexy, dangerous little grin that ignited a spark of heat deep inside her.

And in a low, level voice, he said, "Should I tell you how good it felt to wake up this morning and find you in my bed?"

Dorsey's lips parted softly in surprise that he would reveal such a thing so freely. *No, don't*, she thought. *Don't tell me anything that will make me care for you more than I do already.*

"Should I tell you how sweet you smell and how soft you are?" he added.

No, don't. Please don't.

"Should I tell you how easy you are to hold? How long it's been since I've wanted a woman as much as I want you?"

No, don't . . .

"Should I tell you how incredible last night was?"

Oh, Adam . . .

He seemed to sense her distress, because his smile fell some as he asked further, "Or would telling you all that be revealing too much, too soon?"

Dorsey's languid pulse had begun to vibrate like a ket-tledrum with every soft, seductive word he spoke. Surely he wasn't serious about all that, she thought. Surely he was only saying these things to her now because he was still under the influence of the warm, rosy afterglow that came on the heels of lovemaking. Surely he wasn't tell-ing her what he seemed to be telling her. Surely last night had been no more important to him than any of his other sexual conquests had been.

Then again, he was looking a little conquered himself at the moment, she thought. She never would have guessed that Adam Darien was the kind of man who would bring a woman breakfast and roses in bed.

She swallowed hard. "Uh, no," she said with some difficulty. "Um, that's, uh . . . that's fine. You can say that."

His smile returned, confident, affectionate, and very, very sexy. "Then should I tell you how often I'd like to wake up that same way?" he asked further. "Or would it scare you off if you knew just how badly I want you?"

Had she thought her pulse was rapid before? Heavens, she'd had no idea her blood could rush so fiercely through her body without making her unconscious. Then again, she *was* beginning to feel a little dizzy.

"I, uh . . ." she stammered, "I—I don't know. Would it?"

His smile turned a little sad as he considered his an-swer. "Yeah," he finally said softly. "It probably would. So I don't think I'll tell you that part. Not yet, anyway."

She felt strangely disappointed that he didn't, then told herself not to be. If his intentions would scare her, then she didn't need to hear them. She was much too fright-ened of what lay ahead as it was.

Adam seemed to sense her misgivings, because he

stretched out alongside her, propping himself up on one elbow, cradling his head in his palm. For a moment, he only gazed at her, as if he were trying to imprint her appearance on some part of his brain so that he would never forget this moment. Then he lifted his other hand and twined a single auburn curl around his forefinger.

"I'm glad you stayed last night," he said simply.

She hesitated only briefly before assuring him, "I'm glad I did, too."

He unwound the curl from his finger and then brushed his bent knuckles lightly along her jawline. "We should do it again sometime," he told her.

Dorsey let out a shallow breath before asking, "Should we?"

He nodded, then skimmed his fingertips across her lower lip. "Mm-hm. Soon."

His tender touches, so seemingly innocent, so utterly arousing, made it impossible for her to think clearly. "I . . . okay," she capitulated easily.

He grazed the back of his hand down the slender column of her throat, then turned it to dip his middle finger in the delicate hollow at its base. "Like tonight maybe," he suggested.

"To-tonight?" she asked huskily.

He nodded again. "I have to be in Evanston this afternoon, but I should be done there by six. I could swing by your place on my way home and pick you up. We could grab a bite to eat, maybe go hear some nice jazz, and then come back here. What do you say?"

Frankly, Dorsey couldn't say anything. Because she'd heard little past the word, "Evanston." Although tiny bonfires had exploded inside her every time, everywhere, Adam touched her, a cold, brittle weight now wedged itself tight somewhere between her stomach and her heart. And she couldn't quite make herself breathe around it.

"You, uh ... you're going to Evanston this afternoon?" she asked, amazed that she'd managed to form the question, so numb was she feeling. "What for?"

He dropped his hand to the mattress, and Dorsey felt both gratitude and regret for his retreat. "Lauren Grable-Monroe is speaking at Northwestern today," he muttered distastefully. "And since I've had no choice but to submit to the American public's demands and include a piece on her in *Man's Life*, I figure the least I can do is try to wrangle an interview with the woman."

Telling herself not to sound too interested, but helpless not to pursue the matter, Dorsey asked him, "Why don't you just call her publisher and set something up?"

He didn't seem to think the question odd, because he answered quite readily, "I was going to do that, but there's just something about ambushing the woman that appeals to my baser instincts. So I thought I'd catch her by surprise after her lecture this afternoon."

Oh, no you won't, Dorsey thought. *You've just blown your advantage. She is on to you, mister. Bigtime.*

And she tried to forget how he had been on her—in her—only hours ago. Unfortunately, memories of last night came roaring up to overwhelm her, and Dorsey realized that, regardless of where he was in the world, Adam would always be inside her. Even if she lived to be one hundred years old, she would never forget a moment of what they had shared last night. Especially since it was looking unlikely that they would ever have a chance to repeat it.

Because she had forgotten that there was a woman standing between them. Namely, Lauren Grable-Monroe.

Now what? she wondered as a cool lump of dread settled inside her. What on earth was she supposed to do? She'd just spent the most glorious night of her life with a man who might very well prove to be someone special, and Lauren Grable-Monroe was about to step right between them and shove them apart. She had to tell him the truth, she thought. She couldn't keep carrying on with the charade. Not where Adam was concerned. How could she keep lying to him after what they had shared last night?

But what if he blew her cover? she asked herself. Yes, the two of them had just shared a wonderful night together, and yes, the future for them looked very bright. But what if, when he learned the truth, Adam became angry? Angry about the deception, angry that it was Dorsey who had penned a book he reviled? What if he became angry enough to forget what they had just shared? Angry enough to expose her as Lauren? Angry enough to disrupt her life even more than it had already been disrupted?

In spite of everything, she honestly didn't know him all that well. What the two of them had discovered together was still so new, so fragile, so uncertain. She wanted to believe he would never do anything to hurt her. But she wasn't sure she could make that leap of faith. Not yet.

"Adam, I—"

Dorsey never found out what she was going to tell him, because the hand he had dropped to the mattress moved to the sheet she'd wrapped loosely around herself. With a gentle tug, he freed it from her shoulder, baring one breast. Then, without hesitation, he opened his hand over her naked flesh and palmed her with easy possession. The sensation that shot through her was a keen mixture of heat and cold, of desire and foreboding, of wishing and warning. But the former quickly overrode the latter in every case, and Dorsey lifted a hand to run her fingers through his hair.

He was so handsome. So tender. So wonderful. And she simply did not want to do anything that would jeopardize the tentative feelings that seemed to have come out of nowhere last night. Surely, later they could talk, and she would find some way to make sense of it all. Surely, later she would find some way to explain. Surely later—

"I want you again," he said softly.

But he did nothing to alter his leisurely posture. He only watched her face intently as he rubbed his open hand back and forth over her breast, rousing in her fire and heat and need. Dorsey curled her fingers around his nape and lay back on the bed, pulling him down with her until his mouth hovered just above her own. Then, with one more gentle nudge, she caught his lips with hers, nuzzling them, nipping them, before running the tip of her tongue along the seam that parted them. He opened to her willingly, and she drove her tongue inside, tasting Adam and the promise of a languid Sunday morning.

For now, that was enough, she told herself. Because a languid Sunday morning with him was more than she had ever had with anyone else before. If what she suspected was happening between them was actually happening between them, there would be time for explanations later.

She only hoped there wouldn't be a time for regrets, too.

When Lauren Grable-Monroe took the stage at Northwestern at precisely three-thirty that afternoon, Adam was glad he had arrived early enough to snag himself a seat up close. Not just because the crush of people—

mostly women ... mostly college women ... mostly rabid college women—behind him were so enthusiastic, and not because he might have had trouble hearing otherwise. But because she was dressed in va-va-voom red that really did bear seeing up close.

The short, slim skirt hugged legs encased in sheer black silk, and the shorter, slimmer jacket hung open over a scooped-neck, snug black top. Adam got the impression of dangerous curves and not much else, and if he closed his eyes, he could almost smell the elusive, erotic scent that must surely surround her.

She was an eyeful, that was for sure. *Eye candy*, he thought further, having heard the phrase from Lucas and finally understanding what it meant. Lauren Grable-Monroe, with her blond, blond hair and dark, dark eyes and red, red mouth—not to mention that do-me-baby body—was every man's dream. And once she was front and center onstage, Adam was glad he'd made the trip to Evanston. Because her front and center was just too nice to miss.

Of course, he hadn't been so glad earlier that day, when he'd had to leave the warmth of his bed and Mack to shower and change and return to the real world. He hadn't been lying to her when he'd told her it had felt good to wake up and find her in his bed that morning. Actually, that had been a lie, he backpedaled now. Because waking up beside Mack had felt infinitely more than good. It had felt extraordinary. Incredible. Amazingly right.

As consciousness had gradually dawned on him that morning, Adam had opened his eyes to the indolent, erotic sensations of soft, round breast cradled in one hand and soft, round bottom nestled against full erection. He'd been nearly overcome by the warm, rosy reality of having her in his bed, had wanted to enter her right then, that way, with their bodies spooned back to front as he moved in and out of her from behind.

Instead, he'd only lain there and held her, enjoying the peaceful, innocent feel of her in his arms. She really was very easy to hold. So easy, that he hadn't wanted to let her go. Ever. And that, more than anything else, had shaken Adam to his core. It was one thing to want a woman as much as he wanted Mack. It was another thing entirely for that wanting to go so deep and for that wanting to go on forever. Yet way down deep inside himself, he was beginning to think that he wanted her in just that way. Soul deep. For all time. And he couldn't for the life of him understand why.

Yes, she was a beautiful, intelligent, passionate woman. But there was certainly no shortage of those in Chicago. Why did Mack make him feel so different from how other women he had dated—other women he had bedded—had made him feel? There shouldn't be any more to his relationship with her than he'd had with anyone else. But there was. He couldn't quite put his finger on what, but there was definitely something more there.

The only thing that had kept him from spending the entire day in bed making love to her had been the fact that she, herself, had had to leave, even before he did. She'd never told him specifically where she was going that afternoon. Nor had any amount of coaxing or cajoling on his part been able to make her stay. And boy, had Adam coaxed. Boy, had he cajoled. He'd unsheathed— so to speak—every amorous weapon—so to speak—in his more than ample—so to speak—arsenal, hoping to convince her that nothing could be more important than the two of them spending the day together alone. Preferably in bed. Preferably naked. Preferably insensate with wanting.

But something had been more important to Mack. Because nothing he'd said or tried or done would make her change her mind. And no matter how many times he had asked her, or in how many ways, she wouldn't tell him where she was going.

You wouldn't be interested, she'd kept saying. Or *It's no place special*. Or *It's just something I have to do. A prior commitment*, she'd tried to explain. *I can't get out of it*.

Adam told himself that her reluctance to reveal her destination—and who might be waiting for her at that destination—shouldn't bother him, that she was entitled to her privacy in that respect. In spite of the spontaneous combustion the two of them had generated the night before, whatever was happening between them was still too new and too uncertain for either of them to start making demands on the other. Whatever appointment Mack had been required to meet, she'd made it before last night. And if it was with another man, well . . .

Well, then Adam would just have to find the other guy and break his neck, that was all.

Once Mack had left that afternoon, Adam had seen no reason not to complete his day in the way that he'd initially planned, and he had halfheartedly driven to Evanston to ambush Lauren Grable-Monroe. He expected her to speak at length about the writing of her book, then hawk the publication like snake oil. Instead, she spent much of her time discussing the psychology of men and women and the sexual politics inherent in any romantic relationship. She was surprisingly astute, Adam had to admit, and remarkably animated.

Clearly, she loved the subject matter about which she

had written. Her talk was laced with humor, but many of her observations were unexpectedly pithy. She was obviously well versed in the whole man-woman dynamic. Then again, considering how she'd made her way in the world, he supposed that wasn't surprising. All in all, though, the author's presentation was remarkably informative.

Man, he should have invited Mack along today, Adam thought as he listened. She really would have gotten into this. Of course, she'd had other things—another man?—to do, he recalled uncomfortably. Then again, he'd be seeing her tonight, he remembered, heartened some. Even if he hadn't been able to convince her to stay at his place that morning, he'd won the concession from her that they would see each other again this evening.

He could hardly wait.

After Lauren Grable-Monroe concluded her speech, she opened the floor to questions, thereby bringing Adam back to the matter at hand. There were only a smattering of inquiries at first, but gradually, several people in the auditorium began raising their hands. Many eventually started waving them quite adamantly in their demands to be recognized. Ms. Grable-Monroe took her time when selecting her interrogators, though whether that was because she was trying to be fair or because she was trying to weed out anybody who might be too challenging Adam had yet to decide.

"Yes, here in front," she said now, directing her attention to a young woman who had a hand extended in the air.

The girl—for truly, Adam noted, she couldn't have yet completed her freshman year—wore the standard university uniform of baggy cargo pants and massive, long-sleeved T-shirt. She tossed back her ebony curls and adjusted wire-rimmed glasses as she asked, "Ms. Grable-

Monroe, would you say a word or two about the Cinderella complex? About how women wait around for Prince Charming to come and rescue them from their unhappy lives and make them feel complete?"

"Oh, I'd be happy to speak at length on the Cinderella complex," the author said cheerfully. "Especially since you don't seem to have a clue what it's really all about."

The student's mouth dropped open in surprise, but before she could defend herself, Lauren Grable-Monroe began to talk again.

"Traditionally, a woman with a Cinderella complex, instead of taking charge of her own life and creating her own destiny, assumes that a man, a Prince Charming, will eventually come and sweep her off her feet and carry her to his palace, and then the two of them will live happily ever after. He becomes, in that respect, her rescuer. That's the popular—and erroneous, I might add—interpretation of that fairy tale. I'd suggest we look at it a different way. Ask yourself who needed whom more in that relationship?"

The student seemed stumped. "I'm not sure I'm following you," she said.

Lauren Grable-Monroe tented her fingers thoughtfully on the dais before her and said, "Cinderella, poor drudge that she was, was, nevertheless, a reasonably happy person. A person who really lacked nothing in her life. She had a family—albeit a dysfunctional one, but hey, who doesn't, right?—and a roof over her head and food on the table and steady work. One might argue that the work was a bit too steady, but still. She had a relatively good life, considering the time period with which we're working here. She needed nothing more. Had Prince Charming never come along, she would have survived quite adequately in her world.

"Prince Charming, on the other hand," she continued, "did need something in addition to his family, his roof, his food, and his work. He needed an heir. No self-respecting prince of the time would be without one. He would be far too easy a target for his enemies. And there was only one way for the prince to get an heir. He needed a woman. Enter Cinderella. She was his rescuer in that respect. *She* was *his* rescuer," the author reiterated. "Not the other way around. Technically, Prince Charming had nothing to offer Cinderella that she didn't already have. She, however, did have something that he didn't—a womb. He couldn't have survived without her. She, however, could have managed quite nicely without him."

"But what about love?" the student asked.

Lauren Grable-Monroe smiled. "Ah, now that's an entirely different question. And an entirely different scenario. If you want to bring love into the union, then you have a much more equitable balance of reward and rescue. Which is entirely the point to my book."

That had Adam out of his chair, arm extended, before he even realized he had intended to take exception. "Ms. Grable-Monroe," he called out, unwilling to wait for her to recognize him.

The author, along with a few hundred other people in the room, turned to look at him, her expression impassive. "You had a question?" she said.

"No," he told her. "An objection."

She arched her dark eyebrows in surprise. "To what?"

"To the fact that you just claimed that your book is about love," he said.

"Actually, Mr. . . ."

"Darien," he identified himself. "Adam Darien. I publish and edit *Man's Life* magazine."

Her smile brightened at his admission, and something

inside him responded on a very basic, very masculine level. "So you do," she murmured in that husky timbre that still made his blood run a little too hot for his comfort.

"You're familiar with the publication, then," he said. It was a statement, not a question, because Adam hadn't a single doubt that she was familiar with his publication.

"Of course," she replied. "But you misunderstood me a moment ago. I'm not saying love is what's at the heart of my book. I'm saying that a balanced relationship is what's at the heart of my book."

He barked out a laugh that was completely lacking in good humor. "You can't be serious."

Her expression grew faintly puzzled. "I can't? Why not?"

"In your book, you tell women to use plotting and inveigling and entrapment in order to land themselves a wealthy man who will take care of them for the rest of their lives."

She seemed vaguely amused by his analysis. "Really? Is that what I'm telling them to do?"

"Of course it is."

"I had no idea. How about that?"

"Do you deny it?" he asked.

Instead of answering him, Lauren Grable-Monroe posed a question of her own. "Tell me, Mr. Darien, have you even read my book?"

Adam shifted his weight uncomfortably from one foot to the other. "Actually, no," he confessed. "But that's—"

"That's what I thought," she finished before he had the chance, a knowing little smile playing about her lips.

"That's beside the point, Ms. Grable-Monroe. The point is—"

"The point, Mr. Darien, is that you haven't an inkling

what my book says, therefore you can't possibly object to it. At no time do I advocate plotting, inveigling, or entrapment. Nor do I suggest that women land themselves a wealthy man to take care of them. What I encourage women to do is to find a mate worthy of them and to use the tools they have at their disposal to ensure an equal power base in that relationship."

"And you don't think that's plotting?"

She shook her head. "No, I don't. I think it's taking advantage of an opportunity women have overlooked in the past."

"I'm afraid I don't understand."

The author tented her fingers in that thoughtful way again, tilted her head to one side, and observed Adam in a way that made him slightly uncomfortable. "For millennia," she said, "men have entered into relationships with women and claimed all the power in those relationships for themselves. They've been able to do this because of their superior physical strength and because the laws—*man*-made laws—have been in their favor. Today, in our more *enlightened* times," she continued, clearly tongue in cheek, "those laws are slooooowly changing. In the meantime, I think women are within their rights to effect changes in the balance of power where they can—in whatever way they can—to make the relationship a more equitable one."

"I'm sorry," Adam echoed, "but I still don't understand."

The author smiled at him again. "Read my book, Mr. Darien. Then call my publisher. We'll chat."

And before he could say another word, she turned her gaze to a student who had flagged her down, thereby dismissing Adam with all the interest she might have given to a glob of gum stuck to the heel of her shoe.

Damn. Well, that hadn't gone well at all, had it? Instead of him ambushing Lauren Grable-Monroe, she'd just mowed him down like a weed.

Reluctantly, Adam sat back down in his chair and mulled over the Cinderella complex thing. He had to concede that she'd made a good point with the rescuer/reward thing. Sort of. But what was this balance of power in a relationship business that she kept going on about? And why did this conversation seem so familiar for some reason? Furthermore, why did Lauren Grable-Monroe seem so familiar for some reason?

Because she did seem familiar somehow. Adam couldn't quite put his finger on who, but she definitely reminded him of someone.

"Which is why we can conclude that it is Beauty who truly holds the most power in her relationship with the Beast," the author was saying now. "It is she who rescues him. He needs her in order to break the spell he's been under. She doesn't need him for anything. Unless," she said meaningfully, "you want to bring up the subject of love again. When love—honest, genuine love—enters the picture, the power base of any relationship shifts and grows more equitable."

Adam itched to raise his hand again, but after the last dressing down he'd received at her hands—and boy, was that an interesting way to put it—he was hesitant to draw her attention again. Fortunately, someone else asked the very question he'd wanted to pose himself.

"Why does the introduction of love into a relationship change the balance of power?" a young woman who stood up a few rows in front of him asked.

The author seemed to give much thought to what she was going to say before she began speaking again. "Very few people would argue," she began slowly, "that men and women are entirely different creatures. There's all kinds of evidence to support the truth in that assertion. The genders simply approach life in completely different fashions. That doesn't mean one is better than the other," she hastened to qualify. "It just means they're different."

Hmm, Adam thought. This was sounding familiar, too.

She paused for a moment, thinking, then continued, "Many theorists would have you believe that each gender's reason for entering into sexual relationships likewise differs, and that both reasons are engendered by basic instincts that are throwbacks to primitive times—the man because he needs to procreate, and the woman because she needs protection from natural dangers. I would propose, however, that, like so many other human traits and characteristics, through evolution those primitive urges have changed. They've evolved. Nowadays, I think men and women enter relationships looking to fulfill a need that is identical, regardless of gender—the need to give and receive love."

As he listened to Lauren Grable-Monroe discuss her hypothesis, Adam found himself conceding—with much reluctance—that he found the subject matter to be . . . well, fascinating, actually. More than that, he found the speaker to be fascinating. As irritating as he had thought the author before, he now found her to be more than a little intriguing.

She was clearly an educated woman. Nobody could expound this stuff with the confidence and articulation she claimed unless they were familiar with the subject matter on an academic level. She must have at least one college degree, but why would a professional mistress bother with an advanced education? Especially since Ms. Grable-Monroe's bio from her own publisher—which, granted, he was certain was complete hooey—had stated that her family had lost everything? How could she have afforded to go to college? And why would she have wanted to, if she'd already decided to make herself available to wealthy men for a living?

Moreover, she was, without question, a Chicago native, as Adam deduced from her distinctive accent, which was indigenous to this part of the Midwest. And why would a woman who'd made her living on her back— and who demanded anonymity—continue to live in a city where she could easily be exposed by one of her former benefactors? Especially since her book was turning her into a very wealthy woman, one who wouldn't have to make a living on her back anymore? She could be sunning herself in Rio de Janeiro or skiing the Alps instead.

Too, she was definitely one hot tomata, a fact to which Adam himself could testify. And hot tomatas were notoriously hard to keep under wraps. They were, by nature, attention-seekers, spotlight-grabbers, and paparazzi-bait. How could this woman be making a life for herself in Chicago yet be seen nowhere except at the public appearances arranged by her publisher? Because she was never seen anywhere else. Adam was certain of that. Although he hadn't been following her career with a microscope, he'd definitely taken notice of her appearances. And the only time Lauren Grable-Monroe appeared anywhere, it was at her publisher's behest, in order to promote her book. Otherwise, she was nowhere to be found.

And he himself had hit nothing but brick walls in his efforts to find out more about her. Her publisher guarded her true identity well, and no amount of investigation had turned up anything substantial that might offer a clue as to her real identity.

What he had determined, and only by personal observation, was that Lauren Grable-Monroe was a well educated and beautiful Chicagoan who was currently at the height of celebrity, yet she was never seen anywhere in town outside her arranged public appearances. At a time when everyone in the country wanted to know more about her, no one had come forward claiming to have any particulars about her background. No former school-mates, no former boyfriends, no former benefactors. No distant relatives coming out of the woodwork in need of a buck. No disgruntled wives hoping to expose a home wrecker.

Just who the hell *was* Lauren Grable-Monroe? he wondered. He really, really wanted to find out.

Damn, he thought. This meant he was going to have to read her book. Then again, maybe it would give him a couple of pointers. Because even if he wasn't out to trap himself a tycoon, Adam was definitely looking to catch something. He just hoped what he caught, when he caught it, wasn't contagious.

"I think I have time for one more question," the author suddenly piped up. "Is there anything we haven't covered here yet today?"

"I have a question about something we haven't cov-ered, Ms. Grable-Monroe," a woman called out from down front. When she stood, Adam saw that she was in her mid to late fifties, was stylishly attired and had an elegant demeanor. Her graying hair was caught at her nape in a sophisticated twist of some kind, her beige suit appeared to be haute couture. She rather reminded Adam of his own mother.

"Yes?" the author asked the woman, her smile en-couraging. "What would you like to ask?"

"What I'd like to ask," the woman said, "is how can you sleep at night?"

The author's smile fell—which, Adam supposed,

wasn't exactly surprising, all things considered. "I beg your pardon?" she replied quietly.

"I said," the woman reiterated, considerably louder than before, "I want to know how you can sleep at night. In fact, I'd like to know how you can live with yourself."

But still Lauren Grable-Monroe seemed to have no idea how to respond. Because all she did was stammer, "E-excuse me?"

"Oh, come now, Ms. Grable-Monroe," the woman taunted. "You've had no shortage of analysis and philosophy for any of the other questions asked today. Surely this one can't stump you that badly. It's fairly straightforward. Unlike your own deceitful self."

The author straightened and seemed to recover some of her own elegance and sophistication. "No, you're right, of course. And it's not that I'm stumped for an answer. I'm just trying to fathom how you can be so frightfully rude."

"*I'm* rude?" the woman echoed incredulously, splaying a hand over her heart. "Me? *I'm* not the one who's responsible for leading good, decent men astray. *I'm* not the one who's made my living on my back. *I'm* not the one who's caused countless marriages to fail and left children fatherless. Home wrecker!" she cried defiantly in conclusion.

Oh, wow, Adam thought. This was getting good. With much anticipation, he turned his attention to Lauren Grable-Monroe, wondering how she was going to talk her way out of this one. Evidently, he wasn't alone. Because the entire auditorium had gone absolutely silent, every eye in the place riveted to the two women's exchange.

For a moment, the author said nothing, only returned her interrogator's angry gaze with a slightly less caustic one of her own. Then, very softly, very evenly, she replied, "I'm not responsible for any of those things, either. I'm *not* a home wrecker."

"Oh, the hell you're not," the woman countered. "How can you stand up there, an admitted mistress, a woman who's confessed to countless adulterous affairs, and say otherwise?"

"I can say that," the author replied in clipped tones, "because I never held a gun to any man's head and forced him to be unfaithful to his wife. The men who seek such relationships do just that—seek them. If their marriages fail as a result of that search, then it's their own fault. And I might add that their marriages must not have been very solid to begin with, if these men took it upon themselves to look for fulfillment elsewhere."

Ooo. Score one for the home wrecker, Adam thought.

The other woman, however, clearly wasn't willing to let the author off so easily. "How dare you," she said coldly. "How dare you suggest that a man would willingly turn away from his loving wife to follow after a cheap bit of skirt like you. And how dare you stand up there and encourage these young women to lure respectable men into illicit affairs."

A murmur went through the audience at that, and Adam was fairly certain that more than a few of them were in support of the woman's accusation. Man. It was amazing how quickly a tide could turn.

The author sighed heavily. "Obviously Mr. Darien isn't the only one in the room who hasn't read my book yet feels qualified to comment on it at length."

Oh, fine, Adam thought. Just bring that up again, why didn't she?

"Because clearly, Ms. . . . ?" the author left the remark unfinished, her request obvious.

"It's *Mrs.*," the other woman corrected her crisply, standing more erect than before. "Mrs. Harrison Enright."

And why did Adam get the impression that *Mr.* Harrison Enright was keeping a hot little tootsie under wraps somewhere? Just a hunch.

"Mrs. Enright," the author continued, her voice softening some. "I assure you that at no time do I advocate anyone entering into an illicit affair. On the contrary, what I'm encouraging women to do is to use their resources to look out for their own best interests. I suggest you read my book and—"

A bitter laugh cut the comment short. Well, that, and Mrs. Enright's cry of "Not bloody likely! I'll not put a red cent into your adulterous accounts. You can return to making a living on your back, as far as I'm concerned. Just stay away from *my* husband."

Yep, Adam thought. Mr. Enright most definitely had a hot little tootsie under wraps somewhere. No question about that.

The author sighed heavily again then lifted a hand to pinch the bridge of her nose with thumb and forefinger. She closed her eyes, shook her head slowly, then, "Oh, boy," she muttered softly into the microphone.

And Adam had to admit that, although he hadn't entirely accepted every hypothesis the author had posed that afternoon, he sure couldn't disagree with her on that one.

Chapter 12

"So there she was, with this absolutely furious woman berating her, and all she could do was sputter some lame comment about not being responsible for wandering husbands."

For the third time in less than a week, Dorsey listened with jaw clenched tight as Adam described—in much too vivid, much too enthusiastic detail—Lauren Grable-Monroe's public flogging at Northwestern on Sunday afternoon. The first time had been bad enough, because it had come almost immediately following the event, when she and Adam had spent the evening together, dining and dancing. And, okay, necking heavily on her front porch after she'd cited exhaustion and a need to get home. This instead of returning to Adam's place for a night of what she was sure would have been raucous and extremely satisfying lovemaking.

The second time she'd been forced to listen to his glowing account of the episode had been two days later, when Adam had joyfully described it to Lindy Aubrey. And Lindy, Dorsey recalled now, had taken an uncommon interest in the event. Which was odd, because Dorsey didn't think Lindy took an interest in anything— except Drake's of course. But she'd laughed without inhibition, and with much satisfaction, at Lauren's unfortunate confrontation. And somehow, Dorsey had felt almost betrayed by her employer as a result.

Now it was Lucas Conaway who was held in thrall by the story, and he was enjoying it more than anyone had a right to enjoy anything. He sat in his usual jeans and usual white Oxford shirt and usual silly cartoon necktie on his usual stool next to Adam's, nursing his usual Tanqueray and tonic as if he had no intention of drinking any of it anytime soon. The working day was over for the two men, but Dorsey's was just beginning, and somehow, the knowledge of that irritated her more than usual. She was really getting tired of working so much. Especially since she seemed to have so little to show for it.

"So Lauren Grable-Monroe is standing there renouncing any responsibility for wayward husbands," Adam went on, "but she's dressed in this heart-stopping, libido-grabbing miniskirt that leaves absolutely nothing to the imagination, and—"

Dorsey cleared her throat indelicately, then arched an eyebrow meaningfully at Adam. "Really?" she said. "You noticed what she was wearing? I didn't think men ever paid attention what a woman was wearing."

He had the decency to look a bit uncomfortable before assuming an expression of total and profound innocence. "They, uh . . . they don't," he told her.

"Yeah," Lucas concurred. "Not unless it's a heart-stopping, libido-grabbing miniskirt that leaves absolutely nothing to the imagination."

"Oh, and by the way, Mack," Adam interjected, "that's a really nice tie you have on tonight."

She shook her head wryly. "Yeah, right. Thanks. I got it at the heart-stopping, libido-grabbing tie store. I thought it might catch your eye."

"It's great," he assured her. Then he turned back to Lucas. "Anyway, Mrs. Harrison Enright was in no way placated."

"I'm not surprised," Lucas said. "Don't you know who Mrs. Harrison Enright is?"

Adam frowned. "No. Should I?"

Lucas expelled a rueful sound. "Man, you call yourself a journalist? You don't know anything that's a current event these days."

Dorsey noticed that Adam spared her a quick—and really, kind of hot—glance before telling Lucas, "Well, I've kinda had my mind on other things this week, okay?"

Boy, did he have his mind on other things, Dorsey thought. Or, at least, on one other thing. Getting her back into his bed. He'd made no secret Sunday night of his intention to do that very thing, and he'd been none too happy about taking her back to her place instead of his own.

And she'd managed to maintain the status quo for the rest of the week, citing work at Drake's or class at Severn to prevent her from seeing Adam socially. They'd been legitimate excuses, all. But now the weekend was upon them, and Dorsey wasn't required to show up at Drake's or Severn for two whole days. More significant than that, though, for the first time in months, Lauren Grable-Monroe didn't have any weekend obligations. She didn't have one single public appearance scheduled.

Oh, she was supposed to have been speaking and sign-

ing books at a large, independent bookstore. But the own-
ers had canceled the signing when a local church group
had threatened to picket the event—with big, hand-
lettered signs labeling the author a fornicator and an adulteress and a Jezebel, who was intent on misleading
today's youth and obliterating family values.

Clearly, Mrs. Harrison Enright wasn't the only one
calling Lauren Grable-Monroe names these days. And
Dorsey was hard pressed to put her finger on when, exactly, or even why things had started to turn so ugly.

"Mrs. Harrison Enright," Lucas continued, catching
Dorsey's attention and bringing it back to the matter at
hand, "is none other than the founder and leader of
WOOF."

"WOOF?" she echoed, even though Lucas had been
speaking to Adam.

He turned to face her now. "It's an acronym for Wives
Opposed to Opportunistic Floozies."

But all Dorsey could manage in response was to repeat, not quite credibly, "WOOF."

"They're actually a pretty well-organized bunch. Mrs.
Enright has been on a couple of local shows, radio and
TV both. At first the group was mostly made up of
women like her—wealthy, idle, husbands who are on the
make, that sort of thing. But she seems to have won herself a pretty substantial following. Certainly she's raised
Lauren-bashing to new heights."

Dorsey gaped at him, unable to believe this bit of
news. But all she could manage by way of a response
was yet another "WOOF."

"And the members of WOOF aren't the only ones
who've had their fill of Lauren Grable-Monroe," Lucas
added. "The guys at *The Harvard Lampoon* have written
a parody of *How to Trap a Tycoon* called *How to Bag a*

Bimbo. So you know the end can't be far for ol' Lauren."

Dorsey closed her eyes and shook her head slowly as she digested all this distasteful information. Certainly there had been people bad-mouthing Lauren since the beginning, but they'd been a minority and had never won any "substantial following."

She'd had no idea there was such a sweeping anti-Lauren campaign developing across the country these days. Granted, she'd been so busy lately that she hadn't had time to be in touch with the media—or with reality, for that matter—but Dorsey still couldn't quite come to terms with the idea that so many people out there hated Lauren so much. Hated *her* so much.

"Oh, and did you read the article in last week's *Rolling Stone*?" Lucas piped up further. " 'Miss Greedyhearts,' it was called. And it was not pretty."

"I cannot believe people don't have better ways to spend their time," Dorsey said. "Whatever happened to having a hobby? Like doing embroidery? Or leather tooling? Or studying alien abduction theory? Those were always good for keeping people off the streets."

"Oh, hey, listen," Lucas said, "you should log onto the Internet some night. Those people are nowhere near as polite as Mrs. Enright and the guys at *The Harvard Lampoon.*"

"I don't want to know," Dorsey said, holding up a hand, palm out, to stop him from telling her.

"It's the typical American paradox," Adam joined in. "This country loves to make heroes out of everyday folk, then once those heroes reach their peak of popularity, this country loves to tear them down again."

"Yeah," Lucas agreed. "And then this country loves to jump up and down on the fallen heroes until they can't get back up again. And then, just for good measure, this country loves to kick them a few more times while they're down." He turned back to Dorsey. "This can't possibly be news to you," he said.

"No," she said with a sigh. "It's not news. But I can't understand why everyone would pick on Lauren Grable-Monroe that way. She's harmless."

"She's famous," Lucas said. "She's gorgeous. She's making a bundle of money. In the eyes of the American public, that makes her fair game."

"I don't think everyone in America feels that way," Dorsey said. "Only a few vocal malcontents, that's all."

Lucas chuckled knowingly, and something about the sound of it sent a shiver straight down her spine. "Yeah, right. Think whatever you want. But speaking for myself, if *I* were Lauren Grable-Monroe, I'd keep a fire extinguisher close at hand. You never can tell about angry, torch-bearing mobs."

Adam stayed at Drake's far later than usual that night, but he just couldn't bring himself to leave. He'd seen so little of Mack lately, and he had wanted her so much. Spending that one night with her had only generated in him a need for more. He hadn't felt satisfied—in any way, even those that went beyond the sexual—since Sunday morning. He'd done everything within his power to lure her to his place, but she'd shot down his every effort. But Adam respected the fact that she was a busy woman. Hey, her dedication to her work and studies was just one of the things he loved about her, after all.

Whoa. Back up. Replay.

One of the things he loved about her ... loved about her ... loved ...

Was that really possible? he wondered now as he nursed a cup of coffee and watched her go about her nightly ritual of closing down the bar. Could he actually be falling in love with Mack?

He hadn't thought he'd loved anyone since his ex-wife, and even she had been remarkably easy to get over. He had often speculated that that was precisely what had been wrong with their marriage—neither he nor his wife had really loved the other. Certainly not the way two people should when they want to be together forever. Neither of them had made any effort to try and work things out. They'd both simply walked away from a decade-long relationship and had never looked back.

For that reason, Adam had surmised that he simply wasn't capable of loving in the truest, deepest, most genuine sense. Not in the way that a person needed to love in order to bind himself to another human being.

But what he felt for Mack was unlike anything he had ever felt for anyone else, so who knew? Maybe he was falling in love with her. *Falling in love . . . love . . .*

Okay, that wasn't so bad. If he *was* falling in love with Mack, so what? That wasn't that scary. Was it? Nor was it necessarily surprising. The two of them had started off as friends—albeit friends who were physically attracted to each other—and then, once they'd both realized and accepted the fact that there was nothing to keep them apart sexually, they'd taken that next logical step to become lovers.

And boy, what lovers they'd become. There had been a dimension and an intensity to their lovemaking the weekend before that Adam had never experienced with another woman. And he could only conclude that it had come about because he and Mack had cemented a relationship as friends and confidantes first. Friendship, after all, was founded on trust. And he'd never had trust with a woman before—not really.

He'd never felt comfortable enough with one to share the kinds of things he'd shared with Mack back when he thought she was married and therefore unattainable. Even when he'd been married, he'd kept a part of himself distant, even separate, from his wife. He just hadn't felt like he could be himself with her completely. He hadn't trusted her the way he trusted Mack.

With Mack, though, from day one, he'd felt totally and utterly at ease. Whether that was because he had thought her married and unattainable or because his first exposure to her had been as a bartender—and therefore as someone with whom a man just naturally shared things—he couldn't rightfully say. But something about Mack had appealed to him—had welcomed him—from the moment they met. Trying to understand that, he supposed, would be pointless.

Reasons weren't important. It didn't matter how his feelings had come about. They were there, and they showed no sign of going away anytime soon. What was important was that he cared for Mack deeply. He couldn't imagine not seeing her on a day-to-day basis. He wanted to bring her more fully into his life. He felt better when he was with her than when he was without her. Simply put, he liked having her around.

He just wished he could get her to come around more often.

"More coffee?" he heard her ask then, rousing him from his ruminations.

He glanced up to find himself gazing into bottomless green eyes that looked very, very tired. In fact, he thought, the rest of her seemed to be pretty worn down, too. She really was stretching herself too thin between Severn and Drake's. And he really did wish he knew why.

"Come home with me tonight," he said softly, impulsively. "Spend the weekend with me."

Her mouth dropped open in surprise at his public invitation. Quickly, discreetly, she glanced first left and then right, to make sure no one had heard what he had said. But the bar was deserted, and Lindy had departed with the register receipts some time ago, so there was no one around who might overhear. Nevertheless, it was with no small amount of caution that Mack turned her attention back to him.

"Adam, I wish I could, but I can't," she said softly.

"Why not?"

She seemed to think hard about that, as if trying to come up with an adequate excuse, one that he might possibly believe. Right. As if. There was absolutely nothing to keep her from accepting his invitation—all right, all right, from obeying his command. Whatever. Nothing except her own fear and uncertainty. Which, he conceded, if they were anything like his own fear and uncertainty, might be formidable foes.

She sighed heavily. "I just can't," she said. "I have a lot of reading to do."

"Bring it with you," he told her.

"I also need to sleep," she added pointedly.

"What?" he asked. "You can't do that in my bed?"

She arched an eyebrow in silent but meaningful comment.

He chuckled low. "Okay, okay. So we haven't done much sleeping in my bed. Look, Mack . . ." He lifted his shoulders and let them drop as he searched for the right words to say. "I just want to be with you," he finally told her. "I haven't seen much of you this week, and I want to spend time with you, doing whatever. I can catch up on some things from the office while you do your read-

ing, and I can sleep when you sleep. We don't have to
. . . you know. I mean, don't get me wrong," he hastened
to clarify. "I'd really like to . . . you know. A lot." He
shrugged again, philosophically this time. "But if you're
tired, then we'll just . . . be together. Alone. It could be
nice."

She eyed him with frank speculation for a moment,
her gaze impassive, her expression inscrutable. Then, finally, slowly, she smiled. "Yeah," she agreed, "it would
be nice. I'll be done here in about fifteen minutes. I'll
meet you downstairs by the elevators. Let's just buzz by
my place first, so I can pack a few things, okay?"

It had been a glorious weekend, Dorsey had to admit a
week following the invitation. Because she and Adam
had done absolutely nothing, had simply basked in each
other's company for two full days and three full nights.
Well, okay, so that wasn't *entirely* true. They had actually *done* a couple of things. She had completed her reading, and he had caught up on some work he brought
home from the *Man's Life* offices. And, surprisingly
enough, they had, in fact, slept. But in between those
times, they'd relaxed. They'd enjoyed themselves.
They'd had fun just being together.

Oh, all right. And they'd made wild monkey love, too.
Every night. And every morning. And once in the afternoon. How could they resist? It had been the triple-fudge
icing on the double-chocolate cake. All in all, the
weekend had been very . . . uh . . . fulfilling. Definitely
time well spent.

Even Monday morning had been surprisingly enjoyable. When Adam's alarm had erupted at five-forty-five,
they'd woken in each other's arms, then smiled and hit
the snooze button to snuggle for ten minutes more—and,

my, but the snuggling one could manage in only ten minutes was quite impressive. When the alarm had sounded again, though, they'd separated and rolled out of bed with identical groans of disappointment, and each had headed for a different bathroom—had they headed for the same one, they never would have made it to work on time. After showering, dressing, and downing a hasty couple of cups of coffee, they'd ridden hand in hand in the elevator to the parking garage in the basement, and, hand in hand, Adam had driven Dorsey to school. It had all been so wonderfully domestic, so utterly couplesome, so totally in keeping with a budding relationship.

Except for Dorsey's deceit and dishonesty when it came to telling Adam the truth about Lauren Grable-Monroe. But, hey, other than that, everything was just peachy.

But she had tried to tell him the truth, really she had. A dozen times she had opened her mouth to say, "Adam, we need to talk" or "Adam, there's something you should know" or "Adam, I've been keeping a secret and it's time you knew the truth."

But each one of those times, she had chickened out, or he had initiated some seductive action that blew her concentration completely. And every time she'd failed to tell him the truth, it had only made it that much harder to try again.

When they parted ways Monday morning, it had only gotten worse. Because the last thing Adam had asked Dorsey to do before kissing her good-bye near her classroom at Severn was to—gulp—meet his mother. Actually, he hadn't quite phrased it that way, but what he'd invited her to do would require meeting both the elder Dariens. They were hosting a holiday open house the following weekend at their Gold Coast estate to herald the arrival of December, and Adam wanted Dorsey to attend it with him.

So now here she stood in the entry hall of his parents' house, a dwelling seemingly larger—and doubtless richer in bounty—than some sovereign nations, immersed in what had formed and molded Adam from day one. As her gaze drifted about the massive, tastefully ornate interior, she could scarcely believe this was the environment in which he had been raised, the environment to which he belonged. The place was like a palace, huge and opulent and classically decorated. The colors were unapologetically bold, the furnishings rich and luxurious and traditional—much like the family, she couldn't help but think. The place just screamed good breeding, good manners, good taste.

According to Adam, five generations of Dariens had lived here, loved here, died here. And Dorsey wouldn't be a bit surprised if many of them still walked these hallowed halls. Because as beautiful and luxurious as the house and its furnishings were, there was a definite creep factor at work, one that made her stomach pitch and roll.

Or maybe that was just a result of her own discomfort, she thought, a result of her own feelings of not belonging here. Wearing her mother's black velvet opera coat, dressed in her mother's strapless, emerald-green cocktail dress, in her mother's pearl choker and her mother's pearl drop earrings, Dorsey felt like . . . She felt like . . . like . . . Well, she felt like her mother.

Oh, fine. As if she wasn't already troubled enough.

Ever since she was old enough to understand what her mother did for a living, Dorsey had struggled to be as different from Carlotta as she could be. It wasn't because she disapproved of her mother or her mother's way of life, that had caused the reaction, however. Although she had never understood Carlotta's choices, Dorsey had never passed judgment on her mother or her mother's lifestyle. It wasn't Dorsey's role to tell people how to live. Carlotta was her own person, responsible for her own actions, responsible for the results of those actions. She had made that clear from day one, and she had raised Dorsey to adopt that same attitude of personal responsibility. As a result, Dorsey had always accepted her mother's lifestyle in the same matter-of-fact way that Carlotta lived it. She didn't understand it. But she accepted it.

And she swore to herself that she would never, ever end up the same way.

From the time that she was a child—and just as Carlotta had taught her to do—Dorsey accepted complete responsibility for herself. And as she'd grown and matured, she had done everything necessary to ensure that she would always be her own person and would never have to rely on someone else to make her way through life. She had worked hard to develop her brain and exploit her intellectual resources. She had played down her physical attributes to discourage unwanted attentions from the opposite sex. She had avoided romantic entanglements that might lead to dependency. She had relied solely on herself in every aspect of her existence. She had created her own happiness, her own prospects, her own opportunities, her own *life*. She'd never needed anyone else.

But even after all this time, after all her efforts, deep down inside, Dorsey couldn't quite erase the fear that someday she would end up just like her mother. And as much as she loved Carlotta, she didn't want to be like her. She didn't want to end up alone and unfulfilled and fearful of what the future might—or might not—bring.

Then again, considering the way she *was* living her life, she might very well end up all of those things. But at least she would be alone, unfulfilled, and fearful on *her* terms. She would be that way because of her *own* actions and not because others had rejected her.

For some reason, though, Dorsey found little consolation in the realization.

As if conjured by her thoughts, Carlotta whizzed into and out of Dorsey's vision then, a brief blur of red in the packed hallway beyond. In the instant that Dorsey saw her, she received an impression of elegance and confidence, of happiness and laughter.

A melancholy smile tugged at her lips. So. She wasn't quite like her mother, after all. Because where Carlotta obviously felt very much at ease in these lush, luxurious surroundings, dressed in the trappings of affluence and grace, Dorsey felt like the worst kind of poser. She had shape-shifted yet again, had metamorphosed into a creature that wasn't quite Dorsey, wasn't quite Lauren, and most certainly wasn't Mack.

Oh, where was a good flannel shirt when you needed one?

"Don't worry. I promise they don't bite."

Adam's reassurance emerged as a soft utterance right by Dorsey's ear, and a shiver of heat danced down her spine at his nearness. As had become his habit, he'd read her thoughts. And, as always, his simple presence made her feel better. Better than better, she decided when she turned to look at him. Because dressed in his faultless black tuxedo and greatcoat, he sent every erogenous nerve she possessed into a tailspin.

"Are you sure?" she asked. She dipped her head toward the gaily dressed crowd milling about the entryway and massive hallway beyond. "I'm not positive, but I think I caught a glimpse of my mother in there."

He smiled as he reached for her coat and withdrew it from her shoulders. "I wouldn't be surprised if she's here," he said. "My parents' open house is always one of the biggest social events of the holiday season. Everybody comes to this thing. But none of them bite," he reiterated with a grin.

She reserved comment on that score as she relinquished her coat and watched Adam shrug out of his. Then he passed them along to a woman who politely curtsied—actually curtsied, Dorsey marveled—first to him and then to her and carried the garments away.

Amazing, she thought. She had never been curtsied to in her entire life. And she wasn't entirely sure how to respond. "Uh . . . thanks," she murmured to the retreating woman, battling the urge to bob up and down herself. To Adam she added, "Do we need to get a number or something for our coats?"

He chuckled. "No. Marissa will remember who gets what. That's her job."

The Dariens had a servant whose job was to remember which coat belonged to whom? she thought. Just where did coat-rememberer belong in the domestic hierarchy? Was it above or below the food taster?

Adam extended a hand forward in a silent indication that Dorsey should precede him. A flutter of nerves mamboed through her midsection again at the prospect of entering such a wild, unknown territory, but she forced herself to put one foot in front of the other until she had successfully entered the fray.

One, two, don't trip on your shoes, she thought with fierce concentration as she moved forward. *Three, four, watch out for that door*, she further mused. *Five, six,*

*you're graceful as bricks. Seven, eight, I just can't relate.
Nine, ten, let's try this again.*

Dorsey inhaled deeply, told herself she *could* do this,
and concentrated harder. Adam seemed to sense her anxiety, because as they wove through the crowd toward the
cavernous ballroom at the end of the wide hall, he
reached over and tucked her arm through his, covered
her cold fingers with his much warmer ones, and gave
them a gentle, reassuring squeeze. Then he steered her
gracefully from one couple or group of people to another
to introduce her.

He used only her name when he did that and never
attached a label. He identified her as neither his bartender
nor his . . . his . . . his hunka hunka burnin' love. Whatever. He only smiled whenever he introduced her as Dorsey MacGuinness, and she only smiled in return at the
warm, buttery feelings that pooled in her belly at hearing
the affectionate way his voice wrapped itself around her
proper name.

And she found herself wishing he would call her Dorsey instead of Mack. Not that there wasn't a fun, endearing quality to the nickname, especially now that the
two of them had become lovers. But she wanted Adam
to see her as something other than Mack. She wanted to
be more to him than a bartender, a pal, a confidante. And
she wanted to be more than a lover, too. She wanted to
be a human being with him. She wanted to be a wearer
of flannel shirts. A student. An academic. A woman. She
wanted to be herself.

Gradually, as the party progressed, she began to grow
more confident, began to feel more at ease. And upon
meeting Adam's parents, she started feeling welcome,
too. They were genuinely nice people, she realized immediately. Incredibly rich, but nice. Adam resembled his

mother physically, resembled his father in everything else. Dorsey felt as comfortable with the elder Dariens as she did with their son, and then it became much too easy to fall into the fantasy of thinking she might actually become a part of this world.

Immediately, she shoved the fantasy away and stood firm in her reality instead. She wasn't a part of this world, not really, in spite of her genetic potential in that regard. Yes, her mother floated with ease through this sort of environment, and yes, her father had been born and raised to it legitimately. Dorsey hadn't been. She wasn't legitimate. In more ways than one. And until she could be honest with Adam about her alternate reality as Lauren Grable-Monroe, this would never, ever be her world.

That fact was hammered home the moment she entered the ballroom and her gaze lit on her father. Just like that, there he was, standing not ten feet away from her, engaged in conversation with another man much like himself—tall, fit, tuxedoed, rich. Dorsey's step faltered when she saw him, and she simply could not look away— She stared at him quite openly. Adam must have noted her preoccupation, because he halted abruptly beside her. He trained his gaze in the same direction, then looked back at her.

"Mack?" he said. "You okay?"

She nodded slowly but said nothing, only continued to gaze at Reginald Dorsey. Her father must have felt her watching him then, because he turned to look at her. When he did, his eyes widened for a moment, his mouth dropped open in clear surprise, and he—almost—made a motion to move toward her. But he stopped himself before completing it, hesitated a moment more, then, with clear reluctance, returned his attention to the man with whom he had been conversing. The entire episode lasted only a few seconds. But Dorsey felt as if she had just lived a hundred years.

When she turned to look at Adam, he was still gazing at her, his expression faintly puzzled. "Do you know Reginald Dorsey?" he asked, clearly surprised. "He's a friend of my father's. A local businessman." He turned to look at the other man, then back at Dorsey. "He's a very—" He stopped right there, glanced back at the other man again—probably, she thought, he was looking at Reginald's auburn hair and unusual green eyes—then turned to gaze at Dorsey again. "Dorsey," he said softly. Only this time, it wasn't with the affectionate inflection the word had carried before. This time, it was with a note of discovery

"Yes?" she replied, her heart humming strangely at hearing him utter it anyway.

"No, I mean . . . Dorsey," he said. "You and he are both named Dorsey."

"Yes," she agreed. "We are."

"He's . . . he's your father."

It was a statement, not a question, because Adam had clearly put the facts together and drawn the right conclusion. Hey, he was a smart guy, after all. He knew what was what. Except, of course, for that pesky Lauren Grable-Monroe business.

"Yes," Dorsey told him. "He's my father. My mother's former lover. My mother's former benefactor," she hastily corrected herself.

Adam continued to gaze at her in silence for a moment more, as if this newfound knowledge was hard for him to digest. Well, what had he expected? Dorsey thought. He knew the circumstances of her birth. Just because he'd figured out the identity of her father, what did that have to do with anything?

"Do you want to go talk to him?" Adam finally asked her, dropping his voice to an even softer timbre.

"No." The word emerged from her mouth swiftly, adamantly, finally.

He eyed her curiously. "Are you sure?"

"Quite sure." Again the assurance came out quick, insistent, vehement.

He studied her in a maddeningly assessing way, then told her, "His wife died last year, you know."

"I know," Dorsey said.

"His children are all grown and on their own now."

"I know that, too."

"If they found out about you, it probably wouldn't—"

"They're not going to find out about me," she interrupted him. "He'd never tell them."

"But if you—"

"I'm not going to tell them, either."

"But—"

"Adam, could we please just go into the party now?"

He hesitated a moment, and she silently urged him not to press the issue. Finally, he relented. "Yeah, okay. Whatever you want to do."

Actually, what Dorsey wanted most to do then was go home. She was about to open her mouth to voice that exact intention when her mother, wrapped in a deep-red velvet number with elegant drapes and discreetly plunging neckline, appeared out of nowhere and brushed a quick kiss over her cheek.

"Dorsey, dear," she greeted her. "You look smashing. I told you the green would be perfect for you."

That, Dorsey thought, was entirely open to debate. True, the little—and she did mean little—green dress hugged her body as if made for it. She still didn't feel like herself at all. Then again, she was beginning to wonder if she even knew who *herself* was these days. Could be the dress she had on was just the thing for her. If only she could identify who *her* really was.

"Thanks, Carlotta," she said halfheartedly. "How . . . interesting . . . to find you here."

Her mother waved a hand negligently before her. "Oh, not really," she said. "Anybody who's anybody comes to the Dariens' annual holiday party. Hello, Adam, how are you?" she quickly added, pushing herself up on tiptoe to brush a swift kiss—the kind of kiss any mother-in-law might bestow upon her son-in-law . . . dammit—over his cheek, as well. "Isn't that true?" she added after completing the gesture. "Everyone comes to your parents' party."

He nodded. "I told Mack that very thing myself when we arrived. Which is why I'm not surprised to find you here at all."

Carlotta smiled. "Darling boy," she murmured. Then, "Be a love and fetch me a champagne cocktail," she told him. "I seem to have misplaced my companion."

Adam dipped his head forward in ready and complete obeisance, something that frankly amazed Dorsey. Men just dropped like flies around Carlotta, she thought. She had no idea how her mother managed to so thoroughly and immediately captivate them the way she did, not even after writing a book on the subject, but even Adam wasn't immune. Carlotta just had *it*. Whatever *it* was. And Dorsey was surprised by the faint thread of envy that wound through her at realizing she'd never master *it* herself.

"One champagne cocktail coming up," he said. "Mack? What can I get for you?"

"Just a glass of wine would be fine," she told him.

He nodded again—with much less obeisance this time—and headed off on his quest.

"Stand up straight, dear," Carlotta whispered to Dorsey the moment he was out of sight. "Men don't like to see a woman slouching."

Dorsey frowned but obediently squared her shoulders. "Yeah, well, at least for once I *am* a woman tonight," she told her mother. "Usually, when I come to something like this, I'm a bartender."

Her mother made a soft tsking sound. "Darling. To a man, you're always a woman. So long as your body has produced estrogen at some point in your life, it doesn't matter if you're dressed as a bartender or a nun or a sheep or a dairy maid or a Marine Corps drill instructor." She paused for a thoughtful moment, then added, "All the better if you're dressed as one of those, actually. You'd be amazed at some of the things I've worn over the years. Why, I remember one time when the president of a local bank asked me to dress up like his fourth-grade teacher, Miss Applebee, and spank his—"

"*Carlotta*," Dorsey interrupted, dropping her voice to a nervous whisper. "This is *not* the kind of conversation you should be having with your daughter. Or any other human being we might claim as a mutual acquaintance," she added further.

Carlotta ran a few fingers over the sparkling gems that encircled her throat. "Actually, darling, I think it would have simplified things enormously if we'd had more conversations like this a long time ago. You have so many strange hang-ups about sex."

"*Carlotta*," Dorsey hissed again. "Keep your voice *down*."

"Well, you do."

"Yeah, well . . . it is . . . you know . . . *sex*," Dorsey

said—very quietly—in her own defense. "It's kind of important, after all. Who doesn't have hang-ups?"

Her mother exhaled that quiet sound of disappointment again. "Sex is *nothing*," she told her daughter. "I can't imagine where you get the idea that it's important."

Dorsey gaped at her. "How can you, of all people, say that? You've made your living with sex."

Her mother eyed her with much disenchantment. "Sex is *not* how I've made my living," she denied coolly.

"Oh, please. Carlotta, I know exactly what goes on in a relationship like that. And you've never bothered to hide it. Don't even try to tell me you didn't have sex with the men who kept you."

"Well, of *course* I had sex with them, darling. Don't be an imbecile."

"Hey!"

"But sex isn't why I stayed with them."

"Well, that goes without saying, doesn't it?" Dorsey remarked.

"And sex wasn't why they stayed with me, either."

Now Dorsey eyed her mother with much confusion. "Then why did they?"

Her mother sighed heavily, shaking her head in maternal disapproval at her daughter. "Oh, Dorsey. You just don't get it, do you?"

"Obviously not."

Suddenly, Carlotta smiled, a wicked, playful, salacious little smile. "Then again, you *have* been getting it more than usual lately, haven't you?" she fairly purred. "And from that nice Adam Darien, too."

"*Carlotta.*"

As always, her mother ignored the admonition. "You'd do well to rein him in, dear," she said instead. "And I can tell you how to do it. I didn't reveal *all* of my secrets in *How to Trap a Tycoon*, you know. I kept the best ones to myself. Not every woman would be able to handle them. I think you would, though. You are, after all, my daughter."

As if Dorsey needed reminding. "Thanks, Carlotta, but I don't think there will be any reining in going on in my relationship with Adam." Mostly, she added to herself, because that relationship was about to go careening off a cliff, and any reining one way or another would be pretty much pointless after that.

Carlotta sighed again. "Oh, well. Easy come, easy go," she philosophized.

"Easy is as easy does," Dorsey countered, unable to help herself.

But instead of being offended, Carlotta only smiled brightly. "*Now* you're getting it. Or, at least, you could be. On a much more regular basis than you are now, at any rate. Have you even *tried* the crème de menthe thing with Adam yet?"

Dorsey squeezed her eyes shut tight. Why, she wondered, did these society parties always seem to go on forever? As usual, it was going to be a long night.

Chapter 13

"You are a total disgrace to your gender, you know that?"

Edie muttered the words with frank disappointment, shook her head dismally at Lucas, and wondered what on earth had possessed her to think she could help him in his quest to trap himself a tycoon.

Oh, sure, he looked gorgeous and yummy and totally edible in the charcoal, pin-striped Brooks Brothers suit she'd forced him to buy when she'd taken him shopping that afternoon. And his new hundred-dollar haircut had evened up his shaggy locks just *soooo* nicely, making his razor-straight hair seem even silkier and shinier and blonder than before. And the sapphire-colored necktie knotted expertly at his throat set off his blue eyes in a way that was rather . . . Edie sighed deeply in spite of herself. Rather breathtaking, actually, if truth be told.

Unfortunately, with his bad attitude, he'd be lucky if he trapped himself a staph infection tonight. And, dammit, she'd gone to a lot of trouble to finagle a couple of invitations to Mrs. Simon Preston's fundraiser for the Chicago arts that was being held at a small Halsted Street art gallery.

Actually, Edie amended hastily, it wasn't so much that she'd gone to a lot of trouble. Mr. Davenport from Drake's had been more than happy to help her out when she'd asked him if he knew anybody who would be attending the well publicized, though very exclusive, event. Arty occasions like this one were notorious for bringing out society's women without their men, and Edie had figured it might be Lucas's best shot to land himself a tycoon.

And Mr. Davenport had been delighted to offer his assistance. He'd grinned with much pleasure, had confessed that he'd also been invited, and had promptly used his cell phone to call Mrs. Preston herself—Aunt Bitsy, to him, Edie had been surprised to hear—and have Edie Mulholland and escort added to the guest list.

Now, of course, Edie felt beholden to the man for performing the favor, and she really didn't like feeling beholden to anyone. Especially a man. Even if Mr. Davenport had made absolutely no mention of collecting on the debt anytime soon. Or ever, for that matter. He'd just been happy he could help out, he assured her. Edie did, after all, need someone to take care of her.

But she was confident that the day would come when Mr. Davenport did indeed ask for repayment in one form or another. She just hoped he didn't make any requests of her that were too sordid or icky. Because she'd left her sordid, icky days long behind her.

And now, after all her efforts, Lucas didn't even appreciate the opportunity Edie had presented to him. All he'd done since their arrival at the gallery was complain.

First about how he felt like a friggin' GQ toy boy in his new friggin' suit. Then about how friggin' much he'd spent for a friggin' haircut. Then about how they weren't even serving friggin' Bud in a friggin' bottle at this friggin' shindig. Then about how the alleged friggin' artwork on the friggin' walls was giving him the friggin' willies.

Except he hadn't used the word "friggin' " per se, and Edie was friggin' tired of hearing him complain.

Honestly, she thought, watching him slug back a mouthful of very expensive champagne as if it were, well, friggin' Bud in a friggin' bottle. If it weren't for the fact that she had Lucas shackled to her side, she'd be enjoying herself very much. The Mershon Gallery, though small, was strikingly if unconventionally decorated. Plum-colored walls were offset by a midnight-blue ceiling liberally dotted with white Christmas lights made to twinkle like stars, and the hardwood floor beneath was painted a lovely shade of . . . well . . . black.

The artwork adorning the walls was likewise dramatic, a mix of watercolor slashes in various jewel tones reminiscent of Mark Rothko and some heavier splashes in primary colors à la Jackson Pollock. The effect, on the whole, was very arresting and in no way traditional. Edie liked the paintings and her surroundings very much.

The crowd enveloping her, on the other hand, was *very* traditional—and not all of them likable, she had to confess—the elite of Chicago society decked out in the finest evening wear that money could buy. Edie tried not to think about how she herself had made do with a consignment shop purchase, a simple black, strapless cocktail dress that she'd accessorized with an inexpensive choker and drop earrings made of jet beads. And she told herself it didn't matter that everyone else glittered with far greater light than she.

"A disgrace to my gender, am I?" Lucas muttered beside her, tugging uncomfortably at his necktie. "Just how do you figure that? No self-respecting member of my gender would submit to attending this kind of event, I guarantee you that." He glanced around surreptitiously. "No self-respecting heterosexual member, anyway."

"Oh, please," she countered. "Attending this kind of event would work wonders for the heterosexual members of your gender. Most of you are hungering for aesthetic nourishment to feed that vast artistic wasteland in your souls."

"Wow," he replied blandly. "You're a real poet, you know that? Maybe you could feed me sometime. 'Cause, sweetheart, I have an appetite that's just—"

"And here I've gone to all this trouble," she interjected quickly, "to help you plant your mercenary hooks in some decent, unsuspecting *rich* woman, and you can't even rise to the occasion."

At her closing comment, he threw her a look that was rife with all manner of bad taste. But he offered no verbal response. Not that any was necessary, Edie realized belatedly. Any simpleton could see exactly what he was thinking. And seeing as how she was presently serving as the mayor of Simpleton, she understood much too well.

"You know what I mean," she said, feeling heat seep into her cheeks. Honestly. With a single look, Lucas Conaway could make her feel hot and cold at the same time. How was that possible? And how could she find such a sensation enjoyable?

"I still can't believe I let you talk me into this," he said distastefully. "The last time I wore a suit was to my uncle Fenwick's funeral. I was twelve, if memory serves."

"Oh, will you stop complaining?" Edie muttered right back. "If you want to trap a tycoon, you have to look like you're already a success yourself. Women don't take to gold diggers the way men do. Men don't care *why* a woman is attracted to them, so long as the woman *is* attracted. Women *care* about the whys."

"Yeah, go figure."

"Women want to be wanted not because they're wealthy," she continued, ignoring him, "but because they're desirable as women. And anyway, how can you say you're using *How to Trap a Tycoon* in your quest? It's in chapter one, for heaven's sake, that Lauren Grable-Monroe discusses the importance of looking good. And you look much more handsome—not to mention successful—in that suit than you do wearing those silly cartoon neckties you usually wear."

He turned to gaze at her with clear surprise. "You don't like my neckties? How can you not like my neckties? I have *excellent* taste in neckties."

Edie rolled her eyes. "Oh, please. You have *no* taste in neckties. You have one with the Scooby Gang on it."

He gaped at her. "Hey, the Scooby Gang is hot right now, I'll have you know. An old Scooby Doo lunch box just like the one I used to carry to school went for more than two hundred bucks on eBay not too long ago."

Strangely, Edie didn't find this information particularly impressive. Go figure. "You carried a Scooby Doo lunch box to school?" she asked, battling a smile, but not very hard.

This time Lucas was the one to blush. "Yeah. Well. It was a hand-me-down from my older sister, okay?" he defended himself. Then he quickly turned the tables. "What kind of lunch box did you carry? I'm guessing Barbie. Pink and purple plastic, am I right?"

"Actually," she said, "I attended a school where the lunch was covered by the tuition, so I never carried a lunch box at all."

"You went to a private school?" Lucas asked, his interest obviously piqued—and quite a bit more than she would have suspected, too.

Damn. She really hadn't meant to give him any details about her past, but the words were out of her mouth before she'd realized she meant to say them. Resigned to the fact that he wouldn't let up until he had the answers he wanted—she'd seen for herself that he could be tenacious when his curiosity was roused—she reluctantly nodded. "Yeah, I went to private school," she told him.

"Catholic school?" he asked. " 'Cause you know, I have a real fondness for those uniforms, with their little plaid skirts and those shirts with the little round collars and those knee socks and—"

She held up a hand to cut him off before he started to drool. "Not Catholic school," she told him. "But we did wear a uniform."

He wiggled his eyebrows playfully. "Plaid?" he asked hopefully.

She shook her head. "Navy blue."

"Little round collars?"

She sighed with much resignation. "Yes."

"Knee socks?"

"Yes."

"I bet you were on the field hockey team, weren't you?"

"Well, if you must know—"

"Oh, I must."

"Yes. I was on the field hockey team. We were undefeated my sophomore year."

He said nothing for a moment, but a look came over

his face that was positively sublime. Finally, "Oh, I would have liked to see that," he said softly. "You running around a field in one of those short skirts, all sweaty and intense. I bet every boy in school was after you."

"There were no boys at my school," she told him. "Just girls."

He squeezed his eyes shut tight in what she could only liken to sheer ecstasy. "Oh, stop," he murmured. "You're killin' me. I'm not gonna get a wink of sleep tonight."

"But then, we were talking about *you*," she said suddenly, turning the tables again. Something about the ecstatic look on Lucas's face wreaked havoc on her system, made her heart trip-hammer erratically behind her ribs, made her entire body hum with something she figured it really shouldn't be humming with. Not in mixed and polite company, at any rate.

Lucas eyed her with much interest for a moment more, then replied, "Yeah, we were talking about how I've always been way ahead of my time when it comes to fashion."

She rolled her eyes again. "Oh, please," she said. "You're a walking, talking Fashion Don't. I can't imagine how you've made it through life this long with your taste. Or lack thereof. Then again," she added, not a little maliciously, "you haven't made it, have you? Not lately, anyway. And certainly not with a tycoon."

He gazed at her mildly. "There's no need to be crass, Edie."

She ignored that comment, too, and continued blithely, "That's why you've had to enlist *my* help tonight."

He smiled lasciviously. "You're going to make it with me? Why, Edie, I wish I'd known. I would have worn clean underwear."

She frowned at him. "That's not what I meant, and you know it."

"What I know is that there's something in your voice when you talk about my making it with a tycoon . . ." He arched his pale-blond eyebrows with much speculation. "Could it be jealousy?" he asked smoothly.

A funny little shimmer of heat went dancing down her spine at the glint of frank appraisal that lit his eyes. "Don't be ridiculous," she told him. But her voice came out sounding thin and uncertain, even to her own ears. "Why on earth would I be jealous of you?"

"Not jealous *of* me," he said. "Jealous *over* me."

"I have no idea what you're talking about."

His smile turned knowing, and that funny little shimmer of heat slipped deeper inside her, simmering in her belly. "Don't you?" he asked. "Your lips say no, but your eyes . . ."

"My eyes say, 'Stuff it,' " she told him. "Why would I ever feel jealous over you?"

"Just a shot in the dark here, Edie, but maybe because . . . you like me?"

His question didn't even bear commenting on, so she turned her back on him and sipped her champagne and pretended to be taken with the painting closest to where they stood, a spatter of purple and gray against a background of dark blue that was actually . . . Wow. Really, really cool. Beautiful, even. Just for the heck of it, she bent forward to check the price of the piece. Oh. Only twenty-two hundred dollars. Well, gee. What a bargain.

"You actually *like* that?" Lucas asked when he noted her interest.

She nodded and continued to gaze at it, not quite able to pull her attention away from it. "Yes, I do. I like it very much. It reminds me of a patch of violets after a summer rain. It's very soothing."

When she finally turned to look at Lucas, he had tilted his head to the side in a way that would have been comical had he not been genuinely trying to figure out the painting. Finally, he straightened again and shook his head. "I don't see it," he said. "It makes me think of a boxer whose face has just been beaten to a pulp."

She expelled a soft sound of derision and turned her attention back to the painting, feeling instantly soothed. "Naturally," she said softly. "Men always see something violent where they could find beauty instead."

This time when Lucas tipped his head sideways to ponder the nature of something, it was Edie whose nature he was pondering. She turned back to find him studying her with much interest, his eyes narrowed, his lower lip caught between his teeth. Strangely, she found herself wanting to nibble that lip herself, and it was with no small shock—and no small fear—that she acknowledged the reaction. Why on earth would she want to nibble anything on Lucas Conaway? As if she could ever get close enough to him without bolting in the first place.

"Why do you naturally assume a man will find something violent?" he asked.

She shrugged. "Because men are violent creatures, that's why."

"Not all men."

"Yes, all men."

He gaped. "Well, that's a sweeping sexist statement if ever there was one."

"It may be sweeping, but it's not sexist," she countered. "It's a statement of fact."

"You think I'm violent?" he asked frankly.

The question surprised her. Edie told herself it

shouldn't. Naturally, being a man and therefore the object of her charge, he would challenge it. But it surprised her even more to find herself wanting to reply to the question in the negative. Lucas, for all his sarcasm and the hint of bitterness that surrounded him, didn't seem inherently violent. Yet he was clearly male. Too male. And therefore, he must, by nature, be violent. Right?

"Yes," she replied, even though she didn't quite believe herself. "I think you have the capacity to be violent."

"That's not what I asked you, Edie."

"Isn't it?"

He shook his head. "Everyone has the capacity to be violent, male or female. What I asked you is if you think I *am* violent."

"Well, not at the moment, no," she hedged.

"Have you ever seen me violent?"

This time she answered quite readily. "No."

"Yet you think me violent, just because I'm a man."

She hesitated, but ultimately replied, "Yes."

His expression remained impassive at her assertion, and Edie suddenly wanted to take back what she'd said, wanted to tell him that no, she was sure he was an exception, that she didn't for a moment think he had the potential to commit a violent act. But she couldn't quite convince herself of that.

She'd known a number of men in the past whom she had been confident would never raise a hand to her, and she'd been left bruised and bloodied as a result. Lucas, for all his polish and control, was essentially no different from any other man. He was as capable of violence—he *was* as violent, she amended reluctantly—as any of them.

"I see," he finally said. But he didn't elaborate. Nor

did he press the subject further. And for that Edie was grateful.

He discarded his empty champagne flute on the tray of a passing waiter, then wrapped his fingers around the knot of his necktie and began to tug it free of his collar.

"Lucas, don't," Edie said, instinctively extending a hand to stop him. She caught herself just before her fingers would have closed over his, genuinely shocked that she had reacted in such a way. She *never* reached out to a man. And she certainly never touched one voluntarily. She couldn't imagine what had come over her to attempt it with Lucas. Hastily, she dropped her hand back to her side. "Don't loosen your tie," she told him. "You need to look perfect if you're going to attract a woman's eye here tonight."

He sighed irritably, but reluctantly fixed his tie. "Edie, we've been here for almost an hour," he pointed out as he completed the gesture, "and I don't think I've seen a woman's eye—or any other body part, for that matter—that I'd like to attract." But he threw her a considering look, as if his statement wasn't quite true and that there was, in fact, one woman whose body parts he would very much like to attract, but she found him violent, so there was little chance of that ever happening now, was there?

"You don't have to like it," she told him, assuring herself she did *not* sound—or feel—breathless. "As you said, it's just for a story. But you know, at the rate you're going with this tycoon trapping business, I think it might be time to break out one of those diaphanous gowns."

"Very funny."

His necktie—and the rest of him—once again looking dapper and sophisticated and dreamy and handsome and gorgeous and luscious and mouth-watering and . . . *Oh, damn*, Edie mused. She'd lost her train of thought.

"Just how did you manage to get us into this thing tonight, anyway?" Lucas asked then, diverting her attention once again.

She shrugged off the question. "A friend did me a favor, that's all."

He eyed her suspiciously. "Which friend?"

"Mr. Davenport from Drake's."

"*What*?"

Now it was Edie's turn to eye him suspiciously. He sounded absolutely furious about her admission. "Is there a problem with that?" she asked.

He gaped at her for a moment before hissing, "You're damned right there's a problem with that."

She gaped back at him. "Well, I'd like to know what it is."

He frowned. "The problem is that I don't trust that guy around you, and now you're telling me he did you a favor, something that puts you in a position of . . . of . . ."

"Of what?" she demanded.

"Of having to . . . you know . . ."

"No, what?"

He gritted his teeth at her. Hard. "Of having to . . . reciprocate. To return the favor. To do something . . . nice . . . for him. If you catch my drift."

"No, I don't catch your drift, Mr. Suspicious Mind," Edie snapped. "Mr. Davenport is a nice man. He was happy to get the invitations for me."

"Oh, yeah, I'll just bet he was."

She expelled a soft sound of surprise when she finally understood what Lucas was implying. And she forgot all about the fact that what he was implying was exactly what she had been thinking herself where repayment of Mr. Davenport's favor was concerned. "You make it sound like what he's going to want from me in return is something . . ."

"Something . . . ?" Lucas prodded.

"Something . . . sordid . . . or . . ."

"Or . . . ?"

"Or . . . icky," she finished lamely. "Like he's going to ask me to do something I don't want to do."

Lucas nodded vigorously. "Yeah. Except he probably won't ask. He'll probably insist."

She shook her head slowly in disbelief at what she heard in his voice. "Now who sounds jealous?" she asked softly.

He laughed darkly. "I'm not speaking out of jealousy," he assured her. "I'm speaking out of fear for your safety."

"Number one," she said coolly, "I can take care of myself, all right?"

"Yeah, right."

"And number two," she pushed on relentlessly, "boy, you don't trust anybody, do you?"

His reply was quick and to the point. "No."

"Not even me?"

He inhaled deeply and released the breath in a slow, thoughtful sigh. "Not since you made me dress up like a corpse and spend more for a haircut than I'd normally spend to get my tires rotated, no."

"It's for your own good, Lucas. You'll see."

In fact, Edie was already beginning to see. A woman standing just behind and to the right of Lucas was inspecting his . . . oh, dear, Edie thought . . . his, uh, his backside with much interest. The woman looked to be in her mid-forties, had an incredible figure and perfectly coifed red hair, was wearing the most amazing sea-green dress cut down to *there*, and was obviously looking to make Lucas's acquaintance—if not his night—very soon.

"Tycoon at ten o'clock," Edie whispered, bending her head toward his.

Lucas's eyebrows shot up in surprise. "What?"

Edie bent in a little further. "There's a woman back there who's been giving you the once-over for the last couple of minutes. And she has some decent body parts you might want to attract. I think she saw us arguing, and she figures you're fair game. I'm going to pop off to the ladies' room," she added when she saw Lucas begin to object. "And when I get back, I hope to find you springing your tycoon trap. Do not disappoint me, Grasshopper. Oh, and no offense, but . . ."

She stepped backward and feigned total and severe outrage, then lifted her hand and slapped him hard across the cheek. "How *dare* you!" she cried. "Lucas Conaway, I *never* want to speak to you again for the rest of my life!"

Without awaiting a reply, and trying not to laugh at his utterly shocked and offended expression, Edie spun on her heel and left him to spring his tycoon trap on his unsuspecting prey. Strange, though, how the look on his face had made him seem so much more the hunted than the hunter. She bit back a smile and hurried along, wanting to get back in time to see the end of the show. It ought to be good. She did so enjoy romantic comedy.

Lucas lifted a hand to his burning cheek and gaped at the hastily departing and extremely attractive back of Edie Mulholland, too stunned to do anything other than . . . well . . . ogle her. She was, after all, more than a little oglable this evening, in her little—very little—black dress and smoky—very smoky—black stockings and high—very high—heels. And that black beaded choker around her neck was simply too arousing for words, because all Lucas could do was imagine what she'd look like wearing nothing but that choker. Boy, could he imagine. And had been for most of the evening. But once he got past all that and recalled what Edie had just done to him, he could not *believe* what Edie had just done to him.

She'd just touched him. Voluntarily. And she hadn't flinched from him when she'd done it.

Okay, so the touch in question had been a slap to his face. That was just a minor technicality. She *had* touched him. In a manner of speaking. It *was* progress. In a way. He just wished he could figure out exactly which way.

"Well, my goodness, but that was dramatic."

Lucas spun around at the sound of the velvety smooth comment to find a truly spectacular—and very oglable—redhead ogling him as shamelessly as he had just been ogling Edie. *Wow.* She was incredible-looking. Tall and slim and—*whoa, momma*—stacked.

How had she escaped his attention until now? he wondered. And how was it possible that his capricious attention wanted nothing to do with her? Because that was exactly what was happening. As appealing as the woman was, Lucas was far too preoccupied with thoughts of Edie to care one way or another about the redhead.

In spite of his appalling lack of interest in the woman, he smiled at her. At least, he thought he was smiling at her. He couldn't be sure, seeing as how half of his face was still numb from the flat of Edie's hand. "Yes. Well. Um," he began eloquently. "I suppose to the casual observer, that might have looked a bit dramatic, yes."

She smiled back and sauntered closer. "Oh, I assure you, my observation was anything but casual."

Lucas took a step backward as he replied, "Ah. I, uh, I see."

Clearly undaunted by something so minor as his obvious retreat, the woman continued with her forward progress and sidled closer still. "And in my not so casual observation," she murmured as she drew nearer, "I've deduced that you're a man who could use a friend—or something—about now."

Lucas took a few more steps backward. "Uh . . . yeah. Yeah, I could definitely use . . . something," he said cautiously. Then, because he knew he was behaving abominably—no self-respecting man would run away from a woman like this . . . unless, of course, he'd just been slapped senseless by Edie Mulholland, which, now that he thought about it, surely explained his utter lack of interest in this woman—he forced his feet to halt their rapid retreat. And he wondered how long it had been since Edie's departure and if she would be back anytime soon and if there would be any of him left unconsumed by this vibrant piranha once she did return.

The redhead stopped, but only when a scant breath of air separated her from Lucas. Then even that scant breath was gone, because he sucked it in quickly and nearly passed out on the overwhelming aroma of Chanel Number Something Really Annoying that accompanied it.

The woman seemed not to notice, though, because she tilted her head in the general direction in which Edie had just departed and said softly, "She seems to be pretty upset."

Lucas nodded. "Yes, she does."

"Looks like you might have your work cut out for you tonight winning her back."

"It does look that way, doesn't it?"

The redhead considered him thoughtfully. "Then again," she purred. Actually purred, Lucas noted. How incredibly off-putting. "You don't seem like the kind of man who needs to keep a woman like that," she finished.

Uh-oh. "No?" he asked.

She shook her head slowly and lifted a hand to smooth out what he was sure was a nonexistent crease in his lapel. "No," she said softly, flattening her hand over his chest. "You look more like the kind of man who needs keeping himself."

Oh, man. "Do I?"

This time she nodded. "Young women are just so excitable, aren't they?"

Lucas swallowed hard. "Uh, yeah. Yeah, I . . . I guesso. Edie can be a little vixen sometimes. A little minx, a little spitfire, a little tigress, a little . . . little . . . Where was I? Oh, yeah. A little firebrand."

The redhead seemed in no way impressed by this revelation. "Yes, she's certainly something," she said blandly. "But it seems to me that what you need is a woman who has a little more patience. A woman who takes her time. A woman who has more experience in . . . handling . . . a man like you."

Yikes. "You, uh, you really think so?"

"Oh, yes," she cooed. Actually cooed, he thought. How incredibly irritating. "Why don't you and I go somewhere that's a little more . . . private?" she added smoothly.

Good God. "Private?" he echoed.

"Private," she reiterated. "I have my car tonight—but not my husband," she told him shamelessly. "We could have a lot of fun together, you and I. And not just tonight, either." She smiled with much satisfaction before concluding, "And it goes without saying that it would be my treat. All of it," she further assured him, "would be my . . . treat."

Unbelievable, Lucas thought. Everything he'd been looking for in a tycoon for weeks, everything he needed for his article, everything, in fact, that he could possibly have ever fantasized about in his entire life . . . It had all just walked right up and introduced itself. All he had to do was open his mouth and agree to this woman's proposition, and he would have both his story for the magazine and one helluva good time. And it even went without saying that it would be her treat.

So he opened his mouth to agree to the woman's proposition. Unfortunately, what came out was, "Thanks, but if you'll excuse me, I really need to go find my date."

And then, as gracefully as he could—which wound up being not very graceful at all—he disengaged himself from the woman's enthusiastic clutches, offered her a smile of—almost genuine—regret, and ran like hell in the opposite direction.

Tycoon schmycoon. What Lucas really wanted more than anything else in the world was Mulholland of Sunnybrook Farm.

"You blew it. You totally and completely *blew* it. I can't believe how badly you blew it. Excuse me a moment while I crown you King Blowing It the First. It just boggles the mind how you blew it."

Lucas waited patiently for Edie to finish berating him—again—and tried to focus on navigating the road ahead of him instead. Ever since leaving the gallery, she had taken enormous pleasure in telling him over and over and over again how close he'd come to bagging his quarry only to fail miserably by letting his tycoon get away. In fact, Edie seemed to take a little too much pleasure in telling him that. Here she'd gone to all this trouble to help him trap a tycoon, and when he'd finally had one in his grasp—or, at the very least, had found himself in *her* grasp—he had let the woman get away, and Edie actually sounded happy about it.

What an interesting development.

"The world isn't a big enough place to hold how badly you blew it," she continued relentlessly. "That big sucking sound you hear? That's you blowing it. I mean, Lucas . . ." She sighed heavily. "You blew it."

"So you've said. Sixty-four times now."

"But you *blew* it."

"Sixty-five."

He braved a glance in her direction to find that she had braced her elbow against the passenger side window and was clutching a fistful of blond curls over her forehead. She looked beat. She looked frustrated. She looked confused. What she didn't look was happy.

"I'm sorry," he said, turning his attention back to the highway. "I know you went to a lot of trouble, and I apologize for not taking advantage of you."

He felt, more than saw, her go rigid.

"It," he hastily corrected himself. "I apologize for not taking advantage of it. You, I would never apologize for taking advantage of. Mainly because I think you'd have as much fun as I would."

"Oh, right. In your dreams."

"Oh, believe me, Edie, we have definitely been enjoying ourselves in my dreams. You can't imagine."

She said nothing in response to that, and Lucas didn't push. He was still thinking about how she had touched him—okay, slapped him . . . details, details, sheesh—earlier in the evening, and he was still wondering how to go about broaching that particular subject with her. Because he did indeed intend to broach that particular subject with her. And he would do it before this night was through. He just hadn't quite decided yet how he was going to tiptoe delicately around it.

"So, Edie, about that little slap you gave me earlier this evening," he began. Okay, so forget the tiptoeing. Steamrollering had always worked much better for him, anyway. "Did you enjoy that as much as I did?"

He glanced over at her again, and this time he found her smiling. Still looking beat, frustrated, and confused, but smiling. It wasn't a big smile, but it wasn't bad. It was something they could work on.

"I enjoyed it more than you could possibly know," she told him.

He smiled back. "I thought so."

"But probably not in the same way you did," she qualified.

"Oh, I don't know about that," he told her. "How does the saying go? A little S and M now and then is relished by the wisest men."

She hesitated only slightly before revealing, "I've never heard that saying."

He feigned surprise. "No? Well, *I* sure have."

"And it wasn't S and M," she corrected him.

"Wasn't it?"

"No, it was F and R."

"F and R?"

"Fun and rewarding."

He threw her a lascivious grin. "So then we did enjoy it in the same way."

She expelled a few halfhearted chuckles. "You are the strangest man," she said.

Her comment stung just enough that Lucas couldn't quite stop himself from remarking, "Oh, and that's something coming from a woman who can slap a man without compunction but can't tolerate having his hand curled innocently over hers."

Once again, he felt Edie stiffen in the seat beside him. "That's none of your business, Lucas."

"Maybe not," he retorted. "But it sure as hell makes it difficult to get to know you better."

"Then don't try to get to know me better."

He kept his gaze trained on the road ahead as he said, "See, now that's going to be something of a problem."

"Why?"

"Because, Edie, I'd really like to get to know you better."

She said nothing in response to his assertion, and from the corner of his eye, Lucas saw her turn her head to look out the window at the quickly passing night beyond. "You'll get over it," she said softly.

"Maybe," he conceded. "But maybe I don't want to get over it."

"You'll get over it," she repeated, more softly than before.

He wanted to tell her that was unlikely, seeing as how he had no intention of even trying to get over her. But the words never formed in his mouth—or his brain, for that matter—which was actually just as well, because they'd arrived at her apartment building. Which was actually not so well, after all, because before the car had even come to a complete halt, Edie was scrambling out of it to rush up the walkway toward the big, rectangular, utterly nondescript brick building.

"Edie, wait!" Lucas called after her.

But the exclamation got lost under the sound of a slammed passenger side door.

"Dammit," he muttered as he reached for his own door. He didn't catch up with her until he hit the second floor of the building and saw her jamming her key into her front lock. Quickly, Lucas strode forward and, without thinking, moved behind her and thrust his hand against the door. It landed spread open wide with a loud thump, and although his body never made contact with hers, at his abrupt appearance, Edie leaped backward. The front door halted her, but that didn't prevent her from crowding herself back against it. And it didn't stop her from looking terrified.

It didn't stop her from *being* terrified.

Because, clearly, she was terrified, Lucas noted. Her lips were parted fractionally, her chest was rising and falling with her rapid respiration, and her eyes were wide with apprehension.

"Don't hurt me," she said softly. "Please."

Lucas's own heart began to pound fiercely then at the evidence of what lay before him. Evidence of what he had suspected since that night he'd had too much to drink at Drake's. Somebody—who knew who, who knew why, who knew how long ago—had obviously mistreated Edie Mulholland and mistreated her badly. It didn't bear thinking about, but he knew that, at some point, he'd have to think about it. At the moment, however, he could only try and see clear of the red haze of rage that clouded his vision and do his best to calm her down.

"Edie, I would never hurt you," he said softly. More than anything in the world, he wanted to reach out and pull her into his arms, but he knew that was the last thing she would tolerate. "You have to know that. I would never—I *could* never—hurt you."

"Just let me go inside," she said. "And then go away. Please, Lucas. Just leave me alone."

As much as he hated to retreat from her when she was like this, he knew she was too frightened for him to try reasoning with her. So he took a giant step back and held both hands up before him, palms out, in a gesture of surrender, of supplication. For a moment, she didn't move at all, only eyed him warily, as if she couldn't believe he'd done what she told him to do, as if she still expected him to pounce. Then, very slowly, she turned to the door again and twisted her key in the lock.

"Edie, let's talk about this," he said as she began to push the door open. "Let's not let the night end this way."

She said nothing as she ducked inside her apartment, but she didn't immediately slam the door and lock it, as Lucas would have guessed she would. Instead, she hesitated, standing framed by the doorway and half hidden by the door she had tucked herself behind. Her breathing was much less rapid now, and her eyes were no longer darkened with fear. But her cheeks were stained with red, and the hand clutching the door was white-knuckled and trembling. She was still frightened, he thought. Maybe not of him, but of something that prevented her from seeing him the way he really was.

"Edie," he said again, curling his fingers into impotent fists at his sides.

She noted the gesture and arrowed her brows downward. Belatedly, Lucas realized how she must have misconstrued his actions. Immediately, he opened his hands again, but it was too late.

"Edie, please," he tried one last time. "Talk to me."

"Just go away, Lucas," she said, her voice thin and cold and much too empty. "Just leave me alone."

There was no rancor, no venom in her command. Just a simple request and a kind of sad resolution. Had Lucas suspected for a moment that he possessed a heart, Edie would have broken it right there. Good thing for him he was such a heartless sonofabitch. The realization, however, brought with it little comfort.

"Edie . . ."

"Good night, Lucas," she said as she pushed the front door closed. "And good-bye."

He said nothing more, knowing it would be fruitless at this point. In spite of her wishes, though, he knew it wasn't going to be a good night. And, as her front door clicked softly shut, he knew it wasn't going to be good-bye, either. Not yet. Not by a long shot.

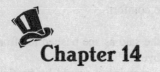

Chapter 14

When Dorsey arrived at work late Monday afternoon, she sensed immediately that there was something very, very wrong. And not just because she'd managed to arrive early for a change, either. But as she changed into her bartender uniform and donned her wedding ring, as she stowed her backpack and teaching assistant clothes in her locker, she just sensed somehow that there was something . . . not right.

In spite of her misgivings, however, she completed her preparations and headed out to the bar and as always, saw all of Drake's regulars lined up in their usual spots. Likewise as always, Adam was already there waiting—watching—for her, with that secretive little smile playing about his lips that Dorsey had come to know and love so well. And as always, Edie stood chatting with Straight-Shot-of-Stoli. But not as always, the other bartender was looking rather morose.

"Hi," Dorsey greeted her as she slipped behind the bar. "You look kinda down. What's up?"

Edie shrugged without much concern and reached behind herself to tug at the strings on her apron. "I'm just not feeling all that great today, that's all."

Which was also totally out of character for Edie, because in all the time she'd worked at Drake's, Dorsey had never known the other bartender to be under the weather at all. Edie's sunny disposition and her a-smile-a-day outlook had always kept even the nastiest germs at bay. Certainly she'd never looked as beaten down as she did now. Her bright blue eyes had dimmed some and were smudged beneath with faint purple crescents. Her mouth was flattened into a tight, joyless line, and her skin seemed paler even than it had before. Her whole body, in fact, seemed more fragile, more limp. Worse than that, though, her spirit seemed almost empty.

Unsure why she did it, Dorsey turned to look at Straight-Shot—not in accusation, but to silently ask for his input on this odd matter of Edie's sudden sobriety. But all Straight-Shot did was shake his head slowly and turn his hands palm up in unspoken confusion.

So she turned back to Edie and asked softly, "Are you okay?"

Edie nodded in a very unconvincing way. "I'm fine," she said, likewise without conviction. Then she sighed with what sounded suspiciously like remorse. "It's just a visit from the seven PMS dwarfs, that's all," she added listlessly. "I'll be okay in a few days."

In spite of the other woman's clear dejection, Dorsey couldn't help but smile at that. "I probably shouldn't ask, but . . . the seven PMS dwarfs?"

Edie did, finally, offer up a small grin in response.

"Yeah," she said. "The seven PMS dwarfs. You know Grumpy, Crampy, Moody, Bitchy, Hungry, Angry, and Doc. What? They never visit you from time to time?"

"Oh, yeah," Dorsey assured her with a chuckle, feeling a little better in light of Edie's—granted halfhearted—whimsy. "And not just when I'm PMS, either. But, gee, I've never seen the little buggers get *you* down like this before," she further observed.

Edie shrugged again, still fumbling with the ties on her apron, which had clearly tangled themselves into a knot. "It's just . . ." She sighed again. "I had to tell someone to leave me alone last weekend, that's all.

Dorsey nodded her understanding. "And he won't leave you alone, huh?"

"No, he *has* left me alone," Edie said unhappily as she fought more fiercely with the apron ties that wouldn't come free. "I haven't seen or heard from him all week."

"And that's a problem?" Dorsey asked, unable to mask her surprise. "I mean, I kind of thought you didn't like to be bothered by testosterone-driven individuals."

"I *don't* like being bothered by them," Edie agreed, increasing her efforts with the relentless apron ties. "I thought it would be *good* that this guy left me alone. But now it turns out that it's not so good. Now it turns out that it's pretty lousy. And I can't understand why it bothers me so much that he's left me alone. I can't understand *why* he's left me alone. I can't understand *any* of it."

With a snarl of frustration, Edie jerked on the uncooperative apron ties with such force that she completely ripped one from its mooring. And with a growl of discontent, she snatched the apron from over her head, wadded it up ruthlessly in both fists, and stuffed it maliciously into the linen bin. Then, when she realized how thoroughly she had lost control, she punctuated the episode with a viciously muttered, "Oh, hell."

Dorsey's eyebrows shot right up to her hairline. She'd never, ever heard Edie Mulholland swear. Not even the harmless ol' H-E-double-hockey-sticks. "Uh . . . why don't you go home and try to get some sleep?" she told the other bartender. "You look like you could use it."

Still staring into the linen bin she had just assaulted, Edie expelled a sound that was at once wistful and hopeless. "Sleep," she echoed. "Yeah, right. What a concept."

Without much enthusiasm, she gathered together her things and slung her backpack over her shoulder. And then, without so much as a see-ya-later, she ducked under the bar and strode away without a second glance.

"That girl needs someone to take care of her," Straight-Shot said, as he always did the moment Edie was out of sight.

But this time, his words carried more concern than they normally did. And this time, Dorsey realized she was in total and unequivocal agreement.

When she turned back around, her concern for Edie was immediately replaced by concern for herself. Because Adam was gazing at her quite openly, hiding none of what he clearly felt for her. And all Dorsey could do was hope that nobody else in the bar could see what she saw so plainly etched on his face—desire, need, affection, perhaps even . . .

Well. At any rate, it was all written there, for all the world to see, and Adam clearly didn't care who saw it.

"Hi," he said as she approached him. Some of her anxiety must have shown on her face, because he added softly, "Rough day?"

"Not really," she said.

Not unless she included the discussion in her eight o'clock Soc. 101 class, anyway. The one where each and every one of Lauren Grable-Monroe's earlier proponents—led by none other than Ms. Tiffany Jennings herself—had proclaimed the author to be a writer of sensationalistic claptrap that pandered to the masses. And an opportunistic floozy. And an adulteress. And a Jezebel.

And then they'd gotten ugly.

On one level, her students' impassioned proclamations had actually restored some of Dorsey's faith that they wouldn't be easily misled by media hype—well, not after a couple of months of behaving like lemmings, at any rate. On another level, their vocal pronouncements concerned her that they *would* be easily misled by angry, torch-bearing mobs. On yet another level, they had offended her intensely as the author of the book they were maligning. And on another level still, she realized they were only echoing some of the very things she had said herself that day in class.

And on a last, very high altitude level, they made her head spin and her stomach hurt. Real bad.

The tide—among other things—had definitely turned against Lauren Grable-Monroe. In her panic, Dorsey had tried to call her editor that afternoon, but Anita had already left for the day. Tomorrow morning, however, first thing, Dorsey intended to pin Anita down, to chat about this matter of turning tides, and to discuss the possibility of having Lauren Grable-Monroe go gracefully into that good night, to get herself to a nunnery, to crawl back beneath the rock whence she had come. Soon.

It was the only feasible thing to do now. Clearly, *How to Trap a Tycoon* had run its course. It was time for the next icon of contemporary American culture to step up to the—admittedly unstable—pedestal. Lauren Grable-Monroe, Dorsey was certain, would be more than happy to surrender her spot. The sooner, the better.

"So then, it was a good day?" Adam asked, bringing her thoughts back to the present—and none too soon.

"Yeah, I guesso," she said. "Good enough, anyway."

"I've had a good day, too," he told her with a smile. Then, dropping his voice a little, he added, "Because I spent most of it thinking about you."

A wisp of something warm and wonderful wrapped itself around her heart and squeezed hard. He was just so . . . so cute, she thought. During all the weeks since Dorsey had met him, Adam had seemed like both the irresistible force *and* the immovable object. He had come across as such an indomitable creature, such a rock-solid wall of conviction.

But tonight he was just . . . cute. Really, really cute. And something inside her turned all warm and fuzzy at the realization that she was at least partly responsible for his transformation.

"What a coincidence," she told him, leaning forward over the bar to draw as close to him as she dared. "I just so happened to spend a good part of my day thinking about you, too."

Her smile, she was sure, was identical to his, because she was experiencing her own share of desire, need, affection, perhaps even . . . Well. At any rate, she didn't doubt that her own feelings were all written on her face for all the world to see, and oddly enough, like Adam, she didn't care who saw them.

His smile turned decidedly lascivious, though, upon hearing her admission. "I can't stop thinking about the last couple of weekends we've spent together," he told her.

"Me neither."

"I think we should spend this weekend together, too."

"Do you?"

He nodded. "What say we get together after your shift and—"

"Dorsey."

Her head snapped around at the summons from Lindy Aubrey, coming as it did from immediately behind her. *Oh, God*, she thought. What if Lindy had just overheard what she and Adam had been—

"Come into my office. Now. You, too, Adam," her employer added. "You might be interested in what I have to say, as well."

Oh, yeah, Dorsey thought. Lindy had *definitely* overheard.

Adam threw Lindy a look that was filled with surprise, curiosity, and not a little resentment. "Hang on a minute, Lindy," he said. "There's no need to—"

"There's every need," Lindy countered. "Your presence in my office isn't absolutely necessary for this," she said. "But you will most definitely find what I have to say interesting."

And then she spun around and walked to her office without a glance backward, fully confident that Dorsey and Adam both would follow her—or else. As, naturally, they would.

"Well," Dorsey said uncomfortably. "That was rather ominous." She inhaled a deep breath and released it slowly, preparing herself for what was sure to come. "I suppose she overheard us talking, and now I'm history here at Drake's."

"Don't borrow trouble, Mack," Adam cautioned. "I don't see how she could have overheard what we said. She came out of nowhere. I mean, granted, I was looking at you, not behind you, but she was definitely sneaking around."

"Which means she *did* overhear," Dorsey concluded.

"Mack," Adam said softly, "if she did . . . Look, I'm sorry if I screwed things up for you here. Whatever happens, I'll help you out however I can."

He reached across the bar to cover her hand with his. Her first instinct was to pull away, but there was little point in objecting to his gesture now. They were made. Lindy was going to tell her to clean out her locker, and that would be the end of that.

It was just as well, Dorsey thought. Not because she had enough research to complete her dissertation reasonably well—which she did—but because she was tired of pretending to be something she wasn't. She was tired of all the deceptions, all the dishonesty, all the lies. She was as tired of being Mack the bartender as she was of being Lauren Grable-Monroe. After she left Drake's this evening she would tell Adam the truth about all of it. About how she'd come to work here in the first place to research her dissertation and about being Lauren Grable-Monroe, too.

Somehow, she would make him understand why she had felt obligated to keep him in the dark about everything. Somehow, she would explain her own fear of exposure and censure and rejection. Somehow, she would make amends for all the deception. And somehow, they would weather whatever repercussions ensued. They would have to.

They would just have to.

"If you want to wait out here," she told Adam, "I'll certainly understand. Lindy's a pretty intimidating person to face. And this really is my responsibility."

"The hell it is," he countered. "We're in this together. We're equally responsible. Whatever happens, Mack, I'm right there with you. And I *will* help you out, however you need it," he added, obviously telling her he'd make up whatever lost wages she might suffer.

She smiled at him, grateful for the rapidity and confidence with which he'd offered his support. She didn't kid herself that she'd have her work cut out for her explaining things to Adam. But she was confident that once the two of them had a chance to talk things out, she'd be able to make him understand. As for her dissertation, she had enough research to complete it, and once it was defended, she was reasonably certain that the sociology department of Severn would find a place for her as a full-time instructor.

It was all going to work out, she told herself as she ducked beneath the bar and joined Adam on the long, long journey to Lindy's office. All of it was going to work out. For the first time in months, Dorsey felt hopeful. She felt peaceful. She felt good.

Until she strode into Lindy's office with Adam right on her heels. Because as he closed the door behind them, Dorsey realized what had felt so wrong earlier, when she'd been in the locker room, changing her clothes. Only now did she recall that her notebooks—the ones containing all of her research on Drake's—had been missing from the top shelf of her locker. She knew that without going back to check.

Because all of them were currently sitting atop her employer's desk.

"I want you to clean out your locker and leave the premises immediately," Lindy stated without preamble. She stood behind her power desk wearing one of her power suits—charcoal with pinstripes this time—her hands fisted firmly on her hips. Normally, it was impossible to tell what Lindy Aubrey was thinking about, because she always kept her features carefully schooled in a bland expression. Tonight, however, her expression held nothing back. Tonight she was livid. Absolutely, utterly, completely livid. Tonight she looked capable of murdering someone.

No, not someone. Just Dorsey MacGuinness.

"I've taken the liberty of beginning the cleaning-out process for you myself," she continued, nodding at the notebooks, obviously straining to keep a civil tongue.

"So I see," Dorsey replied quietly.

"However," Lindy added, jabbing a finger now at the half-dozen notebooks on her desk, "don't expect to be getting these back anytime soon. In fact, don't expect to get them back at all."

Dorsey's lack of calmness quickly shifted to apprehension. "Why not?" she demanded, her own voice nowhere near as controlled as her employer's, regardless of how forced Lindy's control was. "They belong to me. You can't keep them."

"They don't belong to you anymore," Lindy assured her. "Now they're evidence."

Dorsey gaped at her, her apprehension turning quickly to full-blown panic. "Evidence? Of what? I haven't committed any crime."

Lindy thrust both hands in front of herself and enumerated the charges on her fingers. "You've come to work for me under false pretenses. You've lied to me. You've been compiling notes of a dubious nature. You've compromised the entire membership and staff of Drake's."

"Those aren't crimes," Dorsey said instead of denying any of the charges. At the moment, she wasn't entirely sure she *could* deny them.

Lindy glared at her. "We'll let the police decide that when they get here. I just called them."

Oh, jeez . . .

Time to start denying the charges, she told herself. Even if she *was* feeling pretty criminal at the moment. "Okay, I admit that I have been working here under false pretenses and that I've been compiling notes," she began. "And I may not have been totally honest with you, Lindy, but I never lied to you. And I have absolutely no intention of compromising Drake's in any way, shape or form. Those notes are for my doctoral dissertation, that's all. Everyone's identity will be protected, including Drake's. I'd never do anything as malicious as you suggest."

Lindy smiled then, but the gesture was in no way happy. She looked more like a cold-blooded reptile that was about to consume one of its own. "Funny," she said, "but I find that hard to believe, seeing as how authors of sensationalistic, potboiling best-sellers tend to want to follow up with yet another sensationalistic, potboiling best-seller."

Wow. Had Dorsey been thinking that she was panicked a few moments ago? She'd had no idea what panic was then. Because at hearing Lindy's latest charge, what Dorsey had thought was panic surged right into utter and complete terror.

"I . . . I don't know what you're talking about," she lied.

"Oh, don't you?" Lindy asked.

Even though she knew it was probably pointless to deny it any longer, even though she'd just promised herself she was going to come clean and tell the truth, even though she'd just felt liberated by that decision to be honest, Dorsey shook her head. But she couldn't quite give voice to her denial, couldn't quite make herself speak the words that would only wind up being yet another lie.

"Lindy, what the hell is going on?"

Dorsey had all but forgotten Adam's presence until she heard his impatiently uttered demand. And what had started off as concern, then apprehension, then panic, then terror, segued now into stark, stampeding horror. Because Dorsey realized then that nothing was going to work out. Nothing would be all right. She would never be able to make Adam understand. The way Lindy was about to interpret things, there was no way Dorsey would be able to make an adequate explanation of her actions. Once Lindy planted the seed in his brain that Dorsey was going to write a tell-all book about her experiences at Drake's, then Adam would be fully capable of nurturing that idea into fruition all by himself. He would be fully capable of believing that Dorsey was nothing but, well, an opportunistic floozy who cared only for her own success.

Impulsively, she tried to intercept her employer, spinning around to meet Adam's gaze beseechingly. "Adam, we have to talk," she told him.

"Too late," Lindy said from behind her.

"It's not what she thinks."

"Nice try, Dorsey."

"Let me explain."

"No, let *me* explain."

"Somebody had better explain something," Adam ground out roughly, his gaze ricocheting from one woman to the other. "Because I'm completely lost here."

"Adam—" Dorsey began.

But Lindy cut her off with a more loudly offered, "Do you know you've been sleeping with the enemy, Adam?"

And naturally, that announcement would be what caught his attention. Because instead of looking at Dorsey, he shifted his gaze quickly to Lindy. "What are you talking about?" he demanded.

Lindy smiled, a brittle, bitter little smile. Never one to mince words, she said, "We have a celebrity in our midst, Adam. Because Dorsey MacGuinness is none other than Lauren Grable-Monroe."

He expelled a single humorless chuckle. He gazed first at Lindy, then at Dorsey, then back at Lindy again. "You're out of your mind, Lindy," he said softly.

Lindy shook her head slowly, almost sadly. "Although there may have been a time in my life when that was true," she said, "I assure you that these days I never make mistakes. Would that the rest of the world followed my example. We wouldn't get into binds like this one."

"Lindy," Dorsey tried again.

But her employer ignored the petition and continued, "I got suspicious of these little notebooks some time ago," she said, nodding again at the stack on her desk. "So after you left one night, I read them."

Dorsey gaped at her. "You read my work? You violated the privacy of my locker? And you call *me* deceptive?"

"I watch over what's mine, Dorsey. I've worked too damned hard to make Drake's—hell, to make my *life*— what it is. I've made sacrifices and deals you can't begin to understand. And I'm going to make sure no one ever takes all this away from me. I'll do whatever I have to do to protect what's mine. And I'll do whatever I have to do to survive. I always have. I always will. If that means I search a locker or two along the way, when compared to some of the other things I've had to do, you can bet your ass I don't lose any sleep over it."

"But—"

"And when I read those notebooks and realized you

were keeping tabs on me and some of the other employees—not to mention the clientele of Drake's—I had you investigated. Thoroughly."

Dorsey shook her head in silent disbelief. She'd been investigated? Without her knowledge? That was so . . . It was so . . . So . . . gross.

"And imagine my surprise," Lindy continued, "when my investigator came to me this afternoon and told me who you really are. Lauren Grable-Monroe. I must admit, it blew me away." She turned to Adam then. "I didn't believe it, either, at first. But my man had evidence that was indisputable."

"What kind of evidence?"

The question came not from Dorsey, but from Adam. When she turned to look at him, his expression was as blank and guarded as Lindy's usually was. She had no idea what he was thinking. And that, she decided, couldn't possibly be good.

"Photographs," Lindy told him. "Video tape. Audio recordings. And some copies of documents from her publisher."

The revelation made Dorsey's stomach pitch. The realization that she had been followed, photographed, recorded without her knowledge . . . The idea that someone at Rockcastle had betrayed her identity . . . The knowledge that what she had thought was her private life had been invaded and made available to someone else, that it could even be made public . . .

She understood then better why her employer was so outraged. Lindy feared that Dorsey was about to expose her and Drake's in exactly the same way, that she would take what she had recorded in those notebooks and follow up *How to Trap a Tycoon* with a similarly titillating book about private men's clubs in general and Drake's in particular. If Dorsey hadn't already been determined to keep identities confidential in her dissertation, she was certainly going to make sure no one was exposed now. There was little that could make her feel more demeaned or hurt than she felt right at that moment.

"Look, Lindy," Adam said, sounding confused and unconvinced, "there's just no way you can be right about this thing. There's got to be some mistake. Mack can't possibly be Lauren Grable-Monroe."

Lindy turned her attention back to Adam. "Can't she? I have a private investigator who says otherwise."

"Oh, yeah?" he countered. "Well I just so happen to have had Lauren Grable-Monroe thoroughly investigated for a story I wanted to do in *Man's Life*. And my private investigator couldn't uncover the author's identity no matter how hard he tried. How did your guy find out all this stuff?"

"Did you hire a legitimate investigator?" Lindy asked him.

"Of course."

"That's your problem." She turned back to Dorsey. "Not only are you fired, but I'm planning to file every charge available against you. I am likewise suing you for every possible thing I might be able to sue you for. Get out. Now. And expect to hear from my attorneys immediately."

"I haven't committed any crimes, Lindy," Dorsey assured her, her confidence faltering. "And you can't sue me for anything."

In response, Lindy opened her desk drawer and pulled out a fat file folder. Then she opened it and withdrew its contents, fanning the pages out across her blotter. Dorsey's heart sank to the pit of her stomach when Adam stepped up to look at the information before she did, without hesitation and with much interest. She took a few steps forward then and gazed at the sheaves of paper and black-and-white photographs from behind him, around his shoulder.

Her heart plummeted further at what she saw. Lindy had a copy of her book contract, a copy of Lauren's scheduled appearances, even a copy of the payment agreement that stated Carlotta would be the recipient of any and all checks. There were photographs of Lauren entering doors and of Dorsey exiting those very same doors.

Worse than that, there were pictures of her and Adam together, holding hands as they walked down the street, their heads bent together in conversation over dinner, saying—and kissing—their good-byes at Dorsey's front door. She felt utterly and totally violated at seeing their intimacy assailed so ruthlessly. And she could only imagine that Adam felt exactly the same way. Probably worse, because he was an innocent bystander in all this. His privacy had been invaded simply because he had gotten involved with her.

"I have video that will substantiate the stills of Lauren Grable-Monroe and Dorsey," Lindy said when she noted where Adam's gaze was focused. "It was amazing how many times Dorsey emerged from the very rooms Lauren Grable-Monroe had just entered. And just what was she carrying in that backpack every time, hmm?"

"I can explain," Dorsey said halfheartedly.

"You don't need to," Lindy retorted. "You've been working here to collect information for your next book. Any idiot can deduce that. And what a way to follow up something like *How to Trap a Tycoon*. What's the title of the new one supposed to be, Dorsey? Something along the lines of Gloria Steinem's *A Bunny's Tale*? How about

Cocktail? That's kind of catchy. A nice double entendre."

Dorsey was about to open her mouth to defend herself again, but Lindy cut her off by addressing Adam first. "I certainly hope you haven't made her privy to anything you don't want a couple of million people to know about," she told him. "Then again, it might be kind of fun to read all the juicy, intimate details about one of America's most visible bachelor millionaires. Speaking of cocktails, I hope your . . . technique . . . is as good as it's reputed to be. I'd hate to find out you're nothing special. To anyone other than Dorsey, I mean."

The barb hit home, exactly as Lindy had intended. Because Adam's head snapped up from the scattered documents and photos on Lindy's desk, and he spun quickly around to gaze at Dorsey. His expression was still unreadable, but there was something in his eyes that just about broke her heart. She could only guess what he was thinking, what he was feeling. Whatever it was, she figured it was probably pretty awful. Not as awful as what *she* was feeling at the moment, of course, but probably pretty close.

"Adam, Lindy's wrong," she said softly. "About everything." But she could tell just by looking at him that she'd already lost him. In spite of that, she continued, "I would never compromise what you and I have. I didn't get involved with you for the reasons Lindy thinks. And I didn't come to work here for the reasons she thinks, either. I never intended to write a book about Drake's, and I would never, ever do anything to hurt you."

He didn't react to her assurance in any way, only continued to gaze at her in maddeningly thoughtful silence.

"Adam, please," she murmured quietly. "Give me a chance to explain."

"I'm not sure I really need an explanation, Mack," he

said, his voice as empty as his expression. "Lindy's guy seems to have done a pretty thorough job."

He might as well have slapped her, so severe was her response to his remark. Dorsey squeezed her eyes shut tight as an icy fist seized her heart and wrenched every last bit of life out of it. Every emotion she had experienced since entering Lindy's office fused into a cold, dark lump that wedged itself deep inside her, in a place that was darker and colder still.

She had lost him. Just like that. No matter what she said now, things would never be the same between them. Adam had drawn his own conclusions, had unequivocally decided that she'd betrayed him. Even if Dorsey somehow managed to explain her actions, he would never trust her again. And while she was trying to make amends, he might very well see fit to exact a little revenge. He was the kind of man who wouldn't take betrayal lightly. And even though Dorsey hadn't betrayed him, he was quick enough on the trigger to take a bad situation and make it worse.

"I think that's your cue to leave, Dorsey," Lindy said quietly.

Surrendering for now to the obviously heavy odds against her, Dorsey squared her shoulders and stated stoically, "Not without my notes."

Lindy did laugh then, and it almost sounded genuine. "I don't think so," she said evenly.

But Dorsey was already prepared for the response, and immediately executed her own. In one deft, swift maneuver, she scooped up the notebooks and turned to stride out the door. She would not run away, she promised herself bravely. Not unless . . . you know . . . Lindy pulled out her .45.

But Lindy evidently didn't think that was necessary,

because she didn't open fire. What she did do was call out, "Have it your way, Dorsey. I've made copies of them all. You'll be hearing from my attorneys. Soon."

Still not quite convinced that Lindy wouldn't pursue her, Dorsey clutched her notebooks to her chest and hastened to the locker room. *I will not cry*, she promised herself as she went. *I will not cry.* She tugged her apron over her head and tossed it to the floor—God forbid she should be accused of theft on top of everything else—then snatched her backpack from her locker. For one last gesture, she tugged her wedding band from her finger and set it on the otherwise empty shelf.

It was just a cheap bit of gold that symbolized nothing, she reasoned as she left. Not to mention a reminder of a time in her life that she'd just as soon not be reminded of. It was meaningless. Worthless. Pointless.

And hey, it wasn't like she'd ever have use for a wedding ring in the future.

Adam stood in silence as he watched Mack leave, wondering what the hell had just hit him. A truck, he finally decided. A great, whopping-big Mack truck. Traveling at about a hundred miles an hour. With no brakes. And studded tires.

He spared a moment to assess the situation, to try and figure out what exactly he was feeling. And he was surprised to discover that what he felt was . . . nothing. Nothing at all. Or maybe he just felt so many things that he couldn't make sense of any of them, so his brain refused to acknowledge even one. In fact, it was as if his body and his brain both had shut down completely, as if he were just a shadow now of what he had been only moments ago. Even when he turned to look at Lindy, for whom he figured he should feel anger or outrage or resentiment or *something*, there was nothing but a void. He'd never felt so empty in his entire life. And he wondered if he would have to stay this way forever.

Lindy, too, stood silently for some moments, pinned to the spot on the other side of her desk, gazing at Adam with much expectation. He chose his words and his tone carefully before saying anything, genuinely uncertain about what to say or how to say it. How could he know what to say when he didn't even know what to think? How could he know what to think when he didn't even know what to feel?

What he finally opted for was, "You wanted me to be here for this because you thought it would make me angry, didn't you, Lindy? Angry enough to alert all my media friends and expose her. You want me to use my connections—maybe even my own magazine—to hang her out to dry, right?"

"The thought had crossed my mind, yes," she told him coolly. "You're not the kind of man to let a woman take advantage of you, Adam—not for very long anyway. You protect yourself and what's yours, too. You and I are a lot alike in that respect."

Adam mulled that over for a moment. In a way, Lindy was right. He wasn't one to roll over and play dead when someone had betrayed or maligned him. But had Mack truly betrayed him? Had she maligned him? Had that been her intention all along? Or had she been telling the truth? She didn't have much in her favor at the moment, he had to admit. Lindy had some powerful proof sitting there, and Mack hadn't done much along the lines of denying any of it. She certainly hadn't denied being Lauren Grable-Monroe. And from the looks of it, there was a good reason for that.

Namely, because she was Lauren Grable-Monroe.

It all started coming together for him then. Hadn't he himself concluded that afternoon at Northwestern that the author must be an academic? Hadn't he noted a number of common denominators in the author's analysis and thesis and his own conversations with Mack? Hadn't Lauren Grable-Monroe reminded him of someone? And hadn't he experienced an attraction to her that he hadn't been able to understand?

If she and Mack were one and the same, all of that would make perfect sense now. And judging by the photographs on Lindy's desk, that was entirely the case.

"I'll want to study all this documentation thoroughly," he told Lindy, reserving, for now, any decision about what to do in the way of exposure.

"That goes without saying," she replied.

"And I'll want to see those copies of her notebooks, as well."

"Of course. You do figure prominently in some of them, after all."

He wasn't sure how he felt about that, but he supposed he'd find out before the night was through. He planned to read every last word of what Mack had written, study every photograph and document Lindy had in her possession. For some reason, though, in spite of everything that had happened, he felt oddly compelled to protect Mack. He had no idea why. She hadn't done much in the way of protecting herself. And regardless of whatever else she had done, she certainly hadn't been honest with him.

Before he could stop himself, he said, "You know, Lindy, there was probably a better way to go about this."

She lifted her chin defensively, something that gave him the impression that she was looking down her nose at him. "I suppose there was," she conceded. "But where would be the fun in that?"

A couple of months ago, Adam would have probably responded to such a question in exactly the same way. A couple of months ago, he would have drawn his conclusions to Lindy's allegations with a terrible, swift sword. A couple of months ago, he wouldn't have thought twice about hanging Mack out to dry for what she appeared to have done. A couple of months ago, he would have gotten right on the phone to tell all his media colleagues that Lauren Grable-Monroe was actually a young sociology professor at Severn College named Dorsey Mac-Guinness—pass it on. Of course, a couple of months ago, he'd been a ruthless, heartless sonofabitch. Now . . .

Well.

Now he didn't feel quite so ruthless. Now he didn't feel quite so heartless. In fact, whereas a few months ago he'd been certain his heart was gone for good, over the last few months he'd somehow managed to recover a good portion of it. It hadn't been easy, of course. He'd had to have some help, some guidance. And the search was by no means over. Right when he'd started gathering up the remaining bits and pieces, his guide had jumped off the beaten path and disappeared into the underbrush. And he wasn't sure now if he would ever see her again.

So that kind of sucked.

He supposed now that there was only one thing for him to do. He'd have to figure out exactly where his guide had gone, exactly what her intentions were, exactly where her origins lay. He'd have to decide for himself whether she had been in it only for herself, or if she'd truly found the same thing he had along the way. And then . . .

Well. He'd cross that bridge—or machete down that jungle—when he came to it.

He gestured toward the pile of papers and photos fanned across Lindy's desk. "Mind if I take all this and a pot of coffee out to the salon?" he asked her. "I have a lot of reading to do tonight."

"Not at all," she replied. "But I think you should know, Adam, that if you don't expose Dorsey for the conniving little fraud that she is, I plan to do it myself. In spades."

Adam sighed wearily. That, he thought, was exactly what he had been afraid of.

Chapter 15

It was after dark by the time Dorsey arrived home. Not that she noticed. Not that she cared. Not that the sun would ever rise in *her* personal reality again. She might as well get used to the total absence of light, she told herself. Because the only plans she had for the immediate future—or the long-range future, for that matter—involved going to bed and pulling the covers up over her head.

As if in anticipation of her dark arrival, no lights had been lit inside the townhouse she shared with her mother. Which was odd, Dorsey thought, because when she'd come home to eat lunch and change clothes that afternoon, Carlotta had been hip-deep in cleaning out closets, and it had been clear that she would be shoulder-deep by nightfall. And even cleaning out closets, her mother had, as always, looked elegant and sublime, dressed in Ralph Lauren blue jeans and chambray shirt, her platinum hair tied back with a Laura Ashley scarf.

In spite of her melancholy humor, Dorsey smiled at the memory. How on earth had she turned out so differently from her mother? She supposed that was one of those mysteries of the universe that no one would ever be able to solve.

"Carlotta?" she called out to the house at large.

"I'm up here, Dorsey!" came her mother's reply. "In the attic!"

Well, that would explain the absence of light, she thought. No telling how long Carlotta had been up there.

Contrary to her mood, Dorsey did deign to switch on a Tiffany lamp as she dropped her backpack onto the plum-colored velvet sofa. Then she made her way across the living room—as posh and feminine as Carlotta's bedroom was, with purples replacing the pinks—and up the stairs. She paused beneath the rectangular opening in the hallway ceiling above. The stairs had been unfolded into the corridor, and a faint yellow light spilled down over them.

"Hel-loooo up there," she called.

There was a rustle of sound in response, then her mother's head appeared over the opening. "Come on up. You'll never guess what I found when I was cleaning today."

Without hesitation, Dorsey pulled herself up the collapsible stairs and found her mother sitting on the attic floor with a flurry of dust motes dancing around her. The minute particles caught and refracted the pale light from a single naked bulb overhead, giving Carlotta the appearance of an enchanted maiden encircled by fairies. Baskets and trunks and cartons containing no telling what surrounded her, and familiar pink lacquer boxes sat open on the floor in front of her.

"Oh, wow," Dorsey said with a smile as she crossed

to where her mother sat. "You found my old Barbies."

Genuinely delighted by the discovery—and not just because it gave her something to focus on besides Adam and Lauren and Lindy and disaster—she sat down beside her mother and ran a finger through the thin film of dust that coated one of the bright-pink box tops.

"I can't remember the last time I looked at these," she said wistfully. Oh, to be a little girl again, she thought, and have to worry only about which plastic shoes to put on Barbie's rubber feet before she went out adventuring with Skipper and Christie and Ken.

"I remember," Carlotta said. "It was the summer before you started seventh grade. You put them away just before junior high school, because you insisted you were much too old for things like Barbie."

Dorsey nodded, her smile broadening. "That's right. I remember. I was just *so* mature at twelve."

"I, of course, thought you were being silly, because no one is ever too old to play with Barbie."

"These days, I'm inclined to agree with you," Dorsey said, picking up one of the dolls to run a finger over the smooth nylon hair. Carlotta had dressed the doll in an elegant, sapphire-colored evening gown, which Dorsey immediately began to remove.

Her mother gaped softly at her. "You? Ms. Feminist? Playing with Barbie? I thought you'd be one of the ones flaying her for her unbalanced, bulimia-inducing figure."

Dorsey waved a hand negligently before her, then reached for an outfit to clothe the now naked doll. "There are a lot of reasons for women to have eating disorders," she told Carlotta. "But Barbie isn't one of them. I mean, do you ever remember me as a little girl looking at Barbie and saying, 'Gee, I wish I had enormous hooters and a tiny wasp waist and tippy-toe feet like Barbie does'?"

"Not once," Carlotta confessed.

"Exactly," Dorsey concurred with a fierce nod. "It was the *clothes*. Nobody gets that. The clothes and all the adventures we used to send Barbie on. Remember?"

Carlotta laughed. "Oh, yes. I remember. I was always sending *my* Barbie off to Rio de Janeiro and Monaco and St. Moritz to meet movie stars and princes. Or," she added, holding up a GI Joe dressed in commando black, "to meet GI Joe, who was off on leave. You, on the other hand," she continued, "were always sending *your* Barbie off to logging camps and rain forests to fight deforestation or to Amnesty International conventions."

Dorsey laughed, too. "My Barbie had a social conscience."

"Whereas my Barbie had a good time."

Dorsey glanced up at her mother, who had put down GI Joe to dress her own blond Barbie in a peach-colored peignoir set. "Carlotta?" she asked.

"Yes?"

"Are you sure I wasn't switched at birth with some other, princessy, baby that should have been yours?"

Her mother looked up at her and smiled. "I'm absolutely positive. Once you emerged from inside me and they put you in my arms, I never once let you out of my sight."

Dorsey smiled back. "Truly?"

"Truly."

"Thanks."

"You're welcome, dear."

They said nothing more for a moment, only sat in comfortable silence dressing, undressing, and redressing their dolls. Then, out of nowhere, Dorsey announced, "I lost my job today."

Carlotta's hands hesitated on her doll, and she glanced up at Dorsey. "At Drake's?" she asked.

Dorsey nodded but couldn't bring herself to meet her mother's gaze. "Though the one at Severn, I'm sure, isn't far behind." Quickly, so she wouldn't have to think about it for very long, she added, "I lost Adam Darien, too."

Her mother said nothing for a moment, then asked, "What happened? Did you two get separated at the El?"

Dorsey shook her head sadly. "No. I think the two of us got separated before we ever even found each other."

She heard Carlotta sigh softly. "Do you want to start at the beginning? Or should I just keep asking questions until the whole messy story comes pouring out?"

Dorsey did meet her mother's gaze then, and before she could stop herself, the whole messy story did indeed come pouring out. She told Carlotta about what had happened in Lindy's office, about Lindy's findings and Adam's reaction—or lack thereof—about her employer's threat to press charges and sue, about how Lauren Grable-Monroe—and Dorsey—were going to be crucified for the public's entertainment.

The only thing she didn't tell her mother was how very terrified she was of the impending fallout, nor did she describe the depths of her despair where losing Adam was concerned. Those, she figured, were pretty much a given. Mostly because by the time she finished telling her story, even she thought she sounded terrified and despairing.

Carlotta's first response was adamant. "Lindy Aubrey can't have you arrested, Dorsey, nor can she sue you for anything."

"Are you sure?"

"Absolutely. You've done nothing illegal. Unless you've published your notes and called Lindy and her business all kinds of terrible, ugly names, she can't do anything. And even if you published your notes and called Lindy and her business all kinds of terrible, ugly names, she'd have to prove that she and her business weren't all those terrible, ugly things. And if you ask me, the moment that terrible, ugly woman took the stand, both judge and jury would find in your favor."

"I don't know . . ."

"Lindy was reacting out of anger and frustration and fear, Dorsey. When she speaks to her attorneys, they'll tell her she doesn't have a leg to stand on. You just wait."

"Then she'll probably take out a hit on me," Dorsey said. "I wouldn't be surprised if she has friends in that line of work. She might even pull the trigger herself."

"Oh, stop," Carlotta scolded. "Your work at Drake's and your dissertation are the least of your worries. What about Adam?"

Dorsey had rather hoped to avoid that topic. She should have known better. "What about him?" she stalled.

"What are you going to tell him?"

She scrunched up her shoulders and let them drop. "I'm not going to tell him anything."

"*What?*"

"He won't listen to me, Carlotta. I tried to explain at Drake's, but he's already drawn his own conclusions and sided with Lindy. He won't believe me."

Carlotta studied her in silence for some moments, then asked, "Why did you keep your notebooks at Drake's in the first place?"

It took Dorsey a minute to backpedal that far, but she finally told her mother, "In the beginning, I didn't keep them there, for fear of being discovered. But it was hard to keep my observations in my head until I got home at

309 HOW TO TRAP A TYCOON

night to record them. I just thought it would be easier if I could jot them down when I took a break. And gradually, as I got to know Lindy . . ." She shrugged again. "I don't know. I just pegged her as the kind of person who wouldn't violate another person's privacy. She guarded her own so closely. It was more convenient to keep the notebooks at Drake's, and I just never thought she'd do something like search my locker. I trusted her."

"The same way Adam trusted you," Carlotta said.

"Yes," Dorsey replied softly.

"And now he feels that trust has been violated."

"I know. That's the problem. And he's not the kind of man who'll forgive something like that."

"Oh?" Carlotta asked. "What kind of man is he?"

Dorsey fidgeted, then laid her Barbie on the floor beside Ken. Folding her legs up before her, she hugged them to her chest and settled her chin atop one knee. And she tried not to think about how she'd just curled herself up into a fetal position. What was next? she wondered. Would she be trying to crawl back into the womb, too? Somehow, she didn't think Carlotta would stand for that. Literally or figuratively.

"Adam," she finally said, "is the kind of man who protects what's his. He'll see this as an opportunity to throw Lauren Grable-Monroe—to throw *me*—to the wolves."

"Will he?"

"Oh, Carlotta. You know how much he hates that book. He'll jump at the chance to see me squirm."

"He might have jumped at the chance to see Lauren Grable-Monroe squirm, Dorsey, but not you. You yourself just said he protects what's his."

"I'm not his," Dorsey countered.

"Aren't you?"

She shook her head slowly. "I'm not anybody's." She had meant for the proclamation to sound fierce and proud. Instead, it only sounded sad and lonely.

"Regardless of what you may think," Carlotta told her, "Adam won't throw you to the wolves."

"I can't be sure of that."

"I can."

"Why?"

"Because he's just like you, Dorsey. And you would never do that to him."

"He's not like me," Dorsey denied.

"He's *exactly* like you," her mother retorted. "That's why you're so attracted to him. That's why you respond to him so strongly. You recognize yourself in him."

"No, he's . . . I'm . . . We're . . ." She sighed restlessly and gave up trying to explain something she didn't even understand herself. "He's not like any man I've ever been attracted to," she told her mother. "So why does it hurt so much to lose him?"

Carlotta laughed. "Oh, Dorsey, don't you see? That's always been your problem. You've always opted for Ken when you should have gone for GI Joe."

She narrowed her eyes at her mother curiously. "What are you talking about?"

Carlotta pointed at the Ken doll that Dorsey had dressed after completing Barbie's wardrobe. "Ken is so . . . so passive. He's so agreeable. So bland. He's the kind of man that *I* have always tried to attract. One who's manageable. One who's not much work. One who will behave predictably. Docilely."

"And what, may I ask, is so terrible about that?" Dorsey asked.

Carlotta rolled her eyes. "Oh, please. For me, that kind of man is fine. But he's not for you. You're a strong woman. You need a strong man. You need someone who will be both a worthy adversary and an equal partner. You're not going to find that in Ken. Yet Kens were all you ever dated. Until Adam."

"Ken is *not* that bad," Dorsey defended.

Carlotta sighed. "Dorsey, you always dressed Barbie in career coordinates, yet you always dressed Ken in tennis togs. And you still do. Do you realize that?"

Dorsey looked down at the two dolls she had just dressed, and sure enough, Barbie looked ready to take on the stock market, while Ken was prepared for game, set, match.

"Yeah. So?" she asked her mother. "Ken looks good in shorts."

"So you've never taken Ken seriously, that's what," Carlotta told her. "He's always just been a plaything to your Barbie. GI Joe, on the other hand—" Her mother held up the other doll. "Now *he's* a force to be reckoned with."

She snatched grinning, tawny-haired, totally harmless Ken away and settled intense, stoic, facially wounded GI Joe in his place. "Now look at that," Carlotta said with a smile. "That's what I call a power couple. Barbie has to take GI Joe seriously. He'd never stand for being dismissed the way that lame Ken just was. Ken belongs with *my* Barbie," she added, setting him down beside her peignoir-wearing doll. Dorsey had to admit that the pairing seemed much more appropriate. "My Barbie will be gentle with him," Carlotta concluded. "She'll take good care of him.

"You, Dorsey, you wouldn't be gentle with Ken. And you shouldn't have to take care of anyone, if it's not in your nature. You're a strong woman," she reiterated. "You have power. You have focus. You have drive and ambition. You have complete self-knowledge and self-confidence. You deserve to find someone like that, too."

Dorsey smiled halfheartedly. "I deserve GI Joe, huh?"

Instead of answering, Carlotta studied each of the male dolls for a thoughtful moment. "Then again," she finally said, "Ken and GI Joe are both eunuchs, aren't they? Hmm . . ." She snatched GI Joe away from Dorsey's Barbie, too. "Oh, dear. Look at that. Now Barbie's all alone. She's still smiling, but you can tell she's not really happy. I suppose she couldn't be happy with some boring, emasculated piece of plastic." She paused until Dorsey glanced up to look at her again. "She deserves a man. *You* deserve a man," she said pointedly. "A real man. One's who's like you."

"Adam Darien," she guessed.

Carlotta nodded. "He's a worthy rival for you, Dorsey, and a worthy companion. Strong women, I think, need both." She sighed heavily. "You aren't like me, darling. You never have been. And I'm glad of that. The one lesson I wanted you to learn, growing up, was that you are your own person. We are entirely different beings, you and I. We want entirely different things. But that's not a bad thing, Dorsey. It doesn't mean we don't care about each other. It only means that we are different."

"I think we want a lot of the same things," Dorsey objected.

"Name one," Carlotta charged.

"Security," Dorsey said immediately. "That was the whole point to writing *How to Trap a Tycoon*."

Carlotta shook her head. "That wasn't for security. That was for a financial nest egg."

"What's the difference?"

Carlotta smiled a cryptic little smile. "You'd never understand," she said without a bit of malice. "And just for the record, I don't want security. I want a steady income to get me through my golden years. If security was what I wanted, I would have accepted one of the marriage proposals I received along the way. But I didn't want—"

"Whoa, whoa, whoa," Dorsey interrupted. "Marriage proposals? Marriage propo*sals*? As in plural? As in more than one? As if one wouldn't have been enough to set you up the way you wanted to be set up? For life?"

Carlotta gaped at her in clear disbelief. "Marriage would *not* have set me up," she stated indignantly. "A husband is the last thing I want."

"Carlotta!" Dorsey exclaimed. "What are you talking about? How could you have received marriage proposals over the years and never accepted one? And how could you have never told me about them?"

There was a moment of silence, then, "Well, no offense, Dorsey," Carlotta said, "but the reason I never told you about them was because, quite frankly, they were none of your business."

"*What?*"

"They were none of your business," her mother repeated softly.

"But . . ."

Dorsey told herself to let it go, to just be satisfied with Carlotta's explanation, even if she didn't understand it for a moment, and move on. But one question kept circling around and around in her head. And she simply had to know the answer. There was no way she'd be able to leave it behind until she found out for sure.

"Was one of those marriage proposals," she began carefully, "from my father?"

For a moment, her mother didn't reply, only arranged and rearranged her Barbie's lace-trimmed robe until she had it draping dramatically over one shoulder. Just when

Dorsey thought she would have to ask the question again—because she intended to keep asking it until she received an honest answer—Carlotta glanced back up again and met her gaze levelly.

"Yes," she finally said. "One of those proposals came from your father."

Dorsey swallowed hard but said nothing, waiting to hear the rest.

"The first time he asked me was when he found out I was pregnant with you," Carlotta said. "I adamantly refused."

"Why?"

"Dorsey, the man was married to a woman who was completely reliant on him, a woman who had no idea how to take care of herself, a woman who would have been left with three young children to raise alone. His primary obligation was rightfully to his family. Not to me."

"What about me?" The question popped out of Dorsey's mouth before she could stop it. She knew it sounded selfish and cold, but she couldn't help it. She wanted to know.

"*You*," Carlotta said, "were *my* responsibility. And I made that clear to Reggie."

"But—"

"No buts," her mother interjected. "The world was a different place then, Dorsey. Your father wasn't a strong man, and although his intentions were good, he wouldn't have been able to withstand the consequences of leaving his wife and children to marry his pregnant mistress. It would have ended between us eventually, and it would have ended badly. For all of us."

"But he stayed with you for years after I was born. I remember him."

"Yes, he wanted to be a part of both our lives, and I didn't object to that. But he kept asking me to marry him, kept saying he would leave his wife and children for me and you. I told him no every time. He kept asking, anyway. Finally, I told him that if he asked me again, I'd stop seeing him. He asked again. So I stopped seeing him."

"Oh, Carlotta . . ."

"I didn't love him. I didn't want him forever. I never wanted anybody forever. I know you can't possibly comprehend that, but for my sake, please try. I like *men*, Dorsey. All men. I like the way they talk and the way they move and the way they smell and the way they feel curled up next to me in bed. I like chatting with them, dining with them, flirting with them, being with them, in every way imaginable. But I don't want to keep one forever. I don't want to give up that much of myself to a man."

In a way, Dorsey did understand and she respected her mother's conviction. Her mother was right—they were two totally different creatures. And she would never, ever be like her mother. Because she did want to keep a man forever. She did want to give up that much of herself to one. Provided that man was Adam Darien, and he would give as much of himself to her in return.

Then she realized that he already had given as much of himself to her in return, maybe more, because he'd never held any part of himself back from her. He hadn't kept any secrets. He hadn't pretended to be something he wasn't. And he hadn't lied to her about anything.

Dorsey gazed down at her solitary Barbie lying alone in her career coordinates. Carlotta was right. Despite the little plastic smile, she didn't look very happy. And a great career and a social conscience weren't going to be enough keep her warm at night.

"Oh, Carlotta," Dorsey murmured. "What am I going to do?"

By the time Adam had finished examining Lindy's collection of information relating to Mack and Lauren Grable-Monroe, Drake's had been closed for three hours. Lindy sat at the table across from him—where she had been for the last ninety minutes of those three hours— smoking a cigar and nursing her second snifter of Armagnac, lost in a paperback copy of *Dr. Zhivago*. He'd heard her sniffling and figured she'd gotten to the part where Lara tells the good doctor to take a hike. It had been reassuring to realize that Lindy was capable of feeling something for *some*body.

Her investigator had definitely been thorough. He'd all but recorded Mack's underwear size. Then again, Adam already knew she was size six in panties, size 36B in bras. Happily, he had *some* information that the investigator didn't.

Contrary to what he'd told Lindy, Adam didn't actually read every word of Mack's notes. He wanted to, and he'd intended to, but the majority of those words were so erudite and academic, so theoretical and analytical, that he had trouble following much of what was written. And he might as well admit it—he'd found the material to be pretty damned boring, too. Leave it to a sociology student to take a nice place like Drake's and reduce it to a scholarly dissertation.

Then again, that was exactly what Mack had said she planned to do, wasn't it?

And contrary to what Lindy had said, Adam didn't see himself figuring all that prominently in the notes. At least, he didn't think he did. No one had been identified by name, only with labels like Gray Eminence, Apologist, Wannabe, and Sacred Cow. Then there was the one referred to as Pack Leader, which, he had to admit, he liked to think was him. It must be, he decided, because there wasn't anyone she had termed Hot Stuff.

But if Lindy saw Adam as a major part of this study, then she understood it with far greater insight than he. Because not only could he not see himself threatened by anything that was written there, he sure couldn't see a sensationalistic, potboiling best-seller emerging out of it, either. A sleep aid, certainly, but not much else.

What had actually piqued his interest most were the documents from Rockcastle Books. Sure enough, it was Dorsey MacGuinness's signature that appeared on each of them. First on the book contract, whose advance had been impressive but by no means astronomical. Then on the confidentiality agreement, stating that her identity would be closely guarded by the publisher. And most interesting of all, on the payment agreement stating that all funds generated by the sale of the book would be paid not to Dorsey MacGuinness but to her mother.

That, more than anything else, had convinced Adam that Mack wasn't the soulless, flagrant opportunist that Lindy had assumed her to be. Because even if Mack had done this for the money, it hadn't been for personal gain. She was doing it for her mother. And hell, what could be more noble than that?

All right, so maybe it was still opportunistic. It wasn't selfish. And that was in keeping with the Mack that Adam had come to know and love. Because he did love Mack. He'd figured that out tonight if nothing else. In spite of everything he'd found out about her, in spite of

the way she'd misled him, in spite of the fact that she
had kept so many secrets . . .

Despite everything, he still cared about her. A lot. And
he didn't want to lose her.

He didn't kid himself that there were smooth seas
ahead. She had a lot to answer for and a lot of explaining
to do. And God alone knew what her life was going to
be like for the next several weeks if Lindy made good
on her threat to out Dorsey MacGuinness as Lauren
Grable-Monroe. But whatever pitfalls and potholes he
and Mack encountered on the road ahead, he was fully
confident they could repair them and move forward.

But that wasn't his greatest concern at the moment.
Because at the moment, Lindy was still convinced that
Mack intended to take Drake's down. And at the moment, Lindy intended to take Mack down first. Adam
could try to talk her out of it, but she seemed determined.
She had plenty of contacts of her own to spread the word
that Lauren Grable-Monroe was really Dorsey Mac-
Guinness, and hey, here's her address and her phone
number, and you can find her at Severn College teaching
on these days in these classrooms, and here's where she
catches the El.

As if Lindy sensed his thoughts, she glanced up from
her book and met his gaze. "So?" she asked.

"So what?" he stalled.

"So what are you going to do?"

"I don't know, Lindy," he told her. "I honestly do not
know."

She puffed a few more times on her cigar, then placed
it carefully on a crystal ashtray bearing the Baccarat in-
signia. "Fine," she said. "You think about it. In the meantime, I know exactly what I'm going to do."

Adam nodded without much enthusiasm as he pushed

the materials across the table toward Lindy and wondered what he might say that would possibly talk her out of doing what she'd threatened to do. But all he could think was, *Poor Mack.* Lauren Grable-Monroe's days were definitely numbered. And the number he saw most was, unfortunately, one.

Chapter 16

Edie Mulholland's neighborhood was sort of middle everything, Lucas noted, as he sat in his car outside her apartment building, watching the sun dip low in the sky. Middle class, middle America, middle age, middle ground, middle-of-the-road. There wasn't much to remark about the area except that it was totally unremarkable. And somehow, he got the feeling that Edie lived here for that very reason—it would be easy to fade into the landscape.

A week had passed since she had told him to go away and leave her alone, and Lucas had done his best to abide by her wishes. He'd avoided Drake's during the hours she normally worked. He had curbed his urge to go hangout on the Severn campus. He hadn't dialed her number once when he'd picked up the phone. He'd respected her wishes, had left her alone.

And what had he gotten in return?

He'd gotten frustrated. He'd gotten annoyed. He'd gotten irritable. He'd gotten lonely.

There were just too many unanswered questions about Edie Mulholland, and there was one glaring fact about her that he didn't like at all. She'd been mistreated at some point in her past. Enough to keep her scared and uneasy in her present. Enough to prevent her from seeking a future with anyone who might want to get close to her. Lucas, for whatever reason—and God knew he'd tried to figure out what that reason might be—wanted to get close to her. Close enough to touch her. Close enough to hold her. Close enough to understand her.

Why? He had no idea. All this time, he'd been thinking of her as Mulholland of Sunnybrook Farm, a woman who was all sweetness and light, with no shadows or sharp edges to her at all. He'd been certain she was the perfect product of a perfect union in a perfect place, a woman incapable of knowing what it was like to feel pain or experience the cold bite of reality. To Lucas, Edie Mulholland had always been a one-dimensional icon of all that was good in the world.

With last week's episode, however, he had been forced to acknowledge that there were indeed some shadows in her life. There were sharp edges. Badness had soiled her goodness. Darkness had dimmed her light. Bitterness had tainted her sweetness. And that didn't seem fair at all.

Which was laughable, really, because Lucas Conaway was always the first one to eagerly opine that Life Is Not Fair. It was the banner behind which he stoically marched, the standard he held aloft for all to see. Life Is Not Fair, he gleefully proclaimed to anyone who would listen—and even to those who wouldn't. And that was always followed immediately by his other heartfelt declaration: Deal With It.

But he hadn't dealt with it. Not this time. Not with Edie. And hell, it wasn't even his life that wasn't fair these days. Sure, he'd had his setbacks in the past, too. Poverty, abandonment, despair. But then, life is not fair. He had dealt with it. In his own life, at any rate. Somehow, though, he couldn't accept it for Edie's.

Because with Edie, it just wasn't fair.

He pushed open his car door and unfolded himself from inside, then slowly approached her building. Normally, he'd be home by now, home to his empty apartment, his empty life. Normally, about this time, he'd be sitting down alone to eat dinner, wondering what to do by himself with the long, lonely night ahead. But he'd broken his vow to Edie and stopped by Drake's earlier in the day, only to find that she hadn't shown up for her shift.

Illness, Lindy had told him.

Right, Lucas had replied.

And then he'd gotten worried about her, so he'd decided to swing by her place on the way home to see if she needed anything. Chicken soup. Cuppa tea. Bitter blond guy who missed her.

He hesitated only a moment before rapping hard three times on her front door. He waited a minute before trying again, then another minute before trying a third time. He was about to give up, was about to turn away, when a muffled sound on the other side of the door caught his attention. That was followed by a soft swoosh of something brushing against the door on the other side, and then total silence.

"I know you're in there, Edie," he said, gazing directly at the peephole. "I can hear you breathing."

More silence was his only reply.

"Okay, so now you're holding your breath," he said. "I can wait. Bet you can't."

For another long moment, there was only silence. Then the soft *thump-clunk* of a deadbolt being slowly and reluctantly rotated. Little by little the front door eased inward until Edie's face appeared in the opening. She had obviously just risen from bed. Her hair was a tumble of blond curls that cascaded over her shoulders, and her eyes were rimmed with red and shadowed by dark circles. As she pulled the door open a bit more, Lucas saw that she was dressed in a silky robe that fell to her ankles in a riot of color, a purple background patterned with palm trees and volcanoes and words that seemed to spell out Aloha from Waikiki.

All in all, she looked to him like a fading thirties film star, blond and pale and tragic. And he really wished he knew what to say or do that would make everything in Edie Mulholland's life perfect.

She sighed with much defeat and took one more step backward. "If you're not going to go away, then you might as well come in. I don't want the neighbors gossiping."

"About you?" he asked. "Get real. If the neighbors gossip about you, it's only to talk about what a sweet, decent, courteous, nice, kind, polite, blond do-gooder you are."

She muttered a sound of dubious origin. "Yeah, well, you got the blond part right, anyway."

She closed the door behind him, then gestured vaguely toward the interior in what he guessed was meant to be an invitation. Whatever. He'd take what he could get.

"Look, I know you told me to leave you alone," he

said as he followed her, "and you have to admit that I've done a pretty good job of it."

She paused just inside the living room and folded her arms over her midsection a bit self-consciously. "Yeah, you have," she agreed with what sounded like—dare he hope?—disappointment. Then, furthering his hopes, she added, with what was clearly not disappointment, "But you're here now, aren't you?"

"Yeah, well, I was kind of under the impression that your instructions carried an expiration date, even if you didn't say what it was."

"No, they don't," she said halfheartedly. "They don't expire at all. I want you to leave me alone forever."

Liar, he thought. Aloud, though, he said, "See, now that's going to be a problem for me."

"Why?"

"Because I can't stop thinking about you."

She opened her mouth to reply, but no words came out. So she snapped it shut again, turned her back on Lucas, and made her way silently toward the windows on the other side of the room.

Her apartment was small but tidy, an eclectic mix of secondhand castoffs and make-do pieces that combined to achieve a surprisingly pleasant effect. The sofa was actually a futon in a basic wooden frame, the mattress cover decorated with moons and stars. It was accessorized by an old steamer trunk tipped on its side to serve as a coffee table, and wooden crates plastered with paintings of fruit made up end tables on either side of the futon. The hardwood floors were bare, the walls painted a functional beige. They were brightened, however, by Art Institute posters advertising various exhibits and offerings. She seemed to like Paul Klee and Gustav Klimt a lot.

"You have a nice place, Edie," he said as he folded himself onto the futon.

"Thanks," she replied as she pulled aside a lace curtain to gaze down at the street. When she dropped it again and turned to face Lucas, she seemed a bit distracted somehow. "It's not much, but I call it home."

It felt like a home, he thought. Whereas his own place was artfully arranged and decorated—thanks to a friend of a friend who did that kind of thing for a living—it didn't feel or look much like a home. Edie's place, for all its lack of sophistication, was warm and comfortable and lived in. Plants tumbled from bookcases near the windows, throw pillows had been cast onto the floor, magazines spilled across the steamer trunk, and framed photographs were scattered about everywhere. Whereas Lucas's apartment looked like something from a magazine, Edie's looked like something from real life. It was yet another indication that she did indeed have a nodding acquaintance with reality.

"So how come you missed your shift at Drake's this afternoon?" he asked in as offhand a manner as he could manage.

She didn't answer right away, but he knew it wasn't because she hadn't heard him. She did offer a response in the form of another one of those heavy, resigned sighs. Then she sat down in a bentwood rocker near the window—a solid ten feet from where Lucas had seated himself—and said, "I missed my shift because I haven't gotten much sleep this week, and today it just all caught up with me."

When she sat, her robe fell open above her knees, exposing bare calves and feet beneath. Lucas tried really hard—okay, maybe not so hard—not to notice. "Not, uh, not sleeping, huh?" he echoed—sort of. "Seems to be a lot of that going around. I've been having a rough time of it myself in the sleep department lately." He held her gaze levelly as he added, "I can't imagine why."

Her expression remained impassive as she told him, "Not sleeping usually isn't a problem for me."

"Me, neither," he agreed. "I generally sleep like a rock."

"No, I mean not sleeping doesn't usually bother me," she clarified. "I've always been a bad sleeper. This week, though, for some reason, it's just taken a toll."

He eyed her thoughtfully as he asked, "How come you're a bad sleeper?"

She eyed him not at all as she replied, "I just don't like to sleep, that's all."

"Why not?"

"It's a waste of time."

"Mm."

"You, uh, you're not going to leave me alone until I tell you why I reacted the way I did last week, are you?" she asked pointedly.

No reason to dance around that one, Lucas thought. So, "Nope," he told her frankly. "I'm not going to leave you alone."

She nodded. "Okay, fine. It's not like it's any big secret, anyway. Even Lindy knows about my past. I felt obligated to tell her about my arrest record when she hired me. It was the decent thing to do."

Well, that certainly got Lucas's attention. "You have an arrest record?" he asked, not bothering to mask his surprise. "For what? Jay walking? Double parking? Failing to curb your dog?"

She shook her head, but her expression was inscrutable as she told him, "For prostitution. Burglary. And trafficking in controlled substances."

Lucas's jaw dropped open at her admission. He knew he must look foolish, but it was the only reaction that seemed appropriate. Mulholland of Sunnybrook Farm was suddenly the estrogen-producing half of Edie and Clyde. And *that* was a crime against nature.

Taking advantage of his silence, Edie jumped right to her story. "We talked once, you and I, about having a lousy childhood. You remember that?"

He nodded. And somehow found the wherewithal to finally close his mouth.

"So why was yours so . . . unfulfilling?" she asked. Before he could object to the question, she added, "Hey, if I'm going to spill my guts to you, the least you could do is return the favor."

Okay, so she had a point. Reluctantly, and as quickly as he could, Lucas said, "I grew up on a dairy farm in Wisconsin that never quite turned a profit. Or broke even, for that matter. My father was a dairyman who spent every waking hour trying to eke out a living that never materialized. My mother was an alcoholic who spent every waking hour complaining about her rotten life. She was a mean mom when she was drinking," he said with eloquent understatement, "but my father was never in the house often enough to intercede. One day, when I was eleven, just when I was getting big enough to fight back, she took off and never came back—said she was going to find a man who could afford to keep her. She died three years later—alone—in a Detroit hospital. A few years after that, my father collapsed in one of the barns after a heart attack. The United States government took everything that was left for back taxes. And then my older sister and I pretty much took care of ourselves. Mostly by going hungry in our struggle to survive.

"There," he concluded. "The Lucas Conaway Story, all

nice and neat. Not the greatest Movie of the Week ever made, but, save the absence of a lingering illness or two, not bad. How about yours?"

Edie studied him with much consideration before beginning her own sentimental journey. Finally, she observed, "Interestingly, we seem to have a few things in common. Only it was my father who had the addiction—cocaine, in his case—and walked out on the family. Not that my mother was any prize herself, but she was sober most of the time and had no excuse for her behavior. Then one day, when I was sixteen, she wrapped her Mercedes around a concrete pylon on the expressway, and that was the end of that. It was also the end of the family fortune. After her funeral, I learned that everything was just . . . gone. Most of it, I'm sure, went right up my father's nose. He died of an overdose not long after that."

"So, uh . . . so then what happened?" Lucas asked stupidly.

Edie inhaled deeply and avoided his gaze. "I was supposed to go live with an aunt and uncle who were remarkably like my parents, so I took off," she told him. "It's a long story, but I'll be charitable and give you the condensed version, too. By the time I ran away, I was already a mess. I'd started drinking heavily when I was thirteen or fourteen and was using some pretty serious stuff by the time I turned sixteen. My father's stash was always easy to find. Once I hit the streets, my habit only got worse—and more low class. I pretty much became your garden variety, pathetic little junkie whose sole reason for living was to make that next score."

She paused to take another, less calming, breath. "I, uh . . . I did some things back then, Lucas, that I shouldn't have done. That I wouldn't have done, had I been clean."

Feeling a bit sick to his stomach at hearing such a dark tale about Little Edie Sunshine, Lucas told her, "Edie, if you don't want to talk about this, you don't have—"

"No, I want you to know," she said, snapping her head back up to meet his eyes. "I think it's important that you know." But her gaze wandered from his once more as she continued, "I, um . . . I made a few bucks as a prostitute from time to time. I, uh . . . I broke into people's houses and stole from them. Worse than that, though, as messed up as I was, there are memories of that time that I'll have to carry with me for the rest of my life. And that's a hell of a lot worse than jail. I know. Trust me."

"Edie . . ." he tried again to interject.

But she would have none of it. "You have to understand that people in that kind of situation . . . they aren't thinking straight. They're not thinking at all. They're like animals, driven by instinct—or, at least, driven by their addiction. But I'm not like that anymore," she hastened to add—as if Lucas needed the reassurance. "I haven't been like that for a long time."

He opened his mouth to speak, realized he had no idea what to say, and closed it once again.

"A couple of weeks before my eighteenth birthday," she said softly, still not looking at him, "I got beaten up really bad by a, uh . . . by a *client*," she euphemized. "The cops responding to the call took me to the hospital, and I met a social worker named Alice Donohue there who, God knows why, took a liking to me. She helped me out a lot, Lucas. Got me into some good programs, helped me get straightened out. It wasn't easy for me or her. But Alice stuck with me, so I stuck with me, too."

"Where is she now?" he asked quietly, a bit roughly, still trying to digest all this unpalatable information.

"She, uh . . . she died," Edie said. "A few years ago.

She had breast cancer, and they didn't catch it until it was too late. It wasn't fair," she said a little more softly. "She saved my life, but nobody could save hers." She swallowed with obvious difficulty before adding, "I promised her before she died that I'd—"

When her voice broke off, Lucas encouraged her, "That you'd what?"

"That I'd, um . . . that I'd live a good life for her," Edie concluded quietly. "So that's what I've been trying to do. What I'm going to keep doing. I'm going to live a good life. For Alice. And for me."

Lucas shook his head slowly and wondered what on earth he could possibly say that might brighten her dark memories or lighten her burden. But there were no words that could possibly convey the tumult of emotions tumbling around inside him. He could only imagine the ones that must be tumbling around inside her. The thought that Edie, who was so decent and good and kind, had lived through that kind of hell . . . The knowledge that she had descended to such immeasurable depths, only to rise so high above them . . . The realization that she had witnessed so much badness and darkness and could still cloak herself in so much goodness and light . . .

It took a remarkable person to do that.

And all along, Lucas had been thinking what an easy life she must have had. He'd been convinced she'd never seen the rank underbelly of the beast. He'd been so sure he knew more about the bitterness of life and the grimness of reality than she did. But life didn't have to be bitter, and reality didn't have to be grim. Oh, certainly, it could be and had been for both of them. But Edie had put hers behind her, had risen above it, had gotten on with her life.

Edie, he thought, had dealt with it.

Lucas, however, clearly had not. Oh, he had almost convinced himself that he had. He had been so sure that by winning scholarships to college and achieving academic honors, by writing celebrated stories for a celebrated magazine like *Man's Life*, by geographically distancing himself from the place where he had grown up, by emotionally distancing himself from his sister and what few friends he'd ever had . . . By doing all those things, Lucas had been so sure he was dealing with it. But he still pulled out the distasteful memories of his past and relished their bitterness. He nurtured the wounds and savored the hopelessness, relived the torment and revived the pain.

Hell, he wasn't dealing with it, he thought now. He was succumbing to it. Little by little, a bit more with every passing day. By reliving his past, he prevented himself from enjoying his present. And he certainly kept himself from ever planning for a decent future. He had a long way to go before he could finally say he'd dealt with it. Of course, it would help if he had someone there with him who might show him the way, a person who had traveled the path already and knew what to watch out for. A person who might not mind if, eventually, he took her hand and helped her, too.

Right now, however, he had no idea what to say to that person. So he just remained silent and waited for a cue from her.

"After Alice died," Edie finally went on, "I got it into my head that I wanted to find out where I came from. Where I *really* came from. So I started looking for my biological mother."

"And how's that going?" Lucas asked, grateful for the change of subject, fully aware, however, that what he and Edie had just shared was in no way finished.

"It's going," she told him. "The laws are kind of tricky, and it takes time, but . . ." She shrugged. "I'm hopeful."

So what else is new? he thought.

As grateful as he had been for the change of subject, he was surprised to hear himself pipe up suddenly, "That's why you don't want men touching you, isn't it, Edie? Because you were mistreated so often by your . . . clients."

She seemed as surprised as he—and certainly no more thrilled—by the return to their earlier conversation, but she nodded in agreement. "Among others, yes."

Lucas decided not to ask about those others. Not just because he could, unfortunately, imagine all too well, and not because he didn't want her to relive memories she was clearly unwilling to revisit. But because there was another question he wanted to ask her so much more.

"Edie, will you let me touch you?"

Her eyes flew open wide, darkened by her obvious panic at hearing the question. "No," she told him immediately, adamantly.

He didn't make a move toward her, but he opened his hand, palm up, and began to slowly extend it forward. "Just let me come over there and put my hand in yours, that's all."

She shook her head vehemently enough to send her blond curls flying. "No, Lucas."

"Then let me put my palm over yours."

"No."

"Then fingertip to fingertip."

"No."

"Then—"

"*No.*"

This time he was the one to sigh. "Then will you come over here and touch me?" he asked.

Her eyes seemed to brighten some then, but he saw quickly that it wasn't due to any lightening of her spirit. It was due to the tears that had sprung up out of nowhere. She didn't answer him right away, only continued to gaze at him in silence, her eyes filling deeper and deeper. Then, very slowly, she shook her head again. The motion caused one fat tear to spill over and glide down her cheek, and something inside Lucas twisted tight at seeing it.

"Edie, just touch me," he said softly. "You know I won't hurt you. You *know* that."

"Rationally, I suppose I do know that," she conceded softly. "But it's not my rational mind you have to convince, Lucas. It's the scared, strung-out seventeen-year-old girl who's still living inside me."

"Then bring her out," he said eagerly, "and let me talk to her. Let me touch *her*."

Edie uttered a soft, strangled sound at that. "I wish I could. But she's buried way too deep inside me. You'll never get to her. You'll never convince her."

"The hell she's down deep," Lucas countered. "Edie, she's right there, just below the surface. She's the one who panics every time a man gets near you."

He stood up then, not sure what he planned to do, but unable to sit still any longer. And when he did, the scared seventeen-year-old in Edie reacted, bolting out of her chair, too. Even though Lucas didn't make a single move forward, she strode backward until her fanny made contact with the windowsill. Then she wrapped her arms tightly around herself, as if trying to keep herself from falling apart.

"I won't hurt you, Edie," Lucas said again. "I will never, ever hurt you."

He braved a small step forward and took some comfort

in the fact that she didn't retreat further—not that she had anyplace to go except into the corner, but at least she didn't do that. So he chanced another small step toward her, again with no reaction on Edie's part. She didn't move forward to meet him halfway—or even quarterway—but she didn't withdraw, either.

The third step he took did seem to concern her, though, because as he completed it, her eyes widened a bit in . . . something. He couldn't quite say what. Concerned that she would flee to her room and lock the door, and knowing he was probably pushing his luck, Lucas stole a few more steps toward her, positioning himself between her and escape, until he was close enough to reach out and touch her.

He didn't reach out, though. Because she hastened sideways and crowded herself into the corner created by the window and the wall, cowering in very apparent and very heartbreaking fear.

"I won't take another step forward," Lucas promised her. "But I'm not going to go backward, either."

"Lucas," she said, her voice level and strong, something that heartened him greatly. "I appreciate what you're trying to do, but . . . don't. Okay? Just . . . don't."

"Edie, all you have to do is give me your hand. That's all. Just give me your hand."

She shook her head. "You're asking for too much, Lucas. You might as well be asking for the moon."

"It's next on my wish list," he told her with a tentative smile. "Right after Edie Mulholland's heart."

Edie gazed at Lucas in disbelief, certain she had misunderstood, or, worse, that he was lying to her. But there was something in his eyes as he said what he did, something wistful, something hopeful, something she'd never seen there before. And she had to force herself not to blurt out that he already had her heart. That he'd had it for a long time now, maybe even before that first night, when she'd had to drive him home from Drake's. That he would always have it, because he was the only man she'd ever come close to caring about. The only man she had ever wished she *could* touch. The only man she regretted knowing would never be a part of her life.

She still wasn't sure why she had told him everything she had about her past. For some reason, it had just seemed important that he know. She had no idea why. Really, it wasn't like her history was any of his business. And there was certainly nothing between them that warranted this kind of total, unvarnished honesty. But she had wanted him to know. Maybe because she was tired of him seeing her as Mulholland of Sunnybrook Farm. Or maybe because she was tired of seeing herself that way. Whatever. As difficult and uncomfortable as it had been to revisit all that, she felt strangely good for doing it. Cleaner, somehow. Less tarnished. More human.

And now he told her he wanted her heart. And, oh, how she wished she could give it to him. Totally, freely, without shadows, without pain. She gazed at his outstretched hand, steady, strong, and inviting. Maybe, she thought, just maybe . . .

Before she even realized what she was thinking of doing, Edie found herself lifting her own hand and extending it slowly toward him. Lucas fixed his gaze on the motion, but he didn't move in any way. He didn't reach for her, didn't take a step forward, didn't so much as shift his weight in her direction. So, feeling a little more confident, Edie opened her palm and held it out a bit farther. Her fingers trembled, but she didn't pull back, only focused all her concentration on what she was trying to do, what she *wanted* to do. She forced her feet to join in the overture, shuffling them forward, but still Lucas remained pinned to the spot. When she glanced up at his face, she found him gazing not at her hand anymore, but at her face, her eyes, her mouth. Another step forward brought her body within inches of his, yet still he made no move to intercept her.

So Edie lifted her hand a bit more, not toward his hand, but toward his face, toward his mouth. Very, very carefully, she moved her fingers to his lips. For a moment, she couldn't quite bring herself to make that final contact, couldn't quite cover that last, infinitesimal bit of space. Lucas's lips parted fractionally, his warm breath dancing over her fingers, stirring a desire deep inside her unlike anything she'd felt before.

"Touch me, Edie," he said softly, and the words seemed to wrap themselves around her fingertips, drawing them closer, closer, closer still.

And then suddenly she *was* touching him, brushing those same fingertips over the velvety warmth of his mouth, grazing first his lower lip and then his upper lip, over and over and over again, because she'd never felt anything so soft, so warm, so vital in her life. His eyes fluttered closed as her caresses multiplied, and he sighed softly, the sound nuzzling her palm and purling through her body like a languid summer breeze.

Oh . . . Oh, that felt so good . . .

Her heart hammering hard in her chest, Edie dragged her fingers slowly, gently, from his smooth lower lip to his rough jaw, over the hollow of his cheek, along the high ridge of his cheekbone. Gingerly, she threaded her fingers through the silky hair at his temple, skimmed them across his forehead, over his eyebrow, then traced the elegant line of his nose. But always her fingers returned to his mouth, as if captivated by that feature more than any other.

And Lucas, dear Lucas, stood motionless through it all, save the quick rise and fall of his chest as his respiration grew almost frantic. He let Edie move at her own pace, in her own time, to whatever she wanted to explore next. And Edie realized quickly that she did indeed want to explore more. Not tonight. Not tomorrow. Maybe not even next week. But she did want to know more of Lucas. She wanted to know all of him. She just hoped he could be patient with her. She hoped he would think she was worth the wait.

"I'll wait as long as it takes, Edie," he said softly, clearly reading her thoughts from her expression. "We'll do this your way. However you want. For however long it takes. Just promise me you'll give it a chance."

She nodded as she ran a finger gently over his chin, then down the strong column of his throat. "I promise, Lucas," she told him softly. "I promise."

By the time Lucas left Edie's apartment, he was feeling bewitched, bothered and bewildered, dazed, dazzled and delighted. Not just because of the way she'd touched him, but because of the way she'd opened up to him, too. Because of the way he'd opened up to her. They'd talked for a long time—he sitting on the futon, she perched in the rocker—about everything they had in common and everything they didn't, everything they wanted for the future and everything they didn't.

Then, just before they'd said good-bye, Edie had let Lucas touch her, too. And as he'd slowly, carefully, skimmed his thumb over her warm palm, as he'd felt her pulse beneath his fingertips leap and dance, he'd been stunned to discover that he would wait forever for Edie

Mulholland, if that was how long it took. Judging by the look on her face when he'd told her good night, however, it wasn't going to take forever.

He smiled as he exited her building and headed to his car, parked across the street. And it was only by sheer accident that he glanced toward the corner and saw a figure lurking in the shadows. In the quick glimpse he managed to complete before the figure dissolved into darkness, Lucas formed a hasty impression of a man—a man who was gazing up at Edie Mulholland's windows. With a brief glance over his shoulder, he saw her silhou-etted behind the lace curtains, and somehow, he knew— he just *knew*—that whoever was lurking across the street was there because of Edie.

Whistling under his breath, Lucas did his best to look like he was just moseying on over to his car to head home and had no idea that some sleazy sonofabitch stalker was creeping around not fifteen feet away from where it was parked. But instead of reaching for the driver's side door handle, he bolted for the shadow into which he'd last seen the figure merge. And then, suddenly, almost as if he had fallen into a dream, he was chasing a man down the street.

A surprisingly well-dressed man, he realized when he caught up with him and grabbed a fistful of very fine gabardine wool. A man he recognized, he realized fur-ther, as he jerked viciously on that fine wool and pulled the man backward, then slammed him maliciously up against a brick wall. A man he shouldn't be at all sur-prised to see here, he realized even further, as he thrust his forearm against the guy's throat. Hard.

"Davenport," he muttered scornfully. It figured he'd be the sleazy sonofabitch who was stalking Edie. Unable to keep that particular observation to himself, Lucas added, "You sleazy, sonofabitch stalker. Who the hell do you think you are?"

"I'm not a stalker," Davenport denied as he tried to free himself from Lucas's brutal grip. Just to show him what for, however, Lucas shoved him more sternly up against the wall. The other man grimaced when his head made contact with the brick.

"You were the one following Edie after Adam's party that night, weren't you?" Lucas demanded, the memory still much too fresh in his brain for his comfort.

Davenport tried to wrench free the forearm pressed to his throat, but Lucas had rage on his side and barely felt the gesture. "Yes," the other man finally gasped. "That was me."

"And now here you are, hanging around her place," Lucas charged, pushing his arm even more firmly against the other man's throat.

"Conaway, please," Davenport ground out. "Let me explain. I'm not stalking her."

"You follow her around in the middle of the night," Lucas pointed out, "and you stand outside her apartment, looking up at her windows. What does that make you, if not a sleazy"—he shoved Davenport back against the wall—"sonofabitch"—he shoved again, harder—"stalker?" He punctuated the question with a few more shoves.

But Davenport regrouped pretty well. "It makes me somebody who wants to be sure she's safe," he said through gritted teeth. "She wasn't at work today. I wanted to make sure she was all right."

"You wanna take care of the girl, right?" Lucas spat sarcastically.

Davenport nodded.

"You wanna be Edie's sugar daddy, you sonofabitch?" Lucas taunted.

This time, Davenport shook his head. "No. Just . . . just her daddy."

Lucas narrowed his eyes at the man. "What the hell are you talking about?"

"I'm not a stalker," Davenport said for a third time. "I'm Edie's father. Her biological father."

"I was twenty-two when I met your mother, Edie. And she was eighteen."

Lucas listened grudgingly as Davenport spoke, and watched even more grudgingly as Edie pressed a cup of freshly brewed coffee into the other man's hand—without quite making physical contact. Then she retreated to the rocking chair she had occupied before. She was still wearing her robe, her hair still tumbled freely about her shoulders, and she still wore the expression of utter bewilderment that had appeared on her face when she'd opened her front door fifteen minutes ago to find Lucas holding Davenport by the scruff of his neck.

In spite of all that, she seemed like a stranger somehow. There was a desperation about her that Lucas had never seen before, a yearning that went way beyond wishfulness. She'd barely looked at him since he'd come in with Davenport, so fixed had her attention been on the other man after Lucas had shoved him inside and recounted what had happened on the street below, echoing the words that Davenport had uttered. She wanted those words to be true with all her heart, he could see. She wanted more than anything for this man to be her link to the past, her hope for the future. But something inside her wouldn't quite allow that leap just yet.

Her father, Lucas marveled yet again. Unbelievable.

"Go on," Edie murmured from the other side of the room, her voice so soft, so weary, Lucas almost didn't hear her.

Davenport obviously did, however, because he glanced up when she spoke, even if he didn't follow her instruction. Instead of speaking, he curled his fingers more resolutely around his coffee cup and studied her carefully from his place on the futon. Lucas stood midway between the two of them, his shoulders braced against the wall, the rest of his body poised for attack, though why he should feel something like that might be necessary, he couldn't imagine. Not that he didn't trust Davenport, but . . . He really didn't trust Davenport. Not yet, anyway. And he sure as hell didn't want to see Edie get hurt again.

Edie, too, seemed unwilling to surrender her misgivings just yet. Because she didn't smile as she spurred him, "Mr. Davenport?"

He closed his eyes at the formal address, as if he were in no way comfortable with it. Still, what was she supposed to call him, "Daddy"? Even if it were true, that somehow seemed even less appropriate than "Mr. Davenport."

The other man opened his eyes, met her gaze, inhaled a deep breath, and began to recount his story once again. "As I said, we were both young. I'd just graduated from Stanford and was spending the summer with my parents in Chicago before returning to California for graduate school. Your mother was working in one of the department stores downtown. She'd come up from her hometown in Kentucky to look for work, because her family was large and poor and she wanted to help out." He smiled briefly. "I was enchanted from the moment she said, 'May I help you?' She had a charming voice, a beautiful smile . . . She was just a lovely girl all around."

"What was her name?" Edie asked a bit roughly.

"Melody," he said with a sad smile. His blue eyes, too, took on a melancholy cast. "Melody Chance. I loved her name. I loved her smile. I loved everything about her."

"So what happened?" This time, it was Lucas who voiced the question.

Davenport sighed heavily again as he set his untasted coffee on the steamer trunk and dragged a hand through his black hair. "I wasn't exactly engaged when I met your mother," he said to Edie, "but there was an understanding between my family and my wife's family that Lucinda and I would be married after we finished college. And she and I wanted to be married," he added readily. "We'd known each other since childhood, and we were very much in love. But Lucinda was in Europe that summer, touring with her grandmother and great-aunt, and I just . . . I don't know. I suppose I didn't see the harm in spending the time with someone else. I thought Melody would be a nice summer diversion. I had no idea I would fall in love with her, too. I know that sounds terrible, but I truly was just a boy. A selfish boy, to be sure, but . . ."

"And you got her pregnant," Edie said, stating the obvious.

Davenport nodded. "Yes. But I didn't know about it. Melody never told me she was expecting. Apparently, she didn't know it herself until after she returned home. But as summer came to an end, as it came closer to time for me to return to Stanford, she told me she wanted to return to Kentucky. That she missed her family, that Chicago was much too big a place for her to live, that she would rather look for work closer to home. I objected, told her I'd take care of her if she stayed, but she was adamant."

He expelled another ragged breath. "I was young," he

repeated. "Torn between my obligation to and love for Lucinda, and my love for Melody. I knew my family would never forgive me if I didn't go back to school. And I knew I'd be a social pariah if I didn't marry Lucinda, as had always been assumed. But had I known Melody was pregnant . . ."

He stood suddenly, and Lucas jerked away from the wall, ready to . . . Something. But all Davenport did was pace restlessly to the opposite side of the room, so Lucas relaxed and went back to merely being suspicious. Interestingly, though, his suspicion wasn't quite as overwhelming as it had been fifteen minutes ago. Maybe it was just his imagination, but when he gazed at Edie and Davenport in profile, he did detect a certain resemblance between the two. And the other man seemed so genuinely earnest in his explanation. It was hard to stay distrustful of someone who seemed so utterly distraught.

"So where is my mother now?" Edie asked. Her voice was a little stronger now, her doubt, like Lucas's clearly wavering toward belief.

Her question brought Davenport around in a quick pivot, his lips parted as if he intended to speak. But no words emerged.

"Mr. Davenport?" she asked again.

"Look, I know it's inappropriate to ask you to call me 'Dad,' but this 'Mr. Davenport' business really does have to go." He threw her a halfhearted smile. "My first name is Russell. You could call me that, if nothing else."

But instead of addressing him thus, Edie repeated, "Where's my mother?"

Russell Davenport's smile fell. "She died last year, Edie. I'm sorry."

Edie offered no reaction whatever to the revelation,

Lucas noted, only continued to gaze at Davenport in that even, almost unreal, manner.

"She had an inoperable brain tumor," he continued. "The doctors discovered it just two months before she died. It took her six weeks following the diagnosis to find me, and tell me about you. Had she not, I never would have known about you. I never would have found you. But she didn't want to die without giving me the knowledge of my daughter. And I will always be grateful to her for that."

"She's dead?" Edie finally echoed.

The other man nodded. "I'm afraid so. I'm sorry."

Davenport continued with his story after that, but Lucas could see that Edie was only half-listening. So he paid attention himself, certain she'd want to go over the details again later, when she was feeling less . . . Whatever it was she was feeling at the moment. Frankly, he couldn't imagine.

So he listened intently as Davenport described his bittersweet reunion with Melody Chance, and about how he hired a private investigator to find the child he didn't know he had, and about how, nearly a year later, the investigator found Edie tending bar at Drake's, not six blocks from where Russell Davenport worked. Shortly afterward, Davenport had applied for membership to the club, and had started rehearsing his speech for announcing his paternity. But he'd never quite been able to bring himself to make that announcement. He'd been fearful of how his wife and children would react, but worse, he'd been afraid Edie would reject him.

"Reject you?" she said with a gasp when he put voice to the statement, clearly fully focused now on what he was saying. "Why on earth would I reject you?"

"I don't know," Davenport said. "But I was afraid if I told you who I was you'd . . ."

"What?"

"You'd see me as an intruder. Someone who wanted to compromise all the fond memories you had of your childhood and the adoptive parents who raised you. I didn't want you to think I was trying to usurp their roles in your happiness."

She expelled a soft sound of disbelief. But all she said was, "That's not going to happen."

Russell Davenport said nothing for a moment, only gazed upon his daughter with very clear affection. Finally, quietly, he told her, "I have no idea how this is going to play out, Edie. I won't promise you that it will be easy, once I tell my family about you. But I will do whatever it takes to make clear my obligation to you. My responsibility for you. My . . . my love . . . for you."

Edie's lips parted fractionally, and she turned her gaze up to the ceiling in an effort to halt the tears Lucas saw forming there. To no avail. Because the moment she returned her gaze to her father, those tears tumbled unhindered over her cheeks. Still, she said nothing. Not that there was really anything that needed to be said.

"For what it's worth," Russell Davenport continued softly, "my daughter, Sarah, who's only three years younger than you, always wanted a sister, to even the odds with her two brothers."

Edie expelled that odd little incredulous sound again, but this time it wasn't quite as choked as it had been before. "A sister," she repeated. "And two brothers. I've never had any of those."

"It's a good family, Edie," Russell told her. "In the long run, I'm confident everything will be fine. The Davenports stick together. They always have. They always will. Family comes first. In whatever form."

"Family," she echoed softly. But this time she looked at Lucas instead of her father when she spoke. "I never truly thought I would find one of those. Funny how it just came out of nowhere like that."

"Everything will be fine, Edie," Russell said, "you'll see."

She nodded at his assurance, but continued to look at Lucas as she spoke. "You know, funnily enough, I think it will be."

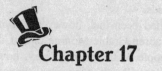

Chapter 17

The media fallout that followed Lauren Grable-Monroe's public outing was nothing short of atomic. Dorsey had concluded that almost three weeks ago on Christmas Day, a Christmas day utterly lacking in gifts, because whenever she or Charlotta had tried to go out of their house, they'd been ambushed by reporters and photographers and talk show host representatives who were intent on roasting something other than chestnuts on an open fire. As a result, there had been little comfort or joy in the MacGuinness household over the holiday season.

Everyone and his—or her—mother had wanted a piece of Dorsey MacGuinness, the sociologist formerly known as Lauren Grable-Monroe. She had been both embraced and reviled, had received both invitations and condemnations. The public reaction had run the gamut. There had been the Hollywood managers and literary agents who wanted to rep her and the conservative newspaper

columnists and politically correct public figures who
wanted to rip her to shreds.

Not all of the news had been bad, however. *People*
magazine had dubbed Lauren Grable-Monroe one of its
Fifty Most Beautiful People of the year. Dorsey, how-
ever, hadn't made the cut. Shortly thereafter, though,
Howard Stern's people had called to specifically invite
Dorsey MacGuinness, sociologist, to come on his show.
Unfortunately, it had only been to remove her shirt.

Dorsey had tactfully declined.

Then *Playboy* had called to invite Dorsey or Lauren—
they weren't particular—to make an appearance. But
they'd wanted her—them—to remove considerably more
than her—their—shirt, or shirts. They'd promised, however, that the photo spread—a term that had made Dorsey
wince—would, of course, be tastefully executed.

Dorsey had tactfully declined.

Then Victoria's Secret had asked them to promote two
of their new bras—Lauren the one called "Tycoon Trappings," a skimpy concoction of black lace and jet beads,
and Dorsey the one called "Social Awareness," a decidedly more modest number. A more modest, *plaid* number. A more modest, plaid *flannel* number.

Dorsey had tactfully declined.

In fact, Dorsey had declined every offer that had come
for her *or* Lauren. Even Anita's encouragements and
Rockcastle's threats would not make her budge. She was
finished with being Lauren Grable-Monroe, finished with
being a cultural icon, finished with being a media magnet.
She wanted an end to the whole fiasco, wanted her life
to revert to normal, wanted the world to go away. She
wanted to forget every last thing about this miserable
chapter of her miserable life.

Well, almost every last thing.

Adam Darien, of course, she would never, could never forget, even if she hadn't seen or spoken to him since that fateful night at Drake's. She'd attempted, without success, to reach him on a number of occasions, only to be told he was unavailable and no, there was no message, she'd just try again later. He'd made no overture to get in touch with her at all. She figured it was pointless to ever hope that the two of them might work things out.

How were they supposed to work things out together when they couldn't even *get* together? And how could they get together when Dorsey's life had become The Truman Show II? It wasn't exactly surprising that Adam had avoided her so steadfastly. What man in his right mind would want to thrust himself into the middle of a media circus? Even under the best of circumstances, they had a lot to work through. But throw in the fact that her life was overrun by chaos these days, and it made the situation pretty near impossible.

For the past month, Dorsey had resisted making any kind of public statement, hoping that if she ignored the media machine, it would eventually run out of fuel and stop working. At first, the reporters and photographers outside her house had multiplied like mold on stinky old cheese. Now, however, it was mid-January, and the media circus, having the attention span of a soap-on-a-rope, was finally starting to break up and leave town. Only a few of the most dedicated members remained, and even they seemed to be asking their questions with considerably less energy than before.

But still, she'd neither seen nor heard anything of Adam. And still she missed him terribly. She missed his rough laughter, his reluctant smiles, his skewed views. She missed the feel of his big body spooned against hers in bed, the sensation of his mouth consuming hers when he kissed her, the heat and friction the two of them generated as lovers. She missed his strength, his irascibility, his challenge.

She missed *him*. And she wanted him. And she needed him, too.

It was so ironic. When she'd had Adam, Dorsey hadn't had time to devote to a relationship, because she'd been too busy trying to be three different people. Now that she didn't have him anymore, she had nothing but time on her hands.

Even Severn College had called her at home just yesterday, two days before the start of the spring semester, to tell Dorsey that—surprise, surprise—they suddenly seemed to have a mysterious surplus of teaching assistants for the spring semester and, so sorry, they were just going to have to take her off the schedule, and could she please come in tomorrow and clean out her study carrel, because they needed it for one of the other TAs?

Oh, of *course*, she could still complete her work on her doctorate, they had assured her. But could she please do it in the library instead of the sociology department, because the media circus was such a disruption, and no one was taking the college seriously while she was working there, but no, of *course* that hadn't had anything to do with why they were letting her go, that was due to the aforementioned sudden—and very mysterious—surplus of TAs. And did they mention that they needed her to come right away and clean out her study carrel so that it would be available for one of the other TAs? Yes, tomorrow would be fine.

Which was how Dorsey came to be spending her Sunday alone, in her soon to be ex-study carrel in the otherwise deserted sociology department, stowing in a cardboard box what few things had fitted inside the tiny space to begin with. Her photo of Ghandi, her desktop gargoyle, her coffee mug that read "Yes, but not the inclination," and a couple of yellowed Calvin and Hobbes and Shoe cartoons she'd taped to the wall alongside her postcard of Marlon Brando as Johnny in *The Wild One*. All went into the box along with pencils, pens, textbooks, and software.

She barely heard the sound of footsteps scraping along the linoleum outside until they were right in front of the carrel door. Dorsey glanced up at the soft sound and suddenly found herself standing face to face—or, more correctly, face to chest—with Adam Darien.

He was leaning casually against the doorjamb, gazing at her with an expression that was utterly inscrutable, his brown eyes framed by pale shadows, his mouth bracketed by faint lines. His leather bomber jacket hung open over a bulky, oatmeal-colored sweater and blue jeans and was decorated on each shoulder by epaulettes of quickly melting snow. His dark hair was dusted with glistening little droplets of moisture, his cheeks were ruddy from the cold day outside, and she wanted more than anything in the world to hurl herself into his arms and kiss him and kiss him and kiss him.

Unable to help herself, she glanced down at her grubby jeans and the plaid flannel shirt buttoned halfway up over a thermal-knit Henley. Her hand flew up to smooth ineffectually over the loose ponytail fixed haphazardly at the crown of her head, but she knew no amount of hasty rearranging would help the errant curls that had spilled out to frame her face. She wore no makeup, no jewelry, had been lucky she remembered to brush her teeth that morning. All in all, this wasn't the way she'd hoped to look when she saw Adam again. She'd rather hoped she would look more like...like...Well, like Lauren Grable-Monroe.

Dammit.

"Hi," she said softly, unsure when she'd even decided to speak.

"Hi," he replied just as quietly, just as uncertainly.

She had no idea why he would come here looking for her. Unless it was to further her humiliation, which she couldn't possibly see being made any worse than it already had been over the last month—unless, of course, Adam Darien showed up.

He pointed to the little plastic sign affixed to the exterior of her carrel, the one that read DORSEY MACGUINNESS, TA "Do I want to know what this T and A stand for?" he asked, the ghost of a smile playing about his mouth.

She expelled a sound that was a mixture of relief and disbelief because he didn't seem to want to strangle her. He didn't seem to want to humiliate her. He didn't seem to want to condemn her. What he seemed like he wanted to do was...

Oh, boy. Maybe there was a chance for them yet.

"It stands for Truly Abominable," she told him breathlessly as, in one swift move, she lunged forward to withdraw the name plate from its metal holder. "That describes my behavior of the last few months quite well, I think," she added as she returned to her original position and tossed the nameplate into the box with her other things. She didn't want to leave it behind, after all. It was the only thing she had left that proved she had ever been a teacher in the first place.

Adam inhaled a deep breath and released it slowly, his gaze never wavering from hers. "Why didn't you tell me?" he asked simply—not that the question required any kind of embellishment.

She opened her mouth to answer him, realized she had no idea how to do that, then closed it again.

Before she realized his intention, he pushed himself away from the carrel door and entered the tiny space, a pretty impressive accomplishment, seeing as how Dorsey herself barely fitted inside the cubicle. Then, even more impressive, he nudged the door closed behind him. He leaned one hip against the counter that had housed her laptop and lamp before she'd put them into the box on the floor, crossed his arms over his chest in a way that looked suspiciously like self-preservation, and continued to study her face.

And just like that, the temperature in the tiny room skyrocketed. Outside Severn College, it might be a cold and snowy morning. But inside the carrel, at that moment, it was a torrid, volcanic afternoon. And she couldn't help thinking then that they were both frightfully overdressed.

Of course, she was probably getting way ahead of herself there.

"Is it hot in here?" Adam asked suddenly.

Then again . . .

He shrugged off his coat and tossed it onto the swivel chair that Dorsey had relegated to the corner—about two inches away. Then he pushed up the sleeves of his sweater, ran both hands briskly through his damp hair, and leaned back against the counter again. And he continued to watch her guardedly.

"Why did you come here?" she asked.

"Because your mother told me I'd find you here."

"You spoke to Carlotta?"

He nodded. "I went to your house first, and she told

me you were here"—he nodded toward the half-full box—"cleaning out your stuff. Ghandi?" he asked before she could comment, noting the framed photograph.

She nodded. "I'm a big fan of passive resistance."

"Is that why you haven't tried to see me?"

She gaped at him. "I tried to call you. You were never in. I just assumed *you* didn't want to see *me*."

"I wanted to see you," he assured her immediately. "But I figured with all the stuff going on in your life in the aftermath of Lauren Grable-Monroe, the last thing you needed was to have me there complicating things. I wanted to give you—both of us—a little time to let things blow over."

She gazed at him with hungry melancholy, wishing she could put words to how very much she had needed him over the last few weeks. Instead, she only told him, "You wouldn't have complicated anything, Adam. I could have used you."

He gazed back at her in silence for a long time, and she wished she could tell what he was thinking. "And did you?" he finally asked. "Use me, I mean?"

She shook her head. "No. Never. Lindy was totally wrong about that. About all of it."

He sighed heavily. "It really pissed her off that she couldn't have you arrested or sue you for anything."

Dorsey wasn't sure she would ever stop looking over her shoulder where Lindy was concerned. Feigning nonchalance, she said, "Did Lindy, uh . . . did she ever say anything about, oh . . . hiring some guys named Vito and Sal to come, gee, I don't know . . . break my legs?"

He chuckled. "Actually, I did hear her on the phone talking to someone name Vinnie who owed her a favor, but . . ."

"What?" Dorsey asked, alarmed.

"Turned out she was just lining him up to do a little landscaping for her."

"Oh."

There was another long, taut moment of silence, then, "Why didn't you tell me?" he asked again. "I mean . . . I thought we were friends, Mack," he added softly. "Hell, we were a lot more than friends. Why didn't you just tell me the truth?"

"I tried to," she said. "I really did. But every time I started to say something, I just . . ."

"What?"

Dorsey sighed. "A picture would pop into my head that was so clear and so scary that it kept me from saying a word."

"A picture of what?"

This time she was the one to study his face, the face she had missed so much over the last several weeks. "I kept seeing you," she told him. "Looking at me the way you're looking at me right now. And I just couldn't bring myself to tell you the truth, because I couldn't stand the thought of you looking at me that way. And now it's not a thought, it's a reality, and you're looking at me that way anyhow, and I . . . I can't stand it, Adam." She curled her fingers into impotent fists at her side. "I hate it that you hate me, and I don't know what to say or do that would put things back to rights."

"Oh, Mack . . ." He reached for her then, pulling her close, folding his arms over her shoulders. "I don't hate you," he assured her. "I could never . . ."

With a soft growl of frustration, he cupped one hand over the nape of her neck, skimmed the other up and down along the soft fabric of her sleeve. He tucked her head beneath his chin and just held her, and Dorsey couldn't believe she had actually forgotten how good it felt to be this close to him. As miserable as she'd been during the last month, she hadn't honestly realized until now all that she had been missing. Because finding herself back in Adam's arms was like living out every fantasy she'd ever had. The scent of him surrounded her, his heat mingled with her own, and his nearness set her heart to racing like a thoroughbred. Never in her life had she imagined anyplace could feel as perfect—as right— as this.

"I've spent the last month trying to figure out what I'm feeling," Adam told her, "and the only feeling I've managed to identify is confusion. You're not who I thought you were. You're not the Mack I came to know and lo—" He halted abruptly, then hastily continued, "And you're certainly not Lauren Grable-Monroe. I thought I knew you so well. And it turns out I don't know who you are at all."

She looped one arm loosely around his waist, then opened her other hand over his chest. And she found some small measure of encouragement in the way his heart was hammering hard beneath her fingertips. "I'm Dorsey," she said softly. "That's who I've been all along. It's all I've ever wanted to be. To anybody."

"Dorsey," he echoed. But he said nothing more, only pulled his head back to look down at her, arching an eyebrow in idle speculation as he studied her face.

"I don't expect you to understand," she told him. "I'm not sure I completely understand myself. But . . . I'm not just Mack. Mack is in there, certainly, and so, I guess, is Lauren Grable-Monroe. But they're both only a part of who I really am. Nobody seems to realize that except me. I'm not sure I even realized it myself until just recently."

Adam gazed at her in thoughtful silence for another long moment, taking in her hair, her eyes, her mouth . . .

and then some. Finally, with a very wicked smile, he said, "Then maybe I need to get to know you—all of you—better."

And before Dorsey—or anybody—could say another word, he lowered his head and covered her mouth with his.

It was *such* a pleasant kiss. Nothing ravenous, nothing demanding, nothing intense, just . . . pleasantness. Tenderness. Entreaty. He plied her lips slowly, softly, gently with his again and again and again. And Dorsey succumbed gladly, entirely, melting against him as if it was where she was meant to be. It *was* where she was meant to be. And it was where she wanted to stay. Forever.

She pushed herself up on tiptoe and roped her arms around his neck, threading the fingers of one hand through his hair, curling the others around his nape. And as she kissed him back, she tasted faint hints of coffee and mint toothpaste and something else . . . something less tangible . . . something less distinct . . .

A promise. She tasted a promise in him. Or perhaps it was in her. In either case, she knew then that everything would work out between them. What they had created together, what they had grown and nurtured during the weeks they'd been together, what they were stirring to life once again . . . It was going to be all right, she told herself. All of it. All of her. All of them.

Adam pulled his head back from hers then, but only far enough so that he could gaze down into her eyes. "I've missed you . . . Dorsey," he said, smiling as he tripped over her name. "That's going to take some getting used to," he added with a chuckle, a flash of merriment brightening his eyes. "But I have missed you. All of you. And I'll do whatever I have to do to get every last one of you back."

He'd do whatever he had to do? Dorsey marveled. Good heavens. All *he* had to do was . . . well . . . say something along the lines of what he'd just said. That and—

"Forgive me," she told him. "If you can do that, then—"

"Done," he replied readily. "Just promise me we will be nothing but honest with each other in the future."

"I promise," she vowed.

"Me, too," he told her. "I should start off by telling you very honestly that I love you. In all your incarnations."

She uttered a nervous chuckle. "Even Lauren?" she asked.

He nodded. "She's a witty dame, and she looks great in a short skirt."

Dorsey laughed. "Better than Mack in a necktie?"

He narrowed his eyes in thought. "Hmm . . . That depends."

"On what?"

"On whether Mack is wearing just a necktie."

Dorsey feigned shock. "You wicked, wicked man."

He grinned, wickedly if she did say so herself. "Hey, baby, you ain't seen nothin' yet," he murmured as he pulled her close again.

It shouldn't be this easy, she thought. After the month she'd spent struggling to keep her life together, finding her way back to Adam should be like hacking a path through the Amazon rain forest at the height of the wet season. With a butter knife. Blindfolded and barefoot. With piranhas nipping at her heels. And a side of bloody beef tied around her neck.

But this . . .

"Actually," he said as he nuzzled the very sensitive

spot just below her ear, "there is one more thing I require of you."

Naturally, she thought. "You want me to get on my knees and beg for you," she guessed.

He pulled back again, arching a dark brow in thoughtful speculation. "Gee, I hadn't thought about that, but now that you mention it . . ."

"Adam . . ."

"Well, maybe later," he relented. "For now, I just require that you tell me how you feel. About me. Honestly, I mean."

His uncertainty was evident in the way he was looking at her, and Dorsey couldn't believe that he would still harbor some doubt about her feelings for him. Oh, well. She would just have to spend the rest of her life showing him *exactly* how she felt. In as many ways as possible. In each and every one of her incarnations. Mack would love him like a cherished friend and confidante. Lauren would love him like a passionate and eager mistress. And Dorsey would love him . . . well, she would love him totally. Irrevocably. Eternally.

And she summed it all up in three little words. "I love you," she told him simply. "There. That was honest."

"It was also," he told her, "very arousing."

Actually, Dorsey had already guessed that, because his arousal was palpable—mostly against her thigh.

"So," he piped up brightly when he realized that she had recognized his . . . palpableness. "Where do we go from here?"

"Well, since Carlotta's home today, I guess there's always your place," she suggested.

He smiled. "We'll get to that soon enough," he promised. "What I actually meant was, where do *you* go from here?"

"Oh." She sighed, hoping her disappointment wasn't too terribly obvious. For now, she contented herself—pretty much—with snuggling more resolutely against him. "Well, Severn has made it clear that there won't be a job for me here. Not in the sociology department, at any rate. They might have something opening up in janitorial soon, but . . ." She tried to chuckle, didn't quite manage it, and so shut up.

"You don't think you might find something with one of the other colleges or universities?" he asked. "There are an awful lot in the area."

"Actually," she told him, "I've already received quite a few offers of employment to teach, both here and out of state."

He pulled back to look at her again, his expression sober. Very sober. "Out of state?" he asked. "You mean, like . . . Indiana?"

She shook her head. "I mean like New England."

"New England?"

She nodded. "Some of the positions even come with tenure."

"New *England*?"

"And good pay."

"*New England*?"

"But they're all positions teaching popular culture or media studies," she finally revealed with a grin of her own, putting him out of his misery. His answering smile was tinged with more than a little relief. "And I don't want to teach those things," she added unnecessarily. She snuggled close to him again. "Frankly, I've had it with popular culture. Not to mention the media. I want to teach, yes, but I want to teach sociology. Nobody seems to think I'll be able to do that with any sort of academic effectiveness. They really can't seem to separate me from

Lauren. I don't know what I'm going to do for a job."

"Why don't you write?" he asked.

She groaned. "Oh, please, Adam, that's what got me into trouble in the first place."

"Yeah, but that's because you were trying to keep Lauren separate from Dorsey and you had to use deceptive practices to do it. Now that everybody knows Lauren Grable-Monroe is really Dorsey MacGuinness, you could write as yourself."

"But write what?"

He pulled back again, and she tipped her head back to meet his gaze. "How about publishing your dissertation?" he said.

She laughed. "Yeah, right. Nobody wants to read a scholarly, sociological treatise on stuffy old-boy men's clubs as microcosms for a male-dominated society."

"They would if you rewrote it and threw in some potboiling sensationalism and gave it a catchy title like *Bottoms Up: My Secret Life as a High Society Serving Wench.*"

"Oh, no you don't," she said. "I don't want Lindy Aubrey hiring those guys from the South Side, no way."

"As long as you don't identify anybody by name . . ."

"No," she said adamantly.

"You can still write about sociology," Adam said. "Just dress it up as popular nonfiction the way you did with *How to Trap a Tycoon.*"

"But—"

"And you could still teach, too," he added enthusiastically, "in a manner of speaking. You could make public appearances the same way Lauren did."

"That wasn't teaching," she pointed out.

"The hell it wasn't," Adam countered. "I saw you in action as Lauren, remember. If she wasn't up there on that stage at Northwestern giving a sociology lecture, then I don't know what she *was* doing."

"Yeah, but, Adam—"

"And you'll never convince me that a part of you didn't like being Lauren," he barreled on. "Because you were too good at it, too convincing. And that could only be because you tapped into something inside you that had been there all along."

"Maybe," she conceded. "But still—"

"And there was something of Mack in all this Lauren business, too," he added further. "There was more than a little bartender advice and wisdom in that book and those talks."

She eyed him suspiciously. "How do you know it was in the book?"

He grinned crookedly. "I read it," he confessed with a shrug. "I thought it was really good, too. You have an interesting way of looking at the world, Dorsey, not to mention a very sharp wit. Oh, and I intend for us to get around to that crème de menthe thing very soon."

Dorsey had never thought of Lauren the way Adam had just presented her, but a lot of what he had just said made a strange sort of sense. As often as she had complained about Lauren, there had been times when she had genuinely enjoyed herself in that guise. Lauren was saucy and sassy in a way that Dorsey had never felt she should be for fear of not being taken seriously. And Mack, too, had been different from Dorsey—more social, more outgoing, more comfortable with strangers. She'd never allowed that side of herself to emerge fully, because it hadn't seemed scholarly. But mix it all up and stir it together, and what resulted was, well . . . Dorsey, she supposed.

Her head was starting to hurt with all the self-analysis

and self-discovery, and she really didn't want to think about all this right now. Not when she had Adam back in her arms. Not when she could make plans—real plans—for the first time where he was concerned. Not when something seemed to be going right after so much had gone wrong.

"Over the last several weeks," Adam continued, oblivious to her focus on *them* instead of *her*, "you've only seen the media as some vicious, hungry beast. But I think maybe what you need to do, career-wise, is approach the media from a different angle. Or maybe," he said further, with a cryptic little smile, "the media needs to approach you."

She eyed him curiously. "What do you mean?"

He studied her with much interest for a moment, as if he was mulling over something of grave importance. Then, very thoughtfully, he said, "Dorsey MacGuinness, I'm going to make you—all of you—an offer that none of you can refuse."

She arched an eyebrow. "Oh?"

He nodded. "Later. Right now, I have a much more important question to ask."

"What's that?"

He grinned *very* suggestively. "Is it true that these study carrels are soundproof?"

She grinned back. "No, I'm afraid not."

"Mm," he replied, clearly unhappy with her response.

"Why do you ask?" she said, already knowing the answer.

"Well, I couldn't help but notice that you're not wearing any shoes."

Okay, so maybe she didn't know the answer, after all. "My, uh . . . my boots were soaked by the time I got here. I set them over by the radiator to dry out." Then, because she couldn't stand it, she asked further, "Why do you ask?"

Instead of answering, though, Adam continued to look thoughtful and posed another question of his own. "Well, if the study carrels aren't soundproof, do they at least have locks on the doors?"

"Noooo," she told him, still not quite certain where he was going with this line of questioning.

"Will that counter hold both our weight?"

Oooh. Okay. Now she knew where he was going. Boy, 'bout time, too. But she replied, with much regret, "Probably not."

Clearly undeterred, Adam asked, point-blank, "Ever made love in one of these things?"

"Um . . . not yet."

"Feel like conducting an experiment?"

"Only if it's for the furthering of my education."

He chuckled. "Oh, Dorsey, the things we can teach each other."

Her laughter joined his. "So what are you waiting for?"

Nothing, as became evident immediately. Because before Dorsey had even completed the question, Adam was tucking her right back into his embrace and lowering his head to hers. This time his kisses were less leisurely than before. This time there *was* hunger, demand and intensity. This time, there would be no retreat for conversation. This time, they would brand each other for life.

Life, Dorsey echoed faintly to herself as she got more and more lost in his kiss. She could hardly wait for that life to begin. Then Adam deepened his kiss even more, tasted her to the very depths of her soul, and she thought, *Um, yeah, okay, I guess I can wait just a little while . . .*

Then that thought, too, faded easily away, because, quite frankly, her brain was the last body part she wanted to be using at the moment. Lifting her hands to his hair, she threaded her fingers through the silky tresses, recalling quickly how much she loved doing this, how good it felt to pull him closer, how very possessive she could be where he was concerned. Adam seemed to sense her thoughts, because he looped his arms around her waist and splayed his hands open over her back to push her body flush with his own. It was an exquisite feeling, touching every inch of his body with every inch of hers, and she reveled in the realization that she would be able to do this forever.

But forever could wait a bit, too, because Dorsey couldn't. Neither could Adam, evidently, because as he pressed upon her—into her—one particularly soulful kiss, he moved a hand forward to curve his fingers unapologetically over her breast. A keen heat shot through her at the contact, and she gasped as she tightened her own fingers in his hair. In response, he, too, clenched his hand tighter, more resolutely, over her, and she was helpless to halt the moan that arose from some deep, dark place inside her.

"Again," she managed to murmur, and immediately Adam obeyed. Several times, in fact.

Without even thinking about what she was doing, relying on simple reaction now, Dorsey dropped a hand to the button of his blue jeans and punched it through its mooring. Hastily, she tugged down the zipper and dipped her hand inside the stiff fabric, until she held him, pulsing and hard, in her palm. He was already slick with his desire for her, and she rejoiced in the knowledge of the power she held over him. Then he caught the fastening of her own jeans in two deft fingers and loosed it, thrusting his own hand inside to easily—and quickly—find the damp, heated heart of her. And when Dorsey's knees buckled beneath her, she understood that that power ran both ways.

Adam roped his other arm around her waist, catching her capably before she would have melted to the ground. But as he held her, he continued the intimate onslaught he'd started with the other hand. Back and forth his fingers furrowed her delicate flesh, drawing erotic patterns and scandalous designs. Over and over he penetrated her, first with one finger, then two, until she was nearly insensate with wanting him.

As his actions intensified, her own exploration of him ebbed, but not so far that he remained in control of himself. As she slowly ran her fingers along the solid length of him, as she methodically rolled her palm over the tip of his shaft, his respiration accelerated and his own ministrations grew more haphazard.

And just when she grew certain that she wouldn't be able to respond in any way other than bursting into flame, somehow, Dorsey found the focus, the energy, to murmer, "Adam."

For a moment, he didn't reply, only stilled his hand and relaxed—a little—his body. Finally, though, weakly, he whispered, "What?"

"I really, really, really want you," she told him.

"That's good," he replied breathlessly. "That's real good. Because I really, really, really, want you, too."

With much reluctance, she pointed out, "But there's no place to . . . I mean, we can't . . . There isn't room here to—"

Before she could even complete the sentence—and in one swift, fluid gesture—Adam withdrew his hand from her jeans, tugged them, and her panties, down over her hips, tossed his leather jacket up onto the counter and deposited Dorsey, bare-bottomed, atop it. The feel of soft leather beneath her naked flesh was an erogenous adventure she wasn't likely to forget anytime soon. She held her breath for a moment, to see if the counter would come crashing down with her upon it, but it held firm.

And so did Adam.

Without compunction or care, he finished removing her jeans and panties and tossed them to the floor, unheeded. Then, without scruple or ceremony, he began to shed his own. Dorsey's eyes widened in wonder at what he clearly meant to do, then a thrill of anticipation shot through her like a lightning bolt.

"Are you sure you want to try this?" she asked. But already she was scooting closer to the edge—to Adam.

"Oh, yes," he readily assured her. "I've been thinking about this for a loooong time. Well, this and about a million other varieties of joining my body to yours. But we can get to them next week," he hastily assured her. "In fact, I've been anticipating this so much lately that—" He reached into his back pocket and withdrew a condom, smiling hugely. "I didn't even bother to put it in my wallet."

Dorsey smiled back. "Gosh, I hope you brought more than one."

He tipped his head back and tented his hands before himself in silent benediction. "Thank you for this woman," he said to some unknown deity. Then he returned his gaze to her face. "Because she is, without question, the answer to every prayer, every wish, every dream I've ever had."

Oh, well, since he put it like that . . .

"I love you, Adam."

His gaze never left hers as he vowed, "I love you, too."

And that was the last thing either of them needed to say. Adam shoved his own jeans down and sheathed himself, and Dorsey opened to receive him. As he stepped between her legs, she settled her arms over his shoulders, curving one hand over his nape. He was warm and alive beneath her fingertips, and he was strong and powerful and sure. Most of all, though, he was hers. He was hers forever.

And she would always be his, she knew, a fact that was only reinforced as he entered her, claimed her, branded her as his own. That first fierce stroke went straight to her heart, to her core, to her soul, filling her so completely that she cried out her response. For one long moment, he stayed buried inside her, as if he couldn't tolerate the thought of parting from her, even that little bit. But then, very slowly, he withdrew, only to thrust himself even deeper still.

Dorsey crowded her body against his, wrapped her legs tightly around his waist, held him as close as she possibly could. Again and again their bodies joined, building friction and passion and need. And with each stroke of that intimate union, their souls merged, too. Together, they formed a unity of spirit as old as time, a spirit that was neither male nor female, but generated by the simple presence of love. And when all was said and done, it was that, and nothing more, that truly mattered.

Epilogue

"I hate summer in the city. It was just too damned hot today. I don't care if it is July."

Adam grinned as Lucas muttered the observation, then passed him the balsamic vinegar for the green salad he was putting together in Adam's kitchen. Both men had just come in from the office and were working in their shirtsleeves to prepare dinner. They had promised Dorsey and Edie that they would actually cook something for a change, instead of picking up carryout on the way home. That had become their habit on the alternating Wednesdays when it was their turn to cook on the weekly dinner date the two couples kept.

Lucas's gripe surprised Adam. He couldn't remember the last time he'd heard the kid complain about anything. Oh, wait a minute, yes, he could. Just last week, Lucas had grumbled something about Edie's decision to have the bridesmaids wear pink, because now he'd have to pin a pink—God, *pink*—rosebud to his lapel at some point in the not too distant future.

Adam chuckled to himself at the recollection and went back to stabbing beef tips and chunks of green pepper onto skewers. A year ago, Lucas Conaway wouldn't have been caught dead within fifty yards of anything pink— not by choice anyway. But after muttering a few more halfhearted lamentations to his fiancée—*his fiancée*, Adam marveled again with a smile—he'd capitulated easily enough to Edie's command. Of course, Adam thought further, seeing as how he was Lucas's best man, he would have to pin a pink—God, *pink*—rosebud to his lapel, too. Hmm . . .

Oh, well. The wedding was still nine months off. Maybe Edie would change her mind. Again.

"So, is Russell Davenport going to give her away?" Adam asked.

Lucas nodded. "Oh, yeah, you bet. He said he wouldn't miss it." He was thoughtful for a moment, then added, "You know, I'm an optimistic man by nature, but even so, it amazes me how quickly Russell's entire family accepted Edie into the fold. Did you know his Aunt Bitsy wrote a letter of recommendation to help Edie get that job at the Mershon Gallery?"

"That was nice of her."

Lucas nodded. "And Russell's arranged a trust for Edie just like the one his other kids have. And he and his wife have already hinted that they're giving us a sailboat for a wedding present. A sailboat," he reiterated with disbelief. "I mean, I wasn't even expecting a *gravy* boat."

"Too bad Edie's biological mother couldn't be here, too," Adam said soberly.

"Yeah," Lucas agreed. "But at least she found Russell and told him about Edie before she died, so he could look for her. Otherwise, Edie would still be alone."

"No, she wouldn't," Adam pointed out.

Lucas smiled. "That's true. Now, if I could just get her to change her mind about those pink dresses . . ."

"Quit complaining," Adam told him. "It's bad for your complexion."

"Oh, is that the latest from the resident *Man's Life* advice columnist?" Lucas asked. "What's Miss Dorsey Manners going to focus on in her girly column this month? Yeast infections?"

Adam chuckled. "No. She's going to address her favorite subject. Pay inequity."

"Oh, well, that ought to be good for spurring sales," Lucas said dryly.

Actually, Adam thought, it probably would be. Although he'd known six months ago that offering Dorsey a job at the magazine was a good idea, he'd had no idea that her popularity would soar the way it had, right out of the gate.

As the author of a monthly column called "From a Woman's Point of View," Dorsey addressed current events and social issues that affected men *and* women, presenting them from a position men normally never saw—a woman's point of view. She'd also contributed a fair number of woman-in-the-street stories for the publication that had met with surprisingly positive feedback. *Man's Life* was still a men's magazine, to be sure, but now it had the added dimension of a woman's touch. And hey, men loved to be touched by a woman. Especially one who wrote with the in-your-face frankness that Dorsey MacGuinness provided so well. Especially one who looked like Dorsey MacGuinness looked in the photo that accompanied her column.

Adam smiled as he reflected on that. Over the last six

months, Dorsey had changed. Not a lot, and certainly not in any way that altered the essence of who and what she was. But the flannel shirts and jeans in her closet had been joined by short skirts and soft colors. There were high heels sitting on the floor alongside her hiking boots, black lace brassieres mingling with the white cotton undershirts in her drawer. And somehow, in embracing both the femininity of Lauren and the masculinity of Mack, Dorsey had emerged a very intriguing creature indeed.

She never stopped surprising Adam. And she never kept secrets. All in all, he was pretty much certain he was the luckiest man alive. But he didn't say so aloud. Lucas, he knew, would take exception.

"So what are you and Dorsey doing this weekend?" Lucas asked him.

"Well, Reginald Dorsey invited us to spend it with him and his kids at his little cottage in the country," Adam said.

"The ten-thousand-square-foot cottage?" Lucas asked.

"That's the one."

"Ah. So are you and Dorsey going to go?"

Adam shrugged and stabbed another chunk of green pepper. "I doubt it. Dorsey's coming around where Reggie's concerned, but she's not there yet. She still feels awkward around her half-brother and half-sisters."

"She'll get there," Lucas said. "It wasn't easy for Edie at first, either, but look how well that's turned out."

Adam grunted in agreement, then went back to work. He was just firing up the gas grill, and Lucas had just tossed the last of the croutons into the salad, when feminine laughter erupted in the other room.

"Our womenfolk have returned," Lucas observed unnecessarily.

It was particularly unnecessary in light of the fact that

the womenfolk in question were entering the kitchen right about then. Each was armed with two grocery sacks, and they stopped dead in their tracks when they saw Adam and Lucas standing amid their dinner preparations.

"You're *cooking*?" Dorsey asked incredulously.

She looked pretty incredible, too, Adam couldn't help but note, dressed in a sleeveless, pale-yellow jumper—only a little bit limp from the heat—and humongous Birkenstock sandals. Her ruddy curls were piled haphazardly atop her head in deference to the heat, and her cheeks and nose were stained pink with a touch of city sunburn. Edie's face, too, showed signs of a long urban walk, as did the damp T-shirt that topped her flowered skirt.

"Of course we're cooking," Adam told them. "We promised, didn't we?"

"Yeah, but there was nothing here to cook when I left this morning," Dorsey pointed out. "Edie and I stopped for groceries, because you and I have been too busy to get any this week."

"Miraculously, I remembered this," Adam replied, "so Lucas and I picked up a few things on our way home. Dinner will be ready in about a half-hour."

"Don't worry about it, Dorsey," Edie said. "You and Adam can save all this for the weekend."

Dorsey chewed her lip thoughtfully for a moment before saying, "We, uh . . . I think maybe we might be in the country this weekend, Edie."

Adam smiled. *Well, well, well.*

"So you and Lucas can take them home tonight, instead," she added.

"Okay," Edie agreed readily. "But I'll stow everything in the fridge for now."

"I'll help you," Lucas offered.

Dorsey opened her mouth to object, but Lucas hefted

the bags out of her arms before she had the chance to say a word. Adam took advantage of her momentary disconcertion to take her hand in his and tug her out of the kitchen, with a hastily offered "We'll be right back" to Edie and Lucas on the way out.

She laughed as she followed him, but her chuckles faded off as he pulled her into the bedroom, closed the door behind them, then pressed her back against it and crowded his big body against her. She immediately looped her arms around his neck and pulled him closer still, opening to him willingly when he covered her mouth with his. For long moments they greeted each other wordlessly after their long—almost a whole afternoon—separation, then, reluctantly, Adam pulled back to gaze at her face.

"Lucas and I have been talking about the wedding," he said without preamble.

Dorsey smiled a dreamy little smile. "Still not happy about the pink dresses, is he?"

"Not a bit," Adam told her. "But I promised him last week that when you and I get married, you'll pick blue."

Well, that certainly got her attention—which, of course, had been Adam's intention. Her eyes widened in surprise, and her mouth fell softly open. "When *we* get married?" she echoed.

He nodded. "What do you say?"

"I . . . Adam . . ." She smiled a little nervously. "You've never said anything about us getting married."

"Neither have you."

"I was waiting to see what you'd say," she said softly.

He laughed. "And here I've been waiting to see what *you'd* say."

She nibbled her lip anxiously. "Actually, I'm not quite sure what to say. I just . . . I don't know. We've just been so happy the last six months, living the way we do."

"But don't you want security?" he asked her.

She smiled. "I have that without being married to you."

He couldn't believe she was actually trying to talk him out of this, he thought. Then he noted the uncertainty in her eyes. Or was she? "But you're here more often than you're at your place," he pointed out. "I found a pair of your panties in my underwear drawer this morning. It was incredibly erotic."

She chuckled. "I'm here so much because I don't want to cramp Carlotta's style. She and her financial advisor have been pretty tight lately. The fact that he's not married has opened up all kinds of freedom in the relationship that she never realized she could have with a man."

Adam chuckled. "Do I hear wedding bells?"

Dorsey hesitated a moment. "I don't know," she said, "do you?"

He pulled her closer, dipping his forehead to hers. "Well, I don't know about Carlotta, but . . ."

"But what?"

"I think you and I should go for it. I love you, Dorsey, and I always will."

"I love you, too," she told him. "And I always will."

"Then let's make that clear to the world at large."

She nodded slowly, smiling hugely. "Okay. But I think I want peach dresses, instead of blue."

"*Peach*?" Adam exclaimed, biting back a gag.

"Or maybe lavender," she amended with a laugh.

He closed his eyes tight. "Fine, dear. Whatever you say, dear. You're the boss, dear."

Dorsey laughed harder. "That'll be the day," she murmured as she pushed herself up on tiptoe to kiss him. "And I look forward to every last one of them to come."